£1.15

28/8/93

PLAYS INTRODUCTION

PLAYS INTRODUCTION

Plays by New Writers

DAVID CLOUGH

NICK DARKE

JOHN FLETCHER

ELLEN FOX

LENNIE JAMES

TIMBERLAKE
WERTENBAKER

faber and faber

LONDON · BOSTON

First published in 1984
by Faber and Faber Limited
3 Queen Square London WC1N 3AU

Filmset by Wilmaset Birkenhead
Printed in Great Britain by
Redwood Burn Ltd
Trowbridge Wiltshire
All rights reserved

All the rights in these plays are reserved by the
proprietors. Applications for professional and amateur
rights should be addressed, before rehearsals begin, to the
following: for 'In Kanada', David Higham Associates, 5–8
Lower John St, Golden Square, London W1R 4HA; for
'High Water', Margaret Ramsay Ltd, 14a Goodwin's
Court, London WC2N 4LL; for 'Babylon has Fallen',
A. D. Peters & Co. Ltd, 10 Buckingham St, London WC2N
6BU; for 'Ladies in Waiting' and 'New Anatomies',
Dr Jan Van Loewen Ltd, 21 Kingly St, London W1R 5LB;
for 'Trial and Error', Lennie James,
c/o Faber & Faber Ltd.

British Library Cataloguing in Publication Data

Plays introduction.
1. English drama—20th century
I. Clough, David
822'.914'08   PR1272
ISBN 0–571–13038–0

CONTENTS

PUBLISHER'S NOTE

The Faber Introduction series, though intended primarily as a showcase for new writers of prose fiction, has in its twenty-four-year history regularly included plays, among them early work by Christopher Hampton, Brian Phelan, John Mackendrick and Alick Rowe, and has also published stories by writers who later made reputations for themselves as playwrights, notably Tom Stoppard and Julian Mitchell.

Having established a series for fiction, we are now publishing our first collection devoted exclusively to drama. Our aims are, first, to publish the work of young writers that would not otherwise appear in print or receive the critical attention and distribution that publication in a book can offer and, second, to reflect as much as possible of the range of current forms of drama.

The publishers wish to thank the Arts Council of Great Britain for financial assistance with the publication of this volume and for editorial help, particularly from Fay Weldon and Robert Woof, with its preparation.

IN KANADA

David Clough

A NOTE ON THE PLAY

Readers, like myself, of contemporary middle-European writers may be struck by the dark spirit of irony and fatalism that seems to pervade much of their work. It is a quality foreign to us: fascinating and elusive. Something of this peculiar 'spirit' is what this play sets out to capture. It is the story of a small, personal tragedy seen against the background of history. The sense of detachment experienced by its hero is a product of just such a perspective and ultimately it causes his destruction.

A word should be said about the Auschwitz episodes which make up an important part of the play. There is no definitive picture of life there – it was many things to many people – nor does the play attempt to give one. What concerns it more is the 'Auschwitz Universe'; a particular state of mind or being. The inmates portrayed here are not especially evil or sadistic. Rather they exist as part of an ordered social structure with its own rules, values and established pecking order. The horror in their lives has become banal, governed by the limits of human response. Therefore the absence of victims in these scenes, like the absence of overt violence, is strictly intentional.

'Kanada' was the name given by the Auschwitz inmates to that area of the camp where the wealth of the dead was stored. It was also used to describe those who worked there; assisting with the unloading of the trains or 'transports', sorting goods and so on. Most of all, in the camp, it signified well-being and prosperity.

In Kanada
Staging

Basically two or three acting areas are required, allowing for a fluid progression. Setting can be minimal. The exception is Beta's apartment which should act as a fulcrum for the other parts of the action. One device used in the first production which might prove useful is leaving BETA on stage to 'witness' the scenes played by his younger *alter ego*, TADEK.

In the original production some of the names were altered to make them more 'Polish'. EWA BALESZKA became 'Ewa Zawadska'; JOSEPH DZADZEK, 'Josef Holubec'; PIA DUKOW, 'Zosia Tauber'. These names might be noted as useful though they are by no means obligatory.

In Kanada is dedicated to Tadeusz Borowski (1922–1951) on whose life story it is loosely based. It must be stressed however that all characters and incidents are purely fictional.

I would like to thank the Polish Library, Hammersmith, and Tomas Karol for their help; most of all my wife, Diana, without whom this play would not have been completed.

D.C.

Characters

BETA (TADEK in 1951; the name is used to
distinguish him from TADEK in the script
only)

TADEK (BETA in his twenties, 1943–5)

MARIA

EWA

KORCZACK

STASZEK

THE FLEA

REUBEN

HONI

THE KAPO

LAWYER

GUARD

PART I

Scene I

Darkness. Music and applause.

Bright spot up on BETA, *standing. He is in his thirties, dressed in a dark suit; holding a piece of paper.*

He lifts a hand, the noise dies away.

BETA: My friends . . .

(His voice, if possible, is amplified. Distorted and slightly disembodied.)

Comrades and fellow workers. *(Smiles.)* Since I seem to be last to speak, I'll try to make my speech brief. I expect you've been wondering what a bunch of newspaperboys from Warsaw could understand about your work? I mean the way you run things here. Not much, it's true. That is why it has been a privilege to visit you all in this factory today. It's a journalist's job to report the facts. And what do we find here that's worth reporting? That's worth telling – not just to the Polish people – but to all our comrades throughout the free world. . . ? *(Waits.)* The answer is simple. *(Slowly)* We see the evidence of a new Poland. A powerful spirit sweeping us forward. The work of men who have found their true purpose. Who have taken history into their own hands and for whom there can be no looking back . . . I won't go on. Here in Poland, in 1951, we have come to know such men well. We recognize their determination. My friends, it is never easy. To haul yourself up by your own bootstraps, to find a real goal for strive for. To do that, you have to defeat yourself. The fear and the greed that is part of our nature – it must be overcome. It takes strength, a conscious effort of will, to remind ourselves we are not alone. To submit ourselves to the will of the People is all

15

that can reasonably be asked of us . . . But, let us never forget, our struggle is not over yet. Out there still exists a world of slavery . . . of labour dedicated to nothing but feeding relentless appetites. Workers still sell themselves to their masters. Daily pour out their honest sweat to maintain injustice and oppression. Cattle, industriously chewing the cud, at least do not know why they are being fattened. Or that – in the eyes of their keepers – they are merely useful gristle and bone. Articles, things to be expended. And I warn you we must remain on our guard. Our freedom's too precious to go unprotected nor is the battle that won it resolved. Opposition is all around us – both inside and without our ranks. Complacency, revisionism, laxness . . . (*With gathering vehemence*) We must be vigilant against them, both in our thinking and our actions. Watchful, suspicious and alert. And we must learn to know the faces of those who will never tire in seeking our destruction . . . (*Quiet*) Study the creatures closely, comrades, for how else shall we know our strength. . . ?

(*The amplification cuts off. Lights soften around him to reveal a small, bare room. Desk with typewriter, bottle and glasses; reading lamp, papers, etc. Chair at desk, door in the wall behind.*)

(*Continuing, slowly, in his own voice*) The Enemy. Yes, my friends. Only through him do we understand. Begin to refine ourselves. Harden. (*Breaking off, he makes a correction to the paper.*) "Racketeering bourgeois . . . (*Writing*) conspiracy of rightist elements . . . etcetera." (*Stops and pours himself a drink. Chuckles thoughtfully.*) Not true? Of course it's true, you idiots. We . . . huddle here – inside the light. Out there – they're roaring and alive! Just so, eh? (*Sits down.*) Comrades, I report the facts. Ah, if you'd come with me to Berlin, then you could have seen it perhaps. Things are back to normal there. Marks and dollars meet on the counters, touch each other with tender respect. Black uniforms roosting in the

cupboards, waiting patiently – you can smell them . . .
(*Shakes his head and inserts a clean sheet into typewriter.
Stares at it for a moment and sighs.*)
New paragraph . . .

Scene 2

*From the darkness, a rumble that becomes the roar of an
approaching train.*

The door behind BETA *opens,* EWA *appears.*

*She is young, dressed drably with a few splashes of colour. She
switches on a light so that the flat brightens.* BETA *turns around.
The train gradually recedes, fades out.*

EWA: I knocked. The door was open.

    (BETA *stays silent.* EWA *poses defiantly in the doorway.*)
    "Liebchen, vy do you look at me zo?"
    (BETA *turns back.*)

BETA: Nothing like her.

    (EWA, *relieved, comes into the room. Now that it is lit, we can
    see packing cases and boxes scattered about.*)

EWA: Liar. I'm very good. Everybody says so. (*Pause.*)
    Anyway, here I am.

BETA: So I see.

EWA: Working?

BETA: No. Talking to you.

EWA: And just now? I heard voices.

EWA: One voice. Mine.

EWA: Talking to yourself? You're going cray-zee, darlingk.

BETA: Not at all. (*Picks up his desk lamp, speaks into it.*) Are
    you there, comrades? Have you heard the rumour that
    Comrade Stalin's ill?

EWA: (*Uneasily*) Cray-zee . . .

BETA: Neither did I. But if we could get one going. (*Putting
    the lamp down*) Ewa. I thought we'd agreed.

EWA: You shouldn't joke. It might be true – even for you.

BETA: Why not me? Even I tell bad jokes sometimes. Ewa, what are you doing here? You know what we said.

(EWA *moves vaguely around the room.*)

EWA: You wouldn't believe how stiff I am. Calisthenics all afternoon. I think that bitch imagines we send actors to the Olympics. I'm going to have legs like tree trunks.

BETA: Ewa.

EWA: Friends, you said. Remember? We could still be friends. What's wrong with a friendly visit?

BETA: You know very well.

EWA: Wait! I forgot to tell you. Guess what's happened? I have been specially selected.

BETA: Is that good?

EWA: Good? From all the others at the Institute, they chose me – Ewa Baleszka* – as "People's Cultural Representative" for the next exhibition. They're sending me to Moscow.

BETA: Congratulations, comrade.

EWA: Pia Dukow† was furious. (*Laughs.*) She has the highest grades, so naturally she assumed . . . They say the Old Man, himself, might be coming. I may even meet him.

BETA: They say he likes them young. And lightly boiled.

EWA: I haven't a thing to wear. Nothing but rags . . . (*Comes to him, seriously*) I want to ask your advice.

BETA: My dear girl, you know you're so exceptionally ugly, it won't make any difference what you wear.

EWA: Not about that. About this . . . (*Takes out a folded sheet of paper. Giving it to him*) You remember Akimov? The one I told you of?

BETA: The lecturer at the Institute?

EWA: The one whom they arrested last month. We thought – that is some of the students – that if we could make a statement . . . about the charges which were brought against him. I mean they were ridiculous!

*See note on p. 13.
†See note on p. 13.

BETA: Ewa.

EWA: (*Angrily*) If we could only make them *see*; to understand
the facts. They'd have to realize their mistake. And now
that I am going to Moscow. Well, there's just a chance, I
meet someone; somebody who would read our petition.
They have to listen to us!

BETA: Ewa, stop. (*Pause.*) You're asking my advice? I'll give
it. Tear this piece of paper up now.

EWA: Why? Why should I?

BETA: Because if you take this paper home . . . or to Moscow
or anywhere at all . . . because if you show these words to
anyone – something is going to happen to you. Do you
know what that something will be?

EWA: Tell me.

BETA: You'll end up in a little room. A room like this one with
a desk. A man will be sitting down behind it. And he will
say to you, quite gently: "Why have you committed this
crime?"

EWA: And I will say: "There is no crime. We ask for justice.
Fairness, a fair hearing. We think that there has been a
mistake. An innocent man was falsely punished."

BETA: And he will say: "How can you know this? Surely you
know the People have decided? Justice belongs to them,
not you. And only they can honestly give judgment. Are
you saying that they are wrong?"

EWA: Yes. No. But sometimes there are things – mis-
understandings and mistakes. I'm only asking that you
listen to us. This man has not been proven guilty . . .

BETA: (*Interrupting*) "So you are right and we are wrong? And
what gives you the right to think that?"

EWA: Because I know the real truth!

BETA: "Ah. Now, at last, we're getting to it. *You* know the
truth and not the People. Reality is as you see it. But we
must disagree with that. Lenin has shown us that it is the
People, the interests of the proletariat which matter. We
see things through their eyes and through their struggle.
Our view is historical and not, like yours, coloured with

19

personal feelings and emotions. Comrade, your crime
is clear and evident. Your ideas are reactionary,
dangerous; a danger to the State and to your other
comrades. By your actions you have shown them and now
our duty is made plain towards you . . ."
(*He finishes, a silence.*)
Do you still want me to go on?
(EWA *shakes her head.*)

EWA: (*Low*) So you are telling me to do nothing.

BETA: (*Painfully*) Ewa, you're young.

EWA: But not a child.

BETA: No. Not a child. (*Pause.*) I'm telling you what will
happen. That's all. (*Pours a drink.*) Perhaps I'm just a
little sentimental. About that clean, young body of yours.
It was nice. A pretty, healthy girl like you. But they can
change all that, believe me. Because of this . . . (*Holds the
paper.*) Forgive me if I don't think that it's worth it.
(*Turns away, busies himself at the desk.*) And now I've still
got work to do. Unless you know a synonym for
productive, we'd better cut this short.
(EWA *drifts away, walks around the room, picking up things,
etc.*)
We had a new recruit sent in today. A smart boy from the
provinces called Korczack. You know, I think he's just
your type. Perhaps I'll introduce you to him.

EWA: Please don't bother.

BETA: He works on the arts page. Still young and sticky with
the right ambitions. He might be useful.

EWA: You needn't try so hard, you know. It looks suspicious.

BETA: (*Smiling*) I thought you'd learned by now. Married
men – we soon turn vicious when our bellies soften.

EWA: Thank you. I deserved that, I suppose. (*Comes
downstage.*) You need curtains on this window. People can
see in.

BETA: Let them. Ewa, you have to go.

EWA: Don't worry, I've gone. (*Comes to the desk, stands behind
him.*) Is it really so difficult now?

BETA: We said a clean break.

EWA: We said friends. Coward.

BETA: You know where the door is, friend.

EWA: Ugh, you've been drinking. I can smell it. Are you drunk?

BETA: Not yet, unfortunately.

EWA: (*Picking up a paper from the desk*) Is this tomorrow's article? Can I see?

BETA: (*Taking it*) No.

EWA: You've spilled booze on it.

BETA: I'll tell the editor it's honest sweat. They taste the same.

EWA: What did you do today? Tell me about your famous writer's life.

BETA: Another time.

EWA: Tell me. Then I'll go, I promise.

BETA: (*Sighing*) We visited a factory.

EWA: Why?

BETA: To make speeches, naturally. I made a speech. We came home.

EWA: What else?

BETA: If you must know: I went to the hospital to visit my wife. After that, I went to the State Security Centre to . . . never mind. I came here. You came. Another famous day. Now, if you don't mind, Ewa . . .

EWA: How is your wife?

BETA: My wife is extremely well, thank you, Miss Baleszka.

EWA: And the baby?

BETA: And so is my daughter. As far as I can make out.

EWA: You had a daughter! Didn't you see her?

BETA: They wouldn't let me. I know she's female and weighs about a kilo. That's all the information that they think a father is entitled.

EWA: (*Moving away*) It would be nice to have some children. A son. I'd like two sons and a daughter.

BETA: Would you find time between performances?

EWA: Don't laugh at me. You're always making fun.

BETA: Am I? I'm sorry.

21

EWA: You think I'm just some empty-headed actress.

BETA: Ewa, I haven't got time for this.

EWA: (*Coming back*) There's one more thing I haven't told you. Josef Dzadzek's* called a meeting – he's the oldest in our class. We're going to pass a resolution. We're going to do something about this. We're going to show them they can't treat us this way; like a bunch of kids or sheep!

BETA: Ewa, haven't you been listening?

EWA: It's not just Akimov. It's . . . *everything*. Who do they think they're dealing with? Idiots? They pick us for our brains and then . . .

BETA: (*Helpless*) Ewa. (*Pause.*) Please don't do this.

EWA: The meeting starts at Dzadzek's place at half-past eight. (*Pause.*) I told them you might sign it . . . if I explained. (BETA *remains turned away from her.*) I'm going anyway. (*Lightly*) Do you know what today is? It's my birthday. (*She waits.* BETA *remains silent.*) "No? Oh, really? Happy birthday, Ewa." I knew you wouldn't remember it, don't worry. I've brought a present for you. (*Producing a small package*) Here.

BETA: You know I can't.

EWA: You'll never guess. Go on, take it.
(*She puts it on the desk.*)

BETA: Thank you.

EWA: Open it then. I won't go till you have.
(*He unwraps it, frowns.*)
Surprised?

BETA: Where did you get this?

EWA: It wasn't easy. Why didn't you tell me that you'd written it?

BETA: Should I have? The libraries're full of war memoirs.

EWA: That's not the point, is it? This book explains too much. And you never explain, do you? If I had read this in the beginning, I might have *begun* to understand. All those things that puzzled me. Why couldn't you just come out and say it: I was in a concentration . . .

*See note on p. 13.

BETA: That's enough! (*Controls himself.*) Ewa, I wish you
hadn't. I really wish you hadn't . . .

EWA: (*Frightened*) I didn't mean . . . I'm sorry.

BETA: (*Managing a lighter tone*) Never mind. Thank you
anyway. (*Rising brusquely*) And now, before I show you to
the door – not to be outdone, I have a present for you.

EWA: Oh, please . . .

BETA: I insist. (*Crosses to a packing case.*) They're in here
somewhere.

EWA: You're moving out?

BETA: A new apartment. And please don't ask me where it is.

EWA: You'll need more room now. With the baby.

BETA: Here. A little dusty but not broken yet. (*Producing a pile
of records*) Benny Goodman, Miller, Waller . . . well, you
take them anyway. All good products of a decadent
culture. Just don't tell anyone where you got them or I
may have to defect.

EWA: No. I couldn't.

BETA: You know I brought them back from Berlin for you.
Frankly this stuff gives me a headache. Maybe this "cat"
isn't "hop" enough?

EWA: It's "hep". And you're a real cool daddy.
(*She kisses him. They smile.*)

BETA: I hope that's complimentary whatever it means. (*Moves
towards the door.*) I prophesy on good authority that in, say,
ten years or so, this "jazz" of yours will replace rational
thought in those poor countries suffering the affliction.

EWA: Hmm. And is that bad?

BETA: Don't laugh. While we talk, a secret team of Soviet
scientists are playing saxophones to rats. Growths of hair
and mild schizophrenia are only some of the side effects.

EWA: Another article?

BETA: Who knows?
(*He opens the door. She hesitates.*)

EWA: You always did say that I stopped you thinking.

BETA: Perhaps that might have been the point.
(*She goes. He closes the door behind her.*

23

*He comes back to the desk. He pulls the paper from the typewriter,
inserts a fresh sheet. Then he notices the petition still lying on the
desk. Turns towards the door, thinks better. He puts it between the
pages of the book.*
*He shrugs, picks up the telephone and begins to dial. The lights
fade around him.)*

Scene 3

Music: Tristan und Isolde.
Lights up slowly on TADEK *lying in bed. He is in his twenties and wears
an army greatcoat. He scribbles in an exercise book. The music comes
from an old fashioned wind-up gramophone next to the bed.*
TADEK *is, of course, a younger* BETA. *The self-conscious irony is there
but not the poise. A shy aggressiveness instead. He wears wire-rimmed
glasses.*
The record sticks. TADEK *ignores it until a rapid pattern of knocks comes
from offstage. He gets up quickly, lifts the needle from the record, goes
out.*
A moment later, he re-enters with MARIA; *a little older, fairly self-
contained but not without humour. She carries a bag.*
TADEK *gets back to bed.*
MARIA: Excuse me. Should I come back later, sir?
TADEK: It's the only way of keeping warm. Unless you'd care to
  join me?
MARIA: No, thanks. Keep your mind on work.
TADEK: I'll try.
MARIA: This place is filthy.
  (*She puts the bag down, sits on the bed.*)
TADEK: Not to mention freezing. Let's skip the small talk. That
  bag of yours – wasn't there something once called food?
MARIA: Not until you've washed. And put some decent clothes
  on.
TADEK: So fair and yet so cruel. You'd better shut your eyes then.
  I suppose you realize that under this (*Lifts the blankets*) my
  ankles are completely naked.
MARIA: I'll light the stove. You get dressed.

(*She goes out.* TADEK *gets up reluctantly. He is about to look in the bag when* MARIA *calls out.*)

(*Offstage*) Honestly, Tadek.

TADEK: What?

MARIA: Listening to Wagner. What would your Nationalist friends think?

TADEK: Nationalists don't think, they just salute. Anyway Wagner is a well-known weapon of counter-insurgency – didn't you know?

(*He begins dressing from a pile of clothes beside the bed.*)

MARIA: (*Offstage*) Know what?

TADEK: Yes. If the SS were outside now, hammering on the door, I just put on my Wagner for them. It's like nerve gas. One whiff and they go all misty eyed and rigid. While they're still standing to attention and dreaming of their "Neue Ordnung" – I'm piling out the back way. Simple.

(*He combs his hair.* MARIA *comes back.*)

I thought you liked Wagner?

MARIA: Not since he took over half our concert programmes. All those glissandos! Do you know what that does to the fingers? The worst kind of German torture.

TADEK: There speaks a patriot.

MARIA: You end up longing for a bit of Brahms. Anything but Herr W. But no he's safe and oh so very Aryan.

TADEK: Maybe they'll find he had a Jewish granny. Why don't you take your coat off?

MARIA: In a minute. I'm still frozen.

TADEK: We said we wouldn't mention that. Come here, I'll rub your hands for you.

(*She goes to him. A brief pause.*)

MARIA: (*Casually*) They've sealed off Stanislau Street again. Taking people off the trams.

TADEK: How did you manage to get through?

MARIA: Somebody warned us just the stop before. I got off and came the long way by the river.

TADEK: Again. Listen, you can't go back tonight. Stay here, please.

(She shakes her head.)

MARIA: I've got a performance. I can't miss it. In any case you're working.

TADEK: They'll cover for me at the factory. Nobody checks on nightwatchmen.

MARIA: No, Tadek. Be sensible. It's far too risky. You lose this job and what? You'll lose your labour card and get deported.

(She breaks away and goes to the bag. Begins unpacking food; bread, sausage, cheese, a few apples.)

TADEK: *(Impatiently)* Who says I won't be anyway? Our German tourists don't care who they take. They cart off "sensible" people every day. By the truck load – careful, sober citizens. Today, they almost got you, didn't they?

MARIA: Leave it, Tadek. Talking doesn't help.

TADEK: Tell me what does help, then? It's all a farce. Each time that you walk through that door, I never know if I'll see your face again.

MARIA: I thought that you were hungry?

(He lets it go. Comes to sit beside her.)

TADEK: I think my stomach's finally given up. Don't you believe those lying French Romantics; no genius works better when he's starving.

MARIA: Eat, genius. You talk too much.

(They eat in silence for a moment.)

TADEK: Have they told you where we're meeting next?

MARIA: I think at Bronski's. It's his turn.

TADEK: Thank you, you've just ruined my meal.

MARIA: He's not that bad.

TADEK: No. "Bad" is too inadequate.

MARIA: Just because you don't like him. You don't like anyone who writes poetry. As well as you, that is.

TADEK: As well as who? I'd cut my throat if I wrote that kind of drivel. He's treated you to his "Sons of Freedom" yet? *(Quoting)* "Proud youth, whose blood is for your country spent. The Tyrant's death shall be your monument . . ."

MARIA: He lost a son, you know.

TADEK: I'm very sorry but that's no excuse. Being sincere just isn't good enough. The Germans are the most sincere of all. You can't compete with that kind of sincerity. Come to think of it, they would love his stuff: "Proud youth, remember, Fatherland knows best. Take care of number one and screw the rest. . . ."

MARIA: At least he finishes his assignments. Not like some students I could name.

TADEK: I have more important things to do.

MARIA: Such as?

TADEK: Such as? You think that I just waste my time, is that it? Well, let me show you something then. (*Dives under the bed and takes out a small package.*) Stealing bits of wood to sell on the black market, suffering bores like Bronski – it's only worth it now. What do you think this is?

MARIA: I don't know.

TADEK: A present for you. Here, take it.

MARIA: For me? What is it?

TADEK: Open it and see. It's for your birthday.

MARIA: (*Unwrapping it*) That was last week. A book.

TADEK: Not just a book.

MARIA: Oh, Tadek.

TADEK: I might let you open it, if you begged me.
(*She opens it.*)
Careful. It's still sticky. I printed it myself on Czeslaw's duplicator. The ink's a bit thin but that can't be helped. He keeps the best stuff for his bomb-making hand-outs. Take a look here on page one . . .

MARIA: I'm not sure that I deserve this.

TADEK: (*Smiling*) What makes you think the dedication's yours? I might know lots of stuck-up girls called "M".

MARIA: Idiot. It's a fine book.

TADEK: A limited edition. Like yourself. Which one shall I read you?

MARIA: Later. Kiss me first.
(*He obeys. They finish and look at each other shyly.* TADEK *gets up.*)

27

Where are you going?

TADEK: A drink. To wet our baby's head. Not mint tea this
time. A real drink. (*Fetches a bottle and a tin mug.*
Formally) I trust you'll join me on this great occasion?

MARIA: An honour.

TADEK: This cost me an unexpurgated Catullus and three
volumes of translated Schiller. Ignore the taste. Just
concentrate on its cultural origins.

(*He pours, offers it to her.*)

MARIA: You first. If it doesn't eat the enamel off your mug, I
might just risk a tiny sip.

(*He toasts, drinks, suppresses the eye-watering effect it has on*
him.)

TADEK: Uh . . . I think you'll be "amused".

(*He passes her the mug.*)

MARIA: My mother should have warned me . . .

TADEK: Your mother should have beat you. Every day.

MARIA: Cheers.

(*She drinks, chokes; coughs and splutters.* TADEK *pounds her*
back.)

TADEK: Is this any way to behave at a party? Really.

MARIA: (*Gasping*) Stop hitting me, you brute.

(*She holds on to his arm, recovers.*)

TADEK: Better. . . ?

MARIA: Umm . . .

TADEK: Lie down a minute. Put your feet up. That's it.
You're obviously not used to high-class life.

MARIA: I am. I drank a bottle of silver polish once. When I
was four.

TADEK: It must have been another vintage.

MARIA: I think I'm going to be sick.

TADEK: You're not. Just close your eyes. All right?

(*He lies beside, holds her hand. A brief silence.*)

Andrei's joined the Left. Did I tell you? They've got him
writing for that appalling rag of theirs now. He must be
mad.

MARIA: I thought you liked him?

TADEK: I sympathize. But, really, have you read that publication? Their prose is clumsier than the Fascists'.

MARIA: I'm lying on something squashy.

TADEK: The cheese. (*Pause.*) I've sent a copy to Vatzeck. Do you think he'll like it? Only the best. I took the old poems out.

MARIA: I went to Saxony Gardens. The swans have gone. I didn't see one in the whole park. What do you think could have happened?

TADEK: They've probably all been deported. Into German stomachs. Killed and eaten. Long ago.

MARIA: How sad.

TADEK: I worry about you.

MARIA: Your ceiling's filthy. Next time I'll bring a broom.
(*Lights dim slowly around them. They keep very still.*)

Scene 4

Lights up on Beta's flat. BETA *is speaking into the telephone while he arranges chess pieces on a board with his other hand.*

BETA: Czeslaw? Yes, it's me. Listen, what are you planning to do tonight? I thought if you weren't caught up in some conference . . . a little game, perhaps? That's right. You can't lose always. (*Pause.*) I see. Of course. No, I understand. Some other time then. (*Pause.*) No, she's fine. I saw her just this afternoon. Yes, the baby's doing fine. Thank you, I will. And give my love to Sacha, too. I understand. Goodbye then . . .
(*He puts the phone down. He looks regretfully at the chess board and is about to sweep the pieces back into the box when a knocking comes from the door. He pushes his chair back to get up as the lights go swiftly down on him.*)

In Kanada

Scene 5

TADEK *and* MARIA, *as before.*
TADEK *reads from his book.*
TADEK: *"No need to bang the table, my loud friend*
   You'll get no disagreement in the end.
   Whatever else – one thing you must concede us
   We're all concerned to bite the hands that bleed us

   Just fetch your grandad's flag and oil his gun
   And let your Great Cause wait until we've won
   Your praise will come from those who follow after
   Over the scrap-heaps – hollow, jeering laughter . . ."
   (MARIA *yawns loudly.*)
   Try and contain your wild enthusiasm. Well?

MARIA: It's gloomy, Tadek.

TADEK: Biting, satiric, sharp, acute – some of the words you might be groping after?

MARIA: It's gloomy, Tadek. You never write anything cheerful.

TADEK: My god, girl. What do you want from me?
   (*He gets up, begins to pace.*)
   Woodland flowers? Rainbows out my arse?

MARIA: There's no need to be crude.

TADEK: It's 1943, Maria. Just look around you. Look what they're trying to do to us. More to the point, just look how they're succeeding. And you know why? Because we still insist that we believe in this glorious Poland left us by our fathers. Some quaint old gentlemen in top hats. The Germans round us up in armfuls; they kill the best and put the rest in camps. In ten years' time, the few of us left over won't even be able to read the books about it – this Poland-relic which we're all defending. Half of us can't believe it's happening, the other half will wave the flag, all right. But what they'd really like is shiny uniforms like the Nazis. They'd like to beat them at their own game – and, secretly, that's really why they hate them.

MARIA: Who doesn't hate them? Does the reason matter?

TADEK: The reason, no. But let's, at least, be honest. Meet force with force and skip the speeches.

MARIA: (*Sighs.*) That's what I mean about your poetry. It's always so political, Tadek.

TADEK: What politics? I haven't got any. I've never written a political poem. That's the whole point. A poet's job – to cut through all of that. He takes a seat and boos at the performers, pricks their balloons. He can't believe in happy endings.

MARIA: I beg your pardon; why can't he? A poet's an artist, isn't he? What about my music? There's happy tunes and sad ones. Even the sad ones can be enjoyed.

TADEK: Maria. Your music isn't real. It's not life. Life is . . .

MARIA: Yes?

TADEK: Life. You don't get me like that.

MARIA: What a giant brain.

TADEK: Never argue with someone who spends half her life vibrating bits of catgut for a living.

(MARIA *consults her watch, gets up.*)

MARIA: Time to go.

TADEK: Not yet. It's early still.

MARIA: I'm due at the concert hall in twenty minutes. They throw a fit if anybody's late. (*Collects her bag, tidies herself.*) You'll come to Bronski's – half-past ten?

TADEK: Why not? I need a lot of sleep these days. (*Sighs.*) What a way to get an education. I sometimes wonder if it's worth it.

MARIA: It's better than having none at all.

TADEK: You know that time we had a false alarm? We thought that drunk had brought the police with him. It's funny, but you know what I was feeling? As we all sat there, petrified like rabbits. Relief. Most of all, relief. They'd got us and the whole thing was over.

MARIA: Tadek, I don't like that kind of talk.

TADEK: I'm sorry. You won't forget we have a date on Tuesday?

MARIA: I won't forget.

31

(*She comes to him quickly for a kiss.*)

I have to say . . .

TADEK: Uh-uh. I'm superstitious too. I'll see you soon.

(*She nods, goes out.*
The lights go down rapidly.)

Scene 6

Lights back up on Beta's flat.

BETA *crosses to the door and opens it.* KORCZACK *stands in the*
doorway. Twenties, dressed in a suit and cheap mackintosh,
carrying a briefcase. A very careful young man.

KORCZACK: (*Apologetic*) I saw the light. I'm not disturbing
you? There was a phone call at the office. I thought
perhaps that it might be important.

(BETA *has returned to his desk. He sits, before speaking.*)

BETA: Come in. It's Korczack, isn't it?

KORCZACK: Stepan Korczack. Yes.

(*He enters, closing the door.*)

BETA: The bright boy from the sticks, eh?

KORCZACK: Well.

BETA: Didn't I read a piece of yours? Social realism in the
theatre?

KORCZACK: "A New Dynamic for the Realist Stage". I hope
not.

BETA: Why?

KORCZACK: Because it wasn't very good. And anyway the
editor cut the best half. (*Quick smile.*) Where I come from,
the "arts" must know their place. Slightly below the
sporting section and only just above the Party news.

BETA: What do you *really* think of Mayakovsky?

KORCZACK: I . . .

(BETA *holds just long enough to embarrass him. Then . . .*)

BETA: You'll join me in a drink?

KORCZACK: Thank you. Perhaps a small one.

(BETA *pours and passes.*)

32

BETA: You'll have to excuse the mess. We're moving house. A new addition to the family.

KORCZACK: Yes, I heard. Congratulations.

He drinks and smiles again. BETA *turns and fixes him with his eye.*)

BETA: So then. What was your opinion?

KORCZACK: I'm sorry?

BETA: Our little act today. Sit down, my dear chap.

KORCZACK: Act? Thank you.

(*He looks around him, finally perches on a packing case.*)

BETA: Our cultural visit. You came with us, I remember.

KORCZACK: Oh. Yes. I found it . . . interesting.

BETA: Inspecting lathes and workers' washrooms? Really, now that does surprise me. But what did you think of the performance?

KORCZACK: It's hard for me to say. It's not been part of my duties before.

BETA: Regretting it already.

KORCZACK: (*Quickly*) No, no. You can't imagine. Compared to where I was before. Warsaw's a hundred, no, a thousand times . . . (*Laughs.*) I dare say I'll catch on.

BETA: (*Dry*) I dare say you will.

(*A pause.*)

KORCZACK: Your speech made in the factory, May I say it?

BETA: Yes?

KORCZACK: I really was impressed. Believe me, I've heard lots of them: high-ups, Party big shots. Tell me a journalist who hasn't. But yours was clear, you got your points across. A touch of humour in the difficult areas. You should give lessons to some people.

BETA: Thank you. But do you think it fooled them?

(*A pause.*)

KORCZACK: (*Startled*) Sorry? Who?

BETA: (*Slowly*) The workers, who else? I don't think it did. They know what really keeps their quotas up. The fellow who needs a new house for his wife; a holiday by the seaside for himself. He sweats it out, gets patted on the

back. And up go all the other schedules. Who's next
to be the Party's pet?

KORCZACK: (*Uncomfortably*) That's one way you could look at
it, I suppose.

BETA: The secret of Socialist Productivity. You said something
about a phone call?

KORCZACK: I wrote it down. (*Takes a scrap of paper from his
briefcase, gives it to* BETA.) Everyone had gone home when
it came. I was off myself so . . .

BETA: (*Reading*) That's all? He said nothing else?

KORCZACK: The name. Oh, and the man said he was sorry.
"It's seven years," he said. "Tell him I'm sorry." (*Pause.*)
Not bad news, I hope?

BETA: No. Something I'd expected.

(*He crumples the paper, throws it away.* KORCZACK *gets up.*)

KORCZACK: Well, I'll be going. I've got some work to do.
(*Hesitates.*) I meant what I said about your speech. I really
was impressed. It's when you meet the good ones that you
realize . . .

(*He laughs self-consciously, moves towards the door.*)

BETA: Do you, by any chance, play chess?

KORCZACK: Chess? A little.

(BETA *gestures at the board.*)

BETA: A friend was going to play a game with me. (*Heavily*)
Unfortunately he had more important business. Perhaps
you'd care. . . ?

KORCZACK: (*Doubtful*) It's been a while.

BETA: A short game only.

KORCZACK: Naturally, I'd be delighted but . . .

BETA: I understand. Your work.

KORCZACK: No. My work is not important . . . (*Comes back
warily.*) I'd be honoured.

BETA: Good. Pull up a seat. You'll have another drink.

KORCZACK: Thank you. Not for me . . .

(*He drags a packing case towards the desk.* BETA *fills both
glasses.*)

BETA: Chess is the only truly Socialist game. Stepan – I may call you that?

KORCZACK: Please.

BETA: You have a girl, I take it.

KORCZACK: As a matter of fact, I don't. Why do you ask?

BETA: (*Smiles.*) No reason. (*Holds out two chess pieces in his closed fists.*) Left or right, your choice.

KORCZACK: The left.

BETA: A wise choice. You begin.

KORCZACK: I'm not too good at this, I must warn you.

BETA: And I should warn you, I am excellent.

(KORCZACK *moves,* BETA *counters swiftly. The game continues as they talk.*)

The editor you mentioned; your former chief. Wasn't his name Dubrowsky?

KORCZACK: Zubrowsky. Tadeusz Zubrowsky.

BETA: There was some scandal, wasn't there? Zubrowsky, yes, now I recall the name.

KORCZACK: He was arrested. Several months ago.

BETA: (*Nods.*) I knew I'd heard a story. Someone denounced him to the Special Section. Zubrowsky – did you know him well?

KORCZACK: I wouldn't say so, no. He was my boss. That's all. Your move.

BETA: And his paper?

KORCZACK: They closed it down. "Politically unstable".

BETA: But you they sent to us. Their loss has been our gain. (*Smiles.*) So to speak.

KORCZACK: I was extremely lucky.

BETA: Cigarette?

(KORCZACK *refuses.*)

Why do policemen go around in threes?

KORCZACK: I beg your pardon?

BETA: Official policy. They always send out one who reads. One to make phone calls. And one is there to keep an eye on two such dangerous intellectuals. (*Pause.*) A joke?

KORCZACK: I see.

(*He smiles weakly.*)

BETA: You knew my phone call concerned the police.

KORCZACK: I had guessed. Yes.

BETA: You haven't asked me what it meant.

KORCZACK: Should I have?

   (BETA *moves a piece*.)

BETA: In check, I believe. My game.

KORCZACK: I can't argue.

   (BETA *begins to reassemble the pieces*.)

BETA: We'll play again.

KORCZACK: If you wish. If you think it's worth it.

BETA: Why not? (*Looks up*.) White always mates. Eventually.
   (*Pause*.) You didn't like my joke. I'm sorry.

KORCZACK: I'd heard it.

BETA: Had you?

KORCZACK: These kinds of jokes are . . .

BETA: Quite so. A minor aberration in our morals. Good, bad
   or simply old – like mine. Harmless – unless you choose to
   take them seriously.

KORCZACK: (*Shrugs*.) Surely a joke is just . . .

BETA: A joke. A pinprick in the seat of power. No one deflates
   a concrete wall that way. Take you, for instance, as a Jew.
   You must have heard a lot of cracks.

KORCZACK: (*Stiffly*) I'm not denying it.

BETA: (*Nods*.) But you don't let fools upset you.

KORCZACK: If some of my so-called comrades whisper
   names – well, that's their funeral. Jews make good
   Communists like other people.

BETA: Only more so, it seems. I don't doubt it. No use me
   calling you "a scheming yid" then? Unless some part of
   you believes I'm right. That makes sense.

KORCZACK: What are you getting at?

BETA: Let's just say I was wondering aloud. If Jews tell jokes
   against the State – is it the Jew or joke that we object to?
   Just how expensive should a joke become?

KORCZACK: Depends on what you think is funny. We're only
   human after all.

BETA: (*Pleasantly*) We crucified the last Jew to remind us.

Compared to that, what's seven years' hard labour?

KORCZACK: (*Slowly*) That name that I wrote down. A Jewish name. . . ?

BETA: My pawn has got your knight at last.

KORCZACK: Who was he? This Jew.

BETA: A humorous man. Yes. Not patient with clumsy liars, I'm afraid.

KORCZACK: A friend of yours?

BETA: You might say that. We both received a similar education.

KORCZACK: You mean you went to school together?

(BETA *fills his glass.*)

BETA: I meant we both have been arrested.

(*Quick blackout.*
Music: Wagner, loud.)

Scene 7

Dim lights up on Tadek's room.
MARIA *sits motionless on the edge of the bed. Her head is bent, long hair falls forward, hiding her face.*
A feeling of unreality, a dumb show.
A man waits beside the gramophone. His clothes are dark, his face anonymous. TADEK *enters, dressed for out of doors. He stops as he sees the man, turns to run. A second man, behind him, grasps his arms.*
MARIA *does not move. The music sticks, repeats.*
Quick fade-out. Crescendo of an approaching train as lights come back on . . .

Scene 8

Beta's flat. KORCZACK *sits alone at the desk. The train passes, fades. A pause.*
KORCZACK *picks up Ewa's book, glances at the title, opens it. He finds her petition tucked inside it. He begins to read it.*
BETA *enters, carrying a bottle. He watches* KORCZACK *for a moment.*

BETA: I take it as a sign . . .

(KORCZACK *starts guiltily.*)

Since Fascists keep their trains on time. It's only healthy ours should be erratic.

KORCZACK: It doesn't bother you – the noise?

BETA: We Poles have had to grow adaptive. But since you ask me, yes, it does. (*Comes to his desk and sits.*) I see you've kept yourself amused.

KORCZACK: I assure you. I didn't mean to pry into your affairs.

BETA: But since you have done, tell me what you think.

KORCZACK: I never knew that you knew Akimov.

BETA: I don't.

KORCZACK: Then why should you be interested in his case? Is it connected with your Jewish friend?

BETA: Not as far as I'm aware. Refresh my memory, what were the charges brought against Akimov?

KORCZACK: The usual kind, conspiracy and sedition. It's all down on this . . . document. You haven't read it? No, of course. Some crackbrain sent it to you, I suppose.

BETA: And if they'd chosen you, instead of me, what would your reaction have been to it?

KORCZACK: It's hardly likely, is it? (*Laughs.*) What would my signature mean on anything? I'm not exactly . . . well, a well-known figure.

BETA: But just supposing that you had been asked. What answer would you have given?

KORCZACK: The obvious one: it wouldn't do any good. (*Quickly*) Besides, how much do we know of the facts? The State never acts without a very good reason.

BETA: A dialectical answer then.

KORCZACK: (*Uneasily*) What else?

BETA: What else, indeed? Though I had different reasons.

KORCZACK: Actually it was the book that caught my interest. I've never seen this one before.

BETA: We all have bits of scribbling, best forgotten.

KORCZACK: I've read your other works, of course. I never knew you'd written on . . . this subject.

BETA: The book was an embarrassing present. Let me tell you, after you have gone, I'll probably use it when I light the stove. Unless you'd like a cup of coffee now?

KORCZACK: (*Shaking his head*) It seems a pity. When was it first published?

BETA: Let's just say: it's been out of print.

KORCZACK: Books on war crimes usually go down well. Perhaps you were just unlucky with reviewers.

BETA: Not at all. My critics were most kind. They spoke at length about my "obvious promise". Unfortunately they all agreed on one thing. They said I had – and here, I quote – a "concentration camp mentality". My book was dangerous for this reason.

KORCZACK: Dangerous? In what way?

BETA: Because it stirred a deep suspicion in them. How could they not suspect the few of us who came back? Returned from Auschwitz, Madjanek and Treblinka. We know a secret that is hideously infectious. Once it was hidden, now it has protruded into the glare of history. Becoming real and therefore justified. And naturally they are correct. The young must feel the earth beneath their feet, not just some thin and dangerous crust.
(*A pause.*)

KORCZACK: Forgive me, but I cannot understand that.

BETA: No?

KORCZACK: You called me a Jew. Yes, that is accurate. One of the luckier ones; still living. My parents packed me off to save my skin. But I lived long enough in the ghetto to see a little of what happened there. The long queues to the loading station, the Poles who looked the other way . . . There was no mystery, no secret. We have no protection from the facts. Some of us cannot afford to be so tidy about the things which we choose to remember. You see, we Jews feel no embarrassment for our debts.

BETA: Guilt is your speciality, it seems.

KORCZACK: Oh no, that's not a Socialist luxury. In Tel Aviv perhaps, not Poland. (*Laughs.*)

I spoke of debts and those who have to pay. I am owed a
few myself.

BETA: And who is getting the bill? The Germans?

KORCZACK: I used to think that. It was stupid. What was
Hitler, anyway? A sideshow for the fat, indifferent
bourgeois. Your articles helped to show me that.

BETA: Who, then?

KORCZACK: Didn't you name them in your speech this
morning? "The Enemy, comrades" – yes, I like that
phrase.

BETA: (*Slowly*) And you believe you know your enemies?

KORCZACK: I am the proof of their existence.

(*A pause.* BETA *refills his glass.*)

BETA: How old are you, Korczack?

KORCZACK: I'm 21.

BETA: When I was your age, I was just as certain. Certain that
I accepted nothing. But then a young man can afford his
nihilism. It's green and bitter, satisfying to him.

KORCZACK: To me, the whole thing's fairly simple.

BETA: Yes, now you've found a cleaner kind of hatred. A
Gentile one. Are you so sure about it?

KORCZACK: I don't think I'm mistaken.

BETA: All right, comrade, then I'd like to ask you—are you
healthy and well nourished?

KORCZACK: (*Puzzled*) Yes.

BETA: You live with civilized people, Party Members. And if
your country so demanded, then I assume that you would
do your duty?

KORCZACK: I suppose so.

BETA: So there are things which you would hold important:
principles, honour and ideals?

KORCZACK: Of course.

BETA: And so you would – forgive the interrogation – place
these above your personal interests. Because you are an
idealist?

KORCZACK: I don't see what . . .

BETA: (*Continuing*) In fact – and please correct me if I'm

wrong – in certain circumstances you would be willing
to fight for your ideals. To suffer and, if necessary, die?

KORCZACK: (*Hesitates.*) If I believed it necessary. Yes.

BETA: Then let me ask you one more question, comrade.
What did you do with your concern for life?
(*A pause.*)

KORCZACK: I'm sorry. I don't follow you.

BETA: Life. Your life; the processes of living. I mean this
breathing animal.

KORCZACK: (*Confused*) But what has that got to do with what
I've told you?

BETA: What you have told me is what you despise – life itself.
It wasn't good enough for you. No, you've already gone to
somewhere better; moved on to somewhere "higher up".
The greatest act you could perform was death. To die or
kill for what you held as sacred. Your ultimate meaning,
purpose – death. Death for the truth, death for the
Revolution; for God, the Fatherland, the Reich . . .
(*Pause.*) I needn't add that you were young and strong.
And therefore bloodier and more vicious in your yearning.
After all, one doesn't speak ill of corpses.

KORCZACK: You can't be serious?

BETA: No?

KORCZACK: Suggesting we're all murderers and oppressors,
because we're looking to improve things. The idea's
quite . . .

BETA: Disgusting.

KORCZACK: Absurd. It's twisted logic.

BETA: A simple paradox, my friend. You shouldn't find them
so hard to digest. Good Communists get lots of practice.

KORCZACK: So how should a man be truly civilized?

BETA: Perhaps you'd care to use my lavatory?

KORCZACK: What?

BETA: The little room, the shithouse down the corridor. No?
And yet you must admit it's useful. Where would we be
without these comforts? A room to eat in and a room for
crapping. You see, my dear chap, it's these little details

that, in the long run, count the most with us.

KORCZACK: (*Grimacing*) That's rather a crude reduction, isn't it?

BETA: I thought it rather kind, considering.

KORCZACK: Progress then adds up to better plumbing?

BETA: There're worse examples I could choose from.

(KORCZACK *laughs.*)

You laugh. But I've seen grown men crying. Because they were forced to soil themselves like babies. It takes a real philosopher, believe me, to tie strings round your trouserlegs and forget it.

(*A pause.*)

KORCZACK: This is some kind of game you're playing.

BETA: Is it?

KORCZACK: You're trying to shock me. That's what I think.

BETA: I'm being perfectly serious, my friend.

KORCZACK: Come now, you can't expect me to believe that.

BETA: No.

KORCZACK: I listened to that speech of yours, remember? "The forward movement of the masses . . . fulfilment of historical destiny . . ."

BETA: The proper sentiments for factories. Since that's where we make our "civilization" these days. (*With increasing irony*) Efficiency, speed, less waste and increased output. Pouring the oil that keeps the engines running, cogs turning round with fine precision.

KORCZACK: We must make use of our potential.

BETA: And when they stuffed our hair in mattresses – wasn't that most practical of all? The logical limits of our usefulness. I'm only surprised that Henry Ford hasn't been struck yet with the possibilities. Destiny, goals, a higher purpose? No one could ride this train we're on without some "glorious destination". As we plunge shrieking into each dark tunnel . . .

KORCZACK: (*Frightened*) Comrade, you shouldn't be saying these things. You will regret it when you're sober.

BETA: Truth is a gift not easily given away. Don't flatter

yourself that I'm wasting it on you now. Two Party
hacks just picking their fleas, that's all . . . (*Fills his glass
again.*) One not *quite* drunk. And only a bit less
mealy-mouthed than the other.

(KORCZACK *gets up.*)

KORCZACK: I'd better go.

(BETA *lifts his glass.*)

BETA: Question: what is alcoholism? Answer: the next stage
after Stalinism. A toast to the Jew who once said that . . .
(*He drinks.*)

KORCZACK: I want to tell you that you have my sympathies.
It's understandable, I suppose.

BETA: What is?

KORCZACK: That you should feel upset. After what happened
to your friend. It always comes as something of a shock.
To find our friends are . . . not quite what they seemed.
As for what's happened here tonight . . . (*Delicately*) I
needn't say it. You can rely on my complete discretion.

BETA: Thank you. (*Evenly*) And would it be too "indiscreet"
of me to ask you if you'd kindly leave? To get the hell out
of my flat?

KORCZACK: I only wished . . . If you wish.

(*He collects his briefcase.*)

BETA: Just crawl off home now, there's a good chap.

KORCZACK: I'm going. (*Moves towards the door, turns.*) This
evening has been quite an education. Of course I knew
that you despised me. I didn't realize quite how far this
"great contempt" of yours extended. To act the way you
do in public and yet to secretly nurse such hatred. I can't
help but feel sorry for you, comrade.

BETA: Whereas we know you don't deserve our pity. Not
while the Party smiles so fondly on you.

KORCZACK: That sounds like an insinuation.

BETA: An observation purely. That Party virtue still goes well
rewarded. They can be fairly generous, can't they? A good
thing too. How else would keen young men get on?
Without the dispensable Dubrowskys?

KORCZACK: (*Mechanically*) Zubrowsky.

BETA: You'd better hope when you sit in his chair there isn't some young jackal underneath it.

KORCZACK: Zubrowsky held reactionary views. His private writings were seditious.

BETA: An anti-Semite too, I bet.

KORCZACK: If you're suggesting it was not on merit that I was appointed to this post . . .

BETA: On merit, yes. Your excellent material, with every qualification for the job. You talk about my "hatred"? God help you, if ever you run out of yours.
(*A pause.*)

KORCZACK: (*Calmly*) I see it's no use talking to you further. It's clear you're not straight in your thinking.
(*He goes to the door and opens it.*)

BETA: I think . . .
(KORCZACK *waits.* BETA *continues; slowly, insultingly, as if he were already alone.*)
. . . I need new curtains on this window.
(KORCZACK *goes.* BETA *remains still. A train approaches. Slow fade-out.*)

Scene 9

The sound of a harmonica. Lights up on an open space. THE FLEA *sits playing it on a pile of blankets. He is dressed in concentration camp uniform, with various additions: a jersey, boots, worker's cap. In his late teens and fairly good-looking. A small sack lies beside him.*

Lounging nearby is STASZEK; *twenties, tough; dressed similarly to the Flea. Even relaxed, he still looks tense and watchful. He wears the armband of a Labour Kommando foreman. Between his legs he holds a pole which he is trimming with a knife. Several others lie beside him.*

STASZEK: Stow it, ass-head. Tell me again.

THE FLEA: (*Breaking off*) I told you. The Russkis have taken Kiev.

(*He resumes his playing.*)

STASZEK: Where did you get this "information"?

THE FLEA: I got it from Louis. It's all over camp.

STASZEK: (*Snorts.*) That lying whoreson.

THE FLEA: It's true. Louis got it from Sergeant Schiller,
personal. They're even saying in the SS barracks the Joe-
Boys have reached Kiev already. They're sending half up
to the front. (*Plays.*)

STASZEK: (*Chuckling*) The Ivans will teach those pigs a lesson.
They'll be no match for decent comrades . . . (*Snatches the
harmonica.*) If this is lies, Flea, it'll be your ass.

THE FLEA: It's true.

STASZEK: It better be. What's the time?

(THE FLEA *takes a wrist watch from his pocket.*)

THE FLEA: Eleven. Still an hour to dinner.

STASZEK: Hey, what's this? A new toy. Let me see.

(THE FLEA *gives him the watch.*)

Who gave you this?

THE FLEA: Kapo.

STASZEK: You sure? Not flashing your eyes at other
customers.

(THE FLEA *shakes his head sulkily.*)

That's good. Remember who fixed you up this little
number. You screw it up, you screw up me as well.
Right?

THE FLEA: Right.

STASZEK: Just concentrate on pleasing one sweetheart. Unless
you want to end up in the sauna.

(*He drops the harmonica, stands.* THE FLEA *retrieves it.*)

If I hadn't picked you off the ramp, believe me, you'd
have gone that way already.

THE FLEA: Staszek.

STASZEK: Uh?

THE FLEA: I don't like it here.

STASZEK: What's wrong? You don't get enough to eat?

THE FLEA: Yes, but . . .

STASZEK: Listen, you think I like this work? It's Funktion,

isn't it? You're sitting pretty. So don't complain to
me about it. There's plenty who would like a piece of you,
without me here to see that you're all right.

THE FLEA: I know but . . .

STASZEK: Yeah, sure, there're others doing better. But that takes
(*thumb-finger 'money' sign*), know what I mean? I'm working
on it, don't worry. Meanwhile you just be careful, right?
(*During this he has been fiddling with the watch.*) Broken. Your
boyfriend's cheated you. Louis might give me something for
this junk. Shit – that means it could be dinner! Pass auf, ass-
head, don't tell him I've been here . . .
(*He runs off quickly.* THE FLEA *hastily puts his harmonica
away and begins to take out of his sack a bottle, a sausage,
bread and cheese. A hoarse bellow from offstage.* THE FLEA
speeds up his movements. A few seconds later TADEK *runs on
stage.* THE KAPO *follows behind him, shouting.*)

THE KAPO: Move, you stupid whoreson! Up! Up! Up!
(TADEK *runs on the spot, knees high.*)
Stop! Down!
(TADEK *throws himself flat.* THE KAPO *puts his boot on*
TADEK'*s back.*)
Sport! Up, down! Up, down! Up, down. . . !
(TADEK *does press-ups.* THE KAPO *hits him with his stick.*)
Up!
(TADEK *leaps to his feet.*)
Arms!
(TADEK *lifts his arms.* THE KAPO *hits them.*)
Higher!
(TADEK *lifts his arms above his head. He is dressed in striped camp
garb; filthy and exhausted. His face is bloody.* THE KAPO *is burly;
black jacket, criminal's green triangle. He crosses to* THE FLEA.)
Where's Staszek?

THE FLEA: (*Shrugs.*) I don't know, Kapo.

THE KAPO: Shit, you don't. You think I'm fucking blind? I saw
the lazy whoreson run from here. He'd better be giving the
soup when I get back. If the shit knows what's good for him!
(*Grabs the bottle from* THE FLEA; *swills from it, stuffs his mouth*

46

with bread.) This one's (*jerks his head at* TADEK) not
getting any grub today. He's lucky that's not all that he's
not getting. The Unterscharführer pays a little visit. And
what you think this dumb-ass Pole does then?

THE FLEA: I don't know, Kapo.

THE KAPO: Answers back when he's not asked to. (*To* TADEK)
Arms up, whoreson! (*Growling*) The old days – they'd have
finished him off right then. (*Throws himself down.*) It's
getting too soft round here for my liking!

THE FLEA: They sent an officer from the camp?

THE KAPO: No need for you to sweat, my pretty.
(*He pinches* THE FLEA's *cheek, painfully.*)
Another Selektion after roll-call. The best thing for these
useless kikes. They're visiting all the Kommandos. The
job's not getting done on time – not quick enough for his
fucking lordship! (*Throws down his food disgustedly, rises.*)
Hitler's arsehole! What do they expect? Look at this
bunch of soft-gutted rabbis they give me. Goddamn
miracles – that's what. These Mussulman shit! They don't
know the meaning of honest work . . . (*Gestures angrily,
working himself up.*) "Here, Kapo, these yids have had it
too good. Now they can work off some that lard." What
use is that, eh?

THE FLEA: No use, Kapo.

THE KAPO: So they want to get rid of the scum? Well, burn
the rubbish, don't give it to me. Whose goddamn skin is
it, let me ask you, if they don't finish their quota on time?

THE FLEA: Yours, Kapo.

THE KAPO: You're goddamn right it's mine! (*Meaningfully*)
And yours too, sweetheart, don't forget that.

THE FLEA: (*Quickly*) I talked to Louis this morning about the
boots. He says he'll send them over later.

THE KAPO: About fucking time. How much is he asking?

THE FLEA: He'll make the deal in the block tonight. There's
another business he wants to talk over.

THE KAPO: (*Grunts.*) That means he's found some way to
screw me. These blood-sucking merchants are all the

same. What's the time?

THE FLEA: (*Terrified*) Quarter-past twelve?

THE KAPO: Time for that Staszek of yours to be finished. You
tell him from me, Flea, he'd better watch out! There's
plenty of ways I can settle his hash . . .
(*To underline this, he whacks his stick across* TADEK's *back
before he strides off purposefully the way he came.*
THE FLEA *sits down again. He picks up the remains of the
Kapo's meal and begins to eat.*
A few seconds later, TADEK *collapses. He drops his arms,
sags, and falls to his knees.* THE FLEA *looks at him with mild
curiosity.*)

THE FLEA: (*Finally*) You . . .
(TADEK *flinches and tries to straighten.*)
Hey, you, Pole. . . ?
(TADEK *turns his head.*)
What are you here for?
(TADEK *tries to answer, opens his mouth.*)
My pal is Polish. Staszek Wozensky. . . ?
(*No reaction.* THE FLEA *is disappointed.*)
Where are you from?

TADEK: (*Hoarsely*) Warsaw.

THE FLEA: (*Pleased*) Staszek is from Warsaw. From Wolska.
(TADEK *nods slowly.*)
Why are you here? (*Pause.*) Why were you put in a Jewish
Kommando?

TADEK: You . . . aren't . . . Jew . . .

THE FLEA: (*Shrugs.*) That is different. This is my Funktion.
(*Pause.*) How long have you been in?

TADEK: Three . . . days.

THE FLEA: (*Understanding*) So. Just a greener? You haven't
twigged yet how we do things here . . . (*Talking as if to a
child*) Listen, friend, you are in Auschwitz now. In
Auschwitz, every Pole gets Funktion. Stay with these
Jews and in maybe two months, you will go up the
chimney – pfft. Verstehen Sie – you understand?
(TADEK *nods.*)

(*Chuckling*) Three days, eh? That's not long. You'll learn.
(*Another prisoner,* HONI, *has entered silently during the last
part of this dialogue. He carries a pair of boots in one hand.*)

HONI: The first day counts as twenty years.

THE FLEA: (*Starting*) Honi! Do you want to kill me?

HONI: Why should I compete with experts?

THE FLEA: Don't creep up on a man like that!

HONI: I couldn't interrupt the lesson . . .

    (HONI *comes forward; small and dark, he wears the yellow
    triangle of a Jew. There might be something slightly wizened
    about him; an irrepressible jester's spirit.*)

THE FLEA: (*Carelessly*) I was explaining to this new
number . . . What are those?

HONI: You're asking me? Your Kapo's boots. Brand new off
that last Czech transport that came in. As Louis says:
"Nothing but the best for favourite customers."

THE FLEA: Let's see.

    (*He examines them critically.*)

HONI: Don't worry. There's not a blood stain on them.

THE FLEA: Still – better shine them up before he sees them.
    (*Takes a rag out, begins polishing.*) So, tell me, is it true
what they've been saying? The Ivans really are in Kiev?

HONI: Some of that sausage – then I'll tell you. You want the
good news or the bad news first?

THE FLEA: (*Tossing him the sausage*) The good. But don't take
too much or he'll notice.

HONI: The good news then: Hitler is dead.

THE FLEA: It's not true.

HONI: No. That's the bad news. "Alive and living in
Kiev" – that's the good news.

THE FLEA: You don't deserve a bite for that.

    (HONI *has cut a piece with Staszek's knife.*)

HONI: No? Good rumours don't come cheap . . .

    (*He catches* TADEK's *eye.* TADEK *looks away.*)
    So give it to him. He looks like he could use it.
    (*He throws the piece of sausage to* TADEK. TADEK *hesitates.*
    THE FLEA *looks up in surprise.*)

THE FLEA: (*Curious*) You know this one?

HONI: (*Shakes his head.*) Never seen him. These aren't the circles that I usually mix in.

THE FLEA: I heard the story. You really told that joke, they said? The one about Ludwig's pet Jewess?

HONI: (*Dryly*) You listen too much to Louis, my friend.

THE FLEA: I heard that Ludwig was out to croak you.

HONI: So, I admit, it was getting unhealthy . . .

(*By now* TADEK *has devoured the food.*)

That's why I fixed up this little vacation.

THE FLEA: You must have been crazy to joke about Ludwig. Where will you get a good Funktion like that one?

HONI: I go back tomorrow. Don't worry, it's settled.

THE FLEA: Back to the camp? And what about Ludwig?

HONI: He won't bother me where I'm going to be working.

THE FLEA: You don't mean. . . ? Shit!

HONI: (*Nods.*) A Scheiss-beglieter. The cleanest place in our Auschwitz home.

THE FLEA: (*laughs.*) Latrine attendant? That's a new one, joker.

HONI: (*Consoling*) Not everyone can afford such ambition.

THE FLEA: I thought for a moment you'd pulled off a fast one . . . Got yourself into a Kanada group. There'll be more shows now? Now that you are back?

HONI: The halt was only due to lousy business. Come to the usual place next week.

THE FLEA: (*To* TADEK) He'll make you crap yourself, this one. He's funny – hah!

HONI: Two breads to get in, just like before. Bring your Pole here, if he lives that long . . .

(STASZEK *enters, in a hurry. With him he pulls or pushes* REUBEN, *an elderly Jewish prisoner.*)

STASZEK: (*To* THE FLEA, *curtly*) Kapo wants you. Better move it, ass-head. He's snuffed three Jews already just for breathing.

THE FLEA: (*Frightened*) What's the trouble?

(STASZEK *has a livid weal across his face. He fingers it angrily, as he speaks.*)

STASZEK: What you think? That goddamn watch of yours. I

gave it to the other Kapo's boy – the one in Louis's block – to give him. The stupid whoreson let our Kapo see it.

THE FLEA: Staszek! I can't . . . he'll . . .

STASZEK: I'll get that ox for this! You see! I know some comrades who can fix his wagon. He'll wish his mother never shat him out!

THE FLEA: Staszek . . .

STASZEK: Why are you still here? Get your stuff and go and sweet-talk to him!

THE FLEA: What do I tell him?

STASZEK: Spin him any line. Tell him the fucking thing was stolen – what do I know? Blow!
(He turns swiftly to REUBEN *and to* TADEK, *who is standing now.)*
(To REUBEN*)* Arbeiten! Get to work! The Kapo needs three stretchers on the double. *(To* TADEK*)* You – help him. And don't screw up or you'll both end up on them.
(They scurry over to the poles and blankets. THE FLEA *is stuffing things back in his sack.* STASZEK *sees* HONI . . .*)*
What's this yid doing here?

THE FLEA: He brought the boots from Louis.

STASZEK: See he gets them. Where are they? *(Picks the boots up, holds them out. They are both the same, left feet. To* HONI*)* What's this? One of your stupid jokes? What fucking use are these to us?

HONI: *(Shrugs.)* So maybe Louis knows your Kapo better.

STASZEK: *(Advancing threateningly)* I ought to break your goddamn neck for this!

HONI: *(Pleasantly)* Pardon me, there's a queue behind you.
(A moment, STASZEK *turns away, back to the emergency he's facing. He throws the boots to* THE FLEA.*)*

STASZEK: Here. Hide these. I'll go back and try to quiet him down. Move it! And make sure you're smiling . . .
(He runs off. THE FLEA *is shaking. He stuffs the boots clumsily into his sack.* REUBEN *approaches deferentially.)*

REUBEN: Flea, we saw the SS man come from the camp. Will there truly be Selektion?

THE FLEA: (*Shrill*) Do I know? Don't bother me now, ass-head.
(*He runs after* STASZEK, *carrying his sack with him.*
REUBEN *has spotted the remains of the sausage, forgotten in the panic. He stoops and slips it under his coat surreptitiously.*)

REUBEN: (*Sighing*) God keep us from it . . . Oy, Oy vey . . .

HONI: I've yet to be convinced that God understands Yiddish.

TADEK: What is Selektion?

REUBEN: Why should you care? It is for Jews.

HONI: A privilege (*Taps his yellow triangle*) "pour la Sémite".

TADEK: Why?

REUBEN: (*Sourly*) He asks why . . . They send the sick ones
to the cremo. All those unfit for work . . .
(*He breaks into a fit of coughing.*)

HONI: Not for nothing are we called "the chosen people".
They choose us and they choose us. Half your group will
go on the trucks tonight.

TADEK: I am sorry.

REUBEN: Shit on your "sorry".
(HONI *gets up.*)

HONI: Don't waste your pity, Pole. These were rich men. In
Kanada they could stuff themselves. Now they must pay
the interest on that debt.

REUBEN: (*To* HONI, *angrily*) Your turn will come too,
whoreson! Soon!
(*He coughs again.*)

HONI: (*To* TADEK) This old Jew wore an armband once. And
shouted – how he shouted, this one. Now he is shouting,
no one listens. I think that's sad, don't you?
(REUBEN *spits disgustedly, turns away.*)
(*Quietly*) Nothing is free in Auschwitz, friend. You pay or
others must pay for you. So long.
(HONI *leaves.* REUBEN *has crossed to the blankets and taken
one.*)

TADEK: What must we do?

REUBEN: You heard him, We must make the stretchers. Some
lucky swine will not be walking back.
(*He spreads the blanket on the ground. It is stitched in half*

with strings attached. TADEK *watches him.*)
What are you doing? You are not working, you are dead
already. Get the sticks.
(TADEK *fetches the poles, lying near the blankets.* REUBEN
*takes two and slips them into the blanket, tying them on. As he
works he mumbles a prayer in Yiddish.* TADEK *fetches the
other blankets and kneels beside him, imitating.*)
Take it from me, Pole. You have been lucky. But do not
tempt God in a place like this.

TADEK: Lucky.

REUBEN: No Jew would have lived after what you did. Lucky to
be born a Pole. You should not spit upon such luck. I say
Kaddish now for someone not so blessed. My uncle, the
Rabbi of Sholev. A famous man, a reader of scriptures.
People would come many miles just to hear him . . . And
what happens? This morning the Kapo gives him one of his
"love-taps". And that is the end of my uncle, the scholar.

TADEK: Why did he do it?

REUBEN: Why? (*Bitterly*) We have a saying here in Auschwitz:
"Hier ist kein Warum" – Here is no "why"! You die.
That's all . . . (*Breaks into another fit of coughing.*) Ach,
why explain. You'll learn, if you live that long.
(*He notices* TADEK *looking at him curiously.*)
Work, Polack, work! Stay alive. Don't worry, your
brothers will take care of you. Not so long now they'll be
making you a Kapo.

TADEK: (*Shaking his head*) Never.

REUBEN: Ah, what a child. Why waste the words? So Honi
has told you: you learn or you pay.

TADEK: Who is this Honi?

REUBEN: Why? Who? You ask too many questions. Don't
talk to me about that joker. A clever monkey, doing tricks
for nuts. We had a Jew like that in my first Kommando.
He juggled bowls. Ate well until he dropped one too.
Then they got bored. Believe me, that is easy . . . (*He
looks expressionlessly at* TADEK.) Look at me, Pole. An old
camp-bird. Two years I have been alive in this place. How

many can say they have done the same? Look
carefully. You have been here three days . . .
(*He straightens, picking up one of the finished stretchers.*
TADEK *carries the other two.*)
Come. We go back now. Soon I will be meeting my uncle
again. Or maybe not soon – if God wills it.
(*They go. Slow fade to blackout.*)

Scene 10

Lights fade up. A hospital room. A bed, side-table, chair. MARIA
*sits on the side of the bed, head bent, in exactly the same pose we
last saw her. She wears a nightdress. A noise makes her look up.
She swings her legs up and gets quickly into bed.*
BETA *enters, dressed in a mackintosh and carrying a small bunch of
flowers.* MARIA'*s head is turned away from him on the pillow. He
approaches the bed, hesitates.*

BETA: Darling? Are you asleep?

> MARIA *doesn't move.* BETA *pulls the chair out and sits. He
> puts the flowers on the table.*

> We only got back an hour ago. The usual trouble with the
> transport. I came straight here. (*Pause.*) How are you
> feeling? (*Waits, then sighs exaggeratedly.*) I'm pretty tired
> myself. You know the kind of thing: speeches to the
> factory workers . . . A lot of effort; to send another
> thousand tractors to the Ukraine . . .

MARIA: (*Without turning*) Why go, if you hate it so much?

BETA: (*Laughs.*) Another rhetorical question. (*Pause.*) You have
a point though. (*Pause.*) Listen, when you get out of here,
we'll take a little holiday. How's that? I can easily get the
time off. Just you and me, mm? If you'd like that. . . ?
(MARIA *sits up in bed and takes a bottle of tablets from the
table. She shakes two into her palm.*)
Here.
(*He gets up solicitously and pours a glass of water for her. She
swallows the pills. He plumps the pillows behind her.*)

Better?

(*She nods. He kisses her cheek.*)

I'm sorry I'm late. Forgiven?

MARIA: Mm.

BETA: Good. (*Sitting on the bed beside her*) Did I tell you when I phoned? I've found us an apartment. It's not much, of course. At least – another room for the baby. I'll take you around to see it later.

MARIA: You did it.

BETA: What?

MARIA: You've been here for five minutes, talking. And now you've finally mentioned your daughter.

BETA: Have I? (*Laughs uneasily.*) How is our new addition then? Not half as pretty as her mother, I'll bet.

MARIA: You haven't seen her?

BETA: I did try. I asked that gorgon of a nurse to let me take a peep at her. But it was hard enough just to get in here – after "visiting hour" that is. (*A thought strikes him suddenly.*) She is all right, isn't she? There's nothing wrong.

MARIA: Your daughter is fine. A healthy baby.

(BETA *clumsily takes her hand.*)

BETA: Darling, really, I'm so happy. When they told me on the telephone, I had to go and put my head under the cold tap.

MARIA: Was it such a shock then?

BETA: No, difficult to believe that's all. My luck – being a father. So banal, isn't it? And yet it's different when they call your number.

(MARIA *begins to cry silently.*)

Darling, what's wrong? (*Pats her arm helplessly.*)

What's worrying you, please. . . ? (*Looks round him irritably.*) This bloody morgue they've stuck you into! No wonder it's depressing you. Things will seem better when you're out of here . . .

MARIA: (*Muffled*) Don't . . .

BETA: My love.

MARIA: Don't patronize me!

BETA: I'm sorry.

(*He gives her his handkerchief.*)

If I've been thoughtless, I apologize.

(*She composes herself.*)

Are you going to tell me? Naturally, if I'm not the father . . .

(*This raises a weak smile.*)

MARIA: I'm being silly.

BETA: No. You're just upset. What is the problem?

MARIA: (*Shakes her head.*) It's not me . . . I know that.

BETA: Leaving myself?

(*She nods.*)

I haven't changed.

(*She looks at him.*)

MARIA: No?

(*A pause. He can't meet her eyes.*)

I do know you, Tadek. Very well.

(*He lifts her hand and kisses it.*)

BETA: My darling.

MARIA: I've never seen you . . . so afraid . . .

(BETA *gets up and walks away a few paces.*)

BETA: Do you remember when I visited you? In the hospital in the Women's Camp at Auschwitz.

MARIA: I was a mess. Don't remind me.

BETA: You were a mess – but still beautiful. Under the eczema and the sores . . . It took my eyes to see that, how beautiful you still were. I said then not to concern yourself. Our children – I said – also would be beautiful with smooth skins and clean healthy bodies.

MARIA: She is. Oh, Tadek. I wish that you could see her!

BETA: I will, I will. (*Comes back to her. Smiles.*) Even if I have to stick my Party card right up your gorgon's nose. (*Pause.*) But you are right. I am afraid of meeting my new daughter. You've no idea how much it terrifies me.

MARIA: Tadek. A baby.

BETA: In Berlin once I saw a film. The worst kind of American trash. There was a scene which had a baby in it. And leaning over him – a monster. The baby sleeps on, unaware the monster's burning eyes are on it. Drops of grey slime fall from the monster's face . . . (*Laughs.*) Rubbish. But it still sticks in the mind. (*Turns to her.*) When my daughter looks into my eyes . . .

MARIA: The young are stronger than you think. They have all kinds of faith.

BETA: I know. But what are we to say to them?

MARIA: Give them the truth and they'll accept it.

BETA: (*Wry*) Too bad. That doesn't make a pretty bedtime story. The truth? That history is a mountain of betrayals . . .

MARIA: Tadek.

BETA: . . . and Papa, he is history's servant.

(MARIA *tut-tuts, puts her arms around him. He allows her to embrace him.*)

MARIA: What a silly little man . . .

BETA: Now who's being patronizing?

MARIA: Why must men always be right? Some things go on no matter what. Can Stalin stop the world going round?

BETA: That depends. I'm not too well up on our foreign policy.

MARIA: If women ran things, there'd be changes. We'd make a better job of it.

BETA: Maybe you'd like that for our daughter? The first woman premier.

MARIA: Not if I can help it.

BETA: (*Chuckling*) That's what a certain Jewish joker claims: "We need a woman in the Kremlin. A female arse to kiss – much nicer."

MARIA: (*Sharp*) No wonder that they locked him up.

BETA: (*Shocked*) Maria.

MARIA: Well. It's not surprising, is it?

(*Their mood is broken.* BETA *moves away.*)

BETA: (*Slowly*) No, not surprising. I'm past being surprised by what's been happening recently.

(*A pause.*)

MARIA: What did the Gestapo say?

BETA: (*Warningly*) The police have said nothing to me. I spoke
to Berman in the end . . . (*Gets up. Suddenly he looks
tired.*) I waited two hours. He was very . . . kind. He said
he'd make "enquiries" for me. But he was afraid that in
"these cases" . . .

MARIA: I could have told you.

BETA: I was granted permission to see the prisoner though.
For half an hour tonight.
(*He looks unthinkingly at his watch.*)

MARIA: I see. Don't let me keep you then.

BETA: You know they've got him in the same place. The one
where all of us were sent. I feel sick each time I go there.
The signs in German in the washrooms. They haven't
bothered to replace them.

MARIA: (*Flat*) How is he?

BETA: Oh, quite at home. I even suspect he's happy.
(MARIA *turns her head away.*)
He hasn't really changed at all . . . And nor have we.
(*Looks at her, an appeal:*) My love?
(*She won't respond.*)
Try to understand a little. God knows, it's hard
enough – but try . . .
(*A pause. He stands.*)
I'll telephone you later then.

MARIA: Tadek . . .
(*He waits. She struggles.*)
These last months . . . since you came back from Berlin. I
know – I'm not allowed to ask. Your work . . . I can't . . .
(*More calmly*) I've been watching you. Committees,
speeches, articles every day. Faster and faster – that is how
you go. Round and round and getting nowhere. (*Looks at
him.*) Tell me I'm wrong. That I don't understand. But
don't tell *me* you haven't changed.

BETA: Darling. Maria, I . . .
(*He stops, can go no further.*)

MARIA: Go to your meeting.
(*He kisses her cheek, goes out.* MARIA *stares straight in front*

58

unseeingly as the lights fade slowly down.
Darkness. Accordian music.)

Scene 11

A bright narrow spot comes up on HONI. *He is dressed in a false beard, shawl and skullcap; a caricature of Shylock Jewishness. He bangs a tambourine and sings.*

HONI: In de liddle town of Schmelz, I vas a boy – oy, oy,
  Lived a lady, name of Sadie, vas my joy – oy, oy,
  Vun day I go propose to her, tell her she's the only vun.
  She says: "Bist du Meshugge? Are you the Rabbi's
   son?"
  Sadie, Sadie – vot a clever lady
  So smart, dot girl, vun day she'll cut herself
  Sadie, Sadie – vot a luffly lady
  The only thing she think of is de geld . . . Oy, oy!

  Dot girl, she broke my heart just like a toy – oy, oy,
  She runs off and she marries with a goy – oy, oy,
  She says: "Vy must I vorry? Every day, I should give
   thanks.
  Vot's wrong with any goyim who's the owner of three
   banks. . . ?
  Sadie, Sadie – vot a luffly lady!
  I ask you, vot a gel to steal your heart
  Sadie, Sadie – vot a clever lady
  Nu – dot Sadie Cohen, she was smart . . . Oy, oy!
(He finishes with a flourish and bows deeply.)
Thank you, thank you . . . So, welcome to our humble entertainment. Some famous faces here tonight, I see. Don't worry, sirs, our lice are strictly kosher. Ah, Guten-Abend, Herr Kapo Rorscher. For you, a proper Aryan greeting . . .
(He raises one hand in a Hitler salute.)
For the boys at the back – the Jewish version. Shalom!

In Kanada

(*He raises the other arm, surrender.*)
If this is your first time . . .
(*He begins removing his beard, etc.*)
Remember one thing only, please – no clapping. If you like
it, just throw something. Preferably something soft . . .
and tasty!
(*He struts up and down as he speaks, a small stick under one
arm.*)
In a moment another song for you. But first I have been
asked to make one or two small announcements
please . . .
(*He stands respectfully to attention.*)
Attention. I must regretfully inform you – a serious theft
has taken place today. Certain Reich property has gone
missing from Kanada Warehouse number two. Eighty
kilos of human hair – that's not a matter we should take
lightly. The culprits shall be found and punished! As I
speak to you now, our highly trained soldiers are slowly
combing the whole of this Sektion . . . Attention! Please.
(*Dropping his voice*) It is with great sorrow that I must now
report a death that has recently taken place. (*Dramatic
pause.*) Mitzi; beloved hound and companion of our own
Oberstandtführer Molz . . . has passed away. Mitzi was a
well-bred bitch – needless to say of purest German stock.
Her death was caused by "heart failure", of course.
Brought on by her love of chasing cats. Abie Katz's widow
has been informed. At a simple ceremony today, Mitzi's
owner's grief was well observed. As that small body was
lowered into its grave. He spoke these moving words
beside it. (*Solemnly*) My heart is full. There are no words I
can find to express it . . . Heil Hitler! (*Flings his arm up in
salute.*) Now the Dog is dead. What a sad story, eh? Yes,
my friends, here you must take the bad with the worst.
And just to prove it, now I'm going to sing . . .
(*Picks up his tambourine.*)
(*Sings*) Why worry when your problems get you down,
  You'll never solve your troubles with a frown.

So turn your head up high, to that bright sun in the
    sky,
  And smile, smile, smile . . .
If you know the words – don't bother!
  It's no use if you're making gloomy faces
  Being moody never gets you places
  So give a cheerful grin, forget the mess you're in
  And smile, smile, smile . . .
*(Faintly but growing louder comes the sound of singing. A
male chorus pounding out a Nazi beer-hall anthem.)*
  Whenever you should feel inclined to curse
  Tell yourself that things could be much worse
  The world is not so bad, you won't feel so sad
  If you smile . . . *(Faltering)* . . . smile . . . smile . . .
  *(The singing swells; triumphant and deafening. The rhythm of
marching feet, beer mugs banging table tops; strident and
relentless, drowning him out. His spot diminishes, fades out.
The music continues as the houselights come up.)*

PART II

Scene 12

Lights come slowly up on Beta's apartment. EWA *sits alone in Beta's chair, now pulled a little way from the desk. Her clothes are dishevelled and her face tear-stained but she is reasonably composed now.*

Suddenly she gets up and comes down to the "window". Her movements are quick and tense. A noise from offstage. She starts and whirls around.

BETA *appears. He sees her expression.*

BETA: The kettle's almost boiled. (*Comes towards the desk.*) Go on.

(*He sits and lights a cigarette.* EWA *turns back to the window.*)

EWA: That's it. It happened after Dzadzek's speech.

BETA: How many?

EWA: (*Shrugs.*) Who counted? Not us. Six . . . twenty?
    (*tight*) We were too busy getting our heads broken.

BETA: Any idea who tipped them off?

EWA: (*Shakes her head.*) No. (*Comes abruptly to the desk and takes a cigarette.*) It could have been anyone. We made no secret . . .
    (*She tries to use Beta's lighter but her hands are shaking.* BETA *takes it gently from her and lights the cigarette.*)
    (*Laughs.*) They broke the door down. That'll please the landlord. Dzadzek's two months behind already.

BETA: What happened then? How many did they take?

EWA: (*Frowning*) I told you. Dzadzek, Jerzy and some others. Mostly the men. They don't think that us women . . .
    (*Breaks off. Flat*) Jerzy was bleeding. Blood all down his shirt. One of them got it on his jacket. I hope it stains it for the bastard.

BETA: You don't know where they took them?
(She shakes her head. BETA *picks up the telephone, begins to dial.)*

EWA: What are you doing?

BETA: *(Dry)* I'm still not entirely without influence. Perhaps this time . . .

EWA: It's no use! Why do you waste the time?

BETA: I could try.

EWA: You think they'll listen? You think they'll ever *listen*!

BETA: No. Perhaps not.
(He replaces the receiver.)

EWA: If you had been there . . .
(She turns away as she speaks but the unintended accusation hits home.)

BETA: Ewa . . .

EWA: You were right. But naturally you were right. It does no good. They've got everything the way they want it. But one day . . . god, one day – we'll make them listen! *(Looks at him.)* And you? Don't you get tired of being right?

BETA: Ewa, I tried to explain . . .

EWA: To think that once I used to think . . . that you had somehow worked it out. You had the answer. What a fool I was! Well, things have become very clear tonight. I have completed my State education. I've passed the course, diploma and all . . . *(Stubs out the cigarette and buttons her coat.)* From now on I see things as perfectly simple. There are only two types of people to deal with. Those that are willing to look up at the sun and those that will sit there and tell you you're blind. *(Moves towards the door, stops.)* Little Ewa is going. And don't worry, comrade, she won't be around causing problems again.
(She leaves. Fade down to blackout.)

In Kanada

Scene 13

Bright lights up on a long narrow wooden box with holes cut in its top. A latrine in Auschwitz. Near to it is HONI, *working with a spade and bucket. He scrapes something into his bucket and goes off whistling.*

TADEK *enters. He looks different, better kept: a wrist watch and a jersey, new boots.* HONI *returns carrying his bucket.* TADEK *waves to him.*

TADEK: Honi.

HONI: Wait. (*Puts down the bucket, scrapes a shovelful into it.*) Don't you know it's bad luck to talk to a man with an empty bucket? So. What did you want?

TADEK: Nothing.

HONI: I'll think it over. Let you know tomorrow.
(*He continues working.*)

TADEK: I have something for you.
(*He takes a pack of cigarettes from his coat.*)

HONI: (*Eyeing him*) So.

TADEK: You don't remember me.

HONI: A Pole who wants nothing for something. That I should remember.

TADEK: My name is Tadek. I brought you this. To pay you for the food. And the advice.

HONI: Advice is free, my friend. Saichel comes extra.

TADEK: Take them, please.
(*A pause. Then* HONI *takes them, opens the pack and sniffs.*)

HONI: The Kapo's sausage has improved. We'll smoke it in good health.
(*He offers one to* TADEK.)

TADEK: You do remember then.

HONI: I see you've come some way since then. How do you like it on the ramp?

TADEK: (*Surprised*) You know my Funktion?

HONI: I know where gifts like yours were "organized".

TADEK: (*Uncomfortably*) I'm . . . not complaining.

HONI: (*Dry*) No.

(TADEK *lights their cigarettes.*)

TADEK: To tell the truth . . . You won't tell anyone? I've put my name down for a different job. Hospital orderly. It's a joke, of course. No proper beds or medicines – and they want to train us!

HONI: I pray you always find it funny.

TADEK: I mean that they should pick us out at all. Two lawyers, one ex-tailor and there's me . . .

HONI: Yes?

TADEK: I am . . . I was a student.

HONI: You don't say. Studying what?

TADEK: (*Embarrassed*) English literature. And poetry.

HONI: So it's true then.

TADEK: What?

HONI: The story that the Poles are allowed parcels now. How nice to pick and choose like that.

(*He moves away, picks up his spade.*)

TADEK: It's not what you think.

HONI: (*Simply*) Tell me. How else should a man get off the ramp?

TADEK: There can be reasons. (*Pause.*) All right. A friend . . . a woman in the FKL.

HONI: (*Amused*) Ah.

TADEK: They say that men go there sometimes. To fetch the bodies here for burning . . .

(HONI *resumes working. A pause.*)

I caught your act. It was really . . . something.

HONI: (*Working*) Sorry, no refunds are given.

TADEK: It terrified me. All of us, I think. We laughed – but we expected any minute . . . Yet here you are. Still making cracks. Why do you do it?

HONI: I tell the jokes. My agent answers riddles.

TADEK: (*Shaking his head*) You must like to live dangerously.

(HONI *looks at him sharply.*)

HONI: And you, you have a choice perhaps? What did you want here, Pole?

TADEK: Nothing. (*Hesitatingly*) To talk then. I was

65

curious . . . Maybe to learn a little.

HONI: That's right?

(*He throws the cigarettes to* TADEK *who catches them, and turns away.*)

I am no teacher, friend. I only shovel shit – not talk it.

TADEK: (*Stiff*) I'm sorry. I wouldn't like to waste your time. (*Puts the cigarettes on the latrine edge.*) I'll push off since you feel that way.

(*He starts to leave.*)

HONI: Hey, Pole.

(TADEK *stops.*)

Do one more thing before you go.

TADEK: What?

HONI: Try to be more honest and less touchy. If that is possible for a Pole.

TADEK: I'll try.

HONI: You have a light, rich man?

(*He takes another cigarette.* TADEK *lights it for him.*)

TADEK: I'd like to ask you one more question.

HONI: So ask.

TADEK: Tell me, what does "saichel" mean?

HONI: (*Chuckling*) It means "good sense" and "circumcision". You don't need it. You were sensible enough to be a goyim. That's one thing that no Jew could teach you.

TADEK: You're not just "a Jew", I think.

HONI: No? I have the scars to prove it.

TADEK: And what you do: is that "sensible"?

HONI: (*Mocking*) So, it's a living.

TADEK: I think they watch you like an acrobat. Waiting for you to break your neck.

HONI: All Funktions are a temporary arrangement.

TADEK: Not the same.

HONI: You think not? (*Crosses to the edge of the area, looks off.*) Come here, my friend, and take a look out there.

(TADEK *comes to him.*)

You see the wooden walkway there between the blocks? (TADEK *nods.*)

66

It's strictly for Prominents and the SS, yes?

TADEK: Yes.

HONI: So who is standing on it now?

TADEK: Some camplings.

HONI: Yes?

TADEK: Three men. That's all.

HONI: No.

TADEK: (*Puzzled*) What do you mean? I can see three people.

HONI: (*Shaking his head*) No. You see some Mussulmans, some bodies. Look closely, friend. Tell me, have you seen "men" that stand like that? Who move their feet, one at a time, like storks. Who stare at the sky, the mud, so calmly – like cows. See, that one has a piece of bread. Take it, he wouldn't notice you.

TADEK: (*Angrily*) I've seen Mussulmans before. What are you saying – that I should feel sorry? Of course I am. But what's the use of that?

HONI: Shh. Look now. Who's that coming, in a hurry?

TADEK: That's Sacher. He's the Kitchen Kapo.

HONI: Watch now.

TADEK: Bastard.

HONI: Why?

(*Comes away.*) The walk belongs to him, he's earned it. You, a Funktioner, should know that.

TADEK: Still, there was no need.

HONI: He is not angry, they were in his way. You think that either of them cares? A Mussulman – who knows what he thinks? He has no shoes and no ambitions. Tomorrow he'll join the pile for burning. But he is already dead inside. His problems solved. For you, they're just beginning.

TADEK: How so?

HONI: You have your boots up on that slippery piece of wood. You join the act – so don't look down again.

TADEK: Which means?

HONI: You have a choice. It's not that different from outside. Except that when the strong fall down . . . (*Smiles.*

Quietly) We like to help them reach the bottom.

TADEK: (*Bitterly*) A very German parable, yours.

HONI: (*Shrugs.*) Even Jews can learn to think like Germans. For Poles it comes much easier.

TADEK: I don't think you believe that really.

HONI: So what do you believe in, clever Pole?

TADEK: In what I understand.

HONI: Then that explains why you believe so little.

(STASZEK *has entered during this, unnoticed. He stands, listening cynically.*)

STASZEK: So here's where you've been hiding, Tadek. (*Comes forward.*) A good spot if you like talking to turds.

(*He lowers his trousers, sits on the latrine.*)

HONI: (*To* TADEK) Better come back. This one is giving birth.

(*He goes back to his cleaning.*)

TADEK: Staszek.

STASZEK: Why do you bother with this Jew? they all talk crap. Not one has got the guts to stand up for his miserable yiddish hide. You've heard the news?

TADEK: No.

STASZEK: A transport's due. They say this one's from Hungary – they're the best. (*Chuckling*) Shit, you remember what we found last time? Two bottles of cognac, French, and two of schnapps. The sons of bitches made us work for it though. Six thousand to get off the trains and into the lorries.

TADEK: Five.

STASZEK: Six . . . five – who gives a damn? The good thing is we're back in business. The boys have been getting pretty worried. It's been three weeks. Not one smell of a transport.

TADEK: Maybe they've run out of Jews to gas.

STASZEK: Goddamn, don't say that! That's not even funny. Where would we be without the stuff they bring us?

TADEK: We still get parcels.

STASZEK: Sure but a man's got duties to his comrades. We must support them in the struggle . . . (*Dropping his voice*)

The Organization doesn't run on air . . . (*He glares suspiciously at* HONI. *Loudly*) It's only Jews who cheat their brothers.

HONI: Maybe that's why: it's only Hitler kept his word with us. He made a promise to you too, I think.

STASZEK: (*Angrily*) Stalin is settling Hitler's hash right now. And when he's finished, you had better watch it. You think we haven't tumbled you, us comrades? We know your slimy Jewish schemes.

HONI: (*Mildly*) What schemes are those?

STASZEK: Ach, don't pretend. We've got your number, Jew. Who do you think makes money from this war? The Jews, that's who. Who are the capitalists behind it? Jews! Who gets rich selling guns to Fascists. . . ?

HONI: The Eskimos.

STASZEK: Why the Eskimos?

HONI: (*Shrugs.*) Why the Jews?

STASZEK: Idiot! Ah, why waste my breath. (*To* TADEK) They'll find out soon what's coming to them. No good crying then . . .
(THE FLEA *runs on breathlessly.*)
Slow down, ass-head, what's the hurry?

THE FLEA: Transport coming! All Kanada groups report! You're wanted at the ramp, Staszek . . .

STASZEK: Hoo, that's more like it! Tell them we are coming . . .
(*He leaps up, pulls up his trousers hurriedly.* THE FLEA *runs off.*)
At last some action, eh, TADEK? *Listen, if you find perfume this time – I've got a little piece I'm after. The good stuff, mind you, nothing cheap . . . Hey, wait, you whoresons! Staszek's coming. . . !*
(*He runs off.* TADEK *turns uncertainly to* HONI. *Their eyes meet for a moment.*)

HONI: What are you waiting for – a blessing?
(TADEK *goes off reluctantly.* HONI *resumes work. The lights fade slowly.*

In Kanada

Fade up, at the same time, the sound of a train approaching and stopping. In the darkness, the groaning and squealing of its brakes seem to go on forever.)

Scene 14

Lights up. A prison interview room; the effect bare, stark and brightly lit. A small table, ashtray and two chairs. Another chair against a wall behind it. BETA *sits waiting, his mackintosh is hung over the back of the chair.*

A GUARD *shows in the* LAWYER *and goes to sit discreetly upstage. The* LAWYER *is elderly and seedy looking. He carries a cheap briefcase and looks tired.*

LAWYER: Ah . . .

(BETA *stands. They shake hands.*)

Yes, they'd told me you'd arrived.

BETA: Sit down?

(*He pulls the other chair out.*)

LAWYER: (*Sitting*) Thank you. Just for a minute. (*Smiles vaguely.*) A little tired, I'm afraid. It's been a long day. For all of us.

BETA: (*Offering*) Cigarette?

(The LAWYER *refuses.*)

How is he?

LAWYER: Fine. Fine . . . as one could expect.

BETA: The hearing?

LAWYER: Oh, over. Finished this afternoon. All a bit of a mess, I fear. Some mix up with the police report . . . (*Sighs.*) A sloppy business. Quite disgraceful.

BETA: And?

LAWYER: Mm?

BETA: What was the result?

LAWYER: Oh, yes. I see. Well, that's what we're not sure of yet. Still waiting till they've got sorted out. Decided the sentence, all that sort of thing.

BETA: He was found guilty? Of the charges?

LAWYER: Oh, yes.

BETA: Of course.

LAWYER: They said they'd telephone me tonight.

BETA: Really.

LAWYER: There's still some evidence they need to consider. Most irregular . . . but there you are.

BETA: You've no idea what they'll give him?

LAWYER: Hard to say. It depends on charges; proof of collusions, tie-ups and so on. Of course I haven't seen this fresh evidence of theirs . . .

(*He trails off. A pause.*)

BETA: (*Heavily*) You don't know then.

LAWYER: (*Evasive*) I wouldn't like to guess. As I say, without the evidence it's hard to be . . . too definite.

(BETA *stands.*)

BETA: You sound just like a doctor – tiptoeing around a fatal diagnosis. (*Walks away a few paces, turns.*) I'm sorry. That wasn't called for. (*Comes back to the table.*) I've just come from the hospital. My wife's just had a baby. She was upset . . . I'm afraid my nerves are still a bit on edge.

LAWYER: (*Sympathetically*) Ah. May I ask you? How well did you know my client?

BETA: You've read my statement. Not well. We met during the war.

LAWYER: And since then?

BETA: He wasn't in Poland then.

LAWYER: You wrote no letters while he was abroad?

BETA: I didn't know where he was. He just turned up one day in Warsaw. Came to see me at the paper.

LAWYER: (*Relieved*) And that was the first time you had seen him?

BETA: Yes. (*Pause.*) Perhaps he should have stayed in America.

LAWYER: (*Tiredly*) It might have been better. Yes.

BETA: Surely all this is academic . . . now?

(*The* LAWYER *takes a document from his briefcase.*)

LAWYER: You'd better read this; the prosecution's statement.

I have two copies. (*Passes one to* BETA, *puts on his spectacles.*) I draw your attention to paragraph four. Were you aware of these facts presented? That my client was an active Zionist before the war. A member of the Betar, the most revisionist of the Zionist groups.

BETA: (*Reading*) No. We never discussed his politics, I'll admit. Unless you count the jokes. It says here he joined in 1937. That means he must have been still in his teens.

LAWYER: Probably.

LAWYER: Rather a long way back to worry about.

LAWYER: Is it?

BETA: We all belonged to something then. Poles and Jews. It was a time for "great convictions".

LAWYER: Some a little less fortunate than others, I fear. (*Clears his throat.*) If I may. . . ? (*Reads.*) "From this we may see at what early age the seeds of the Zionist–Fascist code were planted. Beliefs that would flourish as time passed, becoming more evident in his behaviour. During the period when our countrymen were struggling to rebuild a new and classless society; this man had no compunction in deserting to join his fellow Jewish nationalists in the West. The aims of International Zionism are well known. Whilst we despise issues of creed and race, irrelevant to the proletariat's battle, we cannot blind ourselves to this conspiracy. Their ceaseless efforts to undermine us, to subvert Sovietism and world peace . . . imperialist profiteers . . ." Mm. I'll skip that.

BETA: Please.

LAWYER: "We ask you to look again at the defendant. You see a rootless cosmopolitan whose sympathies we have now established. Since readmittance to this country we have had ample evidence of them. He has been seen frequently in the company of other dubious elements; (*slight emphasis*) Jews, intellectuals, shiftless emigrés like himself. We cannot ignore the threat that he presents to our State security and ourselves . . ." (*Puts the two documents away.*) I thought you ought to know.

BETA: Yes. (*Pause.*) Thank you.

    (*The* LAWYER *rises.*)

LAWYER: And now if you'll excuse me, please. I have another client to visit.

BETA: Of course.

    (*They shake hands.*)

    You'll let me know?

LAWYER: I'll telephone you when I've heard myself. It shouldn't be too late. (*Turns to go, hesitates.*) Tell your friend . . . I'll be speaking to him.

    (BETA *nods. The* GUARD *rises and escorts him out. He returns as the light fades out.* BETA *sits down again.*)

Scene 15

Bright lights up on TADEK, *seated on the ground. His shirt is open and he reads a book. Beside him lies a small cardboard box.*
THE FLEA *enters backwards, followed by* STASZEK, *who is carrying a small sack.* THE FLEA *is impersonating someone for* STASZEK's *benefit.*

THE FLEA: (*High voice; exaggerated*) "Kameraden, this is serious! The regulations are quite clear. No female prisoners in the washrooms . . ."

STASZEK: (*Cuffing him*) Ass-head.

THE FLEA: (*Excitedly*) His face! I'll swear I bust a gut. And you with your pants down, everything hanging out . . .

    (STASZEK *sees* TADEK, *croses over.*)

STASZEK: Hey.

TADEK: Staszek.

STASZEK: Catching some sun, eh? Not so bad.

    (THE FLEA *bounds over.*)

THE FLEA: Tadek, you should have been there! You'd have died. You know our little Adolf in Blockhouse Five? He caught Staszek giving it to a skirt. Right in the washroom under Adolf's nose!

STASZEK: Stow it.

THE FLEA: But Staszek, he just stands there, cool as ice: "Maybe you want to treat the bitch yourself, Herr Doktor. . . ?"

STASZEK: (*Terse*) Flea, shut your fucking yap.

(THE FLEA *dries up. He turns to* TADEK.)

You coming to the block tonight? We're fixing ourselves a little grub.

THE FLEA: Witek's got another parcel. A piece of ham like this (*gestures*) I swear.

STASZEK: We're going to have ourselves a feast. The boys are out now organizing stuff.

THE FLEA: You're coming, Tadek? You'd have to be crazy.

TADEK: I'll see.

(STASZEK *sits down beside him,* THE FLEA *follows suit.*)

STASZEK: Don't forget. (*Takes a tomato from Tadek's box. Grinning*) All contributions welcome.

TADEK: If I come.

(STASZEK *puts his head on one side, looks at him.*)

STASZEK: You play it pretty close, uh, poet? Keep out of sight, I like that.

TADEK: (*Dryly*) I try.

STASZEK: Right. Too many dopes here blowing up your ass. A man can't get a space to breathe, know what I mean?

TADEK: I think so.

(STASZEK *bites into the tomato.*)

STASZEK: Hey, that's good.

TADEK: (*Impatiently*) Stop playing games with me, Staszek.

STASZEK: Who, me?

TADEK: Have you got something for me? Because, if not . . .

(STASZEK *laughs and punches him playfully.*)

STASZEK: You know I used to worry about you? But you're all right in my book, poet. (*To* THE FLEA) He's kosher this one. Don't take any shit.

THE FLEA: (*Eagerly*) Sure. Tadek's got his head screwed on.

TADEK: Well?

STASZEK: Got any more of these? I'll trade you. Three smokes for three. That's fair, now isn't it?

TADEK: Go on. Take them.

(STASZEK *smiles*.)

STASZEK: You want it here?

TADEK: Just give it to me.

STASZEK: No hurry, friend.

> (*Checking around him first, he takes a folded paper from his shirt and passes it to* TADEK *who opens it and begins to read at once*.)
>
> I've seen some crazy on a piece of skirt. But you . . . (*To* THE FLEA) Our Tadek's got a sweetheart in the FKL.

THE FLEA: The Women's Camp?

STASZEK: Writes to her every day. Right, Tadek?

THE FLEA: That so? (*To* TADEK) What's the pussy like? Hey, Tadek, do you write her poems?

STASZEK: (*Amused*) What you think?

THE FLEA: "Oh, darling, it gives me the shits. To think about your lovely . . ."

STASZEK: Stow it, ass-head. Don't insult true love.

(THE FLEA *snickers*.)

TADEK: She says she got the medicine that I sent. One bottle only. I sent two.

STASZEK: So? Maybe one got broke along the way. Listen, you don't like our arrangement. . . ? With me, it's fine.

TADEK: No. You know I have no choice. Now that the women dispose of their own corpses . . . (*Folds the letter up, puts it away*.) Who are you using as the postman?

STASZEK: An electrician friend of mine. A good comrade. They send him there to take care of the wiring.

TADEK: He's going back soon?

STASZEK: Some time. Most days he goes.

TADEK: Then . . . (*Takes a paper from his book and two tomatoes from the box*.) Give him this. And these. A little thankyou.

STASZEK: (*Shakes his head*.) We make no charge for letters here, you know that. But if you wish – there is a something you could do.

TADEK: What is it?

STASZEK: Flea.

> (*He jerks his thumb for* THE FLEA *to keep lookout.* THE FLEA *crosses to the right, looks off.*)
>
> (*To* TADEK) A favour for the Organization. Nothing so hard. You have a patient. Bed number eleven?

TADEK: You mean my Czech? The one with pleurisy?

STASZEK: (*Nods.*) We've got a present for that whoreson traitor. A little gift we'd like you to deliver . . . (*Opens his sack, shows* TADEK *the contents.*) A nice warm shirt to keep him cosy. Don't touch. The owner died of typhus just this morning.

> (TADEK *draws back hastily.*)
>
> (*Grins*) A shame to waste such big fat, hungry lice. They'll make a meal out of your Czech. And when they've finished . . .

TADEK: What did the man do to deserve this?

STASZEK: (*Darkly*) What did he do? That stinking bastard! Sold us! Six of our comrades died because of him. You know what? Even while they stuffed them in the ovens, they still kept shouting for the cause. They were brave men, true Communists. The Czech is getting off too easy.

TADEK: (*Quiet*) Why me?

STASZEK: Because you cured the shit. He trusts you.

> (*A sudden burst of noise offstage.* STASZEK *is on his feet at once. He crosses to* THE FLEA.)
>
> What's up?

THE FLEA: It's nothing. Just the kitchen boys. They caught a Mussulman thieving turnips.

STASZEK: Too bad. (*Comes back to* TADEK.) Well? (*Pause.*) You'll do it?

TADEK: Yes.

THE FLEA: Hey, Staszek, get a load of this! They're really having fun with the poor dope . . . (*Laughing*) Pants off – twenty-five in the ass!

TADEK: I didn't have much choice. Or did I?

> (STASZEK *smiles, holds out his hand.*)

STASZEK: Your letter, lover. I'll see that she gets it.

(TADEK *hands it over.*)

THE FLEA: (*Calling off*) Hey, boys, look out! Your Kapo's coming . . .

(*Chuckling*) That scared the whoresons. Whee, look at them run . . .

STASZEK: (*To* THE FLEA) Leave it, shit-head. Over here.

(THE FLEA *comes back reluctantly.*)

I think you owe our friend. Three smokes.

THE FLEA: Aw, Staszek.

STASZEK: Come on, cough up. We don't cheat on our deals.

(THE FLEA *takes out the cigarettes.* TADEK *holds out the tomatoes but* STASZEK *grabs* THE FLEA's *hand.*)

(*To* TADEK) Bring them to the block tonight. We like to see new faces sometimes. (*To* THE FLEA) Let's go, idiot.

THE FLEA: So long, Tadek. See you at the party.

STASZEK: Don't be a stranger, eh? (*Meaningfully*) Good comrades need to stick together.

(*They start to leave. Suddenly a figure lurches on, knocking them sideways. It trips and stumbles to the floor.*)

(*Angry*) Watch it, whoreson! It'll be your ass.

THE FLEA: Mussulman shit!

(*He kicks the figure. They go.* TADEK *collects his things and the sack. The figure stirs and groans. It is bare-footed, bloody. A klaxon begins to sound. The lights dim gradually.* TADEK *hesitates, crosses to the figure.*)

TADEK: (*Gruffly*) Roll-call, friend. Think you can make it?

(*The* FIGURE *flinches.*)

You should know better. They watch those turnips like eagles. Come to the sick room in the morning; we'll see then . . .

(*He is about to go, notices something, bends and peers. Softly*) Sweet Jesus, what has happened to you, Honi. . . ?

(*He kneels as the lights go swiftly down to blackout. The klaxon continues then stops abruptly.*)

In Kanada

Scene 16

Lights slowly up on the prison interview room, as before. BETA *is standing downstage, smoking boredly.*
A long pause.
BETA *crosses to the table, stubs out his cigarette. He takes another, offers one to the* GUARD.

BETA: Smoke. . . ?

> (*The* GUARD *does not respond.* BETA *shrugs and lights his own.*)
>
> How much longer, do you think?
>
> (*The* GUARD *stays silent.*)
>
> I don't want to cause a nuisance but . . . I've work to do, you understand? (*Pause.*) Important business . . . (*Dryly*) For the State. Another article. This one's about "Colonialist Expansion". Half of the globe's being swallowed up, eaten away by imperialist aggressors. Do you have views about that, comrade? (*Waits.*) No? Well. Perhaps you've read my articles. They come out each week, it's hard to miss them. Front page, three columns, a double heading. It's hard work filling all that space. Oh yes. Believe me it's not always easy. It's not always beer and dancing – for journalists – not by a long, long way . . . (*Pause.*) Haven't I seen your face before? (*Pause.*) You're quite sure you won't have a cigarette?

GUARD: No, thank you, comrade.

> (*As he speaks, he takes one of the proffered cigarettes and, at the same time, lets his eyes travel slowly upwards to where the ceiling would be.* BETA *follows his gaze.*

BETA: I see. (*Pause.*) Well, never mind then. (*Lights the cigarette, comes slowly back to the table. Sits down. Sighs.*) At this rate, I'll probably miss the "expansion". It will have "contracted" before I get out . . .

> *Suddenly the* GUARD *leaps smartly to his feet, stamping out the cigarette in the same motion.* HONI *enters. He is now dressed like a Stalinist detainee; a costume not that much different from his last; collarless shirt, clogs or laceless shoes, a*

78

shapeless jacket.

BETA *comes forward to greet him but the* GUARD *objects. No contact permitted. They sit on either side of the table. The* GUARD *retires.*

HONI *is composed, calm and even slightly amused.* BETA *however betrays deep uneasiness in every word and gesture. They speak quietly at first.*

So, old friend.

HONI: So.

BETA: It's good to see you.

HONI: It was nice of you to come by.

BETA: How are things with . . . (*Stops.*) I mean – are they treating you well?

HONI: I can't complain. But apart from that . . .

BETA: (*Quickly*) Anything you need? I'll try . . .

HONI: A record-player. It would go nicely on the drinks cabinet. (*Smirks.*) A cigarette?

BETA: Of course.

(*The* GUARD *stirs, thinks better of it.* BETA *lights up their cigarettes.* HONI *draws deeply, appreciatively; then begins to cough.*)

(*Worried*) The cough sounds worse.

HONI: It shouldn't. I've been practising all night. (*Controls it.*) So what of the new father then? Which did you get – a boy or girl?

BETA: Girl.

HONI: That's good. A first-born son – now, he would have had to become a rabbi. The mother?

BETA: She's . . . well. She sends her wishes for you.

HONI: And mine for her. Please give them to her.

BETA: I will. (*Pause.*) You're sure there's nothing. . . ?

(HONI *shakes his head. A brief silence.*)

(*Abruptly*) Your lawyer was here.

HONI: Ah.

BETA: We talked a little. Before you came.

HONI: He doesn't know yet?

BETA: No. He says he'll be speaking to you.

(HONI *nods.* BETA *bursts out angrily.*)
What a mess!

HONI: Yes.

BETA: The whole case is quite absurd! I'd never have thought
it would come to this. A job for the censors not the police.
It wouldn't have been the first time either – they've told
some entertainer to clean up his act. It's not as though so
many people saw it.

HONI: A compliment?

BETA: Well. The cabaret show at Morris's Eating Parlour. I
mean, who was there to be subverted? A few deaf
pensioners stuffing themselves with bortsch. Hardly
"dangerous dissidents".

HONI: I've had worse notices before. And better audiences
too. It's true though, it was getting boring. Until the boys
with notebooks came. I gave one of my best
performances . . . Almost like old times . . . (*Chuckles.*)

BETA: They've blown the whole thing up completely! You
realize what these charges mean?

HONI: Morris must book another act. Not easy on the money
he pays.

BETA: (*Exasperated*) How can you be so calm about it?

HONI: (*Gently*) My friend, you mustn't excite yourself. Nice
suit you're wearing, who went for the fitting? You'll stain
it if you get into a sweat.
(BETA *shakes his head.*)

BETA: (*Dully*) This shouldn't have happened. There was no
need, no reason . . .

HONI: Since when did we need reasons? What happens,
happens.

BETA: (*Low*) The lawyer told me you were in the Betar?

HONI: Surprised?

BETA: I never knew that you had politics.

HONI: I had measles too. When I was younger.

BETA: (*Almost an appeal*) Why did you come back from
America?

HONI: (*Sighs.*) America . . .

BETA: (*With bitterness*) Wasn't the "good life" good enough for you? Why couldn't you stay, where you were . . .

HONI: (*Amused*) Harmless? Just "another Jew"?

BETA: What was there left here to come back to?

HONI: You want that I should make a list?

BETA: And Poland, of all places, why?

HONI: Where else is the place not full of Jews?

BETA: Didn't you realize things have changed?

HONI: You mean the old jokes get new laughs?

BETA: Damn it! Why do Jews always answer a question with another?

HONI: (*Smiles.*) Why not?

(*A pause.*)

BETA: (*Defeated*) You should have stayed, Honi. They could afford you in America. They can afford most things that they don't need.

HONI: You talk a lot about America, don't you? What was it? (*Quotes slowly*) "The plump host . . . that feeds the slaves of mindless bourgeois greed . . ." You see, I read the paper.

BETA: (*Tired*) It's my job. Reporting on the "competition".

HONI: So? My cousin Hayim in Chicago, I think he'd be surprised to know he's living in a "moral vacuum". A nice boy, but he's not too bright. For instance, he can't figure out just why they call him "dumb Polack"!

BETA: Some capitalists can be very stupid.

HONI: The Irish run things over there. Now, they are Polish, if you like. They have a new man working for them. A man called Joseph . . . Joe . . . McCarthy?

BETA: I know. A right-wing Fascist.

HONI: This Irish Joe, he doesn't like Hayim. He thinks the Russian Joe would like him. So Hayim, he's in Israel now. He writes and asks me to go out there. Well . . . It's nice and hot. But it seems the Jews take life too seriously; always fighting. (*Sighs.*) That we should lose our sense of humour . . .

(*A silence.*)

BETA: What's going to happen now, Honi? You know that the minimum's four years' hard labour. But with these so-called accusations . . .

HONI: (*Slightly impatient*) So we'll jump off that bridge when we come to it. You'll do a little favour for me?

BETA: Whatever I can.

HONI: Go see Morris. He still owes me money. Tell him I said for you to have it. A little present – for the baby.

BETA: Honi, I . . .

(*He cannot trust himself to speak.*)

HONI: See that cheapskate doesn't cheat you. Two thousand, not a zloty less. (*Smiles.*) So call it payment if you like. For saving the skin of a troublesome Jew.

BETA: If I could do it again . . .

HONI: I know.

BETA: (*Bitterly*) This time I'm not so privileged. Or trusted. In Auschwitz at least, I might have paid. You could buy anything – for a price.

HONI: Don't ever think such things, my friend.

BETA: Why not? I've never felt so helpless!

HONI: It won't be the first time that I've lost a Funktion.

BETA: You told me once that I had a choice. But you never made that choice, did you? To live in the land of milk and honey, in Kanada with the rich and blessed.

HONI: Come now, you don't think I've troubles already? Enough – so you should talk this way.

BETA: That was the lesson that Auschwitz taught me. Marx could have explained what went on there. Two classes – the monkeys who carried the clubs. The others, the fossils, the hollowed-out men. It was quite simple – for years I've believed that . . . (*Looks at* HONI, *a slow realization.*) But you didn't did you? You saw things more clearly. Jesus – you *knew* this would happen to you!

HONI: (*Concerned*) My friend . . .

(*But the* GUARD *has already stood up and is waiting.* HONI *stands slowly.*)

My friend . . .

In Kanada

(*The* GUARD *takes* HONI *impatiently by the arm.* HONI
allows himself to be led a little way. Then he turns back to
BETA.)
There are many kinds of Mussulman, friend. See that you
don't become a fat one.
(*He goes off. The lights dim slowly.*)

Scene 17

A cold light up, suggesting winter. An empty space.
TADEK *and* MARIA *enter, both wearing long overcoats.* MARIA
wears a headscarf as well. MARIA *stops.* TADEK *comes back to*
her.

TADEK: You're shivering. Do you want to go back? Maybe
this was not such a good idea.

MARIA: I'm not cold.

TADEK: (*Worried*) I don't want you getting sick again. Not
now I've just got you with me.
(*Their mood is fragile, cramped by the shadow of recent*
experiences.)
They'll have hot coffee waiting, if we're lucky. One thing
the Americans don't go short of. If they go short of
anything. (*Walks a few paces.*) I suppose it was stupid,
dragging you out here. I wanted you to see this place. I
used to come here in the summer. Sit under that tree, look
down across the river. On clear days you can see almost to
Munich.

MARIA: They let you come here?

TADEK: Not at first. Later they didn't care what we did. Most
had been evacuated by then. It was hardly worthwhile
guarding us few. (*Pause.*) Yes. I could have been in
Warsaw now. If the Red Cross had found you sooner. The
officer who arranged your visit, he says we'll be the next
sent home.

MARIA: When?

TADEK: Who knows? We can't stay here forever. Now that

83

they've closed the business end of Dachau, it's not an
ideal health resort. (*Pause.*) I'm in no hurry. After the
journey here from Auschwitz – eight days in open cattle
cars – I won't mind travelling home in style. What did you
think of our Colonel Shuster?

MARIA: He seems a kind man.

TADEK: Oh yes, a proper gentleman. Even the Germans get on
well with him. (*Dryly*) They like his polite, considerate
manner. The Bürgermeister and him together – fussing
and clucking like mother hens: "Good gracious, mein
Herr, the dirt, the smell!"

(MARIA *moves away, but he continues.*)

In fact, there was only one occasion when I've seen him be less
than tactful. The day of our liberation. As the colonel stepped
inside our gates, a Russian Jew rushed up to greet him. He
flung his arms about his saviour with tears of welcome in his
eyes. The colonel suffered his embrace, but promptly
vomited on his shoes. How long will they let you stay?

MARIA: I don't know. Not long.

TADEK: I talk too much, I'm sorry.

MARIA: Yes.

TADEK: Did I tell you Vatzek liked the poems I sent him? He
says there'll be a job when I get home. Of course the place
is still in shambles, but later, when we get things
going . . . To start rebuilding, that's the main thing. Clear
out the rubbish, start again. You know I'm almost looking
forward to it. Maybe this time, there's a chance . . .

MARIA: A chance for what?

TADEK: To cauterize our national ailment; the Polish heads
stuck firmly in the clouds. They . . . *we* must realize.
This is the twentieth century, there's no room for those
sickly dreams. Don't look at me like that.

MARIA: Like what?

TADEK: You know. Instead look at our "benefactors". Feel
that contempt, if you can bear to. Well, why shouldn't
they despise us? We let ourselves come down to this.
Look at you, pale and sick. You think a Yank would ask

you out? With all those plump and pretty Fräuleins.

MARIA: (*Tiredly*) Tadek, don't.

(*He comes to her, puts his arms around her.*)

TADEK: (*Gently*) I'm only trying to state my case. You know I
don't like politics. Right, so I've been talking to some
people. But what they've said makes sense to me. We have
the future in our hands now, not just some dim and misty
past. I'll say no more. You already know how I feel.

MARIA: I read your letters.

TADEK: Then why not answer them sometimes?

(MARIA *breaks away. She speaks with an effort, gathering
herself.*)

MARIA: I don't know, Tadek. I don't know. You say you want
us to go home. As though it could be the same again . . .

TADEK: No, not the same. But better – maybe.

MARIA: I once had a home, a reason. There's nothing left of
that, I know. You want to . . . start again . . . The people
in Sweden, the ones I live with. They're very kind. It's
quiet there. I . . . (*Trails off, exhausted.*) No more, Tadek,
please . . . I am so tired. Nothing is clear to me now.

(TADEK *gently takes her hand.*)

TADEK: You're not well yet. I'm sorry. It doesn't matter, it
can wait.

MARIA: I'm cold. I'd like to go back now.

TADEK: Yes. Of course. The coffee will soon warm you up.

(*He puts an arm around her. They start to go.*)

I warn you. I'll keep writing letters . . .

(*The lights go down.*)

Scene 18

*Lights up on Beta's apartment. What light there is comes from the
small desk lamp.* BETA *sits at his desk. It is very late at night.
For a long time he remains completely motionless, staring straight
ahead. Then, like a statue coming to life, he speaks.*

In Kanada

BETA: There's been some confusion here.

(*A pause. He smiles slightly.*)

For a moment, let's take a new perspective. A rational viewpoint, if you like.

(*He considers for a moment, then launches himself.*)

Let's say that, like me, you liked to go out . . . to take a short walk on these warm summer evenings. It may have occurred – as it did once to me – that you found yourself wondering what went on around you. Watching the faces that you saw walking by. The people who passed you, intent on their business. Either with humour or total indifference, you might pause to speculate where they are going. . . ? (*Pause.*) But . . . should you then wish, which I wouldn't advise, to look a bit further, to penetrate inwards, what would you find in these parcels of hungers, these little ambitions that brushed up against you? (*Shrugs.*) Well, what? Wells of absurdity, emptiness, intrigue. Pools of murkiness, best unexplored . . . (*Pause.*) Yet each of these creatures persists in believing that he owns possessions, a solitary will. Each of these insects will go on, convinced, that he carries his own world about in his skull . . . While in reality, they own nothing. They live. They move – not by their own volition. And it is *we* who have grasped their being. It is we who have realized finally: the forces that shape them, that carry them forwards – inert on the tides of historical change. And they must understand that too. They must be *made* to see, at last, that history alone can transform them, save them . . . (*Smiles.*) Does that have an ecumenical ring about it? Blame my education. The Jesuit preachers who talked about souls. Redemption – now that's quite a sticky idea. (*Pause.*) I remember one of the sharper brothers was lecturing us on the subject of Hell. "Surely," I asked him, cheekily, "the worst of torments would grow tame – after a thousand years or so?" "My son," he answered, looking shrewd "what do we truly know of suffering? We understand our sins so little. But when we come before His Throne; perhaps for a second or two we'll

know. Then, for a moment, we will bear the burden of our guilt unaided. The agony of remorse that follows will seem like an eternity . . ."
(*He shakes his head, as though to rid himself of this idea.*)
To carry on where I left off . . . You see now why these stale delusions fill us with anger and contempt . . . (*Gets up and begins to move downstage.*) Some days, when I look through this window and watch the young girls in the street below; the children playing in the ruins, the old men sunning themselves and smoking . . . I like to half close my eyes, like this . . . (*Pause.*) Again, I see a wind come out of nowhere. A silent gale that sweeps these creatures up. High, high in the air, over the trees and houses. A tangled heap of arms and legs and mouths . . . until with a last unheard triumphant shriek . . . it drops them to the ground again. Deposits a broken pile of calmness. Stillness and silence . . . absolute.
(*He opens his eyes. He smiles, almost shamefacedly. He turns and goes back to the desk.*)
I don't know who it was once said: "The dead will always outnumber us." Well, I say: The dead may be restless but we owe them nothing. They will never be in the right . . .
(*He breaks off and pats his pockets vaguely as though looking for something.*)
Only the living have that privilege.
(*He turns and vanishes into the darkness. The lights fade. In the blackout, a train approaches and passes one last time.*)

Scene 19

Bird song. Lights back slowly on Beta's apartment. It is morning. The door opens to reveal MARIA. *She is dressed in black and carries a small suitcase. She comes into the room and stops. She looks about her. Leaving her case, she goes back to the door and shuts it. Then she comes back briskly and puts her case on Beta's desk.*
She opens it and goes immediately to a packing case containing clothes. She begins sorting them.

A knock on the door.

MARIA: Come in. It's open.

> (KORCZACK *enters deferentially. He wears a black mourning band.*)

KORCZACK: The driver's asking – will you need the car? He says he's got another job.

MARIA: Tell him to wait. I won't be long.

KORCZACK: You know how tactless these fellows can be.

MARIA: Just a few things to collect.

KORCZACK: You won't be living here then, I take it?

MARIA: I'm spending a few days with my sister.

KORCZACK: No, well.

MARIA: In any case, the kitchen's useless. They turned the gas off at the main supply. Just to be sure.

KORCZACK: I suppose there's still no question. . . ?

MARIA: (*Shakes her head*) You were at the inquest, weren't you? You heard the verdict that was given.

KORCZACK: (*Sighs.*) I must admit . . . I still find it quite difficult to believe.

MARIA: How well did you know my husband? Comrade . . . Korczack, is that right?

KORCZACK: Stepan, please. The first time that we talked together . . . was on the evening of . . . that night.

MARIA: And did he seem upset to you?

KORCZACK: I wouldn't say . . . not *that* upset. Of course – there was that business of the Jew.

MARIA: He told you that?

KORCZACK: A little, yes.

MARIA: I am surprised.

KORCZACK: Perhaps he felt that he could trust me.

MARIA: And what else did you chat about?

KORCZACK: Oh, nothing much. Just academic stuff; art and politics and so forth. I must say I admired his work. We're going to miss him at the paper. Perhaps you've seen today's edition? I took the liberty of bringing a copy . . . (*Producing it*) There's quite a good piece on your husband. A tribute from a literary colleague.

MARIA: Thank you. I will read it later.

(She goes off.)

KORCZACK: I'd better go back and talk to that driver.

(He puts the paper on the desk, goes out, leaving the door ajar. A pause. Then EWA appears in the door. She hesitates and comes into the room. She goes to the desk and picks up Beta's book. MARIA comes back with an armful of linen. She stops.)

MARIA: Can I help you?

(MARIA comes forward, puts down the linen. She holds out her hand wordlessly. EWA gives her the book.)

What are you doing here?

EWA: Nothing.

MARIA: This is my husband's book.

EWA: Yes . . . I . . . I lent it to him.

MARIA: Not very likely, is it? That you would lend him his own book.

(She sees the petition, takes it out and begins to read.)

Did you give this to my husband?

EWA: *(Defiantly)* Yes. I did.

MARIA: You asked him to sign it, I suppose?

(EWA nods sullenly, turns away.)

And he refused, of course. I know. My husband was very careful . . . sometimes. You must be Ewa, then?

EWA: *(Surprised)* Yes.

MARIA: Ewa. And what's your second name?

EWA: Ewa Baleszka. *(Pause.)* Look, I didn't mean . . .

MARIA: How old are you?

EWA: Is that important?

MARIA: Not really. No. Let me see now. You're the actress, am I right? You're not as pretty as I'd imagined.

EWA: I'm going.

(She moves towards the door.)

MARIA: Wait.

(She searches amongst the clutter on the desk for a pen, writes.)

Here.

(EWA takes it uncertainly.)

You'll find my signature next to yours.

EWA: Why?

MARIA: We wives have been known to read the papers. I can remember the Akimov case.

(*She turns back to her packing.*)

Just don't expect me to come to your meetings. I've got a child to take care of now.

EWA: I don't know what to say. When I heard it had happened . . . I just couldn't believe it. We were talking here . . . And afterwards . . . I . . . I was angry because he had stayed so calm. I wanted to . . . tell him, to show him . . . (*Beginning to cry*) It's all my fault. My fault – mine! I'll never forgive what I said to him . . . never . . .

(*She weeps.* MARIA *looks at her with a mixture of sympathy and anger. Her own grief has been deeply buried. Finally she puts her hand reluctantly on* EWA's *shoulder.*)

MARIA: I'm sure that you're mistaken. About things.

EWA: (*Childishly*) Couldn't *you* see what was happening to him. . . ? Couldn't you tell how he was . . . inside?

MARIA: (*Harshly*) What makes you think I didn't know?

EWA: Then why didn't you do something. . . ? Help him. . . ?

MARIA: How?

(*They confront each other.*)

(*Fierce*) How?

(EWA *turns away.* MARIA's *face softens a little.*)

You're very young. You'll get over it. The young heal quickly . . . (*Goes back to her packing.*) Besides you have other battles to fight. I think you had better go now, Miss Baleszka. I have a lot of packing to do.

(KORCZACK *returns.*)

KORCZACK: I've done my best. But I don't think he'll hang around much longer.

MARIA: Just one more minute. I'll be ready.

KORCZACK: (*To* EWA) Hullo?

MARIA: Oh, Stepan, this is Miss Baleszka. She was just

leaving. I won't be a minute.

(*She goes off.*)

KORCZACK: Were you a friend? Excuse me asking. I thought I'd seen you at the funeral?

EWA: No.

KORCZACK: Ah.

EWA: Was it a big occasion?

KORCZACK: Yes. Quite a send-off, I should say. Full State honours, flags and speeches. Most of the big names turned up for it. Well, he'd quite a reputation.

EWA: That's nice. I mean that they remembered. I'd better go.

KORCZACK: Perhaps we can give you a lift somewhere?

EWA: That's very kind. I'll walk.

(*She moves to the door,* KORCZACK *follows.*)

Nice to meet you, um . . . I'm sorry?

KORCZACK: Stepan. Stepan Korczack. (*Smiles.*) Perhaps we will meet again some time?

EWA: Yes. Goodbye.

(*She goes.* KORCZACK *closes the door, comes back smiling.* MARIA *re-enters.*)

MARIA: That's all I'll need now. For the present. (*Closes the case.*) If you wouldn't mind taking that down for me?

KORCZACK: Delighted.

MARIA: You look pleased with yourself all of a sudden.

KORCZACK: (*Abashed*) Do I?

MARIA: No, it's all right. I'm glad someone's smiling. Go down, will you? I'll follow in a minute.

(KORCZACK *exits.* MARIA *straightens a few things. She goes to the desk, sees the paper in the typewriter. She reads a few words, then rips it out. She crumples it, throws it away. She tidies the desk and opens a drawer. In the drawer is a paper bag, inside it, a baby's rattle. She looks at it; puts it back in the bag. Puts the bag in her pocket and goes out swiftly. The room is empty, full of sunshine. From the street comes the sound of children playing. The lights dim slowly, taking the room with them.*)

HIGH WATER

Nick Darke

Characters

SLINGER
GRIFF

Note: the "oo" in "bloomer" is pronounced
short, as in "took".

A small pebbled cove on the north Cornish coast, half an hour
before high water, early in a June morning. The sound of sea,
waves breaking. A pair of wellington boots stands above the high-
water mark, and a large log upended on a boulder, nearby.
SLINGER *walks up from the sea. Mid-sixties, he wears old trousers,*
rolled up to the knees, a faded working shirt with a worn collar, a
holed, knitted waistcoat, and a dirty torn tweedy jacket. A filthy old
wool hat on his head. He carries a very long length of rope, which
he's just picked up out of the sea. It is very tangled, and he spends
the whole play untangling it. He sits on the log and starts to
untangle. He whistles. Not a vague whistle, but a strong one, as
though he's working while he whistles, rather than whistling while
he works. His untangling is quick, deft, and economic, every now
and again there is nylon gut mixed up in it where a fishing-line has
been caught and lost, this he cuts free of the rope with a small
pocket knife. After a while, there is a shout from the cliff and he
looks up.

SLINGER: Aw my Gor.

> (SLINGER *ceases to whistle.* GRIFF *comes up to him, panting.*
> *He is dressed in a bright green tracksuit, and a golfing hat,*
> *with expensive-looking track shoes. He is an energetic talker,*
> *impressionable, open, a young 40. He could pass for early*
> *thirties, because of his behaviour as much as his looks.*
> *Insensitive.*)

GRIFF: Hullo there. Get up all right?

SLINGER: Eh?

GRIFF: Well, I can see you did; I nearly didn't. Alarm didn't
go off, I woke up anyway . . . well, the wife did, she's
very good at waking up. What a morning, eh? Sharp, the
air's so sharp. Nip. Nip in the air this time of morning,
isn't there, even for June. Mmmmmm, no one around. It
really is magnificent. Look at that sea! Do you know? I've

never seen this beach empty? Never. At this time of
year, it's a miracle! I suppose you're used to it, I mean,
out here every morning at this hour.

SLINGER: Most mornings, yeah.

GRIFF: We came down here very late one night once last year
when we were down, the wife and me, full moon, after the
pub shut, and it really was something. The tide was way
out and it was about midnight, and we just walked and
walked, across the cliff, came right out here, sat here and
watched the sea for half an hour and walked back. And
when we walked back, across the cliff, where the main bay
is, we saw this light, flashing, down by the sea, miles
away, right on the low-tide mark, and I thought ay ay,
y'know, how you do, that time of night, few beers inside
you, romantic night, the old imagination working
overtime, and I said to the wife, smugglers. And this light
was flashing away, so I said, you wait here, all deadly
earnest, y'know, I said, keep low. And I leopard-crawled
along the top of the cliff, and the path was all wet with
dew and I kept squashing these slugs, hundreds of slugs,
and I leopard-crawled along the cliff, and when I got
down to the beach, y'know that rock, in the middle, that
big rock with the hole in the middle, y'know the one . . .

SLINGER: Uh?

GRIFF: I made a dash for that, cos it threw a very long
shadow, and I thought, if I get in the shadow of that,
there's a good chance I won't be seen; so I made the rock
all right, and I crept along the shadow, and I was nearly
there, and this bloke was there, didn't see much of him,
but his light was flashing, and I thought, how am I going
to tackle this? Shall I creep up and surprise him, or run at
him shouting, or should I call the whole operation off and
go and get help? And while I was thinking this, he starts
to walk towards me! And I thought, ay ay, and he came
right towards me, and I thought, I know, he thinks I'm
his confederate, his oppo; I'd better get in the shadow and
put on a gruff voice, see if I can pass off as his mate. But

then I thought, and this was all flashing through my
mind very quickly, then I thought, if he thinks I'm his
mate, where the hell's his mate? And I started to look
round, see if I could see his mate, and I thought, oh well,
this is it, his mate's around somewhere and they're going to
thwack me over the head and leave me here to drown, only
hope the wife has the gumption to . . . y'know, so by this
time, there he was, almost upon me, and I wasn't so damn
cocky as I'd been before, and I had squashed slug all over
my jumper, soaked through, best shoes on in the wet sand,
y'know, I really felt uncomfortable, and he came up to me
and said, d'you know what he said? He said, would you
mind holding my torch while I bait up? Yeah, that was it,
he was fishing, bass or something, all night, fanatic . . .
(*Pause.*) That was what the light was flashing.

SLINGER: Best time to fish, midnight.

GRIFF: So that was that. But this is wonderful, dawn, a new
day. Do you know, Slinger, the way I look at this, now
I'm a sensitive man, sensitive to atmosphere, and the way
I look at this, the way I feel, it sounds silly, but you and
me, we, are giving birth. Together. To a new day. This
day is our baby. Ours. No one else's, nobody has been
down here, to spoil it, soil it, I really feel that. I, y'know,
I mean, when I saw the Niagara Falls, the first time, you
go up on a bridge and it's there, and I cried, I cried. I
wept at its beauty. And I could weep at this, it's so
beautiful. But I've got a bit of a hangover. Spoils the
concentration. I got into trouble because I drank too much
last night, the wife, y'know. I was afraid you might have
forgotten all about the arrangement we made, to go
wrecking. But I could see you weren't as drunk as I was.
But the wife wasn't too pleased. She says I talk too much
when I'm drunk. Are you married, Slinger?

SLINGER: Eh?

GRIFF: Married. Are you married?

SLINGER: Was once.

GRIFF: Oh, I'm sorry. Did she die?

SLINGER: No.

GRIFF: Oh. I'm sorry, what, just couldn't get on?

SLINGER: Summin' like that, yeah.

GRIFF: Long time ago, was it?

SLINGER: Years.

GRIFF: Course it was a big thing in those days, I mean,
nowadays it's happening all the time, but in those days, it
took a bit of courage, y'know, to go off and leave your
husband.

SLINGER: She 'ad 'er fancy man, buggered off up country.

GRIFF: Ah. (*Pause.*) Have you had some good wreck?

SLINGER: Ez.

GRIFF: (*After a pause*) Why do they call you Slinger, Slinger?

SLINGER: Cuz I was one. One a the last.

GRIFF: Ah. What is a slinger?

SLINGER: One a the last I was.

(*Pause.*)

GRIFF: What sort of wreck have you found?

SLINGER: 'Smornin'?

GRIFF: Yes.

SLINGER: Aw. All sorts.

GRIFF: Driftwood and that.

SLINGER: Hatchtops, deckin', pallettes, all that lot like.

GRIFF: Quite a selection.

SLINGER: Tidn' only wood washed up, boy. There's all sorts,
tin a sherbert I 'ad once, an' a set of false teeth, all in the
same day.

GRIFF: A set of false teeth?

SLINGER: Yeah. Didn' fit though. Clothes, 'tis like a damn
jumble sale down 'ere after the summer. You'd be
surprised what people d'bring down on the beach and
leave it.

GRIFF: Had any watches?

SLINGER: No.

GRIFF: I lost a watch on the beach once, not here, Southsea,
and I went home after the holiday, to Lincolnshire, I was
still in Lincolnshire at the time, before I was married, and

there standing on the doorstep when I walked up the path,
was a policeman. And he said, are you Mr Griffith Hague?

SLINGER: Big box out there comin' in . . .

GRIFF: Mr Griffith Hague? I said yes . . .

SLINGER: Be 'ere dreckly, wade in, pick 'er up.

GRIFF: And he said . . .

SLINGER: Comin' in on top a the tide.

GRIFF: This policeman . . .

SLINGER: Ab'm bin in the water long, ab'm got that scrubbed
look, no oil on it.

GRIFF: Do you have the time?

SLINGER: What?

GRIFF: Joking you see, about the time . . .

SLINGER: 'Tis about a quarter to six.

GRIFF: I know.

(*Pause.*)

SLINGER: In the mornin'.

GRIFF: I know.

SLINGER: Aw.

GRIFF: And he had the watch, you know.

(*Pause.* GRIFF *ties his shoelace and breathes deep.*)

SLINGER: Good bit a rope this is. Damn waste reely, they
d'get'n all scrawled up like 'at, an' ayb'm overboard cuz
they can't be buggered bow'n out.

GRIFF: Is that the fishermen?

SLINGER: 'Tis all back this, for the lobster pots. They
d'shoot'em wrong, get'n all scrawled. Damn good length a
rope.

GRIFF: Will you give it back?

SLINGER: Eh?

GRIFF: The rope. Give it back, I thought you said you'd give
it back.

SLINGER: Gyat ta hell.

GRIFF: Well, I think we ought to give it back if we know
whose it is.

SLINGER: I knaw whose 'tis, boy, but I arn't givin of 'er back.

GRIFF: Well I'm glad you didn't find my watch, that's all. I

mean, wood off a ship, or even a tin of sherbet, OK, but if
you know who the rope belongs to . . . I bought some like
this, towrope for my car, fifteen foot, cost me nearly five
pounds.

SLINGER: You was done, then.

GRIFF: My wife said that.

SLINGER: Took they false teeth back. To the dentist.

GRIFF: Good.

SLINGER: Didn' fit 'e neither.

GRIFF: No, but they can be identified.

SLINGER: I 'ad armchair washed up 'ere while back, off oil
tanker. 'Ad property of Esso Oil stamped all over'n but I
didn' go up S'Merryn garridge an' say, 'ere, d'y want your
chair back? E'm in my damn kitchen, dryin' out. What
you find on this beach is yours, boy, no bugger else's, an'
if you lift'n over th'igh-water mark, there idn' no bloomer
can touch'n, thass yours.

GRIFF: That's the law, is it?

SLINGER: Thass the law of the land, unwritten, gentleman's
agreement.

GRIFF: Huh.

SLINGER: That box is nearly in.

GRIFF: Ah.

(*Pause.*)

SLINGER: See, if you wade in an' got 'old a that box, an'
auled'n in, thass yours. Tidn' mine, thass yours, no one
else's.

GRIFF: I'm a wrecker then.

SLINGER: Get your feet wet. (*Pause.*) That box ab'm bin in
the water long.

GRIFF: It's a nice box.

SLINGER: 'Tis too clean. No weed. No oil. 'Tis sittin' too high
in the water.

GRIFF: Hoo.

SLINGER: Tidn' waterlogged.

GRIFF: That's amazing.

SLINGER: What?

GRIFF: You're like Sherlock Holmes.

SLINGER: Eh? Who?

GRIFF: Good grief, Holmes. That's Watson.

SLINGER: 'Tis nearly there now. Foreign writing,
hieroglyphics.

GRIFF: That's the writing.

SLINGER: Watertight.

GRIFF: I wish I was like that. I wish I could. Well, y'know.

SLINGER: Brave bit a wreck, that is.

GRIFF: My father was a Cornishman, y'know.

SLINGER: Aw ez.

GRIFF: I never knew him. My mother left him when I was 2.
She never came back. Married a man in Lincolnshire.
Changed her name.

SLINGER: Good Gor.

GRIFF: I was the only child, y'see, by her first marriage. She
died, oo, about fifteen years ago, when I was in my
twenties, and I've often wondered . . . I mean, I
discovered afterwards that her first married name had
been Hicks. But there are hundreds of Hickses in
Cornwall.

SLINGER: There is boy. Hundreds ob'm.

GRIFF: I mean. If I were to ask you your name, your real
name, what would you say?

SLINGER: Me?

GRIFF: Yes.

SLINGER: Hicks.

GRIFF: There you are, you see?

SLINGER: You ab'm never followed up like, more'n that?

GRIFF: I've thought about it, I could find him easily, if he's
still alive, but mother never mentioned him, and, well, he
never bothered to come and find me, did he? People say,
go on, get down there, claim your heritage, get what you
deserve, he could be rich, could own a field of caravans.

SLINGER: No.

GRIFF: No, well, I wouldn't know what to say to the old
rogue, he used to drink a lot apparently, and I don't drink

much, I like a pint but it isn't my MO you see.

SLINGER: What?

GRIFF: MO. *Modus operandi.*

SLINGER: No.

GRIFF: And I wouldn't know what to say to a man who drinks all the time.

SLINGER: What do you do, then?

GRIFF: Me? Oh, I've got a very good job, secure, earn a lot of money, good prospects, I don't need his wealth, y'know, his caravans, he's probably married again, family of his own.

SLINGER: No.

GRIFF: Anyway, that's that. I mean, y'know, curiously enough, I have no desire whatsoever to meet my natural father. I mean, it would upset me to see him now. I was happy with my stepfather, he was a good man, kind, but I've always felt a strong affinity with the Cornish, like I can talk to you now, talk to that Eddy bloke.

SLINGER: Gyat!

GRIFF: But you see you're not easy to get along with, I mean it's not everyone in that pub you would have said, come down wrecking with me tomorrow, is it?

SLINGER: No.

GRIFF: There you are, see, point made.

SLINGER: Tidn' every bugger in the pub would've asked though.

GRIFF: Yes, I admit I asked, and I asked that chap to take me fishing . . .

SLINGER: Eddy?

GRIFF: I think it's Eddy, chap with glasses.

SLINGER: Dun't go fishin' with 'e, boy.

GRIFF: Look at the sun on the water there, isn't it beautiful?

SLINGER: 'E'd take any bugger fishin' 'e would, dun't make no damn difference, 'e never catch nothing.

GRIFF: But you could've refused, you see, that's my point. You could have said no, and probably have, more that once.

SLINGER: Eddy wouldn' say no to no one if 'e thought there
was a pint in it for sayin' yes, boy, dun't flatter yourself.
(*Pause.* GRIFF *looks out to sea. He suddenly cups his hands
round his mouth and shouts very loud and sharp. Cocks his ear
to listen. Repeats the shout;* SLINGER *is put out.*)

GRIFF: Hm. No. Hear an echo sometimes, if you shout on
these beaches. A good echo.

SLINGER: Aw.

GRIFF: 'Course I wouldn't shout if there was anyone lying
around. Ideal time to shout now, no bodies to cushion the
sound, no one on the beach. I must be standing in a dead
spot or something. Have you ever tried it?

SLINGER: Never.

GRIFF: I was talking to that chap last night, he was saying . . .

SLINGER: Who, Eddy?

GRIFF: I think it's Eddy, chap with glasses.

SLINGER: Gyat! Bloody Arab.

GRIFF: Well, he was . . .

SLINGER: Don't knaw bugger all 'e dun't. Dun't do nuthin',
dun't knaw nuthin'.

GRIFF: Pity. Pity about that shout. Would have rounded the
old morning off nicely, a good echo. I used to fly kites, in
Lincolnshire, and we'd shout there, good echo there, but
it's a bit flat, and send messages up the string. Of the kite.

SLINGER: Oo to?

GRIFF: Ha! Hahaha! I like that, who to. No one. Just . . .
huh, the echo I suppose. No, they just used to go up,
y'know, the string. No point to it really . . .

SLINGER: No.

GRIFF: Used to do it for hours. Hours and hours.

SLINGER: Knaw what I used to do for hours an' hours?

GRIFF: What?

SLINGER: Hoe.

GRIFF: Oh. What sort of . . .

SLINGER: Hoe. Day after day after bloody day, boy. An'
y'knaw what?

GRIFF: What?

SLINGER: After we done that, come dusk, used t'milk the cows.

GRIFF: Yes?

SLINGER: An' y'knaw what the call was?

GRIFF: You tell me.

SLINGER: Ho, ho, ho, ho.

GRIFF: Oh.

SLINGER: Yeah.

GRIFF: Must have been wonderful to work on a farm.

SLINGER: Gyat; you dun't knaw, boy, flyin' your damn kite, 'tis too easy for e.

GRIFF: Well, that was leisure time.

SLINGER: I bin Lincolnshire, boy, I knaw what 'tis like up there.

GRIFF: I left. I'm glad I left . . .

SLINGER: I bin Lincolnshire, boy, they'm all flyin' their damn kites up there. They'm all schemy up there, boy. No louster. I can schemy, boy, I dun't louster, but I d'louster as well, I can louster, dun't you worry bout that, id'n' no bloomer louster more 'n me when I d'get goin', but if I can schemy, I wun't louster, bugger it. Leave some bloomer else louster who can't schemy. Now thun . . .

GRIFF: Er . . .

SLINGER: Now you get a big bass and a little bass catched in a net. An' the big bass 'e got three 'ooks in 'er mouth. 'E's schemied. Else 'e never would a grawed big. But 'e also louster, cos 'e got three 'ook in 'is mouth, an' 'e put up a fight, got free, three times, wedged hisself 'tween two rocks, till the gut snapped. But the little bugger. 'E didn' schemy cos 'e got catched an' 'e 'm in the pan, fryin' up. An' 'e also didn' louster. So 'e 'm idle. An' 'e got catched. An' 'tis the idle fish always get catched young, an' they dun't make such good eatin' as the flippy fish, who dun't get catched, cos they got flabby flesh, an' the big flippy ones is all tough with age, like 'orse, so we will never knaw, what 'tis like to eat a flippy bass. An' thass where they d'win out.

104

GRIFF: Hm. Pity.

SLINGER: Intelligent fish, the bass.

GRIFF: Yes.

SLINGER: If 'e can't schemy all that lot out boy, you louster.
An' louster d'mean get your feet wet.

GRIFF: Ah.

SLINGER: An' get your feet wet mean wade in an' catch 'old a
that there box.

GRIFF: Eh?

SLINGER: 'Tis within reach now.

GRIFF: If I get it, I have it.

SLINGER: Ah thass schemy, that is.

GRIFF: Hah! Just schemied, have I?

SLINGER: You 'ad a shot at it.

GRIFF: How did I get on?

SLINGER: Not too good.

GRIFF: So I still have to go and get the box.

SLINGER: Ez you.

GRIFF: Some kind of game, is it? This?

SLINGER: This is the rules you gotta play by, boy, if you
d'come down 'ere wi' me at five o'clock in the mornin'.

GRIFF: Will I be safe out there?

SLINGER: Out where?

GRIFF: Getting the box.

SLINGER: Idn' goin' swim the Atlantic, are e?

GRIFF: No, I . . .

SLINGER: 'Tis only two foot out, boy, get your feet wet, thass
all.

GRIFF: Well, there's a lot of rocks, slippery, and there's quite
a drag there, where it breaks up on to the bank . . .

SLINGER: I'll thraw e a line.

GRIFF: Will it be long enough?

SLINGER: Will be time I've untangled it.

GRIFF: I'd like to help, I'd like to be the man who brought in
the box. I'd like to use it in some way, the beach. As you
said last night, when we were talking, in the pub, the
beach isn't there to be *looked* at, it's there to be *used*. I

mean, look at it, look at the wealth and pleasure you could get, from knowing how to use it.

(*Pause.*)

SLINGER: We 'ad claret washed up. Boat went down off Guernsey, Alderney, an' it all come round 'ere, damn great hogsheads a the stuff, raw claret, Algerian, 'undred an' twenty gallon casks a this Algerian claret, 'undreds an' 'undreds a the buggers, couldn' shift 'em, we was comin' down wi' tin baths, milk buckets, bottles, there wadn' a bottle in the parish, they was all full a wine, no corks, chemist put the price a corks up, shillin' a packet, made a fortune. We was drunk for weeks, all on this claret, all the pubs went bust, closed down cos no bloomer was goin' in 'em, too drunk git out the 'ouse, raw claret, tasted like petrol. Killed two people in Newquay. Methodists pickled eggs with it. Or so they said, but they 'ad a sway to their gait goin' chapel Sundays.

GRIFF: Good grief.

SLINGER: See we didn' 'ang round diggin' sandcastles, boy. We dug claret!

GRIFF: What a life!

SLINGER: You think 'twas romantic.

GRIFF: It still is!

SLINGER: Well 'twadn', boy, cos there was always a squabble who got there first. I come to blows more 'n once.

GRIFF: No gentleman's agreement there.

SLINGER: Eh?

GRIFF: No . . .

SLINGER: An' when the silk come in, off the *Good Samaritan*, at Bedruthan Steps, there was hell up. There was whole families didn' speak for damn decades after that one.

GRIFF: Silence reigned.

SLINGER: So 'twadn' all wine an' roses, boy.

GRIFF: Sounds like there was a good bit of wine.

SLINGER: I still got bottles a that 'ome now.

GRIFF: Have you?

SLINGER: Use it to strip paint.

GRIFF: Hah!

SLINGER: An' now there's that box comin' in.

GRIFF: I'm going to get that box, Slinger. I've decided. That box is going to be mine!

SLINGER: Good boy.

GRIFF: We could leave it and pick it up in Eddy's boat.

SLINGER: Gyat! What the hell . . . 'tis bloody Eddy's then, don't get 'e involved, boy, 'e got 'is damn finger in every pie, boy, an' 'e 'm a damn shyster.

GRIFF: I was only . . . I thought you'd say that.

SLINGER: See Granfer Hawken used ta keep a boat in boathouse, 'long 'ere.

GRIFF: What, this . . .

SLINGER: Just here, next cove on.

GRIFF: With the rock in the middle.

SLINGER: No, thass Totty Cove. Tidn' a cove, not reely . . .

GRIFF: I thought you said you were a Hicks.

SLINGER: Eh?

GRIFF: Hicks, name Hicks.

SLINGER: I am. This is me mother was 'Awken, but 'er granfer was a Hicks, so we're all Hickses an' Hawkens, but they was Hicks Treglissick, we'm Tregolls Hicks, me mother's granfer was a Treglissick Hicks, see? They was all Methodists, come from Bugle. We didn' 'ave nothin' to do wi' they, we was church, they was chapel, not me, see, I arn't church, dun't go church, went church once, get married, but it didn' do no good, an' the Treglissick Hickses all died young, none a they left, so chapel wadn' much better, so I said, bugger it, go up the pub.

GRIFF: Ah.

SLINGER: Ab'm missed a Sunday since.

GRIFF: And he had a boat.

SLINGER: Who?

GRIFF: Treglissick Hicks.

SLINGER: Who?

GRIFF: Your grandfather, Treglissick.

SLINGER: My granfer wadn' Treglissick, 'e was a Jonas.

GRIFF: Well, who was Treglissick?

SLINGER: Jonas Hawken, on me mother's side.

GRIFF: Nice name, Treglissick.

SLINGER: That was the farm. The farm they farmed, the
    Treglissick Hickses. We 'ad Tregolls, or me granfer 'ad.
    Sold'n. Drunk too much whisky, got into debt, gave the
    farm to the landlord an' skedaddled. Went Africa.
    Married several Zulus. They never catched up with him.

GRIFF: I should think they would have eaten him if they'd
    caught up with him.
    (*Pause.*)

SLINGER: What was she like, your mother?

GRIFF: My mother?

SLINGER: Yeah.

GRIFF: Er, talkative, bright, not one for hiding her emotions,
    said what had to be said, no matter what, unafraid,
    colourful in her turn of phrase, religious in her beliefs,
    never went to church but high principled, religious in that
    sense, y'know, naturally cautious, passionate, a true Celt.
    Never lost her accent. It wasn't broad, but it was there,
    the West Country burr. In a sharp way.

SLINGER: What did she look like?

GRIFF: Small. Dark. Black eyes. Why do you ask?

SLINGER: 'Ow old was she, when she died?

GRIFF: Fiftyish. Why?
    (*Silence.*)
    Isn't it wonderful, the rough sea?

SLINGER: Eh?

GRIFF: The sea, I love it when it's rough. I love the sense of
    power behind the waves, it's . . . exhilarating . . . I
    should think a storm here must be fantastic. Incredible in
    the winter.

SLINGER: Storms at sea dun' impress me, boy, no more'n for
    what they can yield. You can shut your eyes an' imagine
    bigger waves'n what God can conjure, boy. You can shut
    your eyes an' imagine taller trees'n what God can grow.
    God's miracles lie in the subtleties a nature, boy, when that

108

sea, out there, is as flat as a pea on a plate, not so much as
a catlap when water touches rock, when that sea, deeper
an' broader'n a preacher's mind, is lyin' there, hundred
thousand million billion tons a water. Still. Flat. Then you
try an' imagine it flatter. You can't do it. Thass subtle,
boy. Thass a damn miracle, boy. When a gale blaw, it
blaw from one direction, North, South, East or West.
When a breeze stroke the sea it whisper, from every
corner of the earth. An' thass the only time I ever come
down this beach juss to look.

GRIFF: I thought you said you weren't religious.

SLINGER: I dun't go church.

GRIFF: Ah.

SLINGER: But I d'knaw what God made, boy. I arn't no fool.

GRIFF: I still think it's pretty magnificent when it's rough.

SLINGER: Gyat.

GRIFF: Eddy was saying it gets rough very quickly.

SLINGER: Gyat, what d'e know?

GRIFF: Well . . .

SLINGER: God didn' make Eddy, boy, thass for certain.

GRIFF: Eddy. Think I remember my mother saying she had a
brother called Eddy. Never saw him. Never saw any of
the family. There was a rift I suppose . . . Funny, talking
about names . . .

SLINGER: Dun't tell me 'er name, boy . . .

GRIFF: What?

SLINGER: That box.

GRIFF: What?

SLINGER: 'Tis goin out. Tide's turnin'.

GRIFF: Right, skipper. Half a ticky, take the old shoes and
socks off. Don't have a towel with you?
(*He takes his shoes and socks off, rolls his track suit up and
walks uncertainly over the pebbles to the sea.* SLINGER
*watches him off. He's gone for a half minute or so, and he
returns with a longish box, made of good wood, with rope
handles, sealed, with Chinese writing on it. Quality stuff.*)
It's very light. I think it's empty.

SLINGER: 'E got summin' in, boy, dun't you worry 'bout
    that.

(GRIFF *dumps the box, looks round it, and tries to open it.*)

GRIFF: Sealed tight, anyway.

SLINGER: 'Ere.

(*He produces a small jemmy from the inside of his jacket.*)

GRIFF: Good grief, do you always carry one of these?

SLINGER: When I'm wrecking. Prise the pallettes abroad.

GRIFF: You open it.

SLINGER: No, 'tis yours.

(GRIFF *opens it. He opens the lid, which is hinged, and takes
    out a pile of straw. They look inside.* SLINGER *delicately
    takes out a moulded wood false top, padded on the inside.
    They look.*)

GRIFF: Good grief.

SLINGER: Hell.

(GRIFF *takes a miniature porcelain Chinese cup from the box,
    holds it up.*)

Put'n back, boy.

GRIFF: What?

SLINGER: You disturb that lot, boy, they'll be all scat up
    'fore you climbed to the top a that cliff. I seed one a these
    afore, they'm packed all proper.

GRIFF: What is it?

SLINGER: Porc'lin. Chinese porc'lin, antique.

GRIFF: Priceless by the look.

SLINGER: Aah, 'sworth a bob or two. Some haul, that is, boy.

(GRIFF *puts the cup back.* SLINGER *replaces the top and the
    straw, then delicately closes the lid, taps round lightly with the
    jemmy, so it's sealed again. They stand, look at the box.
    Silence.* GRIFF *looks at* SLINGER. GRIFF *grins. Suddenly he
    lets out a yell of excitement.*)

GRIFF: Woooohooohoooa!!!

SLINGER: Beginner's luck, boy.

(GRIFF *looks at the box, grinning, shaking his head.
    Disbelief. Pause.*)

GRIFF: Crikey . . . blimey . . . good grief.

SLINGER: An' to think I let you wade in an' fetch the bugger out.

GRIFF: Well, I wouldn't say beginner's luck, I mean, crikey, I mean, I am Cornish aren't I, I've got a bit of the old wrecker in me? Eh? Eh? Ha ha!

SLINGER: Not dressed like that, you ab'm.

(*They study the box some more in silence.* GRIFF *chuckling and musing. At length:*)

GRIFF: I'll have to hand it in, though.

SLINGER: Eh?

GRIFF: Well, I mean . . .

SLINGER: Gittout!

GRIFF: I can't keep it.

SLINGER: What?

GRIFF: It's too valuable. I'll take it to the police.

SLINGER: You serious?

GRIFF: That's valuable. That belongs to somebody.

SLINGER: That somebody is no longer damn with us, 'e ab'm got no box to go floatin' round in, 'ave 'e, 'e'm perished, 'e'm feedin' fishes 'e is, an' that there box is yours!

GRIFF: I'm sorry, Slinger, I wouldn't think of it. If it's mine, I hand it in.

SLINGER: Bugger me.

GRIFF: Supposin' he's still alive . . .

SLINGER: Lost at sea, boy, 'tis the law of the land, ab'm never bin knawed 'and'n in!

GRIFF: I could never sell it, you see . . .

SLINGER: Keep it. Drink your bloody tea out of it.

GRIFF: It's robbing the dead!

SLINGER: You dun't knaw, boy, you can't rob a man you ab'm never seed! 'E've *lost* it.

GRIFF: Look, I couldn't drink coffee out of those cups, I couldn't. All the time I'd be thinking of some poor bastard out there drowning; I'm sensitive, I've got an imagination, I wept at Niagara, lungs full of water, filling up with every breath, ears bursting, eyes popping out of his skull, no, I'm sorry, Slinger, this has turned out to be a bit sick.

SLINGER: Bloody nutcase you are, boy.

GRIFF: I read a story about this in the colour supplement, the bloke eventually went mad.

SLINGER: Soft as bloody sand.

GRIFF: If you want it, you . . .

SLINGER: 'Tis yours!

GRIFF: If that's the way you do things down here, OK, that's OK, but I hand it in.

SLINGER: Gaw Christ.

GRIFF: It's valuable property! It belongs to someone and we don't know if he's alive or dead. It's theft! It's not a tin of sherbert!

SLINGER: Gyaaa.

GRIFF: Look . . .

SLINGER: Gittome.

GRIFF: You said yourself, it's not been long in the water, what if he was saved?

SLINGER: 'E'll be washed in next tide, boy, dun't you worry 'bout that, you come down tonight an' pick the damn body up, see what 'e say to that . . .

GRIFF: That's repulsive!

SLINGER: Thass life, that is, boy.

GRIFF: That's bloody repulsive! My God!

SLINGER: You ab'm seed a little boy strapped in rubber dinghy frozen stiff wi' starin' eyes washed up daid, boy.

GRIFF: Christ!

SLINGER: We get 'em, boy. Down 'ere, at dawn, reg'lar as damn clockwork, dun't you worry 'bout that . . .

GRIFF: It's barbaric!

SLINGER: What do 'e make to all that, then?

GRIFF: I tell you something. When I walk in that pub again I talk to Eddy! All night! and I'll ask him who's lost that rope and tell them where they can find it, and thank you very much for a very nice morning but that's it!

SLINGER: Aw.

(*Pause.* GRIFF *walks away a couple of paces and folds his arms.*)

Tell 'e what, thun.

GRIFF: Eh?

SLINGER: Tide's goin' out. See that rock?

GRIFF: Is this another of your stupid games?

SLINGER: That one there.

GRIFF: There?

SLINGER: No . . . this one . . . here.

GRIFF: Just here.

SLINGER: Thass ob'm.

GRIFF: What?

SLINGER: I'll walk down. An' set this box on top a that rock,
you. If a wave break big enough to wash'n off, we leab'm
float, an' I g'round main bay in the mornin' an' pick 'er
up. If she stays where she's to. 'Tis yours. Hand in.

GRIFF: Hm.

(SLINGER *picks up the box and carries it off to the sea.*
Comes back. Silence. They both look for a very long time at
the box in the distance. SLINGER *takes out a pipe but doesn't*
light it. The sound of the waves can be heard, and a late
curlew or two, flying overhead. GRIFF *picks up a pebble and*
plays with it absent-mindedly. SLINGER *takes out his*
penknife and starts to clean his pipe, keeping one eye on the
box. Then suddenly they both react. SLINGER *smiles slightly*
and folds his knife, puts it and his pipe in his pocket. At the
same time GRIFF *throws the pebble to the ground and stands.*
Looks at SLINGER. SLINGER *turns and looks at him.* GRIFF
turns and walks off without a word. SLINGER *calls after*
him.)

SLINGER: 'Ere, boy.

GRIFF: (*Off*) What?

SLINGER: 'Fore e go.

GRIFF: (*Coming back*) What?

SLINGER: Got summin' for e.

GRIFF: Oh, no.

SLINGER: Watch. (*Takes a pocket watch from his waistcoat and*
hands it out.) Belonged to your granfer.

GRIFF: What?

113

SLINGER: 'E said if I ever saw e, to give it to e.

GRIFF: What the hell are you talking about?

SLINGER: Eddy, boy, is your uncle.

GRIFF: Eddy?

SLINGER: 'Ad a sister called Phyllis. Your mother.

> (*Silence.* GRIFF *looks at* SLINGER. *Light dawns slowly.*)
> An' 'er father, an' Eddy, an' all the damn family never forgived 'er, spoke to 'er nor 'ad nothin' to do with 'er, boy. Disowned 'er. Turned their backs on 'er.
> (*Silence.*)
> But I forgived 'er see, but I wouldn't run after 'er, too proud, see.
> (*Silence.*)
> I never forgived Eddy, see, for not talkin' to she. I couldn' see it, 'er own flesh and blood. Couldn' see the point.
> (*Silence.*)

GRIFF: But . . . you . . .

SLINGER: You take the watch now, boy, wander up the cliff. I'll pick your box up morrer, run'n up police.

> (*They look at each other for a very long time. Then* GRIFF *takes the watch and looks at it. He looks back at* SLINGER.)
> Only wish I could a seed 'er once, 'fore she died.
> (*They look at each other.* GRIFF, *embarrassed, looks at the watch.*)

GRIFF: It's a beautiful watch.

> (SLINGER *turns away, upstage from* GRIFF. GRIFF *slowly walks off as the lights fade.*)

BABYLON HAS FALLEN

John Fletcher

A NOTE ON PRODUCTION

The stage is bare, with only a fairly large wheel of the zodiac above it to suggest, as in the Elizabethan stage, that the stage is the world. The stage should be capable of suggesting various lightings and moods – the bright sunlight of a tropical beach, the darkness of night, the gloom of an *Angst*-ridden blood-letting.

On occasions, it should – either through lighting or props – be capable of suggesting the trunks and leaves of palm trees, the solid geometry of the timbers of a temple. There might need to be a masthead for Slocum, to one side of the stage and intimate with the audience, separate from the structure of the temple and the gallows.

I imagine a close intimacy between actors and audience, with actors on occasion moving among the audience.

A good sound system will be required, in which quite strong sounds, like those of a storm at sea, will not drown out the actors.

There are two examples of American early Puritan shape note music, recently popularized by the Bread and Puppet Theatre in the script. I have a copy of the music of the two songs performed.

J.F.

Characters

SLOCUM
DAVID WORTH
EDITH WORTH
ELISHA BLACK
AUGUSTUS HARE
ANNIE

ACT I

*All six actors come on stage, talking informally among themselves.
To add to the informality I would suggest this was done while the
house lights are still up.* DAVID WORTH, EDITH WORTH, ELISHA
BLACK, AUGUSTUS HARE, *and* ANNIE *are all in a line, facing the
audience.*

SLOCUM *is a short but strong Yankee sea captain, wearing a sort of
donkey jacket and a sailing cap.*

DAVID *is a tall, powerful-looking man, with a black beard, dressed
in black, Puritan clothes and wide-brimmed hat.*

EDITH *is also in sober black clothes, quite small beside his size.*

ELISHA, *also in black, is a lithe, eaten man, physically small but
intense.*

AUGUSTUS HARE, *for the only time in the play, comes on in quite
gay and elegant 1840s aristocratic dress.*

ANNIE, *a negress, is half in tribal dress or sari, half in westernized
Victorian clothes. She is hard, quite young, smoking a pipe.*

The actors tense themselves. The lights in the house go down.

SLOCUM: This stage (*stamps on floor*) is a world. Any world.
Any man, or woman, can make of it what he or she
chooses.
(*He looks at* DAVID *to speak.*)

DAVID: (*Bristol accent*) This ground (*stamps foot*) is strong.
God's earth, bearing me up in my righteousness.
(SLOCUM *looks at* EDITH. *She is a bit shy, takes hold of*
DAVID's *arm and looks at him.*)

EDITH: (*Bristol accent*) This world is a towering black cliff to
which I cling, not daring to look down, not daring to – let
go.

ELISHA: (*Brummie accent*) This world is emotion, blind
nightmare. It is a razor, crystallizing in the darkness
before me.

119

HARE: This world is a football – I kick it about for my
amazement.

ANNIE: This world? (*Laughs raucously, spits.*)
(*All except* SLOCUM *depart.*
Sound of sea starts to come in quietly.)

SLOCUM: This stage (*stamps*) shall represent the Cocos Keeling
Island, a remote atoll in the wastes of the Great Southern
Ocean. Until the start of this play, the year 1845, it
remained happily uninhabited.

I myself – Captain Joshua Slocum – the world's first solo
circumnavigator – will not arrive on this island for another
forty years.
(*Exit* SLOCUM.
*Bright, tropical sunlight, sound of waves beating on the shore.
On to stage from the back comes* EDITH, *a hood over her head,
in black. She looks about her in wonder. As a gesture of
freedom, she sweeps back the hood from her head, luxuriating
in the sun streaming full in her face. She starts to sing, then
dance and skip about the stage to the song.*)

EDITH: (*Sings*) Babylon has fall'n, has fall'n, has fall'n,
   Babylon has fall'n to rise no more.
(*From the back, like Edith in a black, stifling overcoat, comes
ELISHA. Kneels in prayer. Then sees* EDITH, *lips purse in
automatic disapproval.* EDITH *sees this – mocks his
disapproval. He half grins despite himself.* EDITH *laughs,
stops dancing. He undoes two buttons on coat, starts to dance
at* EDITH's *goading, then sing.*
Offstage DAVID *is heard singing first verse, confidently. He
parades on, holding before him a vast flag. As they hear him,
the two stop dancing, automatically tense, unconsciously
returning to previous control system.* EDITH *puts on hood,*
ELISHA *buttons coat.*)

DAVID: Hail the day so long expected,
   Hail the year of full release;
   Zion's walls are now erected,
   And her watchmen publish peace.

ALL: Through our Shiloh's wide dominion

Hear the Trumpet's roar.

(*Chorus*)

Babylon is fall'n, is fall'n, is fall'n,

Babylon is fall'n to rise no more.

(DAVID *sticks flag in ground at back of stage, then processes down to centre downstage,* EDITH *and* ELISHA *taking up flanking positions on either side of him. Suddenly, dramatically,* DAVID *falls on knees, kisses ground. Then looks upward. Others kneel in imitation.*)

DAVID: Jehovah, Yahweh,

Lord of Hosts, God of Gods,

We thank thee.

EDITH and ELISHA: (*Automatically*) Hallelujah!

DAVID: We thank Thee

that Thee have protected we on our perilous voyage.

(DAVID *stands, looks over audience. Others rise.*)

Fifteen thousand miles have we travelled upon the highways of Thy ocean,

against storms, rocks, and monsters of

the deep have Thee protected we, Lord God,

brought we sure and true

to this tiny island, remote from all human habitation,

where we shall build Thy New Jerusalem.

(*Pauses. Admires the view.*)

See the symmetry of the whole,

the mount upon which we shall build Thy Temple

for Thy habitation.

(*Touches earth gently with toe.*)

This-yere blessed earth ant never known the stench of human kind,

'tis the gentlest, sweetest garden

where God hisself, in His awe-ful Majesty

shall shortly dwell,

stately stalk up and down,

passing back and forth atwixt the trees,

thinking, contemplating.

The Lord shall have His silence, His solitude,
in this, His private garden, His private property.
(*Beat.*)
　　Edith, Elisha.
　　my faithful wife, my faithful servant,
　　when I came upon you just now
　　I saw you dancing.

EDITH: Sorry, David.

ELISHA: Sorry, master.

DAVID: Dancing is the mark of Satan.
　　We have cast off this old world,
　　we came to this deserted isle to be free of sin,
　　to prepare the way of the Coming of the Lord.

EDITH: I shan't dance again, David.

ELISHA: Nor me, master.

DAVID: We have work to do.
　　Edith, again our children, that you are meant to
　　discipline, have run away without restraint, shout and
　　scream about the island. Joseph have run up the hill – go,
　　fetch him.

EDITH: (*Going*) Yes, David. (*Exit.*)

DAVID: (*Putting arm round him*) Elisha, faithful Elisha – our
　　faith have come to fruit.

ELISHA: We are free, master, free. I am no longer the servant
　　of great lords, the slave of the whisky bottle.

DAVID: We shall reap the harvest, the Lord shall feast at our
　　supper table.

ELISHA: And us have left behind the filth of England. What
　　did England ever offer me, master, except service,
　　servility . . .

DAVID: Come, let us return to the ship, Elisha, help our
　　brothers to unload. The captain wishes to sail by nightfall.

ELISHA: Yes, master.

DAVID: Do not call me "master" any more.

ELISHA: Master?

DAVID: The Lord is our only master on this island. Call me
　　"David".

122

ELISHA: Yes, mas . . . David.

(*Exeunt.*
Enter AUGUSTUS HARE, *smoking cigar, dressed
extraordinarily in grass skirt and colonial governor's hat,
followed a few paces behind by an unsympathetic* ANNIE.)

HARE: Oh, my back, my poor back. Rub it, Annie, rub it.

ANNIE: Rub it your damned self. Told you that would happen
with those two whores. Fancy mixing together numbers
21 and 37 in the same bed.

HARE: They were like tigers at feeding time.

ANNIE: And they fed on you. (*Taking out book*) What you
want for food today?

HARE: (*Distantly*) Food, food?

ANNIE: Yes, damned food.

HARE: When I was at one of my better public schools, I would
have considered a crust of bread as very paradise.
(*Beat. No sympathy from* ANNIE.)
Very well, venison stewed in port wine. No, fish first,
grilled, then the venison. Then a salad to scour out the
fat. I'll finish with my Stilton. My best Bordeaux to start
with, then a Sauterne to balance the salad, ending with my
second-best brandy and a cigar.

ANNIE: (*Beat.*) And the other?

HARE: Do I have to, Annie?

ANNIE: Forty whores, Mr Hare, all need regular servicing.

HARE: Very well. Give me two hours' rest after my supper,
then send me 3, the Chinese, and 27, the Indian dancing
girl with those wild black eyes.
(ANNIE *going.*)
My back, Annie.

ANNIE: You made this bed – now you must lie on it. (*Exit.*)

HARE: (*To audience*) It was never like this at Eton. Brutal,
terrifying, degrading maybe – but never boring. Take
number 27, my Indian dancing girl.
    Cunning, clinging,
    gentle as a petal,
    tight as a clam.

She rides light and lissome upon me
    until I float, lithe as a dandelion seed upon the wind.
All very well in theory – myself, a single man, alone upon a
desert island with fifty plump and luscious women – but in
practice – boring, infernally boring.

 (EDITH, *offstage, shouts*.)

EDITH: Joseph, Joseph!

 (EDITH *runs on. Each thunderstruck. Pause*.)

Good morning.

 (HARE *too astonished to reply.* ANNIE *rushes on bursting with
 news, stops dead at sight of* EDITH. HARE *aside to* ANNIE.)

HARE: Annie, where did you conjure up this white whore
from? You know I don't like them – especially dressed up
as some damned Quaker woman.

ANNIE: I don't know the bitch. (*Spits*.) A damned ship have
anchored off north shore, lots of men get off with much
cargoes.

HARE: (*Horrified, covering crotch*) Men!

ANNIE: Damned yes.

HARE: (*Pleasantly, to* EDITH) Good morning to you, also, and
what a pleasant one it is too. (*To* ANNIE) Rough men?
Sailors? Lock the girls in the hut, every last one of them.
Get the gun – you know how to use it?

ANNIE: Don't you?

HARE: No. (*To* EDITH) Excuse me but a moment. I greatly
look forward to making your acquaintance in just a
moment. (*To* ANNIE) And get the flag – the Union
Jack – wave it at them – that always impresses sailors.

ANNIE: Where is that damned flag?

HARE: How would I know?

 (*Exit* ANNIE. HARE *turns to* EDITH *who plunges in*.)

EDITH: Since us ant met before, and this-yere ant eggsackly the
place to stand on ceremony, I be Edith Worth, wife of David
Worth, from Bristol. (*Holds out hand*.) How do you do?
(*They shake hands*.)

HARE: A lovely morning indeed, ma'am. Augustus Hare,
delighted to make your acquaintance in such – er –

unexpected circumstances. You are passing through, I
trust, just called in for fresh supplies . . .

EDITH: Thee best ask my husband David 'bout that.

HARE: Oh, David. Are there many of you?

EDITH: Less see? Not countin' my young uns, there be David,
Elisha . . .

HARE: Elisha.

EDITH: Then the eight craftsmen . . .

HARE: Eight craftsmen?

EDITH: Ah – for building the New Jerusalem – and that be
about all – ah.

HARE: There's you.

EDITH: Oh, ah – I were forgettin' myself, s'no.

HARE: You're the only woman?

EDITH: Ah. See, 'tis mainly a man's undertakin' we'm
engaged on yere. We believe, see, that the Lord God shall
shortly reveal His Face, shortly step out agin yere on
Earth, in the presence of we as have prepared a place for
His Coming.

HARE: Really.

EDITH: The Lord God did instruct my husband, David, to
find a private place, withdrawn from all unclean human
habitation, so David did choose, er, here.

HARE: So you came expecting an uninhabited island?

EDITH: Ah.

(EDITH *looks about for* JOSEPH, HARE *for* ANNIE.)

Have you seen my young son, Joseph?

HARE: Afraid I haven't.

(DAVID, *offstage, singing "Babylon has fall'n".*)

EDITH: Caw – Yere be David now. Don't know if ur'll be too
pleased – seein' thee.

HARE: I don't know whether I precisely relish the sight of him
myself.

(DAVID *processes on stage, carrying flag of the New
Jerusalem. Parades downstage, sees* HARE. *Flag and mouth
droop. Inarticulate a second.*)

DAVID: (*To* EDITH) What's this, Edith? Who's this thee gone and found?

EDITH: I weren't lookin' for no one, David, I were lookin' for Joseph – but I found he.

DAVID: What's he doing here?

HARE: Augustus Hare, sir. I might as well ask you what you and your tribe are doing on my island?

(ANNIE *rushes back on, erect Union Jack and gun.* DAVID *stares, his flag grown erect. She places flag in hole centre back, backs off, pointing gun at him, standing defiant behind* HARE. *To prove his defiance,* DAVID *sticks his flag in stage opposite Annie's.* ANNIE *spits.*)

DAVID: (*Angrily*) I, David Worth, be on this soil (*stamps*), this-yere most sacred soil, by the commission of the Most High Lord God.

(ANNIE *laughs raucously.*)

HARE: Quiet, Annie.

(ANNIE *spits.*)

Since you are here on Christ's commission, perhaps I might see the paper this miraculous document is written upon?

DAVID: The Lord duss not sully His hands by pressing inky pen to gross paper.

(HARE *takes out, unfolds, large document.*)

HARE: *My* commission.

(*He hands it to* DAVID. DAVID *cannot read it, turns it round.*) You'll find the confirmation of my commission about here. (*Indicates.*)

DAVID: I cassen read this – 'tis all squirls and puff.

EDITH: (*By his side, helping*) Here, David, see. (*Reads*) "These letters patent and accredited affiliated documents do thus confirm and consense our servant, Augustus Caspar Bulstrode Hare as our true and faithful servant, representative, and consul, wheresoever and whensoever he might tender and present them. In the Name of God, Georgius Quartus Rex."

DAVID: Babble. The bibble-babble of Babylon.

HARE: But, I say, it's signed by His Majesty himself, King

George . . . you know, King of England . . . drives about the place in carriages.

(DAVID *ritually tears paper*.)

DAVID: Pagan filth, scabbed scribble, English lordships. Us did turn our back on all such corruption and privilege. Know that my faith in God be a-damant. It do com-plex and con-firm I in one steady, sturdy root of knowledge, which, like some girt oak tree (*points upward*) do structure and steadfast my whole constitution. This-yere be *my* land. (*Stamps*.)

(*Pause*.)

HARE: As I arose this morning I little thought that by lunchtime I should be facing some fanatic, hot from Bristol, exhaling clouds of godly righteousness. However, it has occurred, and, since it has, I find I must act.

(*He gestures.* ANNIE *passes him gun. He points it at* DAVID.) Now, I shall make my point. While your point may tend heavenward . . .

(DAVID *lowers hand*.)

. . . mine is more down to earth. It is aimed straight at your belly. It is called a gun. My point aims and expels an iron missile at such a tremendous velocity that it will tear through your clothes and your flesh and then several of your more vital organs, finally leaving your body in the company of some of your more precious bodily fluids. This is my island (*stamps*) and *this* is the point of my power.

EDITH: (*Intervening*) Sir, er, Mr Hare . . .

DAVID: (*Restraining her*) Edith!

EDITH: Please understand, we'm peaceful folk.

DAVID: Edith, get back here.

(EDITH *returns. They stare at each other, then withdraw to confer with their women.*)

HARE: The fellow's insane. Are the girls locked up?

ANNIE: You not the only cock on the dung heap no more – yes.

(ELISHA *enters, sees group, stares.*)

127

DAVID: Elisha.

(ELISHA *goes to* DAVID.)

ELISHA: Master, what are these creatures doing on our island? You're sure the Lord God said this exact island?

DAVID: Yes – of course I am.

ELISHA: I seen others. Women, master, women.

DAVID: What?

ELISHA: In a clearing, in the forest. All these women – darkies, Chinks, brownies – all shut up in this hut. (*Shivers.*) Fifty of them, at least.

EDITH: I'll go and release they poor women.

DAVID: Quiet. (*Pause. To* ELISHA) Our ship have left?

ELISHA: You're not thinking of leaving, master?

DAVID: Of course not. Get back to the men at once, order them not to leave the camp.

ELISHA: Keep them away from the women.

DAVID: Exactly.

(HARE *dismisses* ANNIE. *She and* ELISHA *go back upstage, each facing other hostilely, then split, each going own direction.*)

HARE: I presume you're leaving.

DAVID: Never.

HARE: You're not staying.

DAVID: And no more bist thee with the fifty nigger women all locked in thik hut. You'm a slave trader.

HARE: How dare you! You keep your hands and the hands of your dirty sailors off my poor defenceless women – understand?

DAVID: Whores, kept women more like – imprisoned for your sordid delight. Keep them away from my men.
(*Beat.*)

HARE: We have an understanding.

DAVID: God makes no pacts with Satan.

HARE: You control your pure, unsullied men. I shall control my girls. Each might corrupt the other. (*Pause.*) We must meet again, as soon as possible. You have reached an understanding – with the Devil. (*Bows, exits smartly.*)

128

DAVID: But . . . but . . .
(DAVID *stamps, shakes off* EDITH'*s comforting arm, stomps off.* EDITH *follows obediently.*
Lights down, night. Sea sounds up.
SLOCUM *lies full on back midstage staring up.*)

SLOCUM: I lie unmoving as death
as my tiny craft slides lithe through the moving waters,
staring upward into the velvet skies
that stretch massive above I.
I watch each star fluttering, flaming, flaring into life
till all the heavens blaze with godly light.

Can I tell you the weight of that fiery creation
as it wheels and spans above I
– turning, churning, e-volving, re-volving?
It do press immense upon my breast.
I stare up, out into the chasming void
unfolding giddy above me,
till that which was above becomes below;
by sudden, subtle alchemy
I, on my frail craft, hang out above a mighty void,
I, a speck of nothing, float off alone into black infinity,
spiralling, falling timeless through eternity,
Turning slow in the body of my God.

(*Lights down, then up. Still night.*
Small camp fire. Behind it, EDITH *with infant in her arms crying.* DAVID *to one side staring into fire, thinking.*)

EDITH: (*To audience*) Three nights now my young un kept I
up with the croup, nursing, cradling her.
(*Rocks baby. It stops crying.*)
Caw, young uns de draw and drain thee, dunnum?
When they'm babbies they do drag at thy dugs till thy hair
do fall out, thy fingernails crack, and thy bones do ache
like Death have come in.
Then they'm toddling, muggling to and fro, snagging on
thy skirt, tugging at thy scant patience, whining for thy
time.

Then, they'm off, running, fighting, fretting, jagging thy
nerves as thee watch out all day for their safety.
And finally, s'no, 'tis all handsome poses, sulks and
tempers, cutting their cruel blades on thy tired flesh – and
folks de wonder why us de grow old!
(*Smiles.*)

> Young uns do kill thee,
> tread thee down till you'm dust aneath their crowding
> feet –
> but I do love um, s'no,
> for we'm all one flesh,
> rising as others do fall, falling as others do rise.
> The treadmill of humanity,
> motion in an eternal ocean.

DAVID: (*Bitterly*) I be a laughing stock.

EDITH: David?

DAVID: I, who called on God,
> Whom God answered.
> (*Pause. Enter* ELISHA.)

ELISHA: Master, the men won't heed a word I say. "The
master commands you," I say, but they will not bide.
They shall find the whores.
(*Pause.*)

DAVID: Elisha, Edith.

ELISHA: Master?

DAVID: You both know Psalm 68 . . .

ELISHA: (*Puzzled*) Aye?

DAVID: Let us sing it together.

ELISHA: 'Tis wicked, master. A wicked psalm used by the
godless for cursing.

EDITH: David, 'tis evil.

DAVID: Woman – mind thy place. We shall sing it.

EDITH: You want to curse that man, Mr Hare. David – the
Lord Jesus do rule by love, not the sword.

DAVID: This man stand in God's way. King David wrote thik
psalm that its power might smite his enemies – 'tis a godly
psalm!

130

EDITH: No bloodshed, David – swear to I!

DAVID: Not one drop of righteous blood.

EDITH: No blood! I be a woman as have shed her life's blood five times that souls might have life.

(*Pause.*)

ELISHA: Those as sow iniquity shall reap the same.

DAVID: Elisha, do not heed a foolish woman's talk. Look, the Lord Hisself shall walk upon this very ground, His footsteps here (*walks*), yours here (*walks*).

ELISHA: I thought this island a simple Eden.

DAVID: And so it shall be. Come, sing.

(*Beat.*)

EDITH: Blood shall have blood. I shan't hold my babby while Satan is my intimate.

(*She puts baby to one side, it cries. They start to sing Psalm 68 (Moody and Sankey).*

Lights down.

Commotion, HARE *staggers on to stage, holding lantern, adjusting dress.*)

HARE: What has got into these damned women! All the blood and heat run right out of 'em. Take number 17.

Traditionally, as cunning and clinging as a vine – tonight, as arousing as a sheep that's had its arse in the north wind a ten-week.

So, if all else fail, send for numbers 7 and 23, two strapping, lusty nigger girls, full of happy invention and outrageous appetite. (*Beat.*) Stirring as two Scotch spinsters eating porridge.

Witchcraft!

(*Shouts:*) Annie! Annie! (*Takes port bottle from pocket, drinks, scowls.*) Even my finest port wine – dead as ditchwater.

(ANNIE *suspiciously comes on with ledger.*)

ANNIE: You dressed?

HARE: Why should that bother you?

ANNIE: I, a hardworking business lady – not some damned whore. What you want?

HARE: The girls.

ANNIE: They restless – sense the strangers.

HARE: Still locked up?

ANNIE: That just it – "locked up." How many times I tell you,
Mr Hare, we need new lock for hut. See here (*shows him
ledger*), top of damned list. But you, you say what we need
new lock for in middle of Great Southern Ocean? Well,
now old lock broke. (*Beat.*) Your whores is out.
(*Pause.* HARE *stares at her in horror.*)
Got some of your damned shag, Mr Hare?
(HARE *gets out tin.*)

HARE: Finest yellow Virginia, blended specially for me in my
shop in Jermyn Street – my world starts to collapse.

ANNIE: (*Filling pipe*) All for one damned lock.
(HARE *moves to audience.*)

HARE: (*To audience*) Pursued by scandal I've been – since the
beginning. Expelled from Eton for sleeping with two
chambermaids and the Beak's daughter – at the same time.
Sent down from Oxford for being discovered in the
Master's garden atop a handsome whore – property of the
aforementioned Master.

So, my dear papa gave me ten thousand guineas as a start
in the City of London. (*Laughs mockingly.*) Have you
noticed how it is the particular and peculiar fortune of
every rich man to believe himself poor, beastly poor. So,
with my ten thousand guineas I set about persuading some
two hundred stout merchants that my ten thousand
guineas would make them rich, beastly rich – for only two
hundred guineas of their own. Unfortunately my excellent
stratagem was foiled. Had not the then Home Secretary
been my closest partner in this business (*rubs neck*), I fear
I might have danced the Tyburn Jig.

Instead, my friend the Home Secretary became Prime
Minister, and I joined the Diplomatic Service – in haste. I
was posted – post-haste – in a ship which took fifteen
months for the passage, and on which there was not one
female – except for a goat, a very unwholesome, rancid goat.

My fate was to be shipped to the most unknown,
uninhabited atoll known to man. Once a year a
government frigate brings me two hogsheads of mellow
port, a pipe of the sweetest madeira, seven jars of brandy,
two casks of best blended tobacco, plus the widest
selection of preserved foods, luxurious silks, and choicest
extracts from the Prime Minister's private collection of
erotic drawings.

Before my exile, I was permitted to cruise the South
Ocean a six-month, putting in at every port, visiting each
brothel, and there purchasing the hottest, most succulent
creatures on display. Having been expelled from Eton,
Oxford, and London, now it seems I am even to lose my
hot and dusky seraglio.

(HARE *moves softly over to* ANNIE.)

Annie.

ANNIE: What?

HARE: I feel lonely.

ANNIE: Damn you.

HARE: It's dark – I just want comfort.

ANNIE: Keep your damned hands to themselves. I, a manager.
I laid with royalty, damned fine white British royalty. I lie
with no one else.

HARE: I know, I know, but . . .

ANNIE: Only 17, best damned number one whore in whole
East Africa – for white men, Arabs, even damned niggers.
Then His Majesty King Duke of York sail into bay, order
best slap bang up whore in place. I go to his bed, all
through night I only feel little mouse tickle me here
(*indicates crotch*), but next morning he leave me one
hundred damned fine gold sovereigns. With that I set
up best damned whorehouse in whole Southern Ocean –
but no more damned men – not one – just money now,
power.

(*Long pause.*)

HARE: All these strangers on the island make me restless. My
blood won't lie down. They excite me.

133

(*Looks at her, aroused. Moves to her.*)

ANNIE: What got into you? You had whores in your bed all
night.

HARE: I know – but they're so predictable. I want something
real.

ANNIE: What you goin' to do about that lock?

(*Silence from* HARE. ANNIE *snorts, walks off. He shivers.*
Lights down. Blackness.
Lights up. Bright sunlight.
On stage comes DAVID, ELISHA, EDITH. DAVID *places flag*
on ground.)

ELISHA: Master, those men are hunting they whores like dogs
sniffing stinky bitches. You must do something.

(HARE *and* ANNIE *come in from other side.* ANNIE *gives* HARE
black look, plants flag.)

DAVID: Mr Augustus Hare, do you agree to leave this island
immediately?

HARE: On the contrary, you cheap, rabble-rousing
non-conformist . . .

(ANNIE *stops him, points off into opposite side of audience to*
them.)

ANNIE: Damned, damned.

HARE: (*Protesting at interference*) Annie.

ANNIE: Damned sailors! There.

(HARE *sees, shocked. Simultaneously,* ELISHA *sees girls*
coming from other side.)

ELISHA: Look, master, look – the bloody whores are loose.

DAVID: (*Calmly*) Elisha, do not swear.

HARE: (*Shouts at* DAVID) *Do something!*

ELISHA: In a second they'll see each other.

(ELISHA *looks at* DAVID *a second, sees he's not going to do*
anything, runs up aisle closest to him, shouts across audience:)

ELISHA: Bob Stoodley, Zachary Friar – get back. Do you hear
me?

(HARE *has silently ordered* ANNIE *down opposite aisle to*
similar position.)

ANNIE: Get back, you damned whores. (*Raises rifle.*) I

damned shoot you dead if not.

HARE: They've seen each other – oh Jesus!

ANNIE: (*To* ELISHA) Keep your damned men off my whores.

ELISHA: (*To men*) Get back, back. (*Gives up.*)

ANNIE: (*To men*) Right, I shoot.

(HARE *goes to her to restrain her.*)

HARE: Annie!

ANNIE: Who the damned man now!

(*She aims at men, trigger clicks.* ANNIE *furiously shakes it, aims, click. Stalks back on stage.*)

(*Venemously, to* HARE) Damned you, damned you. This your fault. I damned try to run this place business-like and clever. I come to you, say, Mr Hare, I need money so when govmint ship comes I buy good bullets cos old ones be damned dead, but damned you say, tomorrow, tomorrow. Well, now damned tomorrow be damned today!

(*She throws rifle at* HARE, *stalks off.* ELISHA *retreats aghast to stage.*)

ELISHA: God help us, master, they're drawing together, talking, laughing. They touch each others' flesh, and now, they come towards us, right towards us.

DAVID: Take heart, Elisha, remember how Gideon overcame the Midianites.

(EDITH *hears this, looks peculiarly at* DAVID. *Holding his arms wide like an evangelist,* DAVID *addresses audience centre stage.*)

Brothers and sisters, gather about, come hear the joyful word of the Lord. Lord Jesus knows about your struggles, your Babylonian Captivity, the humiliations and tribulations you have suffered, but, he say to me, just as He granted the Elders of the Tribes of Israel many wives, so, now, he grants each of you, the New Elders of Israel, likewise. Look before you. For each of you the gift of five able-bodied, hard-working wives, which he have arranged to be here awaiting you on this holy island. They shall stitch thy clothing, serve thee at thy table, fulfil thy every desire as thee build the New Jerusalem.

Hallelujah, brothers and sisters, thank the Lord for this gift. Come, let us return to camp and celebrate!

(*Sounds of cheers.* DAVID *picks up his flag, leaves ceremoniously, singing "Babylon has Fall'n". As he passes* HARE, HARE *about to protest, but mouth just flaps open. As* DAVID *leaves,* ANNIE *rushes on, carrying ledger book.*)

ANNIE: (*To* HARE) Lost your damned women because even powder in your damned pistol wet. Me going with my book to organize proper damned man.

(*She grabs Union Jack, marches off after* DAVID. EDITH *and* ELISHA *stare open-mouthed after them centre stage.* HARE *downstage right.* EDITH *comes downstage to* HARE.)

EDITH: I ant never afore, in my whole life, spoke out against my wedded husband, Mr Hare, sir, but, I veel . . . all my being do tell I he did wrong. I must apologize for he. 'Twas . . . 'twas a disgrace.

(*She goes back to* ELISHA.)

ELISHA: When we came to this island, I thought the very earth sacred, pure – now, it is as soiled, as filthy as anywhere. (*Pause.*) Mistress?

EDITH: Elisha?

ELISHA: I can't work for the master no more.

EDITH: I understand. The children and I shall miss thee – you were always their best friend.

(ELISHA *comes downstage to* HARE, EDITH *tries the earth in one or two places with foot, sits down on it, foetal position, clasping arms around knees, buries face in knees.*)

ELISHA: You're a lord, some high gentleman. You know, hold your nose above other folk's heads and whiffle your fingers in the air. Twenty years I worked in service, ten as a butler in Grosvenor Square. Always punctual, always discreet – faithful as a hound.

HARE: You appear to be requesting employment.

(ELISHA *acknowledges.*)

I thought you were already employed. (*Indicates* DAVID.)

136

ELISHA: Feet of clay – a filthy whoremonger, sir. I prefer
earthly bondage to spiritual death – though it tears me,
terribly.

HARE: I hire you, Elisha, at unusual rates. My second-best
hogshead of port is under the rush matting in the shed –
take none from my first.

ELISHA: I swore when I first set foot on this island that no
more drink would pass my lips. I still have some shreds of
self-regard.

(ELISHA *and* HARE *exit stage right.* EDITH, *alone on the
stage, watches them offstage right, then looks at David's exit,
left, then buries head in knees again. Slow footsteps, as*
SLOCUM *walks up to her, tests ground with feet, sits beside
her.*)

SLOCUM: (*Addressing audience*) On my solo voyage about the
earth, eighteen days out from Newfoundland I put in at
the Azores, where I rested two days.
While there,
unfortunately I purchased some rich, ripe plums and
white goats' cheese.
On my first evening back at sea,
running before a squally southwesterly for Gibraltar,
when a prudent man would have laid to,
I double reefed the mains'l and gave my sloop the whole
jib,
set her to her course, and went below to enjoy my
cheese and plums.
With dire results.

(EDITH *smiles at him.*)

Within an hour, violent cramps seized my stomach,
wrenched my body to and fro.
I was paralysed, helpless upon the cabin floor,
and all the time I could feel the wind rising,
the sea starting to hammer upon the frail sides of my
yacht.
Untended, it bucked and rolled,
shook and sloughed in the mighty seas.

137

Alone in a vast ocean,
I could not move.
And then, glancing back up the companionway,
I saw a man standing out on the deck,
black-bearded, huge-chested,
holding the wheel of my tiny sloop steady as a rock.
"Who are you?" I shouted.
He answered me quietly (*holds temples*), in my head,
explained he was a member of Columbus's crew
who still roamed these same oceans
helping his fellow seamen.
The pains overcame me, I lost consciousness.
All night I lay thus
but awoke the next morning.
My pains past, I made my way on deck.
Heavy seas were still running,
the decks of my sloop were white as shark's teeth
from the seas running over them.
Everything movable had been swept overboard, and yet,
to my astonishment, I saw in broad daylight that my
tiny sloop still ran truly as I had set her, flying through
the seas.
(*Beat.*)
It was a miracle.
(*Beat.*)
On my subsequent circumnavigation
I have many times felt that seaman's presence,
conversed with him, even.
Sometimes I have left my wheel
untended for two, three weeks,
and always he has steered it
exactly, precisely to my course.
(*He touches* EDITH's *arm, looks left to* DAVID, *right to*
HARE.)
Whichever way you choose, you will finally go where you
were always going.
EDITH: (*Rising*) I must mind my children.

(EDITH *exits stage left.* SLOCUM *exits. Enter* HARE,
downstage right.)

HARE: At Oxford, in between my whoring and high jinks and
the disembursing of the bursar, I opened the odd book or
two. I gained a great affection for the Greeks – Plato
especially. It is one of the wiser maxims of Plato that what
one looks for, one shall find; that this world (*stamps*) has
the peculiar property of presenting for one's discovery
precisely what one goes forth to discover.
Now, I am a man who loves, itches to intrigue. I love a
coterie, a court, a kingdom. I covet one penny infinitely
over a thousand honest-earnt sovereigns. I would rather lie
in one other man's bed than in a dozen of mine own.
Now, see the truth of Plato's observation. With forty
cow-like, carping women about me, stuck exiled on this
lost desert island, it would seem I am doomed to perpetual
vegetation, self-immolation. But, across fifteen thousand
miles of ocean, as unerring as Oedipus to Jocasta's bed,
comes to me a ready cockpit, a seething cauldron, a world
ripe for conspiracy and corruption.
I have been wronged, vengeance is mine. Now gods, stand
up for bastards!
(*During latter part of this speech,* DAVID, EDITH *and* ANNIE
have dragged on a trestle table. EDITH *sits right side of table
sewing,* ANNIE *and* DAVID *pore over plans on left side of
table.* HARE *stays unseen where he was.*)

DAVID: Bob Stoodley got to finish they joists by this
evening – tell him they'm needed for the throne room.

ANNIE: He workin' on great arch.

DAVID: I know – but they joists are more important.

ANNIE: Right – they need varnishing?

DAVID: No, we'll paint 'em when they're standing. And don't
forget to put they tools we lost down in your ledger.

ANNIE: Oh, I haven't forgotten. (*Shows him.*) Here they are.
(*Enthusiastically*) Oh, Mr Worth, it so good working for
you – I write down in book what needed, you say, "Yes,
do it, doublefast," and it done. Damned good!

139

DAVID: Language, Annie.

ANNIE: Sorry, Mr Worth.

> (*They study plans.* HARE *shuffles upstage toward* EDITH, *penitently.* EDITH *looks up, sees him, smiles warmly, strides over to him.* DAVID *and* ANNIE *look up,* DAVID *slightly embarrassed.* ANNIE *scowls.*)

EDITH: Mr Hare, 'tis good to see thee.

> (*She shakes his hand.*)

HARE: (*Mumbling*) Good morning.

EDITH: Come sit down yere. Lookzee, David, Mr Hare.

DAVID: (*Embarrassed*) Aye.

> (ANNIE *spits and marches off.*)

HARE: I hope, after our "experiences", you won't mind my coming over like this. After all, we do have to live on this island together.

DAVID: Yes, yes. Edith, look after Mr Hare here, I got to go get all these-yere plans laid out. Good day. (*Exit.*)

HARE: Good day, Mr Worth.

EDITH: Come, sit down.

HARE: I really don't know whether . . . there's still a lot of ill-feeling about.

EDITH: You'm welcome. It must get very lonely bided over there all by thyself.

> (*She sits, indicates for him to do so.*)

And how've you been keeping?

> (HARE *sits.*)

HARE: It was a bit of a shock. Black, Elisha Black is over there, working for me.

EDITH: Issur drinking?

HARE: No.

EDITH: Good. Elisha be a very kind, feeling body, Mr Hare – behind all his gloom.

HARE: Are the, er, girls all right, Mrs Worth?

> (EDITH *sews faster.*)

I just wanted to know.

EDITH: From what I do see o' they, they'm fine.

> (*Pause.*)

HARE: You've got a lot of sewing.

EDITH: Less see, there be my husband and five young uns, s'no, then all they others – well, they comin' might be good for summat, but they'm no good at stitchin' shirts. Still, I be used to it. Back home in Bristol I allus did dressmakin' – helped make ends meet.

HARE: What – even with all your children?

EDITH: Well, thee cuss allus slip a needle into cloth somewhen. I did a lot afore the young uns woked up, and then some after they'd muggled on to bed. Cor, did my head used to ache from all that sewin' – purdled my eyes right out me head. 'Twas the dark, see. David said us could only afford to burn one candle, and he did need that for his Bible and calkilations. Still, a good seamstress do have eyes in her fingertips, they say. Most stitchin' be done by feel.

HARE: Really?

EDITH: Oh, ah. I cass mind in my mother's day, when I were only a girl, there were this seamstress up Broad Street – blind.

HARE: No.

EDITH: Ah. She did have such a skill at it, see, that if her apprentices did line up a seam, then she could do the rest by feel. She were good, see, cos her touch were so light. She could feel every mesh of the cloth, so her needle did just dip an' nip, dip an' nip. She were famous, s'no, cos seam did lie so close to seam. I remember her starin' out sightless, but her fingers did dance along her seam blithe as spring lambs.

HARE: How interesting.

EDITH: Thee duss mock I.

HARE: No, I don't. Don't ever think that of me.

EDITH: Well, 'tis all past now. None round yere do care how thy stitchin' do stagger about the cloth. Back home in Bristol, see, 'twere only the rich as could afford good stitching – and you'm the only aristocracy us got yere, Mr Hare.

(*He looks down at his dress. They both laugh.*)
Thee did go to a proper school, Mr Hare?

HARE: I did. Learnt to become a gentleman.

(*He does flowery gesture with hand. They laugh.*)
But that, mercifully, is all in the dim, distant past. As you can see, Mrs Worth, it was not precisely the milieu I chose to stay in.

(*They laugh.*)

EDITH: I must say, Mr Hare . . .

HARE: Call me "Augustus".

EDITH: All right, Augustus, I be Edith.

HARE: Edith.

EDITH: Now, as I were saying, "Augustus", I think thee been very good about what happened. Keepin' women like that be sin by my book, but 'twas thy life, s'no, and thee lost un when us came (*snaps fingers*), like that, but thee ant hardly complained.

HARE: The Augustus Hare that you saw, Edith, when you came to this island, might have seemed a happy man – indeed, by the judgment of the world, a man alone on a desert island with forty young women and all the port wine he might drink is in very paradise – but, Edith, the outer man so rarely corresponds with the inner man. (*Beat.*) I was unhappy.

(EDITH *warmly, spontaneously, puts her hand on his arm. Quickly returns to sewing. Beat.*)
Deeply unhappy.

EDITH: Well, there be unhappiness in all our lives, s'no.

HARE: What, Edith, even in yours?

EDITH: Well, less say there be fractures and friction where there might be harmony, companionship.

HARE: What, you're talking about you and . . .

EDITH: Ah, I and my young uns, Augustus.

HARE: (*Disappointed*) Oh.

EDITH: Cor, they'm the devil sometimes. Joseph – thee knows Joseph?

HARE: (*Vaguely*) Yes.

EDITH: Black-haired.

HARE: Ah.

EDITH: Elisha do like he in pertikler.

HARE: Yes – I know him.

(EDITH *springs up, paces up and down.*)

EDITH: Joseph were a happy boy back in Bristol, s'no, played
on droo the streets with his friends, go'ed to the Dame's
School down the street. Allus had his eye stuck in a book,
so ur did learn up a lively tongue in Greek and Latin.

HARE: Quite a gifted little fellow.

EDITH: Well, by all accounts of folk as knows, he were. Then,
us did leave. Joseph didn't want to leave, David did.
Turble arguments. In the end, David did beat ur. 'Twas
turble, Mr Hare, turble. I were sat in the next room, I did
feel each stripe like 'twas my own flesh.
So, Joseph have gone all backkards and contrairy, and
David do blame I for his wildness. 'Tis turble – but, then,
'tis life, iddenur?

HARE: You obviously care deeply for your children.

EDITH: They'm my life.

HARE: The child you were mentioning . . .

EDITH: Joseph?

HARE: Yes. I don't want to butt in, but I thought I might . . .
help. (*Beat.*) You said he was keen on his Latin and
Greek, he missed his books. I, in a very modest way, did
Greats at Oxford.

EDITH: Mr Hare, you'm very kind.

HARE: He could come over to my hut, some afternoons.

(EDITH *puts hand on his arm.*)

EDITH: Augustus. (*Removes hand.*)

HARE: Your husband wouldn't object?

(*Pause.* EDITH *paces up and down.*)

EDITH: My son shall have his education. 'Tis his right. And
p'raps it shall make he to love his father more. (*Beat.*) But
you'm right, David mustn't know. "What worth be
eddication?" ur says, "Christ Jesus be due on earth."
Joseph must come to thee privately.

143

HARE: Yes, secretly.

EDITH: I dussen know how to thank thee, Augustus.

HARE: I must go.

EDITH: 'Tis good to be so open and honest with another soul.
Duss know, Augustus, I ant never talked afore to a man
about my young uns.

HARE: Send Joseph over, tomorrow.

EDITH: I shall.

(HARE *bows, walks over to other side of stage (right).* EDITH
sews.)

HARE: You will have noticed my mistake. It came when I said,
shaking my head, that I was "deeply unhappy". She
warmly touched my arm and said, "Well, there be
unhappiness in all our lives." Now, at the time, I thought
that, rather than being merely a general observation meant
for my consolation and edification, it was in fact her
saying that, like a majority of our human tribe, she was
self-centred, self-obsessed, and wished to talk solely about
herself and her dreary domestic problems. Far from it. I
should have realized that someone so selfless, so used to
the service of others, is never the slightest bit interested in
themselves, but wishes only to talk to and sympathize
with and think concerning others. I should have continued
thinking and talking exclusively about myself and mine
own problems. Still, I was lucky. In my mistake, I happily
stumbled across others she was even more obsessed
about – her children.

Women are a science.
You must spend much time observing their bizarre
habits.
When you wish to board a wench
you must first fathom her,
seek out a loose end – by which you might unravel her –
find a secret crevice by which you might hold her,
from which you might manipulate her.

It is there! I know it is somewhere in this woman, this
admirable woman.

144

He never could understand that.

(HARE *walks over to* EDITH. *She rises.*)

EDITH: Augustus. (*Takes his arm.*) Two weeks thee been
teaching young Joseph.

HARE: Yes.

EDITH: And I seed a diffrince already.

Even his father have noticed and took the credit for tamin'
he.

(*They laugh.*)

Come, sit down.

HARE: Thank you.

(*They sit down.*)

EDITH: Dust think Joseph do show real scholarship?

HARE: He shows great potential, Edith, but it's too soon to
know. (*Pause.*) But I'll tell you something, Edith, having
the child about me reminds me of myself, as a youngster.

EDITH: Yes?

HARE: Things have changed a lot for me – quite suddenly.

(*Sympathetic noise from* EDITH.)

I've started to look back on my life. In the old days I
thought myself sure in what I was doing, but now, I don't
know. Things have changed a lot for me . . . I don't want
to waste your time . . .

EDITH: No, no, Augustus. (*Touches his arm.*) Tell me your
difficulties.

HARE: Young Joseph set me to thinking – he . . . reminds me
of myself, when I was young.

(EDITH *breathes in.*)

Yes, you see, I had a father who was like, well, your
husband.

(EDITH *nods.*)

He wanted me to be one thing; I wished to be another. A
quarrel between father and son (*laughs*), an everyday
incident in the world about us, but, when you're young
and it is you that is quarrelling, then it is as though it has
never happened before, it is as though you – shameless,
sinful you – are shaking down the whole world about your
ears.

EDITH: Ah.

HARE: I started to think badly of myself, you know. (*Directly, sincerely, to audience.*) Do not doubt me, I am sincere in what I say. (*To* EDITH) I used to do things for which I knew I would be punished. Silly things. Then, worse. Steal little household fribbles, and think it the deuce when the servants would get the blame and were dismissed. It sounds terrible now, but then one changed servants as easily as clothes. I used to lie awake at night laughing at their stupid plight. It got to other things – things I shouldn't talk of – women.

EDITH: Oh – I see.

HARE: Even I am now ashamed of certain things I did. (EDITH *looks directly at him.*)

EDITH: (*With feeling*) Augustus, 'tis true I lived a private, modest life – thank God – but as David do say, *all* flesh be senched in sin. I shall listen to thee, Augustus, vor I be no better than any man. The Lord alone dust judge.

HARE: (*To audience*) Oh, the sweet innocence. One worthy woman is worth five hundred whores.
(*Downstage left comes* DAVID, *carrying plan and compasses*, ANNIE *following with ledger. Centre stage they stop. He looks into distance over audience, calculating.* ANNIE *notices* EDITH *and* HARE, *coughs, nudges* DAVID. DAVID *looks.*)

DAVID: (*Embarrassed*) Oh – good morning.

HARE: Good morning.
(DAVID *and* ANNIE *move off stage right. Pause.*)

EDITH: Tell I, Augustus.
(*In his speech, she slowly turns to look at him, stops work, opens mouth voraciously, clasps womb.* HARE *does not look at her.*)

HARE: What's to say? (*Small laugh.*) There were women – lots and lots of women. All the time. One after another. I couldn't stop, you see. I was insatiable – for flesh, feminine flesh. Sometimes it was for simple things, like sweet dimples on the cheek. I would like to touch them, push them in and out, play with them, tickle the ear, brush the hair, back and forth, back and forth. Especially when it layed curled, cupped, clasped in the throat – the delicate, fine-boned, white throat – above . . . the . . . breasts . . . the soft, swinging breasts, white as milk, with their pink nipple dippled in the mound. To lay my cheek against their swelling softness, to cup the gentle mound in my hand, savour the teat, drag, tug it back and forth between my lips, in my teeth, as I were a babe. There's the warmth, the closeness of two fleshes twining, intertwining, striving as one. And you start to feel the lust eat you, shuddering and stuttering in your stomach, enthusing, infusing your embrace, pumping at your heart. Even with whores, even with whores if you pay them enough, you can get that feeling, that feeling as you reach down their backs to the clenched, locked buttocks, mould, kneed them till they loosen and fall flaccid apart and my hand goes down and around, feeling the soft, damp flesh of the inner thigh falling apart, yielding up until you reach the . . .

EDITH: (*Shrieks*:) Stop, stop. No. I sin.

(*Silence. She stares ahead of her.*)

HARE: I'm very sorry. I went too far. I knew I should have stopped – got carried away. (*To audience*) My words carried me away. It's never like that in real life – too much clumsy red flesh rubbing itself raw.

EDITH: No, 'twurden thy fault. I be a knowing ooman, having conceived, carried and born five young uns – I do know each part and function of the body – 'tis all by Nature. Yet, as thee spoke, I did feel Satan e-motion, gout in my body.

HARE: (*Trying to laugh it off*) Come now, surely you don't believe in Satan?

EDITH: What needs belief when thee duss know un, as an adulterous ooman do know her lover in her body. His poison do course my veins – blood shall have blood.

HARE: Look, let's discuss your son's Greek.

EDITH: You mus go now.

Babylon has Fallen

(*Lights dim.*)

Whoss that darkening?

HARE: The sun goes behind a cloud. Goodbye, now, Mrs
Worth. You won't tell your husband any of this, will you?
Please don't get unnecessarily worked up about anything I
might have said.

(*He goes to his side of the stage.*)

EDITH: (*In soliloquy*) When sky-stalking Jehovah up there
    – he who frowns in the midday –
    did con-jure I up from stark naught,
    constituted, configured I vrum rude, random matter
    to a complex of whirling atoms,
    puddled dust, picked ribs,
    and brought I forth
    – conformed my soul to His celestial harmonies,
    framed my fiery being,
    did cohere, cohese I,
    draw I up, a perfect clay figure –
    when He, celestial He (*points up*) did lean over, kiss I,
    inspire life into my moulded form,
    then what were I but a creator's created cray-ture?

(*Beat.*)

Lookzee at the disjuncture, the disfiguration of
wedlock.
    For a ooman, a perfect union be a very free, plain,
    and universal con-fusion of two souls,
    a milling and a melling.
    But for a man 'tis a conjunction, a compaction,
    as two timbers do join, reinforce each the other in a
    greater structure.

(*Beat.*)

    A ooman, 'tis said, do run and flow like water,
    'tis her nature to scatter chaotic if not contained.
    My husband have collected, constrained I to run within
    the sober channels of my marriage,
    so that in our co-mmunion, I might comfort, con-firm
    he, he might rest composed, content upon my still, silent

waters.
And duss see how my marriage, this-yere girt
cumbersome structure have become an engine of
tension, torture, a timbered cross
on which I hang bloody.
My waters do turn stagnant,
poison do churn, dagger my veins,
convulsing I to sedition, foul treason against the estate
of man.

(*Exit* EDITH. *Props removed during* HARE'*s soliloquy.*)

HARE: At this stage, with a normal wench, having thus most
carefully prepared the soil, rolled it, harrowed it, rolled it
again so it lies a trembling, expectant tilth at my feet, I
would cheerfully be readying my plough for much use.
But, with this particular field, this wench, I not only fear
to bring out my stamping, snorting team and parade them
back and forth, I fear even to tread (*treads gingerly on
ground*) upon the ground myself with the lightest of steps.
I fear I might step out only a yard and this earth shall
vomit open, violent black jaws crack apart and swallow me
tumbling down.
This is a most unusual woman, of that I can assure you.
Her flesh is not young and tasteless – she's had five brats
push and shove their way through her – her body is salted
with suffering, tender-tough with experience, and yet her
soul, her soul be as sweet and harmonious as a
fine-tempered clavier. But I sense danger. She is
forbidden – surrounded with taboo, terror.
If I consume her, shall I not be the maggot wriggling in
the apple of this New Eden? (*Beat.*) Augustus Hare,
omniscient and world-weary, admit that now you know
not where you are, and that excitement eats your very
bones.

(*Sea noises up for beach.*

HARE *turns to exit stage right, but* EDITH, *in bright clothes, enters
stage left, skipping and dancing. She has shed her repression,
not like opening scene. Explodes in dance.*

149

*He watches amazed, then makes off, but she cuts him off,
driving him centre stage. He stops, cornered. With final
flourish, she kneels before him, bursts out laughing.)*
Stop this. You have a husband, five children. We can't
behave like this on the seashore.

EDITH: And why not?

HARE: We might be seen. Your husband might find out.

EDITH: David be so busy buildin' his girt temple, us could
love each other on the dinner table afore he, and all ur'd
say to I ood be "Quiet they young uns," and to thee,
"Praise God and pass thik salt." He be stark blind.

HARE: Don't you love your husband any more?

EDITH: *(Smothering sudden agony)* Come, let us dance upon the
shore.

HARE: *(Holding her)* Don't you?

EDITH: Don't ask I. I sheltered aneath ur and his black law,
now I be all adrift, swept upon the great ocean. Thee and
I have met – surf on the shore.

HARE: Your children?

EDITH: They all be organized by thy Black Annie now – wi'
her girt book. Us do have times to mind the children,
times to cook – 'tis all in thik black book. No one shall
miss I.

HARE: You mean you possess freedom.

EDITH: Ah, for the first time in my life. *(Shivers.)*

HARE: Your husband?

EDITH: Cor, some paramour you. 'Tis the intrigue do excite
thee. Thee shall pant more when you'm stood aside my
husband than when you'm laid atop I.

HARE: These sort of things have to be done with finesse.

EDITH: Finesse! I cass see right through all thy intrigues. I
watched thee all the time as thee been trying to turn I
against my husband, gettin' I to talk about my grouses
and hurts, to lean the harder on thy soft shoulder. I see
thee!

HARE: Well, if you find me so naked in my ambitions – why
are you here?

(*He takes her hand.*)

EDITH: You take my hand, I unfasten.

HARE: And so, Madam Quakeress, you always shall.

(EDITH *puts his hand to her breast.*)

EDITH: I be here, because, for all thy fatness and greasy
lechery . . .

HARE: You're so flattering, my dear.

EDITH: . . . thee do draw and hunger I, thy being do interess,
tie and twine I fast till my whole body, in its shame, do
flow alive wi' hot serpent liquids, my eyes flush, grow
dimpsey to thy raw stare.

Veel I, vinger I,

veel my body cleave and climb thee,

tear, devour thee.

I shall sup on thee, thee on I.

Gorge I,

come, slake my shame,

fuck I to flitters.

(*She lies back, pulls him down. He coolly looks at audience,
puts tongue in her ear. She screams and writhes away,
crouching on ground.*)

Stop it, please, stop it. (*Cries.*) Can we stop playing now,
go on home. Forget all this.

HARE: No, I've had enough clever silliness from you, woman.

EDITH: I'm sorry.

HARE: I do not choose to couple here on the beach, in broad
daylight, like some farmyard beast.

EDITH: No.

HARE: You shall come to me at midnight, in the clearing on
top of the hill, where your husband builds his temple. We
shall consecrate it. Understand?

EDITH: Aye.

HARE: I know you, and I know your filth.

(EDITH *goes slowly upstage, lights dimming.* HARE *stays
down, undressing as speaks.*)

No whore might counterfeit this for sport. 'Tis real, 'tis
bloody. No whore, *whatever* the fortune thee pay her,

151

would writhe and welter in her own blood and then thank thee for *thy* pains. This power play ennobles, appetizes me.

(*He hurries into the gloom upstage, where their forms can dimly be seen making love.*

On stage, winsome, wistful, Chaplinesque, waltzes ELISHA, *dancing with a broom. Dances about in immaculate butler's uniform.*)

ELISHA: Unknown to many people, it is a fact that many butlers make very good dancers. A butler, you see, needs a quick, subtle step, full of worldly knowledge, that knows when (*demonstrates*) to glide, pause poised, retreat, or pass by fleet on the other side. His foot must dance swift and svelte as any diplomat, skirting hidden rocks and sudden reefs as careful as any sea captain.

Let me take you through the footwork of a butler, any butler, in some town house about Grosvenor Square, when His Lordship has round to dinner some of his fast friends, and when Her Ladyship is away whoring it in Bath. Early evening, pacing about the household, checking the housemaids have prepared the reception and bedrooms to a perfection. Down the stairs to the stone-flagged kitchen where the chef and his skivvies scurry and scream at each other, back up the stairs, standing by the door as the guests enter, organizing the valets as they collect the coats, then into the main reception room. Pouring out the wine from glass to glass, stepping in between the kicking heels and lounging legs, ignoring the cigar smoke blown in one's face and the obscenities bandied about, stepping over rolling bodies as two young bloods rough it on the floor and set the room in a roar. The meal. Stand by the door, supervising the maids as they set and serve all the foods, checking the meats and wines.

The meal over, the gentlemen sit sated, cigars lolling from their slack mouths. Now the evening's work begins. His Lordship beckons, the feet cross the floor submissive to

his side, the butler gravely leans forward to hear his
instructions, then passes from gentleman to gentleman,
hearing from each the nice and particular details of the
whore – or whores – he desires that night – their
perversions, specialities, dresses and complexions. Gravely
listening, nodding his head, pursing his lips in admiration.
Down the backsteps, out the back door, along the cobbled
mews where they stable whores and horses side by side,
into the Royal Exchange public house on the corner of
Adam's Mews, amid the hob-nailed boots and sawdust to
the pimp set snug in his corner, picking his gold teeth and
breathing onions in your face. Refuse his "kind" offer to
sit down and repeat your list standing stiffly. He beckons
his trusted girl and gives his instruction – detailed, precise
as any great engineer.

She and I go back down the mews, knocking on different
doors till all the night's whores are assembled, tipsy and
giggling, in the scullery. After the guillotine, great lords of
England fear and talk about one subject more than any
other – the pox. Each whore must lean over the table and
I, *I* must inspect their private parts, scrupulous, with a
lighted candle, for sores and diseases. I send them upstairs
and wash my hands, then my face, then my hands again,
very scrupulous.

Then, once more, up the backstairs, into the mêlée with
port and cigars. Stopping precise in amidst the intimate
garments, entwined legs, writhing bodies. Seeing sights,
smelling smells, listening to obscenities – Sodom,
Gomorrah, every night about Grosvenor Square, until the
events on that particular night at Lord William Russell's,
when, next morning, I saw, with my own eyes, the faces
of the Duke of Wellington, Prince Albert, aye, the Queen
herself, peek from round their carriage curtains to see the
famous, infamous Number 14, Norfolk Street.

So you see why a butler's feet are so deft – they cannot
stamp in outrage, kick in anger, trample in
vengeance – they must always be neat, punctual,

subservient.

(HARE *groans in climax.* ELISHA *looks back. On tiptoe, he creeps back, sees them. Comes downstage horrified and goes to one side where he watches.* EDITH *and* HARE *arise and come downstage.*)

EDITH: Have thee finished? Can I go home?

HARE: No, I have not finished with you.

EDITH: David might miss I.

HARE: What, iss the whore snug as a maggot by his side? You are fine game, thing.

EDITH: Can . . .

HARE: No! (*Slaps her.*) Understand?

(*No reaction.*)

I said, do you understand, thing?

(*He slaps her about the stage.*)

EDITH: Yes, yes.

HARE: You go when I say go, thing, you come when I say come, thing.

EDITH: I thought it should only be once.

HARE: Mistress Worth, Quakeress, faithless housewife of Bristol, I shall mount you and raddle you, tup and whore you – on thy eating table, upon your husband's maps, upon the sands, against a tree – as commonly and wantonly as I desire.

Do you understand why I treat you thus? It is because I *know* that your innocent corruption, your stenching womanhood, drives me to my death, inexorably. I smelt death in your body. So, while I live, I shall wreak my vengeance, on you and your purity.

(*They exit.* ELISHA, *shattered, comes centre stage.*)

ELISHA: Oh horror! My mistress and Augustus Hare. The black, black pit of hell gapes for me.

ACT II

Darkness. A spotlight on SLOCUM *downstage, intimate with audience.*

SLOCUM: I sailed from Gibraltar on the twenty-seventh of
August, quickly caught the southwesterly trades
that drove me smoothly down the West Coast of North
Africa.
The sea, though agitated,
was not uncomfortably rough or dangerous,
and as I sat in my cabin I could hardly realize
that any sea was running at all,
so easy was the motion of my sloop across the waves.
On September the third a calm occurred,
usually, in this region, a precursor
of a fierce hurricane or harmattan
– a dust storm from off the Sahara.
The wind came upon us as we lay becalmed, howling
dismally.
Within an hour the sea was stained a reddish brown by
the dust,
the air thick with flying, choking sand.
By evening I saw ahead of us the heads of tornadoes
rising up as a wall is built,
and then the night came down.
(*Subdued lighting on rest of stage. The hints of the palm trees
have been replaced by hints of great solid temple pillars. These
are lit in this passage to make them suggestive of black
waterspouts.* SLOCUM *wanders about them.*)
An hour after the moon came up in a fantastic country.
Great black waterspouts had reared, thrown themselves
up,
immobile, stationary as temple pillars,

swollen, gorged at their tops
they held up the vast stormclouds boiling, turmoiling above.
Through these vaulted arches and pillars fell the shafts of ghostly moonlight
upon the frozen aisles of silent sea;
and through them myself, my sloop
picked our cautious way,
slipping sideways from one path of moonlight to the next,
skirting fearfully these giant pillars
groaning, straining with sea and sky's convulsive copulation.

(*Lights come up for pleasant daylight.*)

Next morning, as I sailed once more upon an open ocean beneath bright, clear skies,
it seemed the sky and sea had always been thus separated – sky above, sea below.
All was in its natural order,
the world went about its business.

(*Exit. Enter* DAVID *with* ANNIE *at his shoulder, her book open. Those on island except* HARE *and* ELISHA *are starting to dress in suggestions of military-type uniform – drab, efficient, like Mao jackets.* DAVID *unrolls plan.*)

DAVID: Our temple soars to the skies.

ANNIE: (*Automatically*) Hallelujah!

DAVID: It hangs in the heavens, s'no, casting its shadow like some girt black eagle.

ANNIE: Praise God.

DAVID: And praise thee too, Annie. This work oodn't never have got done without thee and thy book – thy organizing. Thee told everyone to be here by ten?

ANNIE: Everyone shall be here – or else find their names marked in God's book.

DAVID: (*Uncomfortably*) Annie, duss think Augustus Hare shall come?

ANNIE: Don't know – why?

DAVID: Well, he's about the camp so much recently, allus a
contrite look in his eye, a hang to his head.

ANNIE: Him, Mr Hare, a Christian? (*Laughs.*)

DAVID: Christ's mercy do move in strange ways, Annie.
Maybe Augustus Hare be part of God's plan.

ANNIE: Keep a hard eye on he, master.

(DAVID *looks down into audience.*)

DAVID: Here they come now, streaming up from all parts of
the island – Christ's creatures. Thee left all the young uns
at the camp, Annie?

ANNIE: Yes, master, left them with number 17.

DAVID: (*With deep affection*) I do owe much to thee and thy
good sense, Annie. (*Squeezes her forearm.*) You'm a woman
among women.

(*Intimate atmosphere broken as* EDITH *comes on, very
pregnant. She senses intimacy she has broken, turns away.
Unsure of herself.* HARE *comes on silently.* ANNIE *and
DAVID exchange looks.* EDITH *and* HARE *avoid each other.
To one side of this tableau of four stands* ELISHA. DAVID
steps forward, centre stage.)

(*Sings:*) What wondrous love is this, oh my soul,
What wondrous love is this
That caused the Lord of bliss
to bear the dreadful curse for my soul.

ALL: (*Sing:*) To God and to the lamb, I will sing,
Who is the great I am
While millions join the theme
I will sing.

DAVID: Brothers and sisters in Christ, we have laboured,
for nearly a year now us have laboured that there
shan't be no more time – just eternity – that there shan't be
no more strife nor greed nor lust – just pure heavenly
love.

Brothers and sisters, I spend much time alone on this-yere
island, communing with the Lord. He and I be in-ti-mate.
I dust lie within His bosom, s'no, us be like two lovers
lost in our loving, connexed, complexed, conjoined. He do

entrance, entrance★ I, consume, consummate I. Last
Thursday night, after us wrastled and melled together in
joyous commingling and prayer, after I did lay back all
exhausted and drained from our violent congress, Christ
Jesus, our breaths conspiring in union, did lean over and
whisper in my earhole, "Next Saturday at noon," ur did
say, "I shall step down on earth to reign." Ur did say that
to I. This Saturday, in three days' time. "Ah," says the
Lord, "I ool give thee two things, David, a Father from
heaven, and (*steps over, holds* EDITH *stiffly by arm*) I shall
give this Saturday a son, and I, Christ Jesus, shall stand
here at his baptism as God-Father."
Thus spoke the Lord.
(*All freeze in a line, as at start of play.* ELISHA *shuffles
sideways, like* SLOCUM *at start of play, passing down line.
Looks at* DAVID.)
Heavenly power. (*Stamps.*)
(ELISHA *looks at* ANNIE.)

ANNIE: Earthly power. (*Stamps.*)
(ELISHA *looks at* EDITH. *She looks away helplessly.* ELISHA
looks at HARE.)

HARE: Intimate power. (*Stamps.*)
(ELISHA *looks at audience as others, except* EDITH, *exit.*)

ELISHA: (*To audience, as he drinks from bottle*) All the mighty
of this earth stamp, trample.
I, a servant, have only crept, stumbled in apologetic
dance.
Now, I shall stamp, I shall trample, till the mighty
tremble, tumble.
(*He takes* EDITH's *hand, helps her gently to lie down at edge
of stage. Rises, unseen by her, takes out cut-throat razor*)
(*To audience*) A clean razor shines in much darkness.
(*Exit* ELISHA *carrying razor before him.
Sounds of seashore, but muted.*)

EDITH: I lie upon the seashore,

★Pronounced second time as in "to enter".

my hand in the flowing waters,
my back upon a steady rock,
my feet in the shifting sand
–I be disembodied, dismembered.
See, I do stretch out my hand,
all the oceans and seas and tides of this world
compass upon this one spot,
connex, focus yere to wash
salve solve my sin
so the stain do vlow off
out about the girt ocean,
off into the world.
Endlessly complexing, vortexing,
combining, unbinding,
refining, defining,
de-solving, re-solving.

My emotions fellow-feel the ocean's subtle motion.
Incentric, insorbed,
they scour and course my being,
imbracing, imbreathing, in-forming my child
who sleeps serene within the mound of this turning
earth
(*Pats the ground by her side.*)
as all the waters of the world bring it tribute.
(*Her back arches in the start of labour. Her feet
move.*)
Blind, regardless of all human convenience,
the Earth do start to move,
in its own time, to its own tides and rhythms.
(*She starts to exit left. From right comes* HARE *backwards.
Ignores her.* HARE *in aristocratic dress of first scene.*)
HARE: (*Shouting*) Elisha, Elisha – where are you, man?
(*Enter* ELISHA, *razor in one hand, bottle in other. Watches*
EDITH *exiting.*)
Drinking this early in the morning?
ELISHA: Today is the day when my ex-master, a liar, says

Jesus Christ shall come to earth. (*Stares after* EDITH.)

HARE: Precisely – which is why I want a first-class
shave – never know who I'm going to bump into. What are
you staring at, man?

ELISHA: My past. A small, dear light being extinguished in
much darkness.

HARE: Hurry up!

(ELISHA *subserviently exits. Brings on chair and shaving
gear.*)

This is one event I must not miss. Never may it be said of
me about the clubs of Pall Mall and Piccadilly – "Augustus
Hare? Wasn't he the fellow that missed the Second
Coming?"

ELISHA: You're not religious, master?

HARE: No, Elisha, I am a human man – I love the subtlety of
human drama. What men appear to be, as they strut their
stage all fine poses and splendid uniforms, what I *know*
them to be in their real selves – naked, blind, foolish. It is
a sport for we true kings, Elisha.

ELISHA: Yes, it is a sport.

(HARE *in chair, sheet over him,* ELISHA *with shaving cream
ready.* HARE *leaps up.* ELISHA *swigs from bottle.*)

HARE: And the fault of the sport, Elisha, is precisely that you
might not brag about it. Take a sport like fox hunting.
Well, you're hardly off your nag and snorting your brandy
before you're bragging. "See me shoot Fosser's Ditch?"
(*Staccato laugh.*) "Took Burnham's hedge all right, wot?"
Appalling people, go on like that all night – in between the
eating and the drinking and the fornicating. Come sunrise,
they're all off again – tally ho! (*Pulls face.*) My sport,
Elisha, is the sport of Olympians, looking down on the
struggles of mere mortals from on high.

ELISHA: (*Quoting*) "For His eyes are upon the ways of Man,
and He seeth all their ways. There is no shadow nor
shadow of Death where the workers of iniquity might hide
themselves." The Book of Job, master.

HARE: A very apt quotation. (*Sits down.*) And what, Elisha, is your sport?

(HARE *leans back head.* ELISHA *about to shave, convulsively withdraws two steps. Chokes with emotion.* HARE *stares at* ELISHA.)

ELISHA: (*With difficulty*) Executions, master. I once attended a very memorable execution.

HARE: Really. Can't say I ever followed them much myself – always thought the sport a trifle unsubtle.

ELISHA: The execution I attended, Mr Hare, was a very formal, awe-ful occasion. I wore my best dress clothes, that the scullery maid had especially pressed and laid out for me. I wore a carnation, a red carnation that the head gardener, Jones, had especially cut for the occasion.

HARE: Really.

ELISHA: Most executions, Mr Hare, are rowdy, ill-behaved affairs – very common, very vulgar. For a common murderer – knifed his girl, poisoned a husband – the mob outside Newgate does randy and riot the night away. Not so this night. Silence. Silence, Mr Hare. A great melancholic multitude, exchanging condolences throughout the black, black night. At five minutes to eight the death bell starts to toll. On to the scaffold steps the prisoner, immaculately dressed, his head high, his tread firm.

A sigh escapes the multitude. As one, they bare their heads in salute. The hangman goes about his awe-ful task, the parson recites, the man stands unmoved. For a second, before the bolts are drawn, there is silence, peace. I look about me. I see stood in serried ranks the Marquis of Salisbury's butler, Lord Ashburnham's butler, Lord Hawarden's, Lord Cowley's, Colonel Webster's, Colonel Howard's, the Prime Minister's butler – all, like me, immaculately dressed, red carnations in their buttonholes, staring upwards, transfixed. The bolt cracks, the trap crashes, the body falls, the multitude groans like Israel in its Babylonian captivity. Courvoisier's soul flies free as a dove, his body hangs innocent as a lamb.

161

HARE: Courvoisier?

ELISHA: The murderer, Mr Hare. (*Starts to shave.*) A Swiss man. The butler at 14 Norfolk Street. Have you ever heard of Lord William Russell, Mr Hare?

HARE: What, Old Billy? Hardly, but knew his son, young Billy, at Eton. Why?

ELISHA: He was the victim.

(HARE *stands.*)

HARE: My God. (*Loosens collar.*) I've been a long time from England. What was the fellow's motive?

(ELISHA *invites him to sit. He does.* ELISHA *right over exposed neck with razor.*)

ELISHA: Who can tell, master? The business, the intercourse between servant and master is so intimate, private. A servant sees his master when he lies uncomposed in the morning, naked in his bath, flustered and angry as the world is not allowed to see him. The servant becomes privy to his master's most secret fears and desires, the butt of his cruel wit, the receptacle of his insults and affections. 'Tis a strange, twisted relationship, master – sometimes of love, sometimes of . . . (*Swigs.*)

HARE: Are you going to swig that port all morning?

ELISHA: (*Shaving*) It makes of us half men, always curbing our passions when they should flame, always creeping half shamed in the shadows of the great. If you are a proud man, "master", then it is a thing that is sometimes difficult to swallow. (*Swigs.*)

HARE: Black, take a grip of yourself immediately – get on and shave me.

ELISHA: (*Ignoring him*) And me, I was half daft enough to think if I changed one master for another and sailed half about the world to a new land I might rid myself of my sin, my servility, cleanse my humiliation, that I might even stop my drinking.

HARE: Elisha!

ELISHA: (*Snarling*) Master?

(ELISHA *goes behind him.* HARE, *half scared, starts to rise.*

162

ELISHA *slips rope over him, ties him to chair.*)

HARE: What are you doing? What . . .

ELISHA: A servant should always be silent before his master.
(*Gags* HARE.) A servant should always be on his knees
before his master.
(*Kicks chair so* HARE *is on his knees.*)
(*Intimately*) Now, remember the words of Job, the very
text the prison chaplain used at sweet Courvoisier's
hanging sermon. "For His eyes are on the ways of man,
and He sees all his doings." Master sees servant, servant
sees master. Know that I know.
(HARE *puzzled.*)
A sweet, innocent creature, my mistress, the only mistress
I ever served who gave me joy and love in the act of
service – you, you befouled, utterly ruinated. My mistress,
Edith Worth.
Do you know why every great lord in London shivered in
his bed and the Duke of Wellington, Prince Albert,
Queen Victoria herself came to visit the charnel house of
Lord William Russell, and why every servant and butler
in London stood in awe and reverence at his
execution – because Courvoisier, Courvoisier one morning,
when, like every other servant in creation he shaved his
master, touched flesh to intimate flesh, instead of
skimming his razor above his master's throat as a
tightrope walker shimmers and skims above the abyss,
rather chose – seeing the world, seeing his master –
to plunge that blade straight down into that awe-ful
abyss.
(*Draws back razor, lights out.*
EDITH *screams in labour. Red glow suffuses the stage. Red
spotlight up centre stage.*
Sound of newborn child crying.

SLOCUM: (*Voice over*) To all who sail upon the oceans of the
world, enter into physical, spiritual combat with Raw
Nature – there is one supreme test.
The southern half of our globe is nine-tenths ocean – a

sweeping, rolling tide smoking endlessly around from
West to East,

through thirty clear degrees of longitude,

turbining, compulsing by its anger every other current
and tide about the Earth.

There lies but one obstacle to its regal, trampling
progress

– the grey, granite walls, battlements and towers of the
Andes mountains,

stumbling down suicidal into the wrath and carnage of
Cape Horn.

DAVID: (*Voice over, resonant*) Lord of Lords, King of Kings,
Lord Christ Jesus

step down from heaven,

come, reign in glory.

(ELISHA, *bottle in hand and razor in other, bloody apron,
walks into spotlight. Lights start to come up on rest of stage.*
DAVID, EDITH (*with child in arms*), ANNIE *watching
spotlight.* SLOCUM, *downstage right, detached from action.*)
Elisha? Elisha? Get away from there – Our Master be
about to appear on Earth. (*Stamps.*) Get away.

ELISHA: Thy master have come – hot from judgment.

(*Beat.*) I be thy master.

DAVID: Blasphemy – you'm drunk.

ELISHA: 'Tis the only sober way to see the world.

DAVID: (*Approaching*) Leave this sacred place immed . . .
you'm, covered in . . . blood . . .

ELISHA: "Cut 'em down, saith the Lord, root and branch,
like stubble for the furnace."

DAVID: Urs gone mad, s'no?

ELISHA: Mad as a master, master. I, a poor, humble servant,
be thy master now, for I have knowledge over thee. It is
the duty – the *duty* – of a master to pass judgments upon
his servants, rule justly. I, from my giddy heights, have
seen, have judged – most justly, most bloodily.

ANNIE: (*Approaching* ELISHA) Where you get that blood?

ELISHA: (*To* DAVID) 'Tis the blood, master – (*to audience*)

witness the power of knowledge, see it strike from heaven
like lightening – (*to* DAVID) 'tis the blood of the father of
thy newborn child.

DAVID: (*To himself*) What diddur say? (*To* ANNIE) What
diddur say?

ELISHA: Truth will out, or else where be justice? The blood of
the father of thy newborn child.

EDITH: (*To herself*) Blood shall have blood – old blood for new
blood. (*Hugs child.*)

ANNIE: (*Angrily to* ELISHA) You shut your damned mouth.
(ELISHA *holds her off with razor.*)

ELISHA: (*To* DAVID) Haven't you seen? Art blind? All this
time thee been stickin' thy heaven-topping temple in the
clouds, haven't thee seen at thy feet (*stamps ground
repeatedly*) the maggots turning, gorging, copulating. Thy
wife and Hare.
(DAVID *slumps down.*)

DAVID: No, no.

ANNIE: Shut thy damned mouth.
(ANNIE *slaps* ELISHA. *He shuts up. They both stare at*
DAVID. *Then all three turn to* EDITH *downstage, small and
fragile, hugging and rocking child.*
SLOCUM *sits intimately close to her on stage.*
Lights down behind.)

SLOCUM: My tiny sloop and I
   crept up the Straits of Magellan
   – all the winds and tides of Hell in our teeth –
   past Famine Straight and Crooked Reach,
   mid smoking volcanoes and rubbled cinders,
   snucked past Fury Island
   where not even moss might grow in the wind's ferocity.
   Before us towered Cape Pillar
   bleak sentinel of the Horn.
   Beneath it a carnage/chaos of sea,
   bellowing rollers ripping, tearing white on hidden rocks
   – Hell.

Across this,
across one tiny ribbon of thin clear water,
through this charnel house of slaughter,
We would have to creep and edge.

So intent was I upon this one frail passageway of sanity,
not until the last moment did I look up
(*Looks up above audience.*)
see against the black clouds
the great white arch of an enormous sea.
(*He starts to go back upstage. Lights up, to reveal
cross/halyard/gallows.*)
Open-mouthed, sloth-legged,
I let go all sail,
like an automaton
I felt myself retreat to the mast,
climb stiff-limbed to the main halyard,
(*Climbs to top of halyard.*)
all the time watching Infinity unfold before me,
Eternity uncurl, lazy uncoil careless upon, about me.
My gallant vessel rose and rose
before the moving mountain engorged, submerged it,
and I, upon the halyard,
stood out alone, naked,
in crazy nowhere.
(*Enter* ANNIE *and* DAVID, *leading* ELISHA *with a halter
round his neck.*)

ANNIE: Elisha Black, you been found damned guilty of
murder – how you plead?

ELISHA: Damned guilty – guilty as hell.

ANNIE: It is my and God's judgment you hang by the neck
until you're damned dead.

ELISHA: God's judgment be damned just. My damned soul
shall rest at last – in hell.
(EDITH *puts down baby, runs upstage almost hysterical.*)

EDITH: No, no, it shan't.

ANNIE: Shut your damned whore's mouth.

EDITH: This-yere poor humble crayture shan't hang, he be
less guilty than all o' we yere.

ELISHA: I be guilty.

EDITH: He wanted power less than any man – (*looks at* ANNIE)
or ooman. Lookzee what thee powerful ones did to un –
thee pressed foul knowledge on he till he crippled and
cracked – till he bent to do foul work of thy power. Poor
broken, shamed crayture.

ELISHA: Hang me in my shame.

EDITH: Look at he, Children of Jerusalem – thy sins.
(DAVID *rushes over to her, slaps her to the ground,
downstage.*)

DAVID: Whore, whore.

ANNIE: It is our damned judgment, it is *my* damned judgment
that thee hang.
(*She throws rope over cross, ties it,* ELISHA *standing on a
stool.*)

ELISHA: (*To* EDITH) Remember, mistress, when we first came
to this island, danced free upon the shore. Now at last my
feet shall dance again, free of this filthy earth.
(ANNIE *violently kicks away stool.* ELISHA *hangs dancing.*
ANNIE *comes downstage to* EDITH *with her book open. Lights
down except forestage.* DAVID *with her.*)

ANNIE: (*To* EDITH) Amid husbands and housewives, you, an
adulteress, shall be a damned whore. Never in your shame
shall you look in any eye, but only cast your eyes upon
their feet. You are damned outcast all your life, living in a
hut by the shore.
(*Exit* ANNIE *and* DAVID). Lights down on EDITH *crouching
alone downstage. Spotlight on* SLOCUM, *mast cleared of*
ELISHA.)

SLOCUM: Thus I hung in no time, no place,
upon the face of nothing.
Until, through my feet,
(*Stamps gently on mast.*)
I felt my sloop move,
her timbers tremble, tense,

167

I felt her will pit and push against the sea,
and she rose, glorious,
"Spray" amidst the spray,
shaking victorious like a happy spaniel.

(*He climbs down, comes over to* EDITH, *kneels, puts his arms round her shoulders.*)

Three more days I was in that dreadful storm – and yet not once did I know any more fear – and on the fourth day, with a following wind, I passed out, sailed out free into the Southern Ocean, the peacefulness of the infinite Pacific.

(*Exit* EDITH. *Sea lights up on rest of stage.* SLOCUM *becomes much more limber and fluid as he talks to audience.*)

Across the Great Southern Ocean I set my course for a tiny, remote island, many thousands of miles distant. Drawn inexorably by the emotions of tide and wind, I am carried upon a vast stream where I know the buoyancy of His hand who makes all the worlds.

I cannot deny the comical aspects of this strange life. Sometimes I awake to find the sun already shining in my cabin. I hear water rushing by, with only a thin plank between me and the mighty depths, and I say "How is this?" But it is all right; it is my ship on her own course, sailing as no other ship has ever sailed before in the history of the world. The rushing water along her side tells me she is sailing at full speed. I know that no human hand rests upon the helm, and feel safer than ever in my life.

During the day I sit and read my precious books, mend my clothes, or cook my meals and eat them at peace. One morning, after forty-seven days upon this infinite ocean, I see a white tern fluttering knowingly about my vessel – unmistakable sign of land.

I see palm trees standing out of the water ahead, a tiny smidgen of land amidst this vast blue ocean. It jolts me like an electric shock. During the whole of my forty-seven days' voyage, without one sight of land, I had not spent altogether more than three hours at the wheel, and yet my sloop had carried herself across six thousand miles of ocean to this tiny atoll.

Forty years after the events you have witnessed, I myself arrive at the Cocos Reeling Islands, to find only one character from our saga still alive.

I stagger out upon dry land. There is "land" beneath my feet. Trembling under the strangest sensations, and not able to resist the impulse, I sit on the shore and give way to my emotions – there is land, there is humanity.

(*Sits and weeps. On to stage hobbles* EDITH, *old, blind, but still determined. Wearing colourful patchwork.*)

EDITH: Why are you crying? There's enough salt water about the earth without you adding to it. Fetch my chair and sewing.

(SLOCUM *does so. She sits. He stares ahead, sat on ground.*)
You have been a long time, Captain Slocum.

SLOCUM: I had a long voyage, Mrs Worth.

EDITH: Edith. I have sat upon this shore fifty years now, waiting, stitching the clothing in my hand. (*Smiles.*) They did say that they – the old people, all dead now – ood outcast I forever – but even the strictest Puritan do need his britches mended.

SLOCUM: He especially, ma'am – to hide his hypocrisy.
(*They chuckle.*)

EDITH: And so I secretly worked some colour into the grim tapestry of their lives.
(*Shows coloured patchwork she is sewing. He looks into her face.*)

SLOCUM: I see your noble suffering, ma'am, written in your flesh.

EDITH: (*Smiling ruefully*) My "hot blood" have been cauterized, 'tis true, and all my scarlet passions be but dull blood knocking in my arteries. All youth and fire in my body have gone – (*softly*) I am afraid. Even my eyes have died.

SLOCUM: Not the fire in your soul.

EDITH: Are you looking at me?

SLOCUM: Full in your vital, living face.

(*She puts her hands in front of her face. He gently takes them away, then sits beside her.*)

EDITH: So, you have come at last.

SLOCUM: To learn wisdom at your feet.

EDITH: (*Ironically*) But not upon my body. At last, a man all my being yearns to mix and mell with, without shame nor regret, and – I am too old.

SLOCUM: Solo circumnavigators have, by necessity, found other consolations, ma'am. Teach me, here upon the seashore.

EDITH: Well, this-yere exile upon this-yere shore have learnt I patience, s'no. But, Captain Slocum, they do say (*Approaching incredulity*) that suffering be good vor thy soul, s'no.

"They" – from wheresoever their pertikler armchair of wisdom be set – say suffering re-fines, purifies thee, it do draw and drain thee like leeches set to thy arm. Suffering do anoint thy soul anew with humility, gorgeous humility.

(*Beat.*)

P'raps 'tis true

– if thy soul have been gorged on good living and high sinning then 'tis a quick-sharp purgative, s'no – but if thy soul, thy being do start parched and worn, and then be fed perpetual hard suffering vor its sole Christian sustenance, then how shall a seed spring in such a desert?

Shall forgiveness flower, love blossom?

(*With hint of self-mockery*)

I have been hanged out to dry in a desert wind, Captain Slocum, I be but a wizened, croaking old crone.

SLOCUM: You are beautiful, ma'am.

EDITH: Ah, flattery, I could bathe in it forever.

(*Pause.*)

170

SLOCUM: There is another world, beyond this one here,
 where your noble story is sung and told at every human
 communion
 – in bars and lodging houses from Liverpool to
 Shanghai,
 Tiger Bay to Montevideo.
 Amongst poor sailors
 your story has comforted many poor souls in their
 despair.
 Many tears, ma'am, have been spilt in many beers.

EDITH: 'Tis a mystery, s'no,
 how the suffering of one do, without malice, comfort
 another,
 of how one's happy fellowship do, without envy,
 estrange another.

 (*Pause. She shivers.*)

 Touch my old flesh.

SLOCUM: It would be an honour.

 (*He holds her hand.*)

EDITH: It do warm I, s'no, pro-foundly. (*Beat.*) You'm lucky
 I ant twenty years younger, or the scarlet ooman ood be
 astride thee, demanding satisfaction. In every inch of
 thee I ood find summat to love, treasure – flesh be
 precious.

 (*From left to right across back of stage, in a violently arguing
 mob, stumble* HARE, ANNIE, DAVID, ELISHA, *as second
 generation islanders.* HARE *is blacked up as his son from a
 black woman,* ANNIE *paler,* ELISHA *darker,* DAVID *darker.
 Their clothes are now half colourful patchwork, half ragged
 grey uniforms. They exit as swiftly as they entered.*)

SLOCUM: What was that?

EDITH: An argument. A great emotion sweeping the village
 on the hill. It is said a certain lady so favour a certain
 gentleman above another, while a third gentleman be
 using this pertikler excitement to hide what he is doing
 behind all their arguing backs. (*Beat.*) Nothing changes.
 It would be thought after all the excitements and violence

of forty years ago, the next generation would have learnt
consideration, generosity – but no, the old passions blaze,
the hatred boils. All things stay the same.

SLOCUM: At sea, ma'am,

when you first see those endless, relentless waves,
you think them cruel,
void of all sense and mercy.
But the sea is the sea
– it is what it seems.
If a storm shall destroy you
you see it there before you.
But the land (*taps stage*), is not the land,
it is not as it appears,
for who can say what lurks behind another man's eyes?
All this world might be in another man's mind,
every step upon it might spring a sudden trap.

(*The quartet comes storming back on stage, but this time,
wobbling and seething back and forth, they come to rest centre
stage, behind* EDITH *and* SLOCUM. SLOCUM *speaks above
them.*)

Shall all this great world stop for man?

(*The quartet suddenly freezes, their faces and bodies locked
silently in antagonism.*)

EDITH: No, it shan't.

The waves do yet pound upon the shore,
the old sky do roll on oblivious.

(*Beat.*)

Captain Slocum, fetch my tea,
it is all laid out in my hut.
I shall learn thee some truth.

(*She gets up, goes back toward frozen quartet. As she speaks,*
SLOCUM *brings out tea and cups on small table,* EDITH,
*blind, having felt her way to the quartet. As she speaks, she
feels their faces and bodies with her hand.*)

What be it about humankind, what be it that have taken
so much suffering and striving and skill to embody,
engender it, such love and art to spirit up, inspire it . . .

172

(She breaks off, starts different train of thought.)
    See the human body,
    its nobility, its ingenuity, its infinite beauties and
    subtleties
    – did ever machine or theory match it to the hundredth
    part for exact perfection
    – and yet, with contempt, us do fling it upon the wheels
    of fortune,
    feed its flesh into the jaws of war,
    the mills of industry and profit,
    sacrifice its soul thoughtless upon the altar of ambition,
    pride.
    'Tis the basest, most despised of all us do own, s'no.
    (She shakes. SLOCUM *goes up to her.)*
SLOCUM: Come, sit down again, Missus Worth.
    (EDITH *shakes him off.)*
EDITH: I ood learn the world a simple lesson, s'no, so that
    someday, somewhen it might climb out vrum this vale
    of tears
    – this girt confucious mell –
    and see the heights and glories set around it,
    and, if not rejoice, at least bide easy one hour.
    Why cassen us see, why?
    (To quartet) Blundering, blind young vools!
    (She returns to chair.)
    (Quietly) 'Tis the mystery of flesh, s'no,
    that it do endless knit together, compose strand on
    patient strand,
    and yet, at the fall of careless dice, the stroke of a sword
    it do straight split violent apart,
    rip, tear, fall away, de-compose.

    'Tis the very mystery of holy human communion, s'no,
    that one in violence do throw all friendship vrum he,
    and, in that selfsame moment,
    do crave and strive to have about hc that very flesh he
    banishes.

'Tis an ancient convulsion, s'no,
profound as the girt tides toiling, turmoiling in the
oceans
– I cannot fathom he.
(*Pause.*)
In my frailty
I ood connex, compose all craytures,
that each might complex, interbrace one upon another
until all humanity, all creation
might be a burning union,
a girt, giddy-patterned wheel spinning in flesh and
fusion.
(*Beat.*)
(*Emphatically*) Jerusalem shall be builded here, upon this
very earth (*stamps*).
(*Pause. She turns towards quartet.*)
(*With touch of despair.*) And yet the wheel do rest upon
a fiery cross, a contradiction. There be butchery as
well as blessing in our com-plexion. Pain do flame in all
things.
(*Beat.*)
(*Addressing quartet*)
Come, my loves, us had a hard night's life upon this-yere
stage. A cup of tea vor thy labours?
(*Smiling, they start to relax, grinning, stretching.*)
Come, sit down, rest thy weary bones.
(*Smiling, relaxing, they gather round, helping themselves to
tea.* SLOCUM *passes a cup to everyone. Group face front.
They wait for something.*)
SLOCUM: (*Tentatively*) Shall us have freedom – in the end?
EDITH: In the end, my love, us shall have rest.
The feelings that emotion violent in our blood shall slow
and stop.
Us shall all dissolve,
pass out unknown upon the great waters,
swirl and arc again in the vast womb of creation,
dreaming in the bosom of Our Lord.

Babylon has Fallen

(They all look about at each other and drink formally. EDITH
steps forward.)

>Sweet Lord Jesus, in our pain,
>Do not drive we quite insane,
>Thy mercies vall like gentle rain,
>Help keep us part humane.

(All sing "Northfield".)

ALL: How long, dear Saviour, oh how long
>Shall this bright hour delay?
>Fly swift around, ye wheels of time
>And bring the Promised Day.

>Lo, what a glorious sight appears
>To our believing eyes!
>The earth and seas are passed away
>And the old rolling skies.

>His own soft hand shall wipe the tears
>From every weeping eye;
>And pains and groans and griefs and fears
>And Death itself shall die.

LADIES IN WAITING

Ellen Fox

For Jo-Anne Fraser

Characters

KATE TULL, aged 23
LILY BROWN, aged 23, her cousin
UNCLE, in his early sixties, Lily's father
HARPY (Ruth Harper Graves), aged 24
KERRY HARPER, aged 20, Harpy's sister
GUY LA FONTAINE, aged 25, a French
  Canadian who lives in and helps Uncle
  around the house

The play is set in a small town in Northern
Ontario, Canada, in September 1917.

ACT I

Scene 1

A sitting room downstage with two armchairs, a settee between the armchairs, a small table in front of the settee, a long table behind it. Stairs leading from the sitting room to the upstairs, stage right. A small dining room behind the sitting room (the set is L-shaped) upstage. There is a bay window in the dining room (at the back) and a bay window in the sitting room, stage left. A door to the kitchen leads off from the dining room. A front door is stage left near the bay window; there is a closet near the front door. No wall is necessary at the back of the stage. The window pane could be against a black lit background.

Both the sitting room and dining room are empty and quiet. Then, a scream from outside. LILY, *in a panic, comes running into the house as if being chased, and stands shouting by the dining-room bay window.*

LILY: (*Shouting*) Kate! Kate! There he is!

> (KATE *comes running into the dining room from the kitchen, dishcloth in hand, rushing to* LILY's *side.*)

KATE: Who?

LILY: The boy on the bike!

KATE: Where?

LILY: Over there! See? Through the hedge.

> (*The boy is moving.*)

> There, no there! No there!

> (HARPY *comes downstairs.*)

KATE: (*Looking out the window*) Damn!

HARPY: What is it?

KATE: The boy on the bike.

HARPY: Where's he going?

KATE: He's riding like the devil himself. Look at him go!

HARPY: But where's he going?

179

LILY: (*Panicking*) I can't see him. I've lost him. Where is he?

KATE: Don't panic.

HARPY: When is someone going to trim that hedge?

KATE: (*Searching for the boy*) When someone gets around to it. There he is! There! Harpy, he's coming around the corner.

(HARPY *runs to the front bay window, stage left.*)

Keep your eyes open. Harpy, can you see him?

(KATE *runs to the front window tossing the dishcloth on a nearby chair.*)

HARPY: No!

(KATE *beside* HARPY, *spots him.*)

KATE: There he is! There! (*Puzzled*) He's slowing down.

LILY: Where?

KATE: There. No, wait, he's picking up speed. (*Still confused*) He . . . what the hell is he doing?

LILY: (*Not looking*) What's he doing?

KATE: Riding in a circle . . .

LILY: Oh my God, he's coming here! (*Runs to the screen door, shouts:*) Go away! Go away! (*Closes the door, steps back in, doesn't look back, hoping that's made a difference. Nervous, impatient*) What's he doing now?

HARPY: (*To* KATE) Look, there's your uncle.

LILY: What's the boy doing?

KATE: Smiling and doffing his cap to your father.

LILY: And what's he doing?

KATE: Smiling and doffing his cap to the boy.

LILY: (*Panicking*) Is he stopping here?

KATE: No, he's riding on.

LILY: (*Very upset*) It's not funny, he has no right to do that. No right at all!

KATE: He's gone. Let's try to calm down. (*Looking over to* LILY) I said he's gone, Lily. He's not coming to our house.

HARPY: The bastard. He's going to someone's house. He's taking a telegram somewhere.

KATE: It's not really his fault.

HARPY: No? Then whose fault is it? He saw us watching. He knows we all have men overseas.

KATE: Does he?

HARPY: (*Hurrying to the screen door*) Of course he does. It could've been your husband. (*Opens the screen door slightly and yells down the street:*) What do you do for an encore! You horrible little boy! You think you're clever, don't you? You'll get yours, do you hear me? You'll get yours.

KATE: Be glad we didn't get ours.

HARPY: (*Coming in*) I hate this. When the war's over, that's what I say.

KATE: That's what we all say, but no one's listening. Behold impotence!

HARPY: (*Calmer, relieved*) Soon, it'll be over soon.

KATE: Ah, the promise of 1914, wasn't it? There have been so many I find it difficult to place a date with a promise.

LILY: (*Cautiously*) He's gone to Mrs McNab's house. She's got three sons.

HARPY: (*Coming over to the window, craning her neck to see*) Which one do you think's dead?

KATE: We'll hear soon enough.

HARPY: (*Walking towards to the door*) What a job, eh? (*Opens the door, and yells:*) What a vile rotten job! (*Steps back in.*) I don't think he heard.

KATE: Don't bet on it.

HARPY: (*Wandering back in*) Weren't you making some tea?

KATE: (*Reminded*) Yes, come to think of it, I was. (*Going towards the kitchen, picking up the dishcloth*) Do you want a cup?

HARPY: No, thanks.

KATE: Lily?

LILY: (*Barely audible*) No, thank you.

KATE: (*Flicking the dishcloth at* LILY) Hey! Wake up! Do you want a cup of tea?

LILY: (*Tensely*) No!

KATE: That's all I wanted to know. (*Soothing*) Will you relax. It's over. He's gone.

HARPY: You know, I've never seen the boy's face.

KATE: Does it matter? (*To* LILY) Any mail at the post office?

LILY: No.

(KATE *exits*.)

HARPY: (*Disbelief*) Surely there was something for someone. Did you pick up my mail? You knew I was coming.

LILY: I didn't go.

HARPY: You didn't go?

LILY: No.

HARPY: Where were you, then? Where d'you go? If I had known you weren't going to go, I could've gone myself.

LILY: There was no mail today.

(KATE *enters*.)

HARPY: No tea?

KATE: Changed my mind. (*Looking at* LILY *closely*) Lily, are you all right?

(LILY *gets up and goes to the back bay window*.)

HARPY: Can we discuss the wedding now please?

KATE: The wedding?

HARPY: Yes, the reason for our being here.

KATE: I'm afraid you'll have to plan it without me. (*Playing*) I must prepare to fly from hence.

HARPY: What do you mean "fly from hence"?

KATE: I told you.

HARPY: No, you didn't.

KATE: I'm sure I did. Guy and I are going away for the weekend.

HARPY: You didn't tell me. At least I don't remember.

KATE: There's been a slight change in plans, that's all.

HARPY: But we chose this day.

KATE: If my presence is so necessary we can choose another day. Besides you're better off without me. The last wedding I went to was my own and look how that's turned out. In all honesty I don't think I'm qualified to plan someone else's.

HARPY: And whose fault is that?

KATE: It's not a matter of fault, it's a matter of fact. Lily will

182

help. She enjoys that sort of thing. Oh, Harpy, come on. It's not as serious as all that.

HARPY: I like things organized, keeping to schedule, plans adherred to, punctuality.

KATE: (*Quickly*) I wasn't late.

HARPY: You live here.

KATE: An advantage, I admit. (*Pacing while thinking*) Think of it as fate. It takes you by the hand, it weaves you in and out, and just when you think you know the way, it changes direction and pattern.

(KERRY *enters.*)

HARPY: Can't you sit down?

KATE: I've got all this energy.

HARPY: Well, can't you . . . (*Sees* KERRY.) Ahhh. Lovely, lovely. (*Walks behind her, straightening the train of the dress, always tidying.*) It fits you beautifully. (*To* KATE *and* LILY) Don't you think it's lovely? (*Not waiting for an answer. To* KERRY) I told you.

KERRY: (*Tugging at the waist*) I think it's too tight through here.

HARPY: Let's see. (*Steps around* KERRY) No, it looks fine. (*To* KATE) What do you think?

KATE: I'm not partial to white.

HARPY: Very funny. (*To* KERRY) Turn around.

(KERRY *turns around.*)

Lovely.

LILY: (*Sitting at the back bay window, jumps up, startled, shrieks:*) There's the boy!

KATE: (*Running to* LILY'*s side*) Where? No one's there, look. (*Concerned*) No one. Lily, calm down.

LILY: He was.

KATE: He wasn't. (*Looking at her closely*) What is it? Come sit down.

(LILY *sits down at the dining-room table.*)

HARPY: (*To* KERRY) Walk for us.

KERRY: (*Disbelief*) What?

KATE: (*Playfully to* KERRY, *yet watching* LILY) You heard the lady, walk for us.

HARPY: Ignore her. Walk.

KERRY: (*Shyly*) You've seen me walk.

HARPY: (*Insistent*) Please.

(KERRY *walks.* HARPY *watches.*)

KERRY: I feel stupid.

HARPY: Walk properly. Feel the flow.

(*Behind* KERRY, KATE *outstretches* KERRY's *arms, walks her along.*)

KATE: Flow, two three. (*Abrupt turn in the other direction like a tango of sorts.*) Glide, two, three. (*Abrupt turn.*) Flo – o – ow, two, three.

KERRY: I feel like an idiot.

KATE: Try running slowly, like this. (*Demonstrates.*)

HARPY: (*To* KATE) We need your comments like a hole in the head.

KATE: There's no laugh left in the woman.

(HARPY *goes to the dress to adjust it.* KATE *goes to the dining-room table, sits across from* LILY. HARPY *motions* KERRY *to walk away from her.*)

Are you feeling all right? Did you go to the post office?

HARPY: We've already asked her. (*To* KERRY) Now back towards me.

KATE: (*To* LILY) Did you? Did you go?

LILY: No mail today.

KATE: Lily, please!

HARPY: The girl's becoming a gibbering idiot.

KATE: D'you mind?

KERRY: It's tight through here, you see.

HARPY: (*Tugging at the waist*) It's not tight.

KERRY: Ruthie, I can't breathe.

HARPY: Take small breaths. Little puffs.

KERRY: I'll get the hiccups.

KATE: (*Cautiously*) Lily, did you see Guy anywhere in town?

LILY: No.

HARPY: I'm not surprised. He's probably in hiding.

KATE: What are you talking about?

HARPY: Don't you know, or is it that you don't remember?

KATE: Don't remember what?

HARPY: We're getting the vote today. Women are getting the vote.

KATE: No, we're not.

HARPY: Yes, we are.

KATE: It's a rumour.

HARPY: It's a promise.

KATE: That's what I mean.

HARPY: The government needs us.

KATE: Try again.

KERRY: I want to take this off now please, Ruthie. I'm suffocating.

HARPY: Walk around a bit more.

KERRY: I'm wearing out the rug.

HARPY: Get the feel of being married.

KATE: Oh yes, that'll do it.

HARPY: It's a special dress.

KATE: (*To* KERRY, *in a very small town accent*) I hear tell it cuts off the breathin'.

KERRY: You can say that again, in fact you may have to. I'm going to expire any minute. I thought getting married was supposed to be fun.

KATE: Will somebody kindly set her straight?

HARPY: It is fun.

KATE: I said straight. (*To* KERRY) Do you like going to the dentist?

KERRY: No.

KATE: Same thing.

HARPY: (*Horrified*) It's not.

KATE: Oh, no. It's all so "beautiful".

HARPY: Yes.

KATE: Yes, I thought you'd say that.

HARPY: Sheer bliss.

KATE: Transparent, but only after you take the vows. Once you get up close you can see the confines of the outline. The promise you thought you saw you can't even make out. It's a mistake.

HARPY: You always do this. We were talking about getting married.

KATE: So am I.

HARPY: Yes, but we happen to be a bit more basic than you. We have to set a date, that is if you're quite finished.

KATE: Quite finished.

KERRY: (*Boisterously*) Forget the date – we'll improvise!

HARPY: (*To* KATE) You always have this effect on her.

KATE: Now about the vote.

HARPY: Always. (*To* KERRY) Be practical. The date is important.

KATE: I want to hear about the vote.

HARPY: You plan in advance, thinking that the day is ages away, and then it arrives, almost unexpectedly.

KERRY: I know all that, Ruthie, but it's supposed to be my wedding and you're doing everything. I feel as if I don't have a say in anything.

HARPY: Like what, for instance?

KERRY: The guest list.

HARPY: I've shown it to you.

KERRY: (*Sarcastically*) Thanks very much.

KATE: Lily, did they say anything about the vote in town? Has anyone heard? (*Looking at* HARPY) Either way?

HARPY: We are getting the vote.

KATE: You know even less than I do about politics. Read a pamphlet have you, Mrs Graves?

HARPY: Kate, we are getting the vote. We vote for the Coalition Government; they put through the Conscription Act, the French Canadians are sent to the front; our men are relieved; they all come home.

KATE: And that's that.

HARPY: Your loving Guy will be sent to France. He'll adapt beautifully. He's French. They speak the same language. What's the problem? What would your husband say if he knew about Guy?

KATE: He knows.

HARPY: What would anyone else say?

KATE: Oh, I'm sure everyone else knows too.

HARPY: They don't go into details.

KATE: Why not? I'm sure they go into everything else.

HARPY: As for myself, I don't like being in the same room
with Guy, I'll tell you that now. He's quiet, he stares. I
don't like him and he doesn't like me and don't deny it.

KATE: I wasn't going to.

HARPY: (*Quietly*) Oh. (*Slight pause.*) Your taste in friends is
excellent, your taste in men is appalling.

KATE: And your taste in men?

HARPY: Is excellent. Daniel is special, a rare breed.

KATE: He'd have to be.

HARPY: I will ignore that.

KATE: Please don't.

HARPY: Guy La Fontaine. When I think of him, I think of
arrogance, and you don't need arrogance in a war.

KATE: You fighting one?

HARPY: Daniel is coming back – they are all coming back
home, and we'll live happily ever after.

KATE: You make it sound so simple.

HARPY: It is.

KATE: What about the promise when this war started of no
conscription?

HARPY: (*Laughs it off.*) Oh, that.

KATE: (*Imitates* HARPY:) Oh, that – I knew we'd get her
laughing.

HARPY: Doesn't matter.

KATE: Oh yes, how silly of me. (*Seriously*) No, no. This is far
too important. This is a promise they'll keep.

HARPY: You know how public opinion stands.

KATE: Indeed I do – with a crick in its neck, a sunken chest,
and a pain in its side. But this time . . .

HARPY: I don't know about you, no, no, let me rephrase that,
I do know about you, so I can only speak for myself. I
want my man back.

KATE: He volunteered to go.

KERRY: (*Clearing her throat*) Ahem. Remember me? The bride to be?

KATE: What?

KERRY: This dress . . .

HARPY: . . . is perfect.

KATE: I'm going to get some air.

(KATE *exits out the front door.*)

KERRY: (*Playfully runs up to* LILY.) Oh, you are preoccupied, Lily.

LILY: (*Turning slowly to where* KATE *was*) I have a question Kate, I . . . (*Looks around, quietens up.*)

KERRY: Have you met a tall dark stranger who you're not telling us about? *À faire l'amour*, Lily Brown?

HARPY: It's not *faire l'amour*, you idiot.

KERRY: What is it, then?

HARPY: I don't know, but whatever you said it's wrong.

KERRY: You'd say that about anything I say.

HARPY: Don't be ridiculous.

KERRY: So what is it, then?

HARPY: How should I know? French is not one of my favourite languages.

KERRY: What is, then?

HARPY: Will you shut up.

KERRY: (*Close to* LILY) She's mean, Lily, (*looking over her shoulder at* HARPY) and she can get meaner. She can get downright nasty. She used to pull my hair!

HARPY: (*Coming over to* LILY) I am disappointed in you, Lily. I thought you'd be brimming over with ideas for this wedding.

KERRY: You didn't ask me.

HARPY: Will you shut up.

KERRY: Ruthie!

HARPY: (*To* LILY) You are the only person I know who goes to wedding ceremonies uninvited.

KERRY: (*In disbelief*) You don't.

HARPY: She even went to Lise Bernier's wedding, so I hear. She sat in the front row with Lise's little bastards. How do

188

you think she explains them on her first dates I
wonder – the stork's little bundle, or found them under a
cabbage leaf or a garbage can. It must've been exciting for
them seeing mum married finally, to someone, anyone. I
hear she's due in the spring – for what, one can only
imagine. She used to sit on my stomach during recess, and
Kate used to laugh. I remember it well. They were
friends, co-conspirators more like. Whispering to each
other, giggling. We all know why Lise Bernier left school
at 14. We were young, but not stupid.

KERRY: What do you mean, she used to sit on your stomach?
I never saw.

HARPY: She used to push me down and sit on me. What do
you want, a demonstration?

KERRY: No. Don't get upset. (*Very amused*) I was just
wondering, that's all. And Kate used to laugh?

HARPY: Yes.

KERRY: (*About to burst out laughing*) Out loud?

HARPY: Yes, will you stop it?

(KERRY *starts to giggle as* KATE *walks in.*

KERRY: She sat on your stomach?

KATE: Don't tell me. Lise Bernier again. Don't you ever
forget?

HARPY: My stomach is flat!

KATE: So what? Why complain? Be glad it wasn't your head.

KERRY: (*Laughing*) I can just see it.

HARPY: Will you be quiet! You look "undignified".

KERRY: What?

HARPY: You heard me.

KERRY: It's the dress, it just doesn't suit me. I'll leave it
behind then, shall I?

HARPY: (*Insistent*) It looks fine.

KERRY: Yes, but I've made up my mind.

HARPY: (*Sharply*) Stop it!

KERRY: She wants to be the older sister.

HARPY: I am the older sister.

KERRY: (*Bored*) Yes, Ruthie, we know. And God forbid if we

189

forget because you'll be right there to remind us. You wouldn't know we were sisters, would you, Kate, not really, we don't even look alike.

HARPY: I have the distinct feeling that you are about to embarrass me. I am here today because of you, you know. I could've been doing other things.

KERRY: Like what, for instance?

HARPY: (*To* KATE) Do you know, if she had her way she'd shoot out that door this very minute never to be seen again. She dreams of travelling around the world. Home isn't good enough for her any more, no ma'am. She's been reading some Russian novel or other and came upon troikas.

KERRY: Hmm, with bells. But you need lots of snow. They go whoosh, then they're gone.

KATE: Whoosh?

KERRY: (*Coming over to* KATE *and looping her arm through hers; nodding*) And you're gone.

KATE: What about a toboggan?

KERRY: (*Disappointed*) Oh, Kate, it's not the same. I want the horses and the bells. You sit there with furs on your lap and (*looking at* HARPY) look at her. She's impatient.

HARPY: No, I'm not.

KERRY: When she was younger she used to tap her foot and stand like this. (*Stands with her arms across her chest, visibly pouting, tapping her foot.*) Really, she did. Our mother thought she'd be a dancer, our father thought he'd spank her if she didn't stop, right over his knee, isn't that right, Ruthie? "I'll hit you in a minute, young lady, if you don't stop that," he'd say.

HARPY: *I'll* hit you in a minute, young lady, if you don't stop this. You think you're so smart, you've got it all, the only one with a dream. The world is waiting for you and yours, no doubt. You'll find out. Whoosh indeed.

KATE: I wish I had a whoosh in my day. Lily, what's the matter? You look possessed.

KERRY: (*Hugging* LILY) It's a tall dark stranger, isn't it, Lily?

KATE: Why aren't there any short dark strangers, that's what I'd like to know.

KERRY: Is it the man of your dreams?

KATE: Or dreams of your man. Come on, Lily, snap out of it. (UNCLE *comes in the front door.*)

UNCLE: Kate, is Guy back yet?

KATE: No, not yet. Uncle, could you come in for a minute, please?

UNCLE: No, I've got work to do. The leaves . . .

KATE: The leaves can wait. They're not going anywhere. Lily needs you. Just for a minute.

UNCLE: She's fine. You're there.

KATE: (*Takes a step from where she was standing.*) And now I'm over here. It won't take a minute. Please.

UNCLE: (*Calls to* LILY *from the door*:) You're all right, aren't you, Lily?

KATE: She doesn't bite.

UNCLE: Ah, she's all right. (*Calls to* LILY:) You're behaving yourself, aren't you, Lily Lamb? (*To* KATE) She's fine. She's got you.

KATE: And needs you.

UNCLE: If Guy comes through the back, tell him I'm out front.

KATE: A minute won't make any difference.

UNCLE: (*Apologetic, regretful, impotent*) I've work to do.

KATE: Set a precedent.

UNCLE: (*Backing out the front door*) I've work. (*Exits; the door closes.*)

KATE: For a change.

HARPY: Who will help him when Guy's gone? You're a pillar of strength, everyone says so.

KATE: Maybe they said pillow. And Guy's not going anywhere. He's needed here.

HARPY: He's not a farmer like her man (*referring to* KERRY). William's making a contribution. He's doing something for the country, not like Guy, who's doing nothing.

KATE: Nothing?

HARPY: Except to you, perhaps. With our husbands on their way home, and Guy overseas, your Uncle will have to look elsewhere for help.

KATE: This Union Government, this marriage of convenience if you will, will not allow such a thing to happen. There's a lot of anti-French feeling around, but to capitalize on it is (*lost for words*) vulgar, it's disgusting. It's wrong.

HARPY: What anti-French feeling? Silly buggers. Who cares about them anyway?

KATE: They can't make you have the vote.

HARPY: When are you going to face facts?

KERRY: I'm going upstairs.

HARPY: Be careful with the dress.

> (KERRY *runs upstairs.*)

> (*To* KATE) You're in the minority.

KATE: Then I'll have to shout a little louder. They can take away your rights. They can put through new laws, repeal old ones, tax you, beat you, flog you, but they can't make you have the vote! What are they going to do, twist your arm until you make your mark? It's committing murder, and asking for more accomplices – well, I don't volunteer, I will not be a party to murder.

HARPY: But our men have been away so long.

KATE: I said, I will not be a party to murder! They'll say it's OK, it's all right, it's all been done with their kind consent, meaning our kind consent, but it isn't!

HARPY: My Daniel . . .

KATE: Daniel what? Would he approve? He volunteered to go.

HARPY: Yes, of course.

KATE: Then there's no problem. The problem is here, and the men who don't want to go.

HARPY: Women all over are fighting, struggling to get the vote.

KATE: I don't want the vote. Not on those terms. I will not be made an accomplice!

HARPY: I want my man back.

KATE: Things aren't done that way. Not all women are getting the vote. We're only getting it because we're married to soldiers. And how long do you think they'll let us keep it after the war is over? One week, two? Trust me – it won't happen. It's not even worth the trouble taken in discussing it.

HARPY: A promise is a promise.

KATE: Exactly. I accept that. No vote – no conscription. I want no blood on my hands.

HARPY: Oh God, Kate.

KATE: One murder leads to the next.

HARPY: You read too much, far too much. But your handwriting's beautiful. Will you address the envelopes for the invitations?

KATE: (*Bewildered*) What?

(KERRY *comes downstairs in her own clothes.*)

HARPY: (*To* KATE) The wedding invitations. The envelopes. Will you address them?

KATE: Yes, I suppose I could.

KERRY: Unnecessary, totally unnecessary.

HARPY: No one can read your scrawl, and we agreed to ask Kate.

KERRY: (*To* KATE) Don't feel obligated.

KATE: I don't.

HARPY: I was thinking of having yellow invitations.

KERRY: I don't like yellow.

HARPY: It's my favourite colour.

KERRY: You never wear it.

HARPY: I used to.

KERRY: (*Thinking*),No, I don't like it. What do you say, Kate?

KATE: Personally I don't like it.

HARPY: There's a conspiracy afoot. I sensed it the moment we stepped through the door.

KERRY: (*Sings menacingly:*) Black is the colour of my true love's hair . . .

HARPY: (*Feeling threatened*) Shut up.

KERRY: (*Singing*) White is the colour of his . . .

HARPY: Shut up!

KERRY: Oh, come on, Ruthie. All right, have the invitations
whatever colour you like – chartreuse for all I care. It's
your wedding anyway. With a whoosh I'll be gone. I'll be
surprised if I even get invited.

HARPY: Enough is enough!

KATE: (*Going over to* KERRY, *putting her arm through hers; in a
deadpan drawl*) Well, you know, Mildred, I'm actually
glad, yes glad, we weren't invited to this here wedding
because they would've seated us with the Morgues, real
live wires, and then what would we have done.

KERRY: (*Also in a drawl*) I know, Ethel, I know.

KATE: And the food, Mildred, have you heard about the food?

KERRY: No.

KATE: Well then. That's a sure sign for you. And the music.
Not even toe tappin'. (*Imitates* HARPY's *sulking pose, arms
across the chest, tapping her foot, and pouting; to* HARPY)
You'd never survive, honey.

HARPY: Are you finished? Can we talk about the business at
hand?

KATE: Which hand?

KERRY: Oh, Kate.

KATE: She's such a card.

KERRY: I know.

HARPY: It's pointless trying to talk to you when you're in this
mood, absolutely pointless.

KATE: I am in an excellent mood. I feel very, very good. This
then, ladies, is the Kate Tull declaration of goodness. Yes!
I feel good and do you know why? Do I hear a "why"
from the crowd? C'mon, give me a "why"!

KERRY: A why!

KATE: That's not exactly what I had in mind but it will do.
(*To* KERRY) It's because of your sister – it is, really. She's
made me see that I am right, unbelievably, undeniably,
unshakably right! This must be the "test" one hears so
much about. The old boat rocked to and fro, hither and
thither, side to side. But you see, there are ways of doing
things, and ways of doing things; there are promises and

promises, tactics and tactics; strategies and strategies, and so on and so forth. We are not getting the vote. Guy is not going anywhere, the wedding plans are up to you, and I am going upstairs to pack.

(UNCLE *comes in the front door.*)

UNCLE: I'll be needing the other bushel baskets.

KATE: Good for you. They're out back.

UNCLE: (*Going to the back bay window*) Someone's burning leaves, you can see the smoke from here. Unless of course it's their house. Ha! Can you imagine. (*Bounces over to* LILY, *and hugs her.*) And how's my Lily Lamb? My precious Lily Lamb.

KATE: Unbearably talkative. We couldn't get her to keep quiet.

UNCLE: (*Hugging* LILY, *talking to* KATE) Where did you say the bushels were?

KATE: I think they're out back.

UNCLE: No, they're not there.

KATE: Well, I don't know, then; they're obviously not in here. (KATE *watches* LILY *as . . .*)

LILY: (*Holding on to her father's arm around her neck, singing quietly, slowly and tensely*)

   O soldier, soldier, won't you marry me,
   With your musket, fife, and drum?

UNCLE: (*Winks at the others.*) Thinks she can sing. Listen to this. (*Trying to rouse* LILY, *sings boisterously:*)

   Oh no, sweet maid, I cannot marry thee
   For I have no coat to put on.
   So up she went to her grandfather's chest
   And got him a coat of the very very best
   She got him a coat of the very very best
   And the soldier put it on.

(*Looks to see if he's made* LILY *smile*)

LILY: (*Starts to sing again:*) O soldier, soldier . . .

KATE: Lily!

LILY: (*Singing*) Won't you marry me,
   With your musket, fife and drum?

UNCLE: (*Singing*) Oh no, sweet maid I cannot marry thee
(*Wanders away from* LILY, *singing*) For I have no hat to
put on.
(*Grabs* KERRY *who is by the stairs. They dance as he sings*:)
    So up she went to her grandfather's chest
    And got him a hat of the very very best
    She got him a hat of the very very best
    And the . . . (*Stops, out of breath.*)
The shed!

KATE: What?

UNCLE: Do you think they're in the shed?

KATE: Who?

UNCLE: The bushels.

KATE: I don't know!

LILY: (*At the back bay window, screams*:) There he is!

KATE: Who? Guy?

LILY: The boy on the bike!

KATE: (*Runs to the window, fed up.*) Where? Show me! No one
is there, Lily! Can't you see? No one! (*To* UNCLE) Talk to
her! Tell her!
(GUY *walks in the front door*)
Thank God you're here. I'll go pack. (*About to but stops.*)
What's wrong? What is it?

GUY: You've got the vote.
(KATE *sits down on the window seat,* HARPY *watching her.*
Pause.
Blackout.)

Scene 2

A few minutes later. Only KATE *and* HARPY *are in the room.*

KATE: Well, that's terrific. Just swell.

HARPY: You don't listen.

KATE: (*Not listening*) Hmm? (*Thinking*) I've always believed in
the forces of good overcoming the forces of evil even if I
never actually believed it. (*Smiles to herself.*) Clichéed to

the end.

HARPY: I think you've got your sides mixed up.

KATE: All is not lost yet. Something will happen.

HARPY: You sound as if you've got something up your sleeve. Do tell, Kate.

KATE: I never give away secrets.

HARPY: I don't know.

KATE: You – what do you know? Weddings and local history, the price of butter, and how to iron pleated skirts. Big deal. You know nothing.

HARPY: And you know so much.

KATE: I didn't say that.

HARPY: You didn't have to.

KATE: My humble apologies.

HARPY: You should be more careful.

KATE: Should I?

(KERRY *comes downstairs with* LILY.)

KERRY: It's all done.

HARPY: Did you cover the dress?

KERRY: Yes. I said I would. (*Smiles to* LILY.) I told you.

HARPY: Where did you leave it?

KERRY: On the bed where I said I'd leave it.

KATE: Anyone interested in a drink?

HARPY: I'm just popping upstairs for a minute.

KERRY: Checking to see if I've done everything properly?

HARPY: Don't be ridiculous.

(HARPY *goes upstairs.*)

KERRY: (*Mimicking* HARPY) Don't be ridiculous.

KATE: (*Getting the sherry*) Last chance – anyone care to join me?

KERRY: I'd love a glass, that is, if you're having.

KATE: Oh, I'm having, you can be sure. Lily?

LILY: No, thank you. I think I'll sit on the porch for awhile.

(LILY *exits out the front door.*)

KATE: We're losing them fast. Quick, start singing.

(KATE *gets the glasses out of the cabinet.*)

KERRY: Any requests?

KATE: The 1812 Overture. (*Hands* KERRY *a drink.*) Here.

(KERRY *wanders away, wants to tell* KATE *something.*)

KERRY: I'll miss our "playing".

KATE: Well, you aren't going anywhere for awhile yet.

KERRY: You'd be surprised.

KATE: I've had enough surprises for one day, thank you.

KERRY: (*Fondly*) Oh, Kate. A toast!

KATE: To promises that were once fulfilled.

KERRY: (*Disappointed*) I thought you'd drink to my wedding.

KATE: There's time. Why rush? Enjoy.

KERRY: (*Shrugging her shoulders*) To promises, then.

KATE: (*Sipping her drink*) Promises.

KERRY: (*Sipping her drink*) It's good.

KATE: Hmmm.

KERRY: What is it?

KATE: I don't know. I tend to peel the labels off. I can't tell whether it's daring, or just a nervous habit.

KERRY: Where are the men?

KATE: A question I often ask myself. But if you mean Guy and my Uncle, they're out front, raking leaves.

KERRY: Did he find the bushel baskets?

KATE: I would imagine so.

KERRY: They depend on you a lot.

KATE: They depend on me a lot. (*Toasting*) To ye olde keeper of the bushels.

KERRY: More than that. It'll be strange with Guy not around.

KATE: What does that mean?

KERRY: Ruthie said . . .

KATE: Ignore her.

KERRY: But she said . . .

KATE: Nothing. She doesn't know.

KERRY: (*Excited*) Do you have a plan?

KATE: (*Quickly*) No, do you?

KERRY: It's a funny day, this, isn't it?

KATE: Hysterical.

KERRY: I don't mean funny ha-ha, I mean exciting.

KATE: (*A bit tipsy*) Not the word I would have chosen.

KERRY: Tell me about married life.

KATE: Come again.

KERRY: Please, Kate.

KATE: Ask your sister, she seems to be the expert.

KERRY: (*Laughs.*) Only about weddings. Besides, I'm asking you.

KATE: You're asking me.

KERRY: Yeah.

KATE: Where's the bottle?

> (KERRY *gets the bottle and hands it to* KATE.)
> (*Pouring herself another drink*) Friends who play together won't stay together long with questions like that. They will get into the bad books. Ask me something else. Do you want another drink?

KERRY: No, thanks.

KATE: You know, I knew someone once who drank a whole bottle of turpentine. He's dead. Silly thing to do, anyway.

KERRY: Please, Kate, I've so much to learn in such a short time.

KATE: My, you are in a hurry, aren't you?

KERRY: Yes, sort of.

KATE: (*Frustrated*) Look, Kerry, I'm not a good example. Can't you see that? Don't go by my life. I don't know what you want to know. I feel betrayed. It's not right. It's like a one-way ticket to Moose Jaw, wherever that is, without the luggage. All right for a temporary stop along the way, but permanent, Jesus.

KERRY: It's the drink talking now.

KATE: On an empty stomach sherry can work wonders.

KERRY: (*Reminding* KATE) Moose Jaw.

KATE: You don't give up, do you? It's an evocative name, don't you think? I would describe my marriage as: Moose Javian, too much said, not enough done. (*Sips her drink.*) Christ, this stuff is giving me a headache, and I'm not a drinker, and you would like a serious discussion. I could read that "please be serious" expression from miles away.

It's in the eyes, it's always in the eyes. Take this glass
away.

(KERRY *takes the glass away.* KATE *wanders to the window.*)
Do you think it'll rain or snow?

KERRY: It's not cold enough to snow.

KATE: That's true. (*To the weather*) Stay warm.

KERRY: Why do you feel betrayed?

KATE: A harsh word.

KERRY: It was yours.

KATE: Never quote me to me, it's annoying.

KERRY: Do you feel betrayed by Stephen?

KATE: No, poor bastard never knew what hit him. It has
nothing to do with him. Listen, why don't you go talk
with your sister. After all there's a war going on, as we
have been so rudely reminded, it's difficult to say "rudely
reminded", and lo and behold we now have the vote, and
I need to think.

KERRY: Does Stephen know about Guy?

KATE: Yes, of course he does. We're friends. I tell him many
things.

KERRY: Everything?

KATE: No. I don't think I'd ever tell anyone everything.

KERRY: I would. I want to share everything with everyone,
well, almost everyone.

KATE: (*Amused*) You'd spread the word, would you?

KERRY: What's wrong with that?

KATE: It depends on the word. I come from the school of
thought where one keeps certain things to oneself, that's
all. (*Smiles to herself.*) But not Stephen. Before we were
married he used to write me long, lovely letters. Beautiful
poetry.

KERRY: His own?

KATE: (*Amused*) I wonder. I don't know. Half and half I
should think. It was very good. I had only known "boys"
before, but this I thought was no boy. (*Impressed*) He
writes letters. No one had ever written to me like that
before. I was only 17. Every day a letter came, praising

200

my looks . . .

KERRY: Oh, no.

KATE: (*Smiles and winks at* KERRY.) My talent . . .

KERRY: (*Laughs.*) O God, Kate.

KATE: My cha–rac–ter.

KERRY: What next?

KATE: (*Stops playing.*) And he wrote about life, and love, and need, and want.

KERRY: I'm jealous.

KATE: (*Puzzled*) Whatever for?

KERRY: I've never gotten any letters. A postcard once from Calgary, but that doesn't really count.

KATE: He used to quote all the time. (*Laughs to herself.*) It's funny, I received this letter once where he . . . no. Never mind. Never, never mind. All his lofty ideas, and dreams, and hopes, and dreams, (*becoming bitter*) and visions and dreams, and dreams, and DREAMS! (*Angry*) I was wooed by words, mesmerized by metaphors, seduced by similes! I was only 17! Which is really no excuse, but it's the only one I've got.

KERRY: Oh, Kate.

KATE: (*Smiling at* KERRY, *echoing her sigh*) Oh, Kerry.

KERRY: It'll all work out.

KATE: A happy ending?

KERRY: It's not right. You're being hard on yourself.

KATE: That's funny, I thought I was being hard on Stephen.

KERRY: I'm sure it'll all work out.

KATE: You're missing the point.

KERRY: I think there are several rules we can all follow to find our true happiness. I read about them in a magazine.

KATE: I'd like my glass back now.

KERRY: (*Handing* KATE *the glass*) Do you want to hear them?

KATE: No.

KERRY: I could lend you the magazine if you'd like, but I'd like it back.

KATE: No, it's all right. Really.

KERRY: William and I, we're not going to have any secrets

201

from each other. None. We'll be open and trusting. And we'll be together all the time.

KATE: Weather permitting.

KERRY: Oh, you mean my family. No, it'll be just the two of us. I've never lived on a farm before. I wonder if I'll like it. If not, we can always move back to town. Or travel. I'd love that. But it takes money to travel, doesn't it? But wouldn't it be wonderful? I hate it here. (*Correcting herself*) Oh! Not here, here, you know what I mean. They still call me the baby of the family. They always have to know where I'm going, what I'm doing. If I was in Africa, they'd never know. Kate, I've got this secret, and if I don't tell someone I'm gonna burst. I'm dying to tell you – I told William I wouldn't tell anyone, but it's killing me. He wouldn't mind if I just told you. (*Eagerly*) Promise you won't tell anyone?

KATE: No.

KERRY: Promise.

KATE: I don't want to know.

KERRY: (*Begging* KATE) Please, Kate, let me tell you.

KATE: No. I don't want to know. Keep your secret, I have enough on my plate.

KERRY: I'll give you a hint, just a little hint.

KATE: Kerry, no! You promised William, keep the promise.

KERRY: (*Frustrated*) We shouldn't have come today.

KATE: Doesn't matter.

KERRY: Ruthie insisted.

KATE: I'll bet she did.

KERRY: She said she wanted to see your face. She's very bitter, Kate.

KATE: About what? And what does it have to do with me?

KERRY: I don't know.

KATE: Is she so sure of the outcome?

KERRY: (*Positively*) Yes.

KATE: It's emotional blackmail, this whole thing. It appeals to the baser instincts, cuts to the bone.

KERRY: Does it?

KATE: (*Exaggerated*) Oh, Mr Borden, dear Mr Borden, Prime Minister *extraordinaire*, Defender of the Faith, thank you, thank you, thank you for the vote. You're in with the big boys now, so in you get, there you go. Now put through the conscription bill. (*Cooing*) You do it so well. Your former promise of no conscription? Don't worry about a thing, it's all forgotten (*snaps her fingers*) like that! All taken care of. What's a little breach of promise? Who's gonna notice? Who's gonna care? Just lie back and think of England.

KERRY: You should be on the stage.

KATE: Or in the circus.

KERRY: I guess you won't be voting for Mr Borden.

KATE: How'd you guess?

KERRY: What will happen to Guy?

KATE: Nothing. He won't go.

KERRY: Ruthie says he will.

KATE: And what do you say?

KERRY: Me? I'm not used to being asked my opinion, that's what I say. (*Thinking*) I wouldn't want to be in your shoes. You've got the vote, I guess it depends on how you use it, and what everyone else does with it. I don't know. I can't vote, I'm too young. In a way I feel it has nothing to do with me. I couldn't vote before and I still can't. Big deal, big change in my life. Soon the weather will change, like it always does. The winter will come, and the snow, and if you're lucky, the troikas. Oh, Kate, I don't know. They'll decide without me. What does it matter? I was born a year too late. My hands are tied, and my mouth is gagged.

KATE: I wish that applied to another member of your family.

KERRY: It's a strange friendship you two have.

KATE: We've known each other a long time, which I'm finding out is no criteria for anything. She wanted to see my face? (*Slight pause.*) We went to the same school.

KERRY: Yes, along with a few hundred others.

KATE: I don't know. How does anything come about? Habit, I suppose. I don't know.

LILY: (*Coming into the house*) It looks like rain. It's getting
chilly outside.

KATE: So much for our hopes of an Indian summer.

LILY: (*At the edge of the window, peering through the curtain*)
Don't look now, but Dad is making huge piles of leaves.
(*Giggles to herself.*) He's walking away from them. Oh no,
he's starting to run! He runs so funny. He's jumping into
them! I knew it!

KATE: (*Going over to the window*) Let's see.

LILY: (*Pulling* KATE *out of sight*) No, don't look. He'll think
I've been talking about him. He just wants attention, he
wants us to look.

KATE: (*Peering through the curtains*) Where's Guy?

LILY: There.

KATE: They'll be arguing in a minute about who'll get the last
jump. Look at the two of them. (*Enjoying herself*) Really,
you're both a couple of fools. (*Sticks her tongue out at
them.*) Blah to you too. (*Quickly*) I saw that! (*Laughs.*) Oh,
stop it. Idiots. (*Turns to* LILY *and* KERRY.) For my next
birthday, I want a pair of trousers, do you hear me,
trousers or nothing.

(*Looking outside with envy, then suddenly, sweepingly, boldly,
full of life*)

    Forswear thy skirts!
    Thy lacy blouse
    Forswear thy children
    Homes and men
    And let the wind carry thee.
    For thou art light and adventurous
    Thou canst command a whirlwind stay
    Thou wilt ride the crest of waves
    Thou wilt dance upon a gale
    Thou wilt soar beyond the sun
    And when they cry "but stay"

(*Smiles.*) Fly away.

(*Pacing*) "A voice, a voice," she cried. But how to use it.
Do I just blunder forth? What the hell do I do? Is there

nothing. . . ? (*Looks at* LILY *and* KERRY, *whom she's
forgotten about.*) Don't stare, it's unbecoming and you do
so want to become.

LILY: Kate, I've been thinking . . .

KATE: (*Still looking out the window*) What about?

LILY: About French women. In France.

KATE: What about them?

LILY: About what they say about them.

KATE: What do they say?

LILY: (*Hedging*) You know.

KATE: No, I don't.

LILY: (*To* KERRY) You tell her.

KERRY: Tell her what?

LILY: What they say.

KERRY: Who's they?

LILY: You know. Kate, what do they have that we don't?

KATE: French accents?

LILY: You're teasing me.

KATE: No, I'm not. I don't know what you want.

LILY: I want help. I'm trying to find an answer, to work
something out, and you're not helping any.

KATE: How can I help when I don't know what the problem
is?

LILY: Do you remember the stories my mother used to tell?

KATE: And my mother.

LILY: (*Happily*) Yes, of summer fêtes and balls.

KATE: They're not easy to forget.

LILY: You'd stay the night, and we'd lie in bed talking. My
mother or yours would tap on the door. Stop that in there,
stop that talking and go to sleep, or you won't have your
dreams. My mother told stories of beautiful women in
long lovely gowns, and men in tails – I always found that a
funny expression, men in tails. I used to wonder to
myself, what sort of creatures were those, whatever could
they look like. Did they have ears too? (*Giggles.*) Men in
tails. Demons from the deep, she used to call them, but
that's another story. Only when she was upset.

KERRY: What kind of stories were they?

LILY: Wonderful stories, beautiful stories, about love, and romance.

KERRY: Like the magazines.

LILY: They had a time all their own and a telling. She knew, she knew it all. Such high expectations. (*Bitterly*) And she got everything she expected. And she wanted so much for me. Love overpowering, love all-encompassing, love triumphant. She knew, she knew. Ah, but there were always obstacles in the way that had to be overcome so that love could conquer all – family feuds, wicked aunts, evil uncles, jealous cousins . . .

KATE: I beg your pardon.

LILY: (*Quickly correcting herself*) Step-sisters. Intrigue, sinister goings on. (*Knowingly, excited*) But there were hidden paths that only a few knew about, and meeting places; notes delivered by a trusted messenger, an old friend sworn to secrecy. A time arranged. Deafening silence; the house asleep; a creaking door (*makes the sound of the door*) errrrr. (*Gasps.*) Detected? No. (*Breathes more easily.*) No, a close call.

The rendezvous at midnight, passionate embraces, a full moon, countless stars overhead. Breathlessly vows and promises made, oaths sworn, eternal love pledged, tokens exchanged. (*Whispering*) Don't leave me! Hold me, hold me, just a little longer. (*Pleading*) Stay. (*Gently*) Stay. (*Slight pause. Calmly*) Stay.

They won't notice I'm gone. I'll leave at dawn. Then hide my shoes, wet with dew, under the bed. They'll never know. They've never guessed. (*Giggles.*) You do make me laugh.

(*Suddenly cold*) You said you'd write.

Train to Toronto to see him off. Waving to him from behind the barrier on the pier, while he on the ship's deck waves back, occasionally slapping a buddy on the shoulder. I'm all right, see? I'm all right, he's saying. I see. I see. Oaths loved. Token vows. Lives exchanged.

(*Brightly*) There was music all the time. Waltzes, polkas, brass band. Cymbals, bass drum, snare drum. (*Slowing down*) Streamers, rice, confetti. Music, dancing. (*To* KATE) You threw me your bouquet – but it's been put away. (*Clearing her head*) Upstairs. I have it upstairs somewhere. I think.

(HARPY *comes downstairs*)

(*Giggles.*) Men in tails, women in trails, no trains! Men on ships! (*Panics.*)

KATE: Lily, what is it, what's happened?!

LILY: (*Backing away from* KATE) Nothing!

KATE: (*Worried, shouting at* LILY) What is it?!

LILY: Nothing, please, nothing, please.

(LILY *runs towards the stairs, pushing* HARPY *aside, exits.*)

KATE: Lily, come back here!

HARPY: What's the matter with her – you take her toys away? (*Rubbing her arm where* LILY *pushed her*) For a "little lamb" she sure packs a wallop.

KATE: She was all right before she went out this morning.

HARPY: She said there wasn't any mail. Was she expecting any?

KATE: Aren't we all? But that's nothing new. She was fine before she left – you saw her. (*To* KERRY) Did she say anything upstairs?

KERRY: No, not really. She liked the dress, that's all she said.

HARPY: Maybe the dress brought back memories. (*To* KERRY) I gave it a quick once over with the iron by the way.

KERRY: Maybe she's tired.

HARPY: Maybe she's lonely.

KERRY: Maybe she's ill.

HARPY: Maybe she's nuts.

KATE: (*To* HARPY) You do have a way with words.

HARPY: What do you want us to say? Keep her indoors? Lock up your daughters? She's high-strung?

KATE: Oh, come on.

HARPY: She's excitable. If something's upset her, she'll tell you. You're her mother confessor.

KATE: She usually tells me right away.

HARPY: So today is different. We're here, a lot is happening. She liked the dress, it shows her taste is still intact. What more do you want?

KERRY: Do you want me to go talk to her?

KATE: No, I'll go.

HARPY: Leave her alone. Look, Kate, I know it's your house – I'm a guest, and I don't want to cause any trouble or interfere but . . .

KATE: I knew there'd be a "but."

HARPY: If you don't mind me saying so, they lean on you like there's no tomorrow. Lily Lamb, Little Lily Lamb. It's do this, Kate, do that, where's this, where's that. It must wear you out. Where are the scissors by the way? I couldn't find them.

KATE: Drawer to the right of the sink in the kitchen.

HARPY: Thanks.

(HARPY *exits into the kitchen.*)

KATE: (*To* KERRY) I'd ask you to dance but the dance floor's crowded.

KERRY: That's all right, my card's full.

KATE: Lucky girl. I am impressed.

KERRY: Shouldn't you be . . .

(GUY *walks in.*)

. . . packing?

KATE: (*To* GUY) Shouldn't I be packing is the question on the floor, Mr Chairman.

GUY: We'll discuss it later.

KATE: Packing is not exactly something that needs discussing. You either do it or you don't.

GUY: Kate –

KATE: I mean, it's not exactly an ideal subject for debate.

GUY: Please, Kate, your uncle wants his scarf.

KATE: I didn't ask for requests, but if you insist, what key is it in?

GUY: Where is it?

KATE: (*To* KERRY) He's humouring me.

GUY: Is it in here?

KATE: Nooo. Guess.

GUY: I have no idea. I don't want him to get a chill.

KATE: Over here.

GUY: Thank you. Where are the others?

KATE: Around.

GUY: Well, back to work.

KATE: Wait! Guy, (*Approaching him*) I want to talk to you for a
minute. I feel a bit strange and –

(HARPY *walks in.*)

HARPY: I'll get the dress.

KERRY: Will you forget the dress.

HARPY: I'll just show you what I want to do. It'll only take a
minute.

(KATE *nods to* KERRY *to go upstairs.*)

KERRY: All right, starting now!

(KERRY *darts up the stairs past* HARPY. HARPY *follows her,
after looking at* KATE *and* GUY. KATE *doesn't see her but*
GUY *does.*)

KATE: (*Teasing*) Alone at last.

GUY: That woman doesn't like me.

KATE: That woman doesn't like anyone.

GUY: How long are they staying?

KATE: Meaning when are they going? Soon. They won't stay
late.

KATE: }(*Together*){Guy, I . . .
GUY: }   {Kate . . . No, you go ahead.

KATE: I may talk up a storm, you know me.

GUY: I can always interrupt, you know me.

KATE: I wonder if there's such a thing as mouth-cross'd lovers.

(GUY *laughs. Slight pause.*)

Guy, I feel very strange. Something's happening.

GUY: Nothing's happening.

KATE: Then maybe that's the problem. When are we going to
talk? *Are* we going to talk? I am so confused.

GUY: Sit down.

KATE: I can't sit down! I don't want to sit down. Guy,

something happened out there, and we're all behaving as if it's just another day but it isn't. Lily is behaving oddly to say the least, the others are very sure of themselves, and then there's me, and I feel strange.

GUY: Tell them to go.

KATE: Soon. I will.

GUY: We'll talk later. I've work to do.

KATE: If I hear that one more time, I'll scream. I've work to do, I've work. Stay – somebody – stay still, just for a minute. Please.

(*He stops.*)

I just don't know what to do. I can't stand this feeling. I've always known. I've always had control. I feel lost in my own home, in a fog which I know doesn't make sense but what does, it's all so very –

GUY: Strange.

KATE: (*Smiles.*) You took the words right out of my mouth.

(*Serious*) What is going to happen with this vote?

GUY: We'll talk.

KATE: Now.

UNCLE: (*From outside*) Guy!

GUY: He wants me.

KATE: Yes, well, so do I.

UNCLE: (*From outside again*) Guy!

GUY: It's a tough choice.

KATE: Thanks a lot. Have you tried flattery?

GUY: We'll talk. See you later.

(*He kisses her on the forehead, about to go.*)

KATE: Guy . . .

(GUY *stops.*)

See you.

(GUY *exits with Uncle's scarf.* KATE *turns to the empty sitting room, strikes a very military attitude – at ease, with hands behind her back, rocking on her heels as she surveys the auditorium.*)

I've called you all here today to discuss the war effort. Where's my riding crop?

(She gets an umbrella from where the scarf was, or the sherry bottle from off the table. She turns and faces the audience, tapping the object in her hand.)

Right. Now I hope you all enjoyed last night's manoeuvres, everyone comfortable, I take it. *(In another voice)* "Shells flying overhead. All a bit nasty I thought." Yes, madam! Yes, indeed, and it is precisely for that reason I have decided upon a new strategy. *(Slight pause.)* We're calling the whole thing off. That's right, off. O. F. F. Officially Finished Finally! *(Angry at herself)* Damn it! It's not funny.

(Lights fade to blackout.)

ACT II

Scene 1

KATE, HARPY, KERRY *in the sitting room.*

HARPY: Phew! Planning a wedding is hard work.

KATE: Out of curiosity, why are you planning it?

HARPY: I wanted to. Mother said, fine. She knows I'll do a good job. I've always been a good organizer. I like being in charge, the hustle and bustle of behind the scene planning.

(LILY *comes downstairs.*)

KATE: (*To* LILY) Welcome to the scene.

KERRY: Where's it set?

KATE: Set? (*Thinking*) In a little border town in France, bordering on hysteria in the north . . .

KERRY: Yes?

KATE: Pain in the south . . .

KERRY: Yeah?

KATE: Madness in the east . . .

KERRY: And the west?

KATE: Despair.

HARPY: Really, Kate. Can't you make up any happy stories?

KATE: Population: 4.

LILY: It still hasn't rained yet. I thought it would've by now.

KATE: (*Looking at* LILY) They sit at mid-ocean, playing their lyres, singing sweet music, waiting, watching for a ship to pass.

KERRY: Then what?

KATE: (*Excited, intense*) They see Ulysses tied to the mast, struggling to join them. He hears them and it is too much for him. "We'll be anything you've ever dreamt of – after all, we're not going anywhere, we're chained to this rock." (*An idea*) Ah – take us with you.

212

In an empty street an old woman dressed in black, wearing a headscarf, gathers rocks and puts them in a basket, a red and white checkered cloth on top. A picnic. And all the time they're singing. Guide us, O lady in the scarf, to the man at the mast. Stone him as he sails by. (*Slight pause.*)

Lily, talk to me.

KERRY: (*Captivated by the story*) Do they stone him?

KATE: (*In a Scots accent*) Aye, my lassie, that they do. (*Slight pause.* KERRY *walks over to the window.*) Does it ever occur to you how little we know?

HARPY: No.

KATE: Not at all?

HARPY: I let people like you worry about that sort of thing. I've got more practical things to worry about.

KATE: But there's so much.

LILY: (*Excited*) There's going to be a storm. I can feel it. I love the sound of rain when I'm safe and dry inside.

KATE: Safe and dry. (*To* HARPY:) Yes, let's all be safe and dry. Did you know that turkeys drink the rain as it falls and end up drowning themselves? They don't close their mouths.

HARPY: Turkeys?

KATE: Yes.

HARPY: Where did you get that gem of information from?

KATE: Lise Bernier.

HARPY: A reliable source if ever there was one.

KATE: Her father told her – he was a farmer.

HARPY: Passing it down from one generation to the next. A wonderful legacy. Really, Kate. Knowing her, she probably put the theory to the test and forced their mouths open during some shower, and then on their stomachs to boot!

KATE: They only had cows.

KERRY: What's this? I wasn't listening. Who went around opening cows' mouths, mouths of cows?

HARPY: I refuse to be related to this girl.

KERRY: Oh, c'mon. Hey! What time is it?

KATE: For you too late I fear.

HARPY: She's always in a hurry. Rush, rush, rush, rush, rush. One day the clock'll stop.

KERRY: So, I'll get it mended.

HARPY: You'll see.

KERRY: Oh, no – here comes old Granny Graves. You'd better watch out, Kate, or she'll hit you with her stick.

HARPY: I've had just about enough of you. (*To* KATE) I want to discuss business.

KATE: What business, or should I say whose?

HARPY: I've been giving this vote of ours some serious thought.

KATE: Have you, now?

HARPY: Yes. Have you thought about it at all?

KATE: It has crossed my mind once or twice, yes.

HARPY: We don't agree on much any more.

KATE: The question is, did we ever?

HARPY: The question is, how are you going to vote?

KATE: Not the way you are.

LILY: Hit! It's hit, Kate! (*Stands up.*) The lightning's hit the tree.

KATE: (*Going to* LILY) Where?

LILY: There, look, by the path.

HARPY: You're stubborn, Kate Tull.

KATE: (*To* LILY) That was down before.

HARPY: You refuse to make sense.

LILY: When?

KATE: Days ago. Didn't you see it?

LILY: (*Tensing up*) I didn't notice it. I wasn't sure. The lightning.

KATE: Don't worry about it.

LILY: (*Relaxing*) Look at the clouds, Kate, so dark and heavy. They're just rolling in. It's as if they're going to cover us completely. Do you feel it?

KATE: No. (*Then looking, admitting*) Yes.

LILY: If it rains, how will they burn the leaves?

KATE: They'll simply take them one by one and hang them on the clothes-line to dry.

LILY: That would look funny.

KATE: Yes, well, the neighbours must be used to it by now. (*To* KERRY) We do it every year. (*To* LILY) Don't we?

KERRY: Is it an annual event?

KATE: Something like that.

HARPY: You know, I have the distinct feeling that you're avoiding my question.

KATE: I thought I answered it.

HARPY: You seem preoccupied with clothes-lines and turkeys playing musical instruments on deserted islands. What I want to know is, how are you going to vote?

KATE: I've got a man outside somewhere here, and you're asking me that? You astound me, you really do. Do you need everything spelt out for you? Where are your brains, woman?

HARPY: It's not a matter of that. It's a matter of feeling.

KATE: You've been waiting to ask me all day, haven't you? To pin me down.

HARPY: Guy will go, Kate, they'll all go. Layabouts, stragglers.

KATE: All and sundry. No!

HARPY: You can't deny the facts. We have the vote. Our men will want relief. Guy should be there now. At the front with the others. Just think about it for a minute.

KATE: I have.

HARPY: And what can we each as individuals do about that image that comes to mind when we think?

KATE: Obliterate it.

HARPY: No!

KATE: No. Of course not.

HARPY: Vote. There is a right thing to do.

KATE: And a left.

HARPY: Don't you take anything seriously?

KATE: Yes. This.

HARPY: You wouldn't know it.

KATE: Look – you asked me a question and I answered it. You didn't like the answer and you asked me again. The answer is not going to change.

HARPY: You're wrong, Kate. You're wrong. I'm right, you can't deny the facts. People are –

KATE: Tired.

KERRY: (*Pacing*) Not me. I feel wonderful. Like you, Kate, this morning, I've got all this energy.

HARPY: That's all we need.

KERRY: I could run, jump, anything, everything! I feel terrific. Forget all this. (*Moves towards* KATE.) Think of the future when one day we'll all run away together. (*Looks at* HARPY.) Well, not all. But those of us who will want to, will. We'll leave everything behind. And we'll set up a colony somewhere.

KATE: I don't think that's a very good idea. That's how all *this* began.

KERRY: It'll be different. It'll be us. Oh, Kate, I feel so excited. There's no time for feeling sad or low, or tired. Life is just beginning. (*Trying to convince* KATE) It is.

KATE: (*To* HARPY) I'll tell you what. I'll buy her from you. We can put her in the clock and she can jump out on the hour.

KERRY: (*Jumping*) Cuckoo, cuckoo.

HARPY: Settle down.

KERRY: What's wrong?

HARPY: Just settle down.

KATE: Leave her alone.

KERRY: (*To* HARPY) Cuckoo.

HARPY: Were you even that excited on your wedding day?

KATE: I don't remember.

KERRY: Really?

KATE: It was a long time ago, in a former life. Besides, what does it have to do with anything? You'd think that there was nothing else in life, the way you go on. Weddings, marriages, weddings, marriages, occasionally with the slight variation of marriages, weddings, marriages, weddings, and so on *ad infinitum.*

HARPY: What are you going on about?

KATE: I might well ask you the same.

HARPY: I have been trying to instruct Kerry. A wedding is the
most important event in one's life.

KATE: Your life.

HARPY: Daniel and I had a beautiful wedding. It sealed the
bond between us. Something which you wouldn't
understand, your bonds seem less than binding. He was
marvellous at the ceremony – as always quiet and obedient,
but he can be a tiger when he wants to be.

KERRY: Miaow.

(HARPY *glares at* KERRY.)

LILY: If it rains, my father will get caught in it.

HARPY: Where's his umbrella?

KATE: In the closet, where it always is.

LILY: He'll only say, why didn't you remind me, Kate, just
look at me dripping from head to toe. Tomorrow he'll
remember where he left it two weeks ago.

KATE: In the closet.

LILY: And then he'll forget all over again. He doesn't change
at all, does he?

HARPY: Why should he?

LILY: Yes, why should he?

(*She resumes looking out the window.*)

KERRY: I think I'm going to explode!

HARPY: Will you learn to control yourself! Learn to behave in
someone else's house. And you wonder why people don't
ask us round.

KERRY: (*Looking straight at* HARPY) I don't wonder. I know.
You must always play the older sister. You don't give up.

HARPY: I am the older sister – get it through your thick skull.
I play the role I was given and I take it very seriously.

KERRY: Too seriously. I feel good, and if you don't like it,
lump it. The sun is going to shine today!

LILY: (*Looking out the window*) No, it's not.

HARPY: (*To* KATE) It would be nice if we could be united and see everyone off together. You should have seen Daniel in his uniform.

KERRY: On him it looked more like a school uniform, with that baby face.

HARPY: He looked handsome and rugged.

KERRY: And about 12 years old.

HARPY: (*Ignoring* KERRY) I had a photograph taken professionally.

KATE: For posterity?

HARPY: For the mantelpiece.

KATE: I never thought he was all that eager to go.

HARPY: Of course he was. Do you think they're all like your friend outside? Relief will be sent. They'll be brought home.

(KERRY *goes into the kitchen.*)

KATE: How do you know?

HARPY: They said so.

KATE: So what?

HARPY: They promised.

KATE: A bigger so what. It's a government that has made promises, and then broken them. It's their only consistent policy. We have been kept in the dark so long, we shield our eyes from what little light there is, thus remaining in the dark. We can't go on like forever. If truth be told, we can't go on like this at all. I want to see. I want to know.

HARPY: Oh, come on, Kate. All this and for what? A lover. I'm sure you'll have ample in your life.

KATE: Ample.

HARPY: Yes.

KATE: And that's how you see it, is it?

HARPY: Well, I'm sure, as you say, there are other things involved, as you yourself said, ignorance . . .

KATE: Yes?

HARPY: . . . plays a part.

KATE: The lead I should imagine.

(KERRY *comes in with the tea on a tray, and starts pouring.* HARPY *goes to assist.*)

218

You'll be handing out people's lives like you hand out
cups of tea, other people's tea.

HARPY: Sugar?

KATE: No, thanks.

(HARPY *hands a cup of tea to* KATE.)

KERRY: Lily, tea?

(*No response.*)

KATE: Lily.

KERRY: Do you want some tea? (*Pouring it for her*) She's a
thinker, that girl. (*Takes cup of tea to* LILY.) Gosh, it is
cloudy, isn't it? I don't suppose you've got an ark handy.

KATE: Funny you should ask.

KERRY: I haven't been on a boat for a long time. The last time
I saw the sea was our Georgian Bay trip. Ages ago.

HARPY: That's when I met Daniel, on a boat.

KERRY: I've heard this story millions of times.

HARPY: That is, not exactly on the boat – he gets seasick – we
met beside the boat. He's not one to join in, so I went
over to him to try to get him to come into the group.
"What are you doing here all by yourself?" I asked.
"We're all over here."

KATE: (*Under her breath*) That answers that question.

HARPY: It's remarkable when you meet someone and you like
them immediately. You may know what you want in a
person, but to actually find it is quite miraculous.

KATE: It's not as "divine" as all that.

HARPY: You don't know what I mean. You're told all your life
you're going to meet someone, a very special person, so
you wait and wait, and then one day, just like they said,
there he is – full of promise, and manliness, strength and
consideration, smart suits, clean boots, and a voice so
deep and rich one would expect to hear it only on the
stage.

KATE: I'll take two and you don't have to wrap them. Where
on earth are you going to find one like that, pray tell?

HARPY: What does that mean?

KERRY: Have you been hiding him in your room? Is that why

219

you won't let me in there?

KATE: When do we meet this paragon of perfection?

HARPY: You have. I was describing Daniel.

KERRY: Your Daniel?

HARPY: Of course my Daniel.

KATE: You know, I've never actually seen him like that.

HARPY: And lucky for me that is too.

KERRY: I wouldn't say his voice was exactly deep and rich, it's
more like a (*thinking*) a drone.

HARPY: A what?

KERRY: You know. (*Drones.*)

KATE: I never knew you went in for impressions.

KERRY: Oh, yes. You should hear my horse.

HARPY: Enough!

KERRY: Look, I'm very fond of him, you know I am.

HARPY: You're only picking on him because he isn't here to
defend himself.

KERRY: I am not picking on him, and since when has he had
to defend himself when he's always had you around to do it
for him?

(*During the next four speeches,* LILY, *by the window, sings
quietly*:)

LILY: On a mountain
Stands a lady
Who she is
I do not know.
All she wears is
Gold and silver
All she needs is
A fine young man.
So I call in hmmm . . .

HARPY: (*Ignoring* KERRY, *explaining to* KATE) One has ideals.

KATE: That's true enough.

HARPY: One has ideals!

KATE: I'm agreeing with you, it makes a change, I know. Do
you remember skipping rope to that? Where does she
summon these things from? All she needs is a fine young

man. God help her. Wearing only gold and silver. If you scratch away long enough, you'll find brass underneath.

HARPY: Why scratch? I'd leave it. It's not always necessary to know what lies beneath the surface, Kate. Sometimes it's nice to believe that gold's gold, and silver's silver. You don't have to have your nose rubbed into the filth to know it's there.

KATE: I don't agree.

HARPY: No, of course you don't. I'm not surprised. You revel in the mire. So put your nose into this, Kate: Guy will go, they'll all go.

KERRY: What time is it?

HARPY: Time for you to sit still. Get away from that window.

KERRY: No.

HARPY: I said get away from that window!

KERRY: Stop talking to me like that, Ruthie.

HARPY: I can talk to you how I please.

KERRY: Well, you'd better stop it, or else.

HARPY: Or else what?

KERRY: You'll see.

HARPY: Big deal. Look at me. I'm all a-tremble. Come sit down and learn what it's like to have a civilized conversation.

KERRY: I can sit where I like.

(*She sits down on the window seat.*)

KATE: (*Calmly*) Guy won't go.

HARPY: Oh, he will, one way or another.

KATE: And you're going to see to it, are you?

HARPY: It's my duty, yes.

KATE: Yes, I thought so. Are you now going to tell me how this town ain't big enough for the both of us, like some dime western novel? Is this the showdown, or perhaps we should have a hoedown and dance each other to death. That way no one would be hurt, wounded, scratched or scarred by flying shrapnel or barbed comments from the front lines. Perhaps we should cordon off the room. Or perhaps you already have the house surrounded. No one can leave.

KERRY: (*Picking up on the last line, standing up, worried*) What
do you mean, no one can leave?

KATE: All exits sealed and watched. Damn it! Are you so sure!

HARPY: I can almost promise.

KERRY: If it rains, how do you think the roads will be?

HARPY: Not very good but we don't have far to go.

KERRY: It's not us I'm worried about.

KATE: *How* are you so sure?

HARPY: Because I happen to know where we live.

KATE: Don't get "cute" with me.

HARPY: Certain things one knows instinctively.

KATE: You've got the situation felt out have you? Feel it in
your bones do you? How!? Tell me!

HARPY: (*Amazed*) You're frightened.

KATE: No, I'm not.

HARPY: This is a first.

KATE: I said, I'm not.

HARPY: Do you know what they say about you in town?

KATE: I don't care.

HARPY: Yes, but do you know?

KATE: I don't care!

HARPY: You and Lise Bernier . . .

KATE: Christ Almighty, one childhood incident, one! And
you've marked her for life. She did do good things too,
you know.

HARPY: Not for me.

KATE: Not for you. You wouldn't have remembered if she
had. You are obsessed!

HARPY: And you two are one of a kind, they say, one of a
kind. But you, they say, are the whore with class. She
never had much style.

KATE: (*Disbelief*) I don't believe this. (*To* KERRY) Do you
believe this?

HARPY: With Guy away, you'll be doing yourself a favour.

KATE: Oh, I see. It's all becoming very clear.

HARPY: And the rest of the family.

KATE: God bless 'em.

HARPY: People talk.

KATE: And say nothing! Take yourself for example.

HARPY: Don't you care about your husband?

KATE: New tactics now, is it?

HARPY: My husband, then. I thought you liked Daniel.

KATE: You mean his straight part, dark voice, and deep eyes.

HARPY: What about Lily, then? How often does she sit by that window?

KATE: Today's the first day.

HARPY: And for how many days to come will she sit there like that?

KATE: I'm sure as soon as you leave, she'll return to the land of the living.

HARPY: Lily, how will you vote?

KATE: Leave her alone.

HARPY: No, let her speak for herself. Lily?

(LILY *looks up from the window, looks at* HARPY.)

How will you vote? (*Going towards her, talking as if to a child*) You do want your Joe back, don't you? He's such a lovely boy, and so clever. Everyone adores him. You must be very happy. And he's been gone for such a long, long time. You know, of course, that Guy will have to go in order for Joe to return, but you mustn't concern yourself with that.

(LILY *looks at* KATE, *then out the window again.* HARPY *looks at* KATE.)

He will, you know. It's so simple, so damned simple, and you won't even listen!

KATE: Cannon fodder. Grind the bones with a pestle and mortar. Spread them over the fields and forest. Fertilize the land, impregnate the earth – the gods will smile upon you. Our boys will be home soon.

HARPY: What is it with you?

KATE: With me?

HARPY: You're such a proud, proud woman. (*Slight pause.*) You want them dead.

KATE: Shut up.

HARPY: What is Guy doing here, anyway? What right has he to be anywhere, anywhere at all? He's always here.

KATE: (*Finally losing her patience*) Why, isn't that strange? He lives here.

HARPY: He shouldn't be here. He's a constant reminder to –

KATE: To what? To what, Harpy? Don't stop now. I'm waiting for this great revelation.

HARPY: He's not where he should be.

KATE: And where's that?

HARPY: You know where.

KATE: If I knew I wouldn't be asking. I always thought he should be here with me. But I'm wrong so it seems, that's not so. But you know. You're the expert, so tell me. Where?!

HARPY: My Daniel is at the front.

KATE: Yes, I know.

HARPY: Taking it all, taking it all, taking it all. Not like your . . . not like . . . Do you want to know what I think?

KATE: No.

HARPY: What I honestly think?

KATE: Go home!

HARPY: That people like Guy should be hanged!

KATE: What?

(KERRY *moves closer.*)

HARPY: Why is he better than anyone else?

KERRY: Ruthie!

HARPY: Shut up!

KERRY: Stop saying that to me!

HARPY: No! (*To* KATE) What is he doing here, huh? What? Serving some sort of purpose? What is he doing here? Nothing, nothing, he's nothing! What right has he to . . . I would've signed up right away – no questions asked. No one would've had to force me to go, twist my arm. What's the matter with him? What's so special about him? We all know what he does around here, don't we? Keeping the natives happy.

KATE: (*To* KERRY) Get her out of here.

KERRY: Ruthie, let's go.

HARPY: He's a coward, a damned coward, and you sleep with him. Proud of yourself, aren't you? Proud, proud. What's wrong with you? Are you so desperate – is it so very necessary – is it such a vital part of your life that you can't do without him? What is it with you? What is he doing here? He should be hanged and treated like the (*whispers loudly*) shit that he is. We suffer, we suffer 'cause of him, we suffer, we're the ones. While he struts around like some cock gone to town. Oh, you're so clever, aren't you? So damned clever and you don't even see what goes on in your own home. He's got you in the palm of his hand, like putty. Fool! While we suffer, we suffer, 'cause of you, we suffer, we're the ones.

KATE: Get her out of here now!

HARPY: You know, this is the only place I know where the mistress of the house is really the mistress! You're disgusting. Filth! Can't you see – you're nothing, absolutely nothing. Nothing, nothing, nothing, trash is what you are, trash! Purely functional. Perhaps you'll set him up in business one day. Sell your soul for a quick one in the shed while we suffer, we suffer, damn!

KERRY: Stop it!

HARPY: Wonderful, wonderful, proud Kate.

KERRY: Enough! What has gotten into you?

HARPY: You stay out of this!

KERRY: No!

HARPY: Yes! What do you know? Your life is just beginning. You'll be put on the right road – you have my experience to learn from. Dreams won't be soiled for you some sweaty summer's morning you're preparing to see him off and you can't find him because he's hiding between the sheets, quivering, snivelling, afraid to go. Everyone else had gone – he was the only one left. What was I *supposed* to do?

KERRY: (*Coldly*) Tell Kate.

HARPY: Never.

KERRY: Tell her.

HARPY: No!

KERRY: You tell her or I will.

HARPY: No, you promised.

KERRY: Kate, she –

HARPY: No!

KERRY: Kate, she –

HARPY: Nooooo!

KERRY: (*Calmly, coldly*) She sent Daniel white feathers in the post.

KATE: What?

KERRY: White feathers through the post – twice – anonymously. A few choice phrases here and there, a slogan or two, a threat. He was petrified.

HARPY: You gave me your word.

KERRY: (*Innocently*) Did I?

KATE: (*Exhausted*) I don't believe this.

KERRY: How could I sit back and listen to you go on and on and on . . . Ruthie, you're vicious.

HARPY: *I'm* vicious?

KATE: I think I'm going to be sick.

HARPY: So that's it, is it? Accused, judged, and convicted. All we need now is a sentence.

KATE: (*Numbed, exhausted*) She should be hanged, drawn and quartered. Her head shall be placed on London Bridge for all innocent lambs to gaze upon before going to slaughter.

HARPY: It's not what you think.

KATE: No? (*To* KERRY, *who is by the window*) Shut her up, will you.

HARPY: No, you listen to me.

KATE: No one can ever accuse me of not listening to you. I have heard it all, word by word, syllable by syllable. I'm just surprised there's more.

(*Very loud thunderclap.*)

HARPY: He wouldn't go.

KATE: (*Total disbelief, shock*) I can't believe what you've done. For what? (*Laughs.*) What?

HARPY: Don't you see – he wouldn't go.

KATE: (*Very sarcastically*) Oh, a shame that.

HARPY: When I was a child –

KERRY: You were never a child, Ruthie. You were always the older sister.

(HARPY *just looks at* KERRY, *then to* KATE *to explain again.* KERRY *waves to someone outside unnoticed by* KATE, HARPY *and* LILY. KERRY *lightly kisses* LILY *and walks out the front door quietly, still unnoticed, while* HARPY *is talking.*)

HARPY: When I was a child, I thought things would be so different. It wasn't how I thought it would be.

KATE: And that's my fault, is it? Mine and Guy's. You believed a tale told by an idiot, and it's our fault. And maybe Lise Bernier's, just thrown in, despite her lack of style. Do you ever not pass the buck? Is anything ever your fault? Or are only the "nice" things yours, the "good" things yours, the "real" things yours?

HARPY: Everyone was going.

KATE: Not everyone.

HARPY: No, I forgot myself, not everyone, but almost. It was his chance to prove himself – I would've gone. He was supposed to be strong. Why was he confused all the time, so indecisive? I like a man who asserts himself, who takes the initiative. Why did he need everything done for him? Why couldn't he ever decide? Why didn't he know, just know, the way a man does? Why did he cry, out loud, where I could see him. I was told all those stories of what it would be like – given ideas, expectations.

KATE: And you believed them all.

HARPY: Why shouldn't I, why shouldn't I? Why would anyone mislead me?

KATE: Yes, why indeed – why is the earth flat, the sky green, the sun cold? Why don't the clouds bleed?

HARPY: The stories –

KATE: Were stories!

HARPY: No! (*Pause.*) I want him back!

KATE: So go and get him. Fly overhead, swoop down and

carry him off to safety – but before you do – tell him how
he got there in the first place – tell him! He'll lap it up,
especially the part about the feathers. (*Shouts:*) TELL HIM!
(*Quietly*) Then let him decide. I'm sure he'll be able to
now – but perhaps, just perhaps, he'll prefer to stay where
he is.

HARPY: I would've gone.

KATE: So you keep saying.

HARPY: I would've done what I was supposed to do.

KATE: Supposed to do. Where is that written – show me!

HARPY: You don't understand. (*Slight pause.*) I should've
been a boy, my mother used to say.

KATE: I don't care.

HARPY: I would've been happier, she said, but I don't think
so.

KATE: This is all very fascinating, but it's time.

HARPY: They were feathers from a dove. How do you think I
feel?

KATE: I don't care.

HARPY: How can he cope, I keep thinking to myself. He
might get hurt.

KATE: (*It's too much for her.*) *Get* hurt. Oh, a brilliant piece of
hindsight. God, you know, you make me sick – you make
me physically ill. (*Pause.*) I'm tired. I'm 23 years old and
I'm tired. Which to me is disgusting. It's terrible. I had so
much energy this morning, and you've taken it from me.
No, no, I've let you take it, which is worse. And I feel
graceless. I feel pockmarked and scarred. I've let you
mark me. I loathe you. I felt sorry for you. Children
wouldn't befriend you at school. Being an only child, I
thought it's wrong to be made to feel lonely. I thought,
she can't be that bad, surely she's some "potential",
something to give, something to offer. But I was wrong.
You don't even know what I'm talking about, do you?
And stop glaring at me. It makes you look as ugly as I
feel. Get out.

(HARPY *moves towards the door, looking for* KERRY *as she*

228

leaves. She exits. Silence. Then UNCLE *comes barrelling in.*)

UNCLE: (*Oblivious to all*) Did you hear the thunder? Did you?
Nobody could've missed that. Impossible, absolutely
impossible. Boy, did you miss a scene in town. Sy Falls
fainted dead away in a puddle on Main Street – he can't
swim, he could've drowned. Anyway, he fainted right
beside a cat an automobile squashed. Ugh. And his
missus, Sy's missus that is, not the cat's, froze on the
spot. There were cries of "Judgment has come" and
"This is the end" and a few swear words, after all the
Thomsons had just put up new curtains, but it wasn't the
end. After a couple of minutes, when it looked like no one
was about to be struck down dead, people began to get up
off their knees. It's funny what inspires people to take up
religion so sudden like. They all dusted themselves off and
sheepishly walked away. But you should have see Sy
when he came to. He turned his head to the right, and saw
the cat lying there next to him with it's insides hanging
out, and I bet he jumped higher then than he's ever
jumped in his life. I don't know whose cat it was, it was
hard to tell, I didn't get a very close look. If anyone had a
chance to see, it was Sy, and he ain't talking. It was a bit
of excitement, I'll tell you that. (*Sits down in a heap.*)
Whew!

KATE: Are you quite finished?

UNCLE: Uh–huh.

KATE: Uh–huh. Don't you feel anything? Can't you sense
anything in the air?

UNCLE: A bit of rain.

KATE: A bit of rain. Oh, that's good, that's just fine.

UNCLE: Just what we need.

KATE: I'm thinking of moving, going on a little trip, changing
house, shifting lives, taking stock, bowing out. (*Looks at*
LILY.) A charming pose for a still life, don't you think?
I'm going upstairs. There isn't any dinner.

UNCLE: I thought it was a good story.

(*Blackout.*)

Scene 2

Night. A candle is lit on the dining-room table. KATE *is sitting at the table, stage left, peeling the wax off the candle.*

GUY *enters.*

GUY: Kate?

KATE: Come over and sit with me.

GUY: Have they gone?

KATE: Yes. They left ages ago. For good.

> (GUY *comes over to the table, sits down across from* KATE.)
> It's nice to see you. You're probably wondering what I'm doing in the dark like this. I'm peeling the wax off the candle. Who knows – perhaps I've found a vocation after all. (*Tense*) Will somebody please push the walls apart – they're a little too close for comfort. Thank you. Ever so kind. (*Sighs.*) Oh, Guy. We're not going away for the weekend, are we? (*Irritated*) Decisions.

GUY: Did you know, Kate, La Fontaine is a very old name?

KATE: (*Amused, fondly*) You've often mentioned it, yes.

GUY: Very famous. Is Tull?

KATE: Hmmm?

GUY: Your name. Kate Tull.

KATE: I know it's my name.

GUY: What sort of name is Tull?

KATE: English?

GUY: Figures. La Fontaine was a poet. La Fontaine is a very old name.

KATE: And Old King Cole was a merry old soul. (*Irritated at having said that*) Oh God.

GUY: Do you know any of his fables?

KATE: Guy . . .

GUY: What sort of name is "Arpy"?

KATE: The devil's own – I don't know, why are we talking about names?

GUY: It will help.

KATE: Help. I see. (*Pause.*) I wish –

GUY: What, my Kate, do you wish?

(KATE *gets up and walks away from* GUY, *trying to hold in her feelings, trying not to get upset.*)

KATE: There must've been a time, any time, sometime, when things were simpler. A world where feelings, where life, where dreams, (*angry*) where stories, Oh God, I don't know.

GUY: It's not going to be easy. You've got to be strong.

KATE: Oh, yes. I must be strong, heaven forbid that I crumble, that I become weak, that I fail, that I make a mistake! The armour was tarnished, the horse was a nag; why couldn't I see it? (*To* GUY, *lightly*) Where were you when I needed you?

GUY: Kate . . .

KATE: Look at me waltzing around the room, as my mother used to say. The very foundations are being shaken out from under me! I have no control. I always have control! (*Pacing*) If I'm creating a breeze, let me know.
(*She goes back to the bay window, looks away from* GUY.)

GUY: What do you think of America?

KATE: What?

GUY: What do you think of America?

KATE: North or South?

GUY: It's like this. If I stay, I'll be sent away, and there is every possibility that I get killed. "Il est mort" they'll say. A terrible description of one so young. To fight for "right and freedom" seems a bit comic, when as a Frenchman I am losing those very things here. My only alternative is to leave. You know that. It's not an easy decision. I am as confused as you are. Perhaps this upheaval is a sign that it's time for a change. If it's not a sign, it's definitely a cause. Some get tired of fighting but go on, others just get tired. Are you going to sit down?
(*KATE sits down on the window seat, still looking away from* GUY.)
You know how I feel about you. (*Getting frustrated*) Kate, I cannot see your face.

KATE: And I cannot see any stars! Perhaps they've been sent

231

overseas. Next they'll take the sky, then the sun, then
the moon, then the trees, one mustn't forget the trees. But
not the women, never the women, not that the women
want to go, mind you. (*An anger that builds*) No, let them
wait. And wait. Let them sing their songs, let them play
their games. Let them dream their dreams. Let them
climb the walls, wring their hands, tear out their hair. But
leave them their stars! (*Hushed tone to* GUY) Are you just
going to sit there? What, what do you want, what should I
say – come on, tell me, come on, you tell me – what do you
want? An answer, a solution, a promise, an oath sworn in
secrecy? What do you want? What can I say? Can you not
see at all? Can you not see anything? Help me! Now.
(*Pause.*) *You* say something. Tell me it's going to be all
right when it isn't. I want to hear the words.

GUY: Kate, I promise you that . . .

KATE: No! Promise me nothing! I have had it up to here with
promises, promise me nothing; not a damn thing. I want
nothing. (*Slight pause.*) And everything. (*To herself*) Explain
that one away. Why weren't all those stories true, all that
time ago? (*Lights up.*) We could dress you up as a woman!

GUY: Kate.

KATE: It always worked in Shakespeare.

GUY: You are a nut.

KATE: (*Sarcastically*) Terrific. But then again he always had
characters, dramatis personae, to make grand sweeping
statements about life. So go ahead, say something. (*Silence.*)
No? Come on, sweep me off my feet, along with the rest of
the rubbish. (*Slight pause.*) I bet if you didn't know me so
well, you'd hit me. I'd hit you right back, mind, but still. I'm
sorry, Guy. I love you, you know that. So.

GUY: So.

KATE: Do you know what I felt the first time I saw you?
Everything I should've felt the first time around. (*Slight
pause.*) Look after yourself.

GUY: I will. You too.

KATE: I will.

232

GUY: I'll write.

KATE: I know. I'll write too.

GUY: I'll let you know where I am as soon as I'm settled. I'll get a job, maybe work with my hands.

KATE: Yes, you're good at that.

GUY: Maybe on a farm.

KATE: Where?

GUY: I'll let you know.

KATE: America's a big country.

GUY: I'll be all right.

KATE: I know.

GUY: So will you.

KATE: Always. (*Slight pause.*) I feel trapped, Guy. Shut in.

GUY: I know the feeling.

KATE: I know. (*Smiles sadly.*) Not much help to each other, are we? (*Slight pause. Worried*) How do I shake it off? I can't leave. I'm chained to this rock.

GUY: It's not by choice that I —

KATE: I know. I know. I didn't mean it like that.

GUY: I know.

KATE: (*Fondly*) You know many things.

GUY: Are you convinced yet?

KATE: Getting there.

GUY: Eat.

KATE: Always. Be careful.

GUY: Always. Don't do anything stupid.

KATE: Impossible. (*Slight pause. Excited*) We could hide you in the basement!

GUY: What?

KATE: Nothing. Forget it. It just slipped out. (*Pause.*) Dare I say it?

GUY: What?

KATE: Shit!

GUY: You can say it again if you like.

KATE: I don't think it's necessary. Don't make me laugh, Guy. This is serious. You'd better pack. Governments move in mysterious ways. It's time for you to go. (*Slight pause.*)

233

It's time.

(GUY *goes over to* KATE *but she refuses to look away from the
window.* GUY *exits.* LILY *enters, sits on the stairs, behind the
bars of the banister.*)

LILY: It was at the post office.

KATE: (*Vague, exhausted*) What?

LILY: I was behind the screen door.

KATE: Not now.

LILY: It's torn the screen and that's how I heard they were
talking and laughing the postman with his sack slung over
his shoulder his cap tilted off his head and all the others
were standing around him he had a letter from his son.
Mother lied to me all those stories about men in tails in
tales I don't know any more no don't look this way please
don't look this way. Oh Joe how I've missed you so much.
The underworld don't talk you used to say but they do yes
they do through the mouths of the living. You went away
in faith-lessness never entered conversations but he was
holding his son's letter and showing it around. You're
going to cafés now, having wine, lots of wine but you
don't drink!? You never touch the – (*straining to hear*)
What? Where? Say it again no don't say it again I'm here
overhearing your Sweet Lily Lamb, your Lily Lamb.
With women? What women? They're boys they're lads
and he showed them a photo and said it was you, my son
and young Joe and the women hey hey take a look what
they say – arm in arm, arm in arm. Takes after his dad, let
them enjoy, they're away, and they're young he-he ho-ho
wink of an eye, nod of a head, I wish I were dead, do you
hear me?! Don't you miss me at all?
Who is she? Can't you tell me? Aren't we lovers any
longer? The postman said you had one woman after the
other and he laughed they all did cause I heard every
word.
It's not him! I called out, but it caught in my throat. Left
alone lonely me with post office shrieks. (*About to vomit,
stops herself.*) Lily Lamb your sweet Lily Lamb,

lover-wife-whores?! No more please no more please sorry
ma'am sorry ma'am no mail today no mail today no mail
today.
(*Lights fade to blackout.*)

Scene 3

Early the next morning. KATE *comes into the sitting room from the
kitchen, carrying a cup of tea. About to put it down, she drops it.
The lights aren't on in the room.*

UNCLE: (*From upstairs*) Who's there?

KATE: Me! Me! It's only me.
(*She bends down to pick up the pieces of china.*)
(UNCLE *turns on the light.*)

UNCLE: Who's there?

KATE: It's just me. Don't worry. Look, it's nothing, a cup,
nothing of value.

UNCLE: We don't have anything of value. Mind where you go.
(LILY *comes downstairs.*)

KATE: I couldn't sleep.

UNCLE: I see, so you thought you'd come downstairs and
throw the cups around the room.

KATE: It beats peeling the wax off candles.

UNCLE: What?

KATE: Nothing. I felt a bit restless. I couldn't sleep. It's been
a long day. Hey! Do you know who rang up at midnight?

UNCLE: No. Who?

KATE: Kerry. She was in Toronto, deliriously happy. She
eloped. I think it's marvellous, absolutely marvellous.

UNCLE: Does her sister know?

KATE: Oh, I hope so.
(UNCLE *bends down to pick up a few pieces of china.*)
Leave it. I'll clean it up.

UNCLE: Where's Guy?

KATE: He's gone.

UNCLE: Just like that?

KATE: It wasn't just like that, no.

UNCLE: And your weekend?

KATE: All leave has been cancelled until further notice.

UNCLE: Without a word.

KATE: With several words. He left me this letter. (*Takes a letter from her dressing-gown pocket.*) He said I should add it to my collection.

UNCLE: Where'd he go?

KATE: I don't know.

UNCLE: When will he be back?

LILY: Will he?

KATE: Doubt it.

UNCLE: But the work.

KATE: It's always the work with you, isn't it? He's done the work. He thinks of others.

LILY: Don't be sad.

KATE: I'm not. I'm merely passing through myself.

(UNCLE *walks over to the back bay window.*)

UNCLE: Look at that rain. (*Opens the window, takes a deep breath.*) Wonderful fresh air. Oh, looky there. The boy on the bike.

(LILY *freezes.*)

LILY: What?

KATE: (*Quickly*) Where?

UNCLE: I wish I could ride like that.

(*Lights fade to blackout.*)

TRIAL AND ERROR

Lennie James

A NOTE ON THE PLAY

Trial and Error is set in a community home on the outskirts of London and follows the duration of a mock trial. TONY MICHAELS, having been refused a chance to leave the home, runs away. He is followed by a mute child called DRAY. When the boys return to the home they discover that a fire has damaged the main recreation area. The staff make no link between the boys' disappearance and the fire. However the children at the home are not completely convinced. Under the guidance of a manipulative bully called STALLION and coupled with general boredom, the idea of a trial is born. The trial is used to establish whether TONY is guilty but also serves to examine child care.

Despite the seemingly far-fetched plot, *Trial and Error* is intended to be realistic. The idea of a trial was used to provide a platform where conversation would be open and truthful. It is important, if the play is to work, to capture the internal relationships of the inmates. Children's homes as institutions are sub-cultures, therefore relationships within them are different from the accepted norm.

Trial and Error is not an attack on children's homes. It sets out to be a fair examination of one form of a substituted lifestyle. It highlights real problems and expresses various attitudes towards children's homes. The characters in *Trial and Error* could easily be members of a home, but they are not necessarily a typical cross-section of home inmates. This play attempts to show one event in one home on one specific day.

The character of DRAY has no written dialogue, as he is mute. But his presence and reactions are important. Therefore, I feel it is important that he is constantly monitored and not neglected as a result of the absence of a written part.

L.J.

238

Characters

TONY MICHAELS   An extremely determined 16-year-old who adamantly does not want to be in care. His determination has made him slightly self-centred.

SHIRLEY   Tony's girlfriend. Boyish and attractive. She is very protective towards her brother, Dray, and later becomes protective towards Tony as well.

DRAY   Mute. Apart from his sister, Shirley, the only person to treat him with any respect is Tony and Dray adores him. His muteness has made him an object of ridicule for the other children.

STALLION   A manipulative bully, enjoying life as the "top boy" at the home. All the other children fear him.

MARCUS   Tony's best friend. An intelligent boy, a long-term resident.

NORMAN   A rather aloof middle-class boy, extremely nervous and academic. Although not liked, he is grudgingly respected.

SCOT BRADLEY   A happy-go-lucky ex-resident. Very popular.

WAYNE   Quiet and resourceful. Sincerely convinced of Tony's guilt.

SPIKE   Stallion's side-kick. He tries so hard to be noticed and liked that he becomes an irritation.

BLUE   A rather wide-eyed girl. Short for her age and the home's pet.

PAT   The head of the home, strict and sincere.

GEORGE   A member of staff. Rather young and academic, he relates most of his experience to a text-book of child care.

MARGE   A member of staff. Very strict and with a Victorian attitude to child care.

ANNE JESSEP   Tony's social worker. The "vicar's daughter" type.

SAM MICHAELS Tony's mother. Liked by all the children at the home, apart from Tony. She never had the time or inclination to mother him.

MRS DOREEN WILMOTT Sam's landlady.

STEWART TOWNSEND From Spear's Housing Association.

There are a number of additional parts which can be doubled. For instance, the children can be played by members of the jury. The average size of the cast is thirty-eight.

CHILD I	THREE SCHOOLCHILDREN
CHILD 2	SCHOOL TEACHER
CHILD 3	PUPIL
CHILD 4	MOTHER
THREE READERS	SON

ACT I

The children are gathered with the staff in the main hall. TONY
and DRAY *sit at the front of the hall and* STALLION *stands.*

PAT: . . . and in the future, Stephen, kindly keep your hands
to yourself. If there is to be any hitting in this house I will
do it.

STALLION: I'm sure you would, but I didn't hit Blue.

PAT: Of course you didn't! She often comes running into the
kitchen crying.

STALLION: Blue, did I hit you?
(*Pause.*)

BLUE: Well . . . no!

STALLION: See? She was crying because of something I said.

PAT: Oh, so Blue burst into tears because of something you
said?

STALLION: Yeah. So don't make it look like I bullied her.

PAT: You, Stephen, a bully? The thought never even crossed
my mind. But regardless of how you upset Blue, I don't
want to see it again.

STALLION: What? I already told you I didn't do nothing.

PAT: Christ, but you're an arrogant child, Stephen.

STALLION: That's right, and you're "Little Miss Perfect",
pure as gold and lily-white.

PAT: Just do as you are told.

STALLION: I'll try very hard, Aunty Pat!

PAT: Stephen Shannon, you probably think your witty
comments are very funny, but I personally don't hold with
them. So just sit down and remember what I told you.
(STALLION *sits.*)
Good, now Uncle George has a few announcements.

GEORGE: Fine. As you no doubt know, the gym is temporarily
out of use. We have therefore decided to run a few day

241

trips, out somewhere.

SHIRLEY: Where to?

GEORGE: A museum or something, depending on the cost.

SHIRLEY: Great. What if we don't want to go?

SPIKE: You mean you'd pass up a trip to the museum? All that trouble was taken to place all that knowledge under one roof, and you don't want to go?

SHIRLEY: Very funny, Spike.

GEORGE: Anyone wanting to go, just sign your names on this list. It'll be outside Aunty Pat's office.

SHIRLEY: What happens if we don't sign the list?

SPIKE: You don't go, believe it or not!

GEORGE: Spike, please.

SPIKE: What? It's true, isn't it?

GEORGE: The only alternative to the trip is all day in the Lodge.

SHIRLEY: Great!

PAT: Well, if you come up with somewhere better to go, we will consider it.

SPIKE: What about bowling?

PAT: Yes, if you don't mind paying for it out of your pocket money? As you have probably noticed, both Tony and Dray are back from their little adventure. I will end all rumours here by telling you all neither are being held responsible for the damage caused to the gym area.

(*General moans throughout the hall.*)

WAYNE: You're joking, you must be?

PAT: Hardly, Wayne. The matter is hereby closed as far as you lot are concerned.

(SPIKE *mumbles something.*)

MARGE: Would you like to repeat that, Spike?

SPIKE: No, it's all right.

MARGE: I'm sure we'd all like to hear what you said.

SPIKE: It was nothing. I can't even remember what it was.

MARGE: I'm sure you can't.

PAT: In future, if you have something to say, Spike, say it out loud or not at all.

SPIKE: Yes, Aunt.

PAT: Good. Lunch will be in about one hour. Try and stay out of trouble until then.

(Staff and some children leave hall. Small groups form and conversations break out.)

SPIKE: What a bitch!

BLUE: Who?

SPIKE: Marge. She really made me look stupid.

BLUE and SPIKE: That isn't too difficult . . .

SPIKE: *(Continuing)* . . . I know, but in front of everyone. Cow. Makes me sick.

CHILD 1: No table tennis or basketball or machines for three weeks at least, and they expect us to be happy with a walk round a museum.

CHILD 2: I hate going out in that van anyhow. I mean, it's painted in the council colour, with its name down the side and the number on the doors.

CHILD 3: It looks like a spastics' van.

CHILD 2: Remember when we went into town and we pretended we were flids?

(Slight laugh.)

CHILD 1: Yeah. You were there, weren't you, Wayne?

WAYNE: *(Indifferently)* Yeah, it was great fun.

CHILD 3: You were miles away.

WAYNE: I just can't swallow it. The very day Tony and Dray do a bunk the gym's nearly burnt down.

CHILD 3: And they ain't being blamed for it.

WAYNE: Yeah.

CHILD 1: But Pat said they had nothing to do with it.

SPIKE: I reckon Tony paid Pat off. That would explain where she got the money for that new dress she was wearing.

SHIRLEY: Wages! The staff do get paid for working here. Christ, when are you going to grow up?

SPIKE: Well, you won't say a word against either of them. One's your lover boy and the other's your brother.

SHIRLEY: Anything you say, Spike.

SPIKE: And if Tony did do it, Dray will keep quiet about it.

(*Laughs.*)

SHIRLEY: Just cos he can't speak doesn't mean he wouldn't tell the truth.

SPIKE: Of course not!

SHIRLEY: Go away, Spike, you bore me.

STALLION: All right, they must have looked into it, but they could've been wrong. I mean, Pat has been known to make a mistake.

MARCUS: Tony and Dray had nothing to do with the fire, Stallion, and you know it.

STALLION: Yeah? Prove it.

MARCUS: How? What do you suggest, a trial?

STALLION: Why not?

MARCUS: Be realistic, Stallion, how can we?

STALLION: We'll have our own private trial.

MARCUS: You want to put Tony and Dray on trial?
(*Pause.*)

STALLION: No, you're right . . . just Tony. Dray wouldn't have done it. He wouldn't know how.

MARCUS: Listen up, you lot, Stallion's flipped his lid.

STALLION: Do you like hospital food, Marcus?

MARCUS: Cute, Stallion, very cute.

SHIRLEY: (*To* TONY) I said Stallion wouldn't let it go by.

STALLION: Tony, your friend here has suggested we put you on trial.

MARCUS: You're serious.

STALLION: What about it, Tony?

TONY: What you playing at?

STALLION: Me, playing? It's just a bit of fun!

SHIRLEY: It was a bit of fun that got you put in here, wasn't it, Stallion?

STALLION: Yeah. Well, you're no angel or we never would have met.

SHIRLEY: It's no fault of mine why I'm here.

STALLION: No, it's my fault. Now, what about this trial?

TONY: OK, Stallion, I'll play your game.

STALLION: How kind.

SHIRLEY: Let's hope it stays just a game.

(*General running around. Some more kids come in.*)

STALLION: Court in session. (*Laughs.*) Spike, you can be . . .

MARCUS: The doorman. It was my idea, remember?

STALLION: And so?

MARCUS: And so, I'll be the defence counsel.

STALLION: What about the jury?

MARCUS: Easy enough. (*Counts them out.*) Twelve, isn't it?

STALLION: The prosecution?

WAYNE: I'll do it. I reckon he did it.

STALLION: And the judge?

(MARCUS *pauses and looks around. Smiles.*)

MARCUS: Norman.

STALLION: Norman? Why him of all people?

MARCUS: Because he . . . he doesn't give a damn either way. Will you do it, Norm?

NORMAN: I really haven't time to play let's pretend.

MARCUS: Thanks, Norman! I think we're about ready.

STALLION: Not quite. What about the court usher? There's one in every court.

SPIKE: Stallion should know, he's been in enough . . . Er, sorry . . . I was just . . . I mean . . . eh. I vote Stallion as our court usher, and Norm seconds it.

NORMAN: Eh?

SPIKE: Thanks, Norm, you're a brick.

STALLION: I am appointed court usher by popular demand.

SPIKE: (*Clapping his hands, etc.*) The only person for the job.

SHIRLEY: What a horrible little person you are.

SPIKE: Well, you're no angel or we never would have met!

SHIRLEY: Worm!

MARCUS: Can we get started?

STALLION: Silence in court. (*Pause.*) Well, come on, Marcus.

MARCUS: What?

STALLION: Get started.

MARCUS: How?

STALLION: Christ knows, you must know what happens?

MARCUS: Wayne, you must have seen it on TV.

NORMAN: If I might interrupt, you seem to be at a loss when it comes to court room procedure, as it were.

STALLION: As it were! But I wouldn't have thought your sort had ever seen the inside of a court.

NORMAN: Quite. I suggest that both the defence and prosecutor put forward their respective cases, outlining what they expect to prove in the course of the trial. It may not be right but it'll do for all intents and purposes.

MARCUS: OK. In defence of my client, I intend to prove beyond a shadow of a doubt that he is innocent as charged – of arson – that's what I'll prove.

WAYNE: Your honour, ladies and gentlemen of the jury, my learned friend. I will prove beyond all doubt that the defendant, Tony Michaels, is guilty as charged.

TONY: Mr Rumpole, eat your heart out.

NORMAN: Carry on, Wayne.

WAYNE: Oh, right. (*Whispers to* NORMAN:) What next?

NORMAN: You call your first witness.

(*Pause.*)

WAYNE: Who?

MARCUS: That's a point. Who do we call to testify?

STALLION: Thought you would've figured that one out, scholar boy.

MARCUS: Yeah, I must be falling behind. Remind me.

STALLION: Everyone knew about this Tony and Dray saga, didn't they?

MARCUS: Yeah.

STALLION: So where did they find out from?

MARCUS: All over the place. Bits from you, Spike, May, and things I already knew.

STALLION: So we just put the people who mouthed it around on the stand to testify.

NORMAN: That's remarkably clever, Stallion.

STALLION: Kiss off, Norman. Get on with it, Wayne.

WAYNE: OK. The prosecution calls Shirley to the stand.

STALLION: Now we're getting somewhere. (*To* SHIRLEY) Put your right hand on this book and repeat after me.

SHIRLEY: What is it? I ain't swearing on a school text-book.

STALLION: It's all I could find.

NORMAN: Do you think we could skip the swearing in and proceed with the testimony?

STALLION: Why, of course, your honour!

WAYNE: Shirley, wasn't it you who suggested Tony should run off after the fire?

SHIRLEY: Where d'you hear that? I said maybe he should leave, but it was before the fire.

WAYNE: Could you tell us exactly how this came about?

SHIRLEY: (*Looks at* TONY.) He, I mean Tony, wasn't happy here any more. He wasn't too chuffed to begin with.

WAYNE: About what?

SHIRLEY: About being in a home. He never settled down here. It just came out in a conversation we had.

WAYNE: What was your conversation about?

SHIRLEY: Nothing. It just led to the Lodge and Tony's position here.

(*Again she looks at* TONY.)

TONY *and* SHIRLEY *are sitting at a table.* DRAY *plays cards on the floor.*

TONY: Don't go all quiet on me.

SHIRLEY: I want you to tell me what you mean by "It wouldn't work."

TONY: (*To* DRAY) Don't cheat. You're only cheating against yourself in patience.

SHIRLEY: Is it because you're scared of what the others might say?

TONY: (*To* DRAY) How many times is that? I thought you could only go through the pack three times.

SHIRLEY: That's "Blackpool Patience"! Tony.

TONY: It would be like we were married. I'd see you every day.

SHIRLEY: And what of it?

TONY: Just imagine it. A smile across the dinner table, maybe a quick kiss when no one's looking. We might even get to hold hands, when everyone's watching TV.

SHIRLEY: So we'll just be friends?

TONY: For now, yes. How about a game of blackjack with Dray?

SHIRLEY: Every time you can't handle a conversation with me it's "Let's have a kick about with Dray" or "Coming for a walk with me and Dray?" Will you stop hiding behind my brother?

TONY: What do you want me to say?

SHIRLEY: The truth!

TONY: The truth is as long as I am in the Lodge we will be no more than friends.

(*Pause.*)

SHIRLEY: What, is that the end of it?

TONY: Yes.

SHIRLEY: Why?

TONY: Why?

SHIRLEY: Yes, why?

TONY: Because.

SHIRLEY: Because what?

TONY: Ever since I've been here, everything has gone wrong. I've screwed up my exams, which isn't surprising because I never went to school. It's been downhill ever since I got here.

SHIRLEY: You can't blame the Lodge for all that.

TONY: To make matters worse, now I'm here nobody will give me a second chance when it comes to a job.

SHIRLEY: Yeah, you and three million others!

TONY: Look at the lot that's in here now: Stallion came after beating up a teacher at school, then the Welfare Officer and everyone else who came along. All just for a laugh.

SHIRLEY: There were other factors involved.

TONY: And how about Wayne? Put in here after breaking into a school music department.

SHIRLEY: His mother didn't want him at home any more. And what about the kids from broken homes, or the orphans and neglected kids? Oh, and that boy who tried

248

to burn down his mother's flat.

TONY: That isn't fair!

SHIRLEY: The Lodge didn't mess up your life, you did. The
day you threw a wobbly and set light to Sam's flat is when
you screwed up.

(DRAY *signals*.)

He wants us to stop arguing and play cards. Tony, if you
hate the Lodge so much, leave.

TONY: Sure, I'll up and tell Pat straight away. (DRAY *signals*.)

SHIRLEY: (*To* DRAY) Yes, he can. Trevor left when he was 16.
Got his own flat in London, I think.

TONY: You can't leave until you're 18.

SHIRLEY: You have an option when you're 16. Just get Pat to
see your social worker next time she comes down.

TONY: I just get Anne to see Pat and that's it?

SHIRLEY: I expect so.

The court.

CHILD 1: I remember Trevor, great footballer. Moved in with
his girlfriend, I thought.

CHILD 2: Na, he's living with his dad up town.

STALLION: Silence in court! Put a sock in it.

WAYNE: So Tony tried to burn down his mother's flat?

SHIRLEY: Yes, you knew that.

WAYNE: No further questions.

MARCUS: You said Tony wasn't too chuffed with the Lodge.
Was he angry enough to try and burn it down?

SHIRLEY: No, that would mean more time in here or even
Borstal. What he wanted was to leave.

MARCUS: Thanks, Shirley.

NORMAN: You can stand down now, Shirley.

SHIRLEY: What will you do when you've found out what
really happened?

STALLION: Tell Pat, of course.

SHIRLEY: That's not fair. Pat already said there was no
connection.

STALLION: Yeah, and she could have been wrong.

SHIRLEY: Norman, tell him it isn't fair.

STALLION: Fair? He burnt down the gym. I can't see that as being very fair.

SHIRLEY: Tony, stop this "game" now. It'll go too far.

STALLION: What's the matter, Shirley? Frightened we'll find out you and Tony did more than hold hands in the dark?

TONY: Leave it out, Stallion. Just get on with the trial.

SHIRLEY: What are you doing?

TONY: It's interesting. I'm enjoying it. Now stand down and let Wayne carry on.

SHIRLEY: Why not? I mean, this beats monopoly any day. At the risk of sounding like a killjoy, remember I told you so. Come on, Wayne, continue with the fun!

WAYNE: Prosecution calls Blue. (*To* NORMAN) She's always in Pat's office. She'd say if Tony went to see Pat.

BLUE: Don't I get sworn in or something?

NORMAN: We've decided against it, Blue.

WAYNE: We have heard from Shirley that Tony went to see Pat. Did he?

BLUE: Christ, did he? Pat really got angry with him.

WAYNE: Tell us exactly what happened.

BLUE: I wasn't listening in or nothing. I just heard them cos most of the time Tony was shouting.

NORMAN: Just explain why he was shouting.

SPIKE: Maybe it was because he was annoyed.

NORMAN: Quite. Carry on, Blue.

BLUE: I had to leave the office when Anne, that's Tony's social worker, arrived. I hadn't finished what I was doing, so when I got myself a drink I went back and waited outside. They were hard at it by this time.

NORMAN: Hard at what exactly?

STALLION: What's the matter, Norman, don't she speak well enough for your refined ear lobes? Should I translate for you?

NORMAN: It's all right, Stallion, I understood.

BLUE: What I meant, Norman, was . . . well, Tony was in there now and they were arguing about Trevor.

Pat's office.

PAT: Trevor was a totally different case to yours.

TONY: He left when he was 16 and that's all I want to do.

ANNE: Calm down and let Pat explain, Tony.

TONY: What you mean is, shut up and listen to a perfectly good excuse to explain why I can't leave.

PAT: That is not what Anne meant, Tony Michaels. (*To* ANNE) This boy Trevor left before Tony came to the Lodge. How he got to hear about it I can't imagine.

ANNE: You were saying that Trevor was different from Tony. In what way?

PAT: Trevor was under Section 1 of the present Act.

ANNE: That would be Section 2 of the earlier Act.

PAT: You know, I don't know. I'm completely at a loss with all these extra Sections and changes. What is clear is Tony is under Section 2 of the present Act and therefore in a very different situation.

ANNE: That's true. I expect that if Tony were to leave it would have to go through the Courts.

TONY: Excuse me. Remember me, I'm the Section 2. I have a question, if you don't mind!

PAT: What is it, Tony?

TONY: Am I supposed to understand all the Section 1, 2 and 62 stuff? Cos if I am, I'm sorry, I didn't do my homework.

ANNE: No, we wouldn't expect you to understand it.

TONY: So you slipped into that jargon so I wouldn't understand you?

PAT: Tony, please calm down. We have trouble understanding the different Acts that bind child care. So we can't expect you to comprehend it.

TONY: So explain it, please.

PAT: Section 1 is voluntary care, where a child is placed in care until his home life straightens out or he is old enough to leave. Section 2 on the other hand is a Court Care Order.

ANNE: So in order for you to leave, your case would have to go

251

through the Courts again.

TONY: I can't see any problem.

PAT: Very rarely do they allow a discharge until the person is 18.

TONY: Why should it be down to them?

PAT: It isn't entirely. Both Anne and I have to submit a report on you.

TONY: And you'll say I'm not ready . . . Shit!

ANNE: Tony, please.

TONY: Tony, please what? Go back to my room and stop making your job harder? It was a better excuse than I expected.

ANNE: It wasn't an excuse.

TONY: No?

ANNE: No.

PAT: Don't you like staying at the Lodge, Tony?

TONY: I hate it. It's become a living nightmare. I have to get away from here. Is that what you expected me to say? Was I convincing?

PAT: If you like it here, why do you want to leave?

TONY: Because I don't want to live in a children's home. I don't want to listen to that "children should be seen and not heard" routine. I don't want to share a bedroom with five other kids, one of whom wets the bed. I no longer want to sit down to a meal with twenty other fucking kids . . .

(PAT *slaps* TONY's *face. Pause.*)

Is she allowed to hit me?

ANNE: Tony, we want what's best for you.

TONY: Does that include slapping me? (*To* PAT) You take it as a personal insult because I want to leave the Lodge, don't you?

PAT: No, Tony, I don't, but it annoys me to see you set yourself above the people in this Lodge.

TONY: I didn't mean to offend your Lodge!

PAT: It isn't my Lodge. I'm just the head. I run it for a group of people sitting on a board. Answerable to the Welfare

State.

TONY: I wasn't knocking the system. It works for the majority and good luck to them.

PAT: But it doesn't work for you?

TONY: It's not a matter of working. I don't want to live in care. Is that some kind of sacrilege? Will I be cast into continual damnation for my sins?

PAT: Don't you think you're blowing this a little out of proportion? Grow up. Stop behaving like a spoilt child.

ANNE: After all, this is a very nice place. You should be . . .

TONY: Grateful? Tell me, were you going to finish that all too familiar statement with "grateful"?

ANNE: Yes, I have said it a few times. But still . . .

TONY: Don't patronize me, Anne.

ANNE: Sorry, I don't mean to, I just feel that . . .

TONY: You people amaze me. You think just because you do a worthwhile job you're beyond criticism.

PAT: I wouldn't have said you were in a position to criticize anyone.

TONY: I decide against the plan you and your socially conscious friends have drawn up for me, and all of a sudden I'm a revolutionary.

PAT: Do you realize how utterly paranoid you sound?

ANNE: Tony, what do you really want?

TONY: Oh, sorry, didn't I make it clear? I wish to part company with Pat here.

ANNE: Well, we'll see what we can do. We can't say fairer than that.

TONY: No, better not make any promises. You might have to work to fulfil them.

PAT: I don't believe you said that. After all Anne has done for you? If it weren't for her you would be in Borstal and not in a community home like the Lodge.

ANNE: Where will you go, Tony – if you leave?

TONY: I'll get a job up town, move into a hostel or flat and go to college part-time like Trevor.

PAT: What do you mean, like Trevor? Where did you hear

about this hostel and flat rubbish? Trevor Small
moved back in with his father.

ANNE: You know reconciliation with Sam is totally out of the
question?

(TONY *doesn't answer, just leaves office.* ANNE *starts after him.*)

PAT: He's best left alone.

ANNE: I really don't think you should have hit him.

PAT: Probably did him some good.

ANNE: Or enhanced his desire to leave?

PAT: Yes, there is that. I don't feel he is ready to leave. He
needs more time, I'll see he gets it.

ANNE: Surely that's for the Courts to decide.

PAT: Yes, if it gets that far.

ANNE: I'll see it does. He's obviously unhappy here.

PAT: Obviously!

ANNE: Just when I thought he was settling in here.

The court.

BLUE: They went on about the friends Tony had made. Your
name was mentioned, Marcus, and yours, Shirley. After
that she left. Didn't say goodbye to Tony. Couldn't find
him.

WAYNE: Was that all?

BLUE: Yeah. It was that night he ran off with Dray.

STALLION: It was the night of the fire as well.

MARCUS: But when Tony left, was he upset?

BLUE: He looked as though he was about to cry. He didn't
though.

MARCUS: Are you sure he wasn't angry?

BLUE: Yes. I made a joke about something, but he just walked
by as if I wasn't there.

MARCUS: You can step down, Blue.

STALLION: (*To* TONY) You let her land one on you and did
nothing?

CHILD I: He probably would have hit her back.

TONY: Oh, you would've hit her back, I suppose?

STALLION: I couldn't just stand there. I wouldn't let nobody slap me like that. It's out of order.

CHILD 1: Remember Lena?

CHILD 2: Yeah, but does Stallion?

MARCUS: What do you suggest he should've done?

SPIKE: He shouldn't've just stood there, that's out of order!

TONY: It was over before it had begun. There wasn't time to do anything.

CHILD 1: It was old Stallion's first day as well.

CHILD 2: First day in the Lodge and Lena made him sit on her bed and watch her undress.

STALLION: What?

CHILD 2: Oh, nothing. We were just saying.

STALLION: You didn't even kick up a fuss. Once she's seen she can do it once, she'll be landing them on you left, right and centre.

TONY: You really believe that, don't you?

CHILD 1: He kept turning away from her. But Lena kept moving around the room.

SHIRLEY: Of course, hitting people is what Stallion knows most about.

STALLION: Wondered when you'd start up. You're like his guardian angel.

CHILD 1: In the end, Stallion just sat and watched her.

CHILD 2: So she beat him up for peeping at her while she was changing.

STALLION: Cupid's dart well and truly got you.

SHIRLEY: Are you jealous or worried?

CHILD 1: And if that wasn't enough, Lena told him not to come downstairs until he was smiling.

STALLION: I'm worried old Cupid's probably got his sights on Tony next.

CHILD 2: You should've seen his face trying to stop crying by forcing a smile.

SHIRLEY: That's not funny in the slightest.

CHILD 1: That's what Stallion said when we took the mickey out of him.

STALLION: Course it's not funny, it's sad. Poor Tony falling for a semi-delinquent.

TONY: Come on then, Stallion. What makes you think Shirley is a delinquent? We're all busting to hear.

STALLION: Well, just between you and me, I reckon that she's a bit loopy. I mean, Dray couldn't have taken all the insanity in their family.

SHIRLEY: I'd tell you that the only thing wrong with Dray is that he can't speak. But there isn't enough scope in that for picking fun. So you carry on imagining there's something else wrong with him.

STALLION: Or you imagine there isn't!

SHIRLEY: That isn't funny.

STALLION: What's this repetition and you usually being so sharp?

SCOT: Here he is, appearing for one day only, that legend in his own lunch-time, Scot Bradley!

(*All silently look at* SCOT *and then carry on.*)

Hello, Scot, how are you? Oh, I'm fine, how about you? Oh, I am sorry to hear about that.

SHIRLEY: What are you doing down here again? You spend more time in here now than you did before you left.

SCOT: It's nice to see you, too, Shirley.

TONY: How are you, Scot? Long time no see.

SCOT: That too is funny.

STALLION: What's happened to this trial? Come on, Wayne.

SCOT: Oh, you're having a trial. Can I play?

STALLION: When did you say you were leaving, Scot?

SCOT: I heard you had a fire here a couple of days ago.

SHIRLEY: What do you think all this trial palaver is about?

SCOT: "Palaver"? The wonders of speech therapy. You know, Norman, not so long ago she would have said "trial shit is about".

NORMAN: You're quite mad, you know?

SCOT: Yes, but I'm keeping it from myself. Was it a big fire?

SPIKE: Yeah, if I hadn't told Pat we might all be dead.

SCOT: Burnt to a crisp on your National Health mattresses. So it wasn't that big then?

SHIRLEY: No, but the gym's out for a few weeks.

SCOT: Who did it?

SHIRLEY: They're trying to blame Tony.

SCOT: Why?

TONY: Because me and Dray ran off the same night.

SCOT: So?

STALLION: What do you mean, so?

SCOT: So, the even-if what-then use of so.

SPIKE: Most of us know Tony did it.

SHIRLEY: I wouldn't say most.

SPIKE: You might believe all that crap about not wanting to
live in care. But I reckon he ran away pure and simply
because he started the fire. And I saw him running off.

MARCUS: How did you know it was him?

SPIKE: It had to be him, who else was out at that time?

MARCUS: What about Dray? Did you see him go as well?

SPIKE: No, but he could have left with him.

MARCUS: Why do you think Tony took Dray with him?

SPIKE: I don't know. Why not? They're always together.
They can't stand being apart.

TONY: What's that supposed to mean?

SPIKE: Come on, you two are always together.

STALLION: What's the matter, frightened people might start
talking?

TONY: Just explain what you meant, Spike.

SHIRLEY: It was probably something Stallion had said. Spike
just repeated it in a convenient place.

STALLION: Maybe it was. Yeah, as a matter of fact it was.

SPIKE: (*To* SHIRLEY) That's funny, coming from someone
who's loopy.

TONY: (*To* STALLION) OK, then, what did you mean by it?

SHIRLEY: (*To* SPIKE) I'd keep quiet, Spike, if I were you.

STALLION: I probably only meant that maybe you're having a
sexuality problem.

SPIKE: But you're not me and there's no history of insanity in
my family.

TONY: (*To* STALLION) You get worse, Stallion. Your petty

comments used to annoy me, now they just make me laugh.

SHIRLEY: (*Lashing out at* SPIKE) You should know now when not to repeat after Stallion.

SCOT: (*Grabbing* SHIRLEY) Please, children, take a hold of yourselves.

NORMAN: I think it's time we got back to the trial.

SCOT: Now's as good a time as any.

NORMAN: Wayne, next witness.

WAYNE: Prosecution calls Spike.

NORMAN: Have you been asleep for the past few minutes? We've had his entire testimony.

WAYNE: I thought there was more.

NORMAN: How much more do you want?

(*Enter* GEORGE.)

GEORGE: May, telephone, in the office.

CHILD I: (*Getting up to leave*) Who is it?

GEORGE: Your social worker, I think. Shirley, you haven't forgotten to lay the tables, have you?

SHIRLEY: No, just call me when you're ready.

GEORGE: (*Looking around*) Why so quiet?

STALLION: No reason.

SPIKE: When will we be allowed back in the gym?

GEORGE: About three weeks, as you were told. What have you all been doing, then?

STALLION: Oh, nothing much.

SCOT: Now, come on, Stallion, you know that's not true. We're all waiting for George to leave so we can carry on with the trial.

STALLION: Well done, rent-a-mouth.

SCOT: George, you weren't listening in on my conversation with Stallion, were you? Shame on you.

GEORGE: And who, pray tell, is on trial?

TONY: I am, for the fire.

GEORGE: Pat explained that neither Tony or Dray were to be held responsible.

TONY: Well, they don't believe it.

GEORGE: You can't put him on trial over an accident.

NORMAN: Was it an accident, though?

GEORGE: Norman, I credited you with a little more sense.

NORMAN: I was press-ganged into it. Couldn't you take the stand and explain why no connection was made?

MARCUS: He's not a prosecution witness, surely.

NORMAN: Yes, but he's here now and may not be later. Both of you can question him, therefore.

WAYNE: OK. What steps were taken to see if there was any connection between the fire and Tony's disappearance?

GEORGE: You know I can't tell you everything. Pat told you as much as you need to know.

NORMAN: Please tell us as much as you can.

GEORGE: Sure, Norman. I mean your honour!

STALLION: This is pointless. He's just taking the piss . . . I mean, mickey.

GEORGE: I'm trying to be serious, but I can't believe at your ages you're still playing let's pretend.

STALLION: I would've thought it was the fairest way.

GEORGE: No offence, Stallion, but I wouldn't have thought the word "fair" was in your vocabulary.

STALLION: Oh, I forgot – what is it, I'm a mindless moron who makes people scared of me as a kind of ego-trip – was that right, George?

GEORGE: As you say, Stallion. But come on. Court, at your ages. Could you not find anything else to fill your time?

SHIRLEY: Like visiting a museum, you mean?

GEORGE: Something like that. I mean, the idea of child care . . .

(*General mumbles and moans.*)

. . . is to put you lot on an equal par with those who had a normal home life.

STALLION: Can't you hold a conversation without slotting in the pros and cons of the Welfare State?

GEORGE: Stallion, do you see this as your home or some kind of stop-off point in your life?

STALLION: I live here, don't I? I can't see what difference it makes.

GEORGE: (*To the group*) You treat it like a youth club.

SHIRLEY: How would you like us to treat it?

GEORGE: Like your home!

MARCUS: Oh, shut up. I'm sorry, but how can you expect us to treat the Lodge that way? What do you want us to do? Call you lot mum and dad? Most of us can't handle aunty and uncle. We can call each other brother or sister – it might be a breakthrough for the multi-racial society, but isn't it a little far-fetched?

GEORGE: What I meant was, identifying with the Lodge.

MARCUS: How long have you been here, George?

GEORGE: Two years!

MARCUS: Marge has been here five, David four, Michael about one year and Sue for only six months. And all of them came from other homes and will probably move on to another place.

GEORGE: I was thinking of doing probation but . . .

MARCUS: How can you expect us to identify with the Lodge when it's forever changing? Come back a few years from now and you won't know a soul.

SPIKE: Except Pat. She won't leave. They'll have to kick her out.

GEORGE: Point taken, Marcus. But surely you can make some effort?

SCOT: Leave it out. You keep saying "We can do this" and "You should do this." It ain't down to us.

MARCUS: We don't have a "home" model. We take the table tennis and gym and the mixed group and the only comparison we have is a youth club.

GEORGE: That's amazing – that idea is spot on. Well, I'm glad you've learnt something and understand your situation. And still you do nothing about it?

STALLION: (*Laughs.*) You're not stupid, George – but Christ knows how many kids are in care and . . .

NORMAN: A hundred and twenty thousand – 1979 figures.

STALLION: (*Staring at* NORMAN) Yeah, right – and with

120,000 in care the problem is with the "system".

SHIRLEY: I read somewhere that kids' homes were supposed
to be a temporary substitution for home life. Sounds a bit
stupid when you think most of us have been in one home
or another for most of our lives.

SCOT: Pat says we're living in a second society because the first
one couldn't cater for us. If you ask me, this one's having
catering problems.

GEORGE: Granted it isn't perfect. But Lord only knows how
much was spent last year on . . .

NORMAN: Over £150 million in England and Wales. This is all
very interesting but now is hardly the time to discuss the
drawbacks of child care.

TONY: God, but you're callous, Norman.

NORMAN: Quite! George, were any connections made between
the fire and the disappearance?

GEORGE: As I said, I'm not really at liberty to say. But – the
fire could have been started by anything from a cigarette
end to that useless electric heater in there.

WAYNE: Could Tony have dropped the cigarette?

GEORGE: It's only a possibility. And anyhow he doesn't
smoke.

MARCUS: So you don't think he dropped it?

GEORGE: If that's how the fire was started, it would be a little
pointless.

WAYNE: Why? He could have wanted to shift the blame.

GEORGE: Hardly, because by running away blame would go
straight back to him.

(MARGE *comes in.*)

MARGE: George, May needs to make an appointment with her
social worker. Could you sort out times?

GEORGE: Yeah, sure. (*Leaving*) We should set something up
where we can talk more about what you brought up.

(*General mutters of mixed opinion.*)

MARGE: You lot are very quiet today. Hope you have not done
anything. Hall looks in order. Dinner will be soon and it's
boys' turn to wipe up. Don't let me have to chase you up

about it please.

(*She leaves.*)

SPIKE: Yes, Marge, no, Marge, go sit on a drill, Marge.

MARGE: (*Poking head in*) Power or hand drill, Spike?

SPIKE: (*Embarrassed*) Nothing – I – was – it was nothing, honest.

SHIRLEY: Unlucky, Spike. (*To* TONY) Are you going to talk with George about "the points we brought up"?

TONY: Yeah, I reckon it's a good idea to get us to think about our situation.

STALLION: "Our situation"? I thought you wanted to leave. Child care wasn't your scene.

TONY: Give it a rest, eh?

(WAYNE *and* NORMAN *whisper to each other.*)

What are you two up to?

SCOT: Three. (*Laughs.*) Get it? What are you up to? Three.

STALLION: That isn't funny.

NORMAN: We've decided the next witness should be Dray.

SHIRLEY and STALLION: No!

SHIRLEY: (*Continuing*) You'll only get at him.

STALLION: (*Hurriedly*) Anyway, what can he tell you?

WAYNE: I think Dray saw Tony start the fire and that's why Tony took him along.

SHIRLEY: I don't care, he isn't going up there.

STALLION: You have to – er – consider his – er – capability. I mean, we all know he's a little lacking!

SHIRLEY: You see? He's started at him already.

MARCUS: Shirley's right. It's hardly worth the bother.

NORMAN: I think he is an important witness.

SHIRLEY: No, and that's final!

SCOT: So says you.

SHIRLEY: What's that supposed to mean?

SCOT: Look, everyone has their little part to play in our quaint court, except Dray. We get to play judge, jury, take the stand – bring it back!

(*No one laughs.*)

But not Dray. He was even excluded as a possible villain.

And why? Because big sis says so. His self-appointed
guardian angel decides against it so he doesn't get to play.
You won't always be there to protect him, Shirley. He has
to learn to fend for himself. Let him stand on his own two
feet.

SHIRLEY: No!

SCOT: Couldn't you have waited a little? The rest of the gang
might have wanted to applaud or something. You killed a
worthy speech with a one-syllable word.

SHIRLEY: I'm serious.

SCOT: So am I.

STALLION: How is he going to communicate?

NORMAN: As he always does, through Shirley. Dray, if you
would . . .

SHIRLEY: No, I said, and I meant it.

SCOT: Do you let him go toilet on his own yet?
(DRAY *takes the stand.*)

WAYNE: Dray, do you mind being up here?
(DRAY *shakes his head.*)

STALLION: Is it going to be nods and shakes all the way
through? (*Through a laugh*) It's like the trial of a Martian.

SPIKE: Might as well be one for all we'll get out of him.

SHIRLEY: Don't waste any time, will ya? Just keep digging at
him – get your satisfaction from it, do you?
(STALLION *gives her a shallow smile.*)
Well, sorry to spoil your fun but Dray's had enough.

MARCUS: No, wait. Dray, did you see who started the fire?
(DRAY *keeps his eyes fixed on the floor.*)

STALLION: (*Pause*) Well, answer the question, Dray. Cat got
your tongue?

TONY: All right, Stallion, a joke's a joke . . .

STALLION: I don't know I take Dray very seriously. (*To*
DRAY) Well, let's see the sign language this lot marvel at
and Shirley pretends to understand.
(DRAY *fixes on* STALLION.)

SHIRLEY: You bastard. I'm warning you.

STALLION: Of what? I'm doing nothing wrong, am I? (*Taking*

DRAY's *wrists and trying to move them*) Come on, Harpo,
  tell us your all. (*Standing back*) Teach me how to do them
  signs. How would you say "pillock" or "berk"? (*Laughs*)

SHIRLEY: (*Shouting*) Stop it, for Christ's sake.

STALLION: Or yours, whichever we best identify with.

  (DRAY *holds back his head to stop the tears.*)

SCOT: Christ, do something, Dray!

STALLION: Be fair, Scot, what's he to do? Hit me?

SHIRLEY: Shut you up if he did?

STALLION: Do me a favour, a decent fight from anyone round
  here would be a turn up for the books. How about it,
  Dray? You must want to. Go on, lay one on me. Give it
  your best shot. Well, come on, you mightn't get another
  chance.

  (DRAY *lifts hand as if to protect himself.*)

  Not to worry, you're safe for now.

SHIRLEY: (*Moving towards* DRAY) Don't listen to him, he ain't
  worth it.

  (DRAY *starts to cry.*)

MARCUS: (*Almost embarrassed to carry on*) Who started the fire,
  Dray?

TONY: Do you know, Dray?

SHIRLEY: Tell me, Dray, who? Do you know?

  (DRAY *starts to nod his head maniacally, now crying hard.*)

  No, don't, we didn't mean it. It doesn't matter.

STALLION: Look out, he's throwing a fit. Hope it wasn't
  anything I said!

SHIRLEY: He's probably too scared to say anything anyways.

STALLION: I didn't think he had anything to say.

SHIRLEY: Keep the game running smoothly, won't you? You
  don't give a fuck about anyone bar yourself. Not an ounce
  of feeling in you.

STALLION: Yeah, but you're full of it. Lapping it up no
  matter who it comes from. Even if you have to steal it on
  route to Dray.

TONY: Leave it, you'll work yourself up for nothing.

SHIRLEY: I said to stop it, didn't I? Are you still bloody

enjoying it?

(*No answer from* TONY. MARGE *comes in.*)

MARGE: Lunch is ready now. Shirley, it was your turn for the tables.

SHIRLEY: Yeah, I know, but . . .

MARGE: Well, May's done it now. So you'll have to help serve up. Come along.

SHIRLEY: OK. In a minute.

MARGE: No, child, now. If you could all move now, it would be helpful.

(*General moans as they leave.*)

SPIKE: What's on the recipe today, then?

MARGE: Pat made her special meatballs as she knew you'd be in for lunch.

SPIKE: Just for little old me, well, Lordy be!

MARGE: (*Smiles.*) Um, Dray, do you intend to eat today? Or will you stand there until you take root?

(DRAY *shakes his head, gradually moving towards a maniacal state, still crying. Lights pick up his face and slowly fade to blackout.*)

ACT II

Lights pick up corner of stage. A BOY *sitting at a table, his* MOTHER *standing over him.*

SON: I'm not out that much.

MOTHER: I don't know why you don't just move out completely. It was unheard of in my day for a 15-year-old to be out all hours of the night.

SON: Isn't it a little early for you to start on at me?

MOTHER: Look at you. Have you been to school? I don't think you have. You didn't go to school with your hair in that state?

SON: No, Mum.

MOTHER: Are you getting a hair cut? And your neck. My mother wouldn've beat the high heavens out of me if I had a neck like that.

SON: Yes, Mum.

MOTHER: No doubt you've been getting into trouble with that boy of Mrs White's – he's twice your age.

SON: Yeah, right.

MOTHER: Beats me why he doesn't get a job, grown boy like that.

SON: Right, I'm off.

(*He stands up from the table.*)

MOTHER: You've only just got in.

SON: Got things to do, ain't I?

MOTHER: You'll come to no good. Carry on the way you are and it's down the welfare for you, my lad . . .

SON: Yeah, right, Mum, see you later.

MOTHER: See if they can't do something for you in one of those council homes. And wash your neck before you leave.

(*Lights fade.*)

Trial and Error

Lights up on the opposite corner of the stage. SCHOOL CHILDREN *walking home.*

CHILD 1: That new kid in school lives in a home.

CHILD 2: The one on Hanson Estate?

CHILD 1: Yeah.

CHILD 2: There's been a lot of trouble since they set up that home there.

CHILD 3: You mean the home's been blamed for a lot of the trouble.

CHILD 2: Come off it. You got to admit it got worse since they moved in.

CHILD 3: No, I ain't. One of my mates lives in the Hanson and he says the idea was to set up homes in community areas and not stick 'em out in the country somewhere.

CHILD 1: They'd do less damage in the country.

CHILD 2: Does your mate like it in the home?

CHILD 3: I think so, he hasn't complained.

CHILD 2: I'd quite like to live in one of those places for a while. I'd do anything to get away from my lot right now.

CHILD 1: I heard they got a full-size pool table and table tennis. That one at Hanson Estate is mixed, ain't it? (*Child 3 nods.*)
What could be better?

CHILD 2: I heard they've got to be in bed by 9 o'clock, but most of them have got TVs in their rooms.

CHILD 3: Where d'you hear all that?

CHILD 1: That new kid told us.

CHILD 3: Well, he's winding you up.

CHILD 2: Oh you'd know, would you?

CHILD 3: Yeah, as it happens I do. I told ya, my mate lives in one.

CHILD 1: Well, how d'you get to live in one?

CHILD 3: (*Pause*) You get sent!
(*Lights fade.*)

Lights up on centre stage. A TEACHER *is talking to a* PUPIL *who lives in a home.*

267

TEACHER: Not to worry, Julie, you're not in trouble.

JULIE: Why did you keep me behind then, Miss?

TEACHER: Well, actually – I – you know. Last night was parents' night and – well, I – it's stupid really, but . . .

JULIE: Somebody did come, didn't they?

TEACHER: Yes, of course. It just – I didn't know you were in care. You never told me, Julie.

JULIE: What's to tell? It's the one over the back of the cemetery.

TEACHER: You must be very lonely.

JULIE: With fifteen other kids, hardly.

TEACHER: What I meant was – I didn't mean to – it's just, you have no family?

JULIE: I got David and Janice. They're my brother and sister.

TEACHER: And do – David and Janice live at the home?

JULIE: No, David's left. He lives with his girlfriend. And Janice is in Wales.

TEACHER: Wales?

JULIE: Yeah, she didn't want to stay around here.

TEACHER: How sad – I mean I – well, do you see her?

JULIE: Yeah, at Christmas and school holidays.

TEACHER: I was wondering if you would like to maybe go out somewhere?

JULIE: Like a museum, you mean?

TEACHER: Well, actually, I was thinking of a play or maybe ice skating, but if you want to . . .

JULIE: No. No, that sounds fine. Can I give you an answer tomorrow?

TEACHER: Yes, that will be OK.

(*Lights fade.*)

Lights up. the kids of the Lodge are in the main hall with
GEORGE.

GEORGE: There, we've read three scenes from this book by Martin Jacobs. Any comments?

STALLION: Where's this leading to? You don't want us to act out those scenes, do you?

SPIKE: Remember that disastrous play he got us to do for the old people's homes?

MARCUS: You forgot your lines, didn't you, Norman? You came running on full of energy, took one look at the audience and said Mary's lines.

NORMAN: I was wrongly cast as the Angel Gabriel.

GEORGE: I'm sure you were, Norman, and I'm sorry, but a nativity play is not the point at hand.

SHIRLEY: We read the scenes from this book. What else is there?

GEORGE: (*To* SHIRLEY) Have you never experienced any of these situations?

SHIRLEY: I had a couple of teachers and a Brownie leader feeling sorry for me, but hasn't everyone?

GEORGE: Were they feeling sorry for you or was it just lack of understanding?

TONY: Understanding of what?

GEORGE: Child care. Maybe they thought of the home as a scene from *Oliver*.

SHIRLEY: The Brownie leader definitely did.

GEORGE: How did you react towards them?

SHIRLEY: At first I was very polite and even went to the zoo with one of the teachers. Then it started to annoy me so I told them care was great and I didn't need any pity.

GEORGE: Is that what you really feel?

SHIRLEY: Sometimes. I enjoy it even at times.

TONY: Yeah, it's a bundle of laughs.

STALLION: Well, we know your views on the matter. Care "doesn't agree with you", poor child!

NORMAN: Agrees with you, though, Stallion. Carved out quite a notch for yourself.

STALLION: I make the best of it!

NORMAN: That you do, Stallion.

GEORGE: Don't we all, though? Surely you "make the best of it"?

NORMAN: In a way, yes, I suppose I do. It's suitable for me at present. Later, I'll probably shun care.

GEORGE: Why?

NORMAN: Stigma!

SCOT: (*In manner of chatty housewife*) No, wouldn't do to have people knowing, would it?

STALLION: Especially in the circles he'll revolve in.

SCOT: Not so much revolve as quietly spin!

NORMAN: Sharp, Scot, very unlike you.

SPIKE: I'm glad I'm in care!

SCOT: Oh, are you, and pray tell us why.

SPIKE: I'm a lot better off than I would've been at home.

SCOT: How d'you know? You were only at home for three years.

SPIKE: I had my dad knock me and my mum about. I reckon I've got a fair idea.

SHIRLEY: Wondered where you got your charm from.

SPIKE: Aren't we the funny one?

GEORGE: When you two have finished, we'll continue.

STALLION: What for? We've been through it before. I want to get this trial thing finished with.

GEORGE: Oh, right, mustn't forget the court! Well, maybe, if you can draw yourselves away from persecuting Tony, we'll carry on at a later date.

STALLION: If you like.

GEORGE: Look, I've got a couple of copies of this "Why Care?" booklet. It's young kids in care speaking out. Anyone like to read one?

NORMAN: I'll have a swot through it.

GEORGE: No one else?

TONY: Yeah, I will. When do you want them back?

GEORGE: (*Leaving*) There's no hurry. Say a couple of days.

(*Kids run around resetting courtroom.*)

MARCUS: Are you lot ready to start?

NORMAN: Yes, right – er – Wayne, any further questions?

WAYNE: No, I feel I've produced enough evidence, at present, to justify my belief in Tony's guilt.

NORMAN: Then, Marcus, the defence counsel may begin.

MARCUS: Firstly, I'd like to call Scot to the stand.

STALLION: You're joking!

MARCUS: Why? He will act as a character witness.

STALLION: He'll act the fool, more like.

SHIRLEY: He knows Tony no better than we do.

BLUE: Yeah, but he's neutral. (*Slightly embarrassed*) What I meant was, he's not living here – but – er – still knows Tony . . . that's all.

MARCUS: Blue's right. He isn't affected by the fire and can therefore offer an objective testimony.

NORMAN: Must we have this constant arguing before every witness?

STALLION: What happens when he starts putting on his one-man show?

SCOT: Well, I'll bow at the end and you can applaud.

MARCUS: Take the stand, Scot.

STALLION: And no mucking about.

SCOT: OK, Stallion, I'll speak in plain English and if you can't understand I'll shout.

MARCUS: How long have you known Tony, Scot?

SCOT: As long as he's been here, about two and a half years.

MARCUS: Were you good friends?

SCOT: We got on. He's a very difficult person to get to know.

MARCUS: How do you mean?

SCOT: Well, he seemed reluctant to make friends in the Lodge, as if he had erected some barrier.

MARCUS: Wasn't he this way with everyone?

SCOT: No, he made friends easily outside of the Lodge. It's strange, but I found it harder to make friends outside of the Lodge.

NORMAN: I find that hard to believe.

SCOT: Believe it or not, inside we've got this ready-made environment. When I left, I had problems adjusting to being fostered and being outside.

MARCUS: Why do you think this was?

SCOT: I think it's to do with Tony not wanting to be in care. He's almost frightened of it.

STALLION: What's there to be frightened of?

SCOT: That's my point. We don't see as there is anything to be scared of.

STALLION: Are you muck-arsing around, Scot?

SCOT: Can I explain? When we come into care there's a lot of changes to home life.

BLUE: Some of us don't remember home life.

SCOT: We have to adapt to these changes: loss of emotional bonds, the constantly changing people, things like that. I was in three other homes before coming to the Lodge.

SPIKE: I'd been in four.

SCOT: You've got one up on me, but how many social workers have you had?

SPIKE: Only two.

SCOT: Unlucky. I've had five, not counting the welfare officer.

STALLION: Great, so you're leading in the battle for the most social workers, but what does it show?

SCOT: All these things don't bother us any more. Most of us have accepted them as normal.

NORMAN: You mean we're institutionalized?

SCOT: That's the word, I couldn't remember it.

NORMAN: It means we've taken on the characteristics of this institution, the Lodge. We've fully adapted.

SCOT: And we find it difficult to relate outside of it.

SHIRLEY: Rubbish.

(*Pause.*)

SCOT: Is that it? No more? Oh, I see, it's word association. OK, dustbin.

NORMAN: Scot, please.

SHIRLEY: Just because you found it difficult doesn't mean we will.

SCOT: OK then, how many of you lot belong to any outside clubs?

SHIRLEY: What's the point? We've got everything here.

SCOT: Exactly. We've got the games, machines, the gym, gals. Everything is provided right here.

MARCUS: Carry on, Scot.

SCOT: Remember when we went to that holiday camp? We

kept to ourselves for the first week and then when we did
make friends it was with kids who were in another home.

STALLION: Is that why you're always down here, Scot? Scared
to face the outside world?

SCOT: Maybe. Much the same reason why you're reluctant to
leave.

MARCUS: Any more?

SCOT: Pardon? Oh, yeah, in this present environment we've
even taken on a new language.

SPIKE: Now you are talking rubbish.

SCOT: You reckon? We talk about being "inside" or
"outside". Blue, go and get us a pen from Pat's office.

BLUE: It's out of bounds, you know that.

SCOT: And if you're caught you'll have "loss of privileges".
Hey, May, how about coming to the pictures with me on
Saturday?

CHILD I: You'll be lucky. Anyway, I'm on home leave.

SCOT: "Out of bounds", "home leave", "visiting rights",
"loss of privileges", "subject to Section 2", and so the list
goes on, all part of this institution's vocabulary.

MARCUS: So what you're basically saying is Tony isn't
institutionalized and is also aware of it. But does that
explain why he didn't start the fire?

SCOT: Yes, I think it does. You don't do something that will
effectively mean you'll spend more time in a place you
don't want to be. Anyway, no offence, Tony, but he's so
busy looking after number one and absorbed in himself
that he wouldn't burn down the gym.

WAYNE: Could it be, in your expert opinion, that Tony hated
the Lodge and the fire was an expression of this hate?

SCOT: Maybe, but he doesn't exactly hate the Lodge. He
doesn't want to live here is all.

STALLION: (*To* SCOT *and* MARCUS) You two must have
worked hard on that little explanation.

MARCUS: How d'you mean, Stallion?

STALLION: You can tell me. It won't go further than these
four walls. It was a load of bull, wasn't it?

MARCUS: It was all facts, Stallion.

SCOT: If you could read, we'd give you the book to read up on it.

STALLION: And what does that mean?

SCOT: Poor child can't understand English, either.

NORMAN: You'd better stand down now, Scot.

SPIKE: Yeah, that last remark was below the belt.

SCOT: Yeah, well, Stallion looks like something below the belt, doesn't he?

STALLION: (*Moving towards* SCOT) What was that?

SCOT: Hearing difficulties as well? My dear boy, you really are plagued with afflictions.

SHIRLEY: Leave him alone, Stallion.

SCOT: That's right, leave me a loan. Make it two quid.

STALLION: (*Hitting* SCOT *in the stomach*) Ha bloody ha!

SCOT: (*Curling up in pain*) You bastard!

STALLION: (*Bending down to* SCOT) You're not crying, are you?

SCOT: No, I'm not crying. I can't draw the breath to cry, you pig-headed fool . . .

(STALLION *hits* SCOT *once more.*)

Don't hit me again, Stallion, please. The first time did the job. I'm sorry I opened my mouth. (*To the other kids*) Do one of you want to stop him? You must know the procedure by now. Hail words like "Don't, Stallion" or "You've done enough, Stallion."

STALLION: Maybe they're so institutionalized they see this as normal!

(*He leaves.*)

SCOT: How right you are.

NORMAN: Should we – er – continue with the trial?

SCOT: Oh, that's a new approach. Pretend I'm not here. Carry on "business as usual"!

NORMAN: With all due respect, you were warned.

SCOT: So, Stallion is now something to be warned against, avoided like the plague.

NORMAN: Something like that.

Trial and Error

(SPIKE *starts to leave the hall*.)

NORMAN: Where are you going, Spike?

SPIKE: Oh, nowhere, I'm just going to see something.

SHIRLEY: Where the master goes so he shall follow!

SPIKE: Go play with a whisk, Shirley.

(*He leaves the hall*.)

NORMAN: Charming, I'm sure. Are you OK, Scot?

SCOT: Me? I'm just fine, never felt better!

CHILD 1: If you ask me, he deserved it. He's always talking rubbish.

CHILD 2: If you think about it, what he was saying was true.

CHILD 3: What makes you say that?

CHILD 2: Who took those "Why Care?" booklet things of George's?

CHILD 1: Tony and Norman. But Norman's forever reading.

CHILD 2: And what about Tony? He isn't so keen on reading but he took it.

CHILD 3: And you think it's because he wants to know more about his situation?

CHILD 2: Yes.

CHILD 3: Rubbish!

CHILD 4: (*To* BLUE) What's the time?

BLUE: I don't know, about two, I suppose.

CHILD 4: Can't see the point in carrying on.

BLUE: We don't know if he did it or not yet.

CHILD 4: Do me a favour. You said you saw him upset after the barney with his social worker and Pat, and Spike said he saw him running away from the fire. That's pretty decisive, don't you think?

BLUE: Might just be one of Spike's tall stories.

CHILD 4: Maybe he's got a mental problem with fire.

BLUE: If you're going to be stupid . . .

CHILD 4: No, straight up. The way I heard it, it was after a barney with his mother that he put the match to her flat.

SHIRLEY: (*To* TONY) I said it would go too far, didn't I?

TONY: OK, no need to gloat about it. All the same, you can't say it wasn't eventful.

275

SHIRLEY: Stallion's worked his way through Dray and Scot. I wonder who's next on the list.

TONY: I meant apart from Stallion.

SHIRLEY: Oh, apart from the spots and the scratching, chicken-pox is all right.

TONY: What?

SHIRLEY: Nothing, I was just saying.

TONY: Only one complaint so far. That's you going up there and telling everyone about us.

SHIRLEY: I knew all you were worried about was what they'd say.

TONY: It isn't that. You still don't understand.

STALLION: (*Re-entering*) Still having those stomach pains, Scot?

SCOT: My, but that was funny!

STALLION: Not half as funny as the sight of you curled up on the floor begging for mercy.

NORMAN: (*Pause, hesitantly*) I think we should carry on now.

SCOT: Yet again you save the day, Norm.

MARCUS: Tony, will you take the stand?

TONY: (*To* SHIRLEY, *while moving away*) You don't understand, but I'll explain it later.
(*He takes the stand.*)

MARCUS: (*To* TONY) Please explain what happened the night of the fire. Starting from . . . (*looks at notes*) . . . the argument with Anne and Pat.

TONY: It wasn't exactly an argument, more like a heated discussion. I had got the idea from Shirley that leaving would be easy. When they started bombarding me with opposition I was disappointed and upset.

MARCUS: Not angry?

TONY: No. A lot of what they were saying I would've accepted under normal circumstances. I just wasn't in an understanding mood.

MARCUS: Was it just the disappointment which caused your mood?

TONY: I didn't think it was fair for a judge who didn't know

276

me, but from a file, to decide my life.

MARCUS: Did you leave straight after leaving the office?

TONY: No, I went down to the old air-raid shelter. It's somewhere to cool off.

STALLION: Is that where you take Shirley for some privacy?

MARCUS: (*Annoyed at the interruption*) You obviously didn't cool off.

TONY: Not really. I had a lot of thinking to do. I came out of the shelter around eleven and went to my room. Marge shouted something at me but I wasn't listening.

MARCUS: How long did you stay in your room?

TONY: About ten, twenty minutes. I was just pottering around trying not to wake Dray up.

MARCUS: Talk us through exactly how you left.

TONY: Out the back via the kitchen, then out past the gym and over the back wall.

MARCUS: Taking Dray with you?

TONY: What makes you say that? I didn't take him, he followed me.

MARCUS: But you made no attempt to send him back?

TONY: I did, but I was down by the cemetery before I noticed him.

STALLION: You could've still made him come back.

SCOT: You're right, Stallion, he could have beat him over the head with a blunt instrument, say a trombone . . . and then dragged him back into the Lodge for Pat to find.

STALLION: Pardon?

SCOT: Nothing.

TONY: Dray can be very stubborn when he wants to be.

MARCUS: Where did you go, Tony?

TONY: Is that important?

MARCUS: It might be.

TONY: I went to the flat.

MARCUS: Sam's flat, even after you were told you couldn't go home?

TONY: I went to see a friend, Mrs Wilmott.

MARCUS: Wasn't that the lady who brought you to the Lodge

277

on your first day?

TONY: Yeah, she's the resident landlady at Sam's.

MARCUS: Why did you want to see her?

TONY: She's a friend. She chats a lot and some might see her as interfering, but she gives good advice. Whether she knows she does, I don't know.

MARCUS: Did you get to see her?

TONY: In a way, not exactly how I wanted to.

(*Lights dim on the court.*)

Lights dim on court and spot picks up MRS WILMOTT *walking on to the stage. She is standing as if in a doorway and speaking as to* TONY *and* DRAY.

MRS WILMOTT: Tony, is that you? My, haven't you grown? And, Dray, what a nice surprise. Isn't it a little late for you two to be away from the Lodge? Still, I expect there's good reason. Just the other day I was saying to . . . Mrs Lockwood, I think, how long it was since I had seen you. Not that I didn't want to, mind you, but I have been so busy of late. Well, now, I can't get over how you've grown. Did your mother not answer the bell? I swear she's getting as bad as my old man. Still, I'll call her for you, I think she's in. (*Takes step backwards as if into passageway and shouts:*) Samantha, your boy's here. Tony's come to see you.

SAM: (*From upstairs*) Sorry, Mrs Wilmott, who's there?

MRS WILMOTT: Your boy, Tony.

SAM: At this time of night? Is he with the Lodge people?

MRS WILMOTT: No, just himself and Dray. (*To* TONY) Hope nothing is the matter, T. You getting on OK at the Lodge place, are you? I always said it was the best thing that ever happened to you. You be sure and make the most of it. Mark my words, it's the best thing that ever happened to you. Nothing's wrong, kid?

SAM: Mrs Wilmott, can you deal with him, I'm busy at present.

MRS WILMOTT: (*To* SAM) He's obviously come to see you.

SAM: Not now, Mrs Wilmott.

MRS WILMOTT: You're always too busy, that's your problem, never had any time for your own flesh and blood. (*To* TONY:) Nothing's changed, or will it, if you ask me. (*To* SAM) You hurry up and get down here. He hasn't come all this way to be told you're busy, now then.

SAM: Doreen, please. I can't, not now. I haven't the time.

MRS WILMOTT: What time does it take to come see him? God, woman, it's your son.

SAM: Can he not come back tomorrow?

TONY: Doreen was right, nothing had changed. I couldn't stay there so I just walked away, Dray in tow. Doreen called after me . . .

MRS WILMOTT: (*Turning as to face* TONY) Listen, Tony, I'll . . . Tony, wait, please . . .

TONY: But it wasn't worth it, I couldn't handle going back.

MRS WILMOTT: (*Walking off stage as if into house*) Could you not have come to the stairs, at least? You never cease to amaze me. Your own son.

SAM: Sorry, Mrs Wilmott, what were you saying? You'll have to speak up.

(*Lights fade out on* MRS WILMOTT.)

Lights up on court.

MARCUS: (*To* TONY) Did you come straight back to the Lodge?

TONY: I started feeling responsible for Dray. He was worried about something, didn't know what.

MARCUS: Finally, Tony, did you start the fire in the gym?

TONY: No, I had nothing to do with the fire.

MARCUS: No further questions.

WAYNE: You said you were worried about Dray. In what way?

TONY: He seemed preoccupied. He had something on his mind. As I said, I don't know what.

WAYNE: Did you start the fire?

TONY: No, I didn't.

WAYNE: You said you weren't in a very understanding mood

the night of the fire. Could it be that your lack of understanding made you seek revenge on the Lodge?

TONY: Isn't that a little melodramatic?

WAYNE: You said you left about eleven? That was around the same time as the fire.

TONY: So they say.

WAYNE: Was it you who Spike saw running away from the gym?

NORMAN: He's hardly in a position to know who saw him, is he?

WAYNE: Why didn't you leave straight after the heated discussion?

TONY: I didn't plan to leave. I went to cool down. My chain of thoughts just led me to running off.

WAYNE: Did you see any sign of the fire?

TONY: No.

WAYNE: But you just said you were at the gym around the same time as the fire.

TONY: I just assumed I was there because of what had been said.

WAYNE: In much the same way you assumed you wouldn't be suspected of the fire if you came back, I suppose?

TONY: I told you, Wayne, I had nothing to do with the fire.

WAYNE: So it's mere coincidence that you run away on the same night and the same time as a fire nearly guts the gym?

TONY: It must be.

WAYNE: You said you went to see Mrs Wilmott? But you led Mrs Wilmott to believe you had gone to see Sam. Why was this?

TONY: Apart from the fact that I couldn't get a word in, Doreen doesn't like to think she's come between me and Sam. She's very adamant about it. Doreen prefers to be the comforter rather than the replacement.

(SPIKE *re-enters the court.*)

SPIKE: Right, Scot, still having those stomach pains?

(*He laughs. The others groan at the repetition of the bad joke.*)

280

Oh, Tony, I just saw Sam coming up the drive.

TONY: Do what?

SPIKE: Yeah, Marge is showing her into Pat's office.

SHIRLEY: (*To* TONY) What do you think she wants?

TONY: Doreen probably gave her a parental pinch.

(MARGE *enters the court.*)

MARGE: Tony, your mother is here.

TONY: Yeah, I know.

MARGE: She's talking at present. When she's finished, will you come out or shall I send her in?

TONY: Suit yourself.

MARGE: Is that the right attitude to adopt?

TONY: I think so.

MARGE: And do you want her to see you playing children's games?

TONY: I don't think I care.

MARGE: No, I don't believe you do. You have proven you care about very little except, of course, Tony Michaels. You don't realize how well off you are, none of you do. You are all, without exception, better off at the Lodge than you would've been elsewhere. But still some of you take it upon yourselves to criticize and pick holes. Thinking you're too good for the Lodge.

SHIRLEY: You've lost us, Marge.

BLUE: What brought this on?

MARGE: It just annoys me to see certain members of the Lodge non-appreciative of the work being put in on their behalf.

BLUE: Like who, for instance?

MARGE: That is not for your ears. I'd just add that a hell of a lot of work is done for you children. All right, you might not notice it right away, but if only you knew the half of it. Do you hear, Tony Michaels?

TONY: (*Slightly embarrassed*) I don't understand, but, yes, I'm listening.

MARGE: Good.

(MARGE *leaves in the midst of confusion.*)

281

SPIKE: What was all that about?

SCOT: I think she felt hard done by, because you let George testify but not her.

TONY: No, it was something else.

NORMAN: I think we'd better break for a while so that Tony can see Sam.

TONY: I want to know what all that with Marge was about.

SHIRLEY: She'll probably be in the office by now.

(TONY *leaves the hall and the lights fade.*)

Lights up on TONY *standing alone on stage waiting for* SAM. MARCUS *crosses the stage with* NORMAN.

MARCUS: Haven't they finished in there yet?

TONY: No, they've been in that office for ages now.

NORMAN: What's happening in there?

TONY: I don't know but they're all in there; Anne, Sam, Pat and Marge.

NORMAN: Only George left holding the fort.

MARCUS: Hold on, something's happening.

(*Talking offstage between the group, then* SAM *and* MARGE *enter.*)

MARGE: I'll see you through to the hall. Oh, he's come out. Well, just call when you're ready to leave.

(*She exits. Edgy pause as* SAM *and* TONY *stare at each other.*)

SAM: Is that you, Marcus? And Norman? Haven't you both changed so?

MARCUS: Yeah, we have a bit. How have you been, Sam?

SAM: You know me, never say die.

NORMAN: It's good to see you, Mrs Michaels. Well, we'd better be off.

SAM: Oh, don't go. Where are the others? It's awfully quiet.

TONY: Safety in numbers!

SAM: Hello, Tony. I didn't see you there.

TONY: No, you wouldn't. I blend in with the background so well.

(*Slight pause.*)

SAM: And how's work, Norman?

NORMAN: (*Still wanting to leave*) Fine, Mrs Michaels.

TONY: Miss!

SAM: Marcus, if you must leave, you couldn't get me a cuppa, could you? Only I don't like asking straight out. That Marge's not too keen on me.

TONY: Good judge of character is Marge.

MARCUS: Yeah, OK, Sam. Two sugars, isn't it?
(SAM *nods.* MARCUS *and* NORMAN *disappear offstage rather hurriedly.*)

SAM: I see you haven't lost your sense of humour.

TONY: If you don't laugh, you'll cry.

SAM: I'm sorry about the other night, T.

TONY: No, you're not, but apology accepted.

SAM: I had company and it would've been awkward.

TONY: Why did you come down today?

SAM: (*Ignoring his question*) Mrs Wilmott said you called but left no message. Still, you never was one for writing. Remember your first school report?

TONY: No.

SAM: That Mr Pegg just wrote "refuses to write in my lessons" and you getting "A"s in all the other subjects.

TONY: Don't.

SAM: Don't what, Tony?

TONY: Don't pretend.

SAM: Pretend? You've lost me, son.

TONY: Don't pretend you're besotted with memories of me as a child. Just busting to tell everyone how proud you are of your only son.

SAM: Must we go through this again?

TONY: Yes, because we never get past this point. You always brush past the subject. It's OK, Sam, we're alone. You can be yourself.

SAM: What's that supposed to mean?

TONY: It's a struggle for you to say one decent word to me.

SAM: That's not true, and you know it.

TONY: What are you to me, Sam, mother or older sister?

SAM: Tony, please, people will hear.

283

TONY: Doreen says this is the best thing that ever happened to me.

SAM: What does she mean by that?

TONY: I got free from you, I suppose.

SAM: That's not fair. (*Half whispering*) I did my best for you.

TONY: No, not your best. You did as much as you could be bothered to do.

SAM: How dare you? I'm your mother.

TONY: So they tell me.

(MARGE *enters.* SCOT, DRAY, SHIRLEY *and* BLUE *run behind her.*)

MARGE: I'm sorry, but you'll have to keep your voices down or move into the office.

SCOT: How are you, Sam?

MARGE: Scot, please leave, and you other three.

TONY: It's OK. Sam doesn't mind them being here and I love crowds.

MARGE: I think you should come into the office.

TONY: Marge, what are your views on motherhood and the role of the mother?

MARGE: Have you no respect for anyone?

TONY: I find it very difficult to respect anyone who refuses to respect me. It's a two-way thing.

MARGE: Never have I heard a boy talk to his mother in such a way.

TONY: Sam's never been a mother to me. If you chalked up all her motherly qualities, I doubt you'd get past two.

SAM: I've got used to the way you speak to me, but I draw the line at being insulted in front of these people.

TONY: You defend your honour with such grace. It's a shame I'm going to take no notice of it.

MARGE: Tony Michaels, stop it. You've gone much too far!

(NORMAN *enters with a cup of tea.*)

NORMAN: Here is your tea, Mrs Michaels.

MARGE: Cups are not allowed through here, Norman, you know that.

SAM: It's my fault, I asked him to bring it through.

MARGE: Oh, I just don't want it to be habit-forming, you understand.

TONY: (*To* NORMAN) Where's Marcus?

NORMAN: He won't listen to any more pointless fighting between you and your mother.

TONY: Did you see "my mother" when she walked in? She held a conversation with you before she even looked at me. "Oh, Tony, I didn't see you there." How couldn't she see me?

SHIRLEY: You make it difficult for her.

SCOT: If she does say anything, you put her down. What d'you expect?

SAM: You're embarrassing yourself and everyone else.

TONY: Shut up, Sam. (*To* SHIRLEY) Why do you defend her? Isn't she able to explain herself to me? Answer me . . .

SHIRLEY: She hasn't anything to explain.

TONY: No? How about me always being second in her life? Why she never gave us a chance to be a normal family? And what made her decide on this form of child-rearing? (*Slightly embarrassed at maybe having said too much*) They're just for openers.

SAM: I will not explain myself to a 16-year-old who should know better.

TONY: (*Trying to be calm*) His name was Mr Pedge. Pedge, not Pegg. I refused to read in his lessons, not write. I came running home with a near-perfect report and, like always, you weren't there. I had to show Doreen and she told you about it in the morning. Mr Pedge, not bloody Pegg! I had to bring up the subject before you'd say anything about it. As if it wasn't important.

SAM: I find it very difficult, Tony.

TONY: No, I don't think you do!

NORMAN: Would you like us to feel sorry for you?

TONY: No, Norman, I want you to understand I have reason to feel this way towards Sam.

MARGE: You had no reason to say the things you said to your mother. You wear your self-pity on your sleeve.

TONY: This isn't a quest for pity, it's . . .

SCOT: Lack of understanding and compassion?

TONY: Yes.

SCOT: Yeah, now we've hit on it. (*As gospel preacher*) We have seen the light. I been to Mount Zion and I've seen the burning bush.

SHIRLEY: Scot, don't, this is serious.

SCOT: Too bloody serious.

NORMAN: I was reading this "Why Care?" booklet George gave us. There is a chapter on reasons for care. It struck me that any of these reasons could have been our explanation for care. I'll read some. (*Reads:*) When I was 9 my parents died. . . .

(NORMAN *continues to read in silence as Children come on to tell their own stories, possibly spotlighted.*)

CHILD 1: My mother killed my father, well that's what the police said. I don't believe my mum would've done that. I don't want to know the truth. The police said Mum killed my dad on the Tuesday and committed suicide on the Wednesday. I was only 9, I didn't know who to hate, the police for telling me or my mum for leaving me alone. I ended up hating and blaming myself.

CHILD 2: Brace yourselves, my story's a bit complicated. I was adopted a little after I was born and when I was 4 my adopted mother died. After that I lived with my adopted father and his sister, my aunt. We moved from one crisis to another. My aunt used to say we were fated. My adopted father got married again to a lady I couldn't stand so I stayed with my aunt. She wasn't very well and unfortunately she died. Everything was getting better when it happened. I went to live with my adopted father but I kept running away. Finally, I did a little tea-leafing and got put in a reception centre. Life has been pretty normal ever since.

BLUE: Bad luck always comes in threes, or so they say. Stage one, my father is told by doctors he is paralysed from the waist down. My mum had to look after him, but life was all right. Stage two, my mum had a heart attack and died. My dad couldn't look after us so we went into care. Then they split me and David up. I only got to see him twice a year.

CHILD 3: When I was born my parents weren't married and neither of them could look after me due to their careers. So I was fostered. I still saw my dad but then he left and went to Canada. Mrs Marsden, my foster mother, was white and I was a black boy growing up in a white family. I'd look at my hands sometimes to convince myself I was black. I was really mixed up and I started taking it out on Mrs Marsden. She'd say do this but I'd ignore her or do something else.

NORMAN: (*Reading out loud again from booklet*) She was the only person I had around, but we couldn't make it work so I was put in care. (*Pause. Looks at* TONY.) There's another about a child who had two nervous breakdowns before she was 13 and another who watched her mother try and kill her baby. (SCOT *sniggers*.) Did I say something funny, Scot?

SCOT: It was just the way you said it. As if it happened every day.

NORMAN: Maybe not every day, but still very common, too bloody common. (*To* TONY) You're catering to the wrong audience. We can't contend with your problems on top of our own.

MARGE: I think you owe your mother an apology, Tony.

TONY: Why? Because Norman decides I've an axe to grind against my mother?

NORMAN: Well, haven't you?

TONY: No, I haven't. I'm sick of being seen as the ungrateful son.

MARGE: Some of the remarks you made were very untoward. We'll all leave. You won't have to do it in our company.

TONY: You think I've got a problem and you're too busy to help me. But you will take the time to set me back on the straight and narrow.

MARGE: I don't want to hear any more. We all think you have said quite enough for one day.

TONY: You haven't heard the worst of it. Anything I said, Sam will get over.

SAM: You won't change, Tony Michaels. You're ungrateful and disrespectful.

TONY: What have I to be ungrateful for?

(MARCUS *enters.*)

MARCUS: Tony, Pat wants to see you in her office. She's with Anne and some other bloke.

(*Lights fade to blackout.*)

Lights up on TONY, *standing, as if having just left Pat's office.*
MARCUS *walks up behind him.*

MARCUS: How did it go?

TONY: What?

MARCUS: The meeting. Was it good news?

TONY: Why aren't you in the hall?

MARCUS: My chief witness has vanished.

TONY: Couldn't be helped, I'm afraid.

(*An edgy pause.*)

MARCUS: Penny for your thoughts.

TONY: That man you saw in Pat's office was a Mr Stewart Townsend or something. He was strange. He's got a really condescending manner and he spoke in a half whisper.

MARCUS: Sounds pretty strange, I suppose.

(*Spotlight picks up* TOWNSEND, *standing upright, and speaking as if to* TONY.)

TOWNSEND: I am Stewart Townsend and I'm from the Spears Housing Association, the S.H.A.

TONY: They deal with homes for kids leaving care. They get three kids leaving homes at the same time and set them up in their own flat.

TOWNSEND: We understand that large step from child care to independent life. The S.H.A. hopes to soften the inevitable blow.

TONY: He said it as if he were trying to sell a "Brand X" floor cleaner to a housewife.

MARCUS: I thought you wanted to leave.

TONY: I do, but I don't want to jump at the first chance that comes along just for the sake of it.

MARCUS: I can understand that but this idea sounds worth a try.

TOWNSEND: Now on to the rent. Six pounds seventy-five plus five pounds for bills. We treat you as normal tenants and expect regular weekly payments.

MARCUS: How do you expect to pay the rent?

TONY: Anne said the social services would pay it until I got a job or whatever.

MARCUS: Where is it? The flat, I mean.

TONY: It's in London – er – Finsbury Park, he said.

MARCUS: That isn't that far, but it's still quite a move. What if you get homesick or something? (*Laughs.*)

TONY: (*Through a smile*) Pat said I could come back any time.

TOWNSEND: Either myself or a Miss Stacy Potter will call for the rent each week. We are voluntary workers but we will be on hand for you if any problems arise. Miss Potter is a school teacher and I am a lawyer.

TONY: I wanted to ask Mr Townsend so many questions but he kept rattling on . . . I just got bowled over.

(*He continues speaking to* MARCUS.)

TOWNSEND: (*Starting during pause in* TONY's *sentence*) Two hundred and fifty pounds will be awarded for the furnishings to your bedroom. A further four hundred and fifty pounds will be awarded to the flat as a whole to furnish the front room.

TONY: It sounded a lot but he assured me there was much to buy.

MARCUS: You always land on your feet.

TONY: Nothing is final until a meeting on Friday week. I get to meet my flatmates and see the flat.

(MARCUS *begins to smile.*)

What are you smiling at?

MARCUS: It just clicked. I just figured out why Marge really bit your head off about work being done for you.

TOWNSEND: You are very lucky to be chosen for the flat. We have quite a long waiting list. If it wasn't for the diligence of Anne here, you might not have been considered.

MARCUS: What's bothering you really?

TONY: I'm just a little taken back by it all. It happened so fast.

MARCUS: It's something else as well.

TONY: It's what I want, but I'm just a little dubious. I don't like being vulnerable and when I leave that's what I become. Open to the elements, if you like. Everything is custom built in here to cushion every blow from the real world. When I leave I'll be too proud to come back. Oh, I'll visit, but not for help. Remember Vicky? She left the Lodge in an air of self-confidence. Three months later she was back pregnant and homeless. Pat bought her a pram, baby-bath and clothes out of her own pocket and she just lapped it up as if she was still entitled to them. The air that I'll leave under won't let me come back. It'll be saying "See if I can do better for myself." It scares me. I can't cook. Christ, you've tasted some of my attempts. I've got burning toast down to a fine art. When I went to Court, over the incident with Sam, the judge told me he was putting my life in my own hands and I should make the most of it. Then he handed me over to the care of the council. When you reach my age you naturally grow away from your parents. Who are my "parents"? I'm the legal ward of the council. When I grow away from that it increases the overall paperwork, causes rushed reviews, means more running around and bargaining for Anne and upsets the daily running of Pat's Lodge completely. It's all blown out of proportion. Yet they never seem ready for it. It always, somehow, comes as a great shock. Causing a sudden fit of panic . . . When I lose this cover I become so bloody vulnerable.

(*Blackout.*)

Lights up on court. The kids are standing around talking.

CHILD 1: Looks like we've got to burn down the Lodge in order to leave.

CHILD 2: When I want to leave I think I'll flood Pat's office.

CHILD 3: I'd prefer to paint the kitchen with graffiti.

CHILD 4: The fact that he's leaving obviously shows he had nothing to do with the fire.

CHILD 1: Not really. They might just be telling us he's moving into a flat, but he may be going somewhere else.

CHILD 3: Vicky told everyone she was going into a hostel but ended up living with her bloke. You see, you never can tell.

SPIKE: (*To* SHIRLEY) How much would you like to bet Pat had something to do with Tony's leaving?

SHIRLEY: (*Preoccupied*) She has to, she's head of the home.

SPIKE: Not in that sense. I mean, on the quiet. Come on, how much?

(*No reply.*)

Hello, Shirley, wakey, wakey. I said . . .

SHIRLEY: Shut up, Spike.

(*She walks away.*)

SPIKE: (*Shouting after her*) Isn't that rude? I thought now you were a changed woman, you'd learnt some manners. Blue, I know what happened.

(SPIKE *moves off to talk to* BLUE. MARCUS *and* TONY *enter the court.*)

NORMAN: Ah, Marcus, we've been waiting. Can we try and get this wrapped up, please?

MARCUS: Seeing as you asked so nicely.

SHIRLEY: (*To* TONY) Why am I always the last to find out things about you? Why didn't you say you were leaving?

TONY: I only just found out myself. Nothing is finalized.

MARCUS: I think the best way to prove Tony is innocent is to show who did start the fire. I'd like to cross-examine Spike.

STALLION: Is it customary to question the doorman?

MARCUS: In this court anything and everything is customary.

(SPIKE *reluctantly takes the stand.*)

Where were you when you saw this person running away from the gym?

SPIKE: I was out in the back garden.

MARCUS: Doing what?

SPIKE: Having a smoke. Pat still won't let me smoke in the house.

MARCUS: You said "It had to be him" – meaning Tony – "who else was out at that time?"

SPIKE: Something like that.

MARCUS: Word for word, actually. But Dray was out at that time. Could it have been Dray you saw?

SPIKE: It was Tony.

MARCUS: Where in the garden were you?

SPIKE: By the sundial.

MARCUS: About seventy-five yards from the gym. You want us to believe you can see specific people over seventy-five yards in near darkness?

SPIKE: I told you, it was Tony.

MARCUS: How convenient! I put it to you that the person you saw was Dray, not Tony.

(DRAY *leaves the hall, glancing at* STALLION.)

SHIRLEY: Dray, where are you going? Dray! (*To* MARCUS) My brother wouldn't start a fire.

STALLION: No? Then why'd he leave so fast?

MARCUS: Because he's scared, of course. He followed Tony out of his bedroom and into the garden. On passing the gym he saw somebody starting the fire, how I don't yet know. Then he ran and caught Tony up by the cemetery.

SPIKE: You're just guessing at that.

MARCUS: Not really. Spike, take an educated guess at who Dray saw.

SPIKE: (*Avoiding* STALLION'*s stare, mumbling*) I don't know.

MARCUS: Pardon?

SPIKE: I don't know. You tell me.

MARCUS: OK . . . Stallion, you have a try.

CHILD 3: I knew it was Stallion.

STALLION: (*To* MARCUS) Sorry, I can't think of anyone.

CHILD 2: (*To* CHILD 3) I half wish it was Tony.

MARCUS: (*To* STALLION) It was you, wasn't it?

CHILD 3: (*To* CHILD 2) What makes you say that?

STALLION: (*To* MARCUS) What makes you say that?

CHILD 2: (*To* CHILD 3) Well, I'm not going to tell Pat Stallion started the fire, will you? No, I didn't think so.

CHILD 3: (*To* CHILD 2) You're right. Stallion wouldn't be too pleased, would he?

SCOT: (*To* STALLION) You started the fire and then tried to blame Tony.

STALLION: Not exactly. It was Marcus's idea for the trial.

MARCUS: You've been running this charade from the start.

STALLION: No harm's done.

SHIRLEY: What do you call Dray and Scot, or aren't they classed as harm?

TONY: I want to talk to you, Shirley.

SHIRLEY: He isn't even bothered by being found out.

TONY: Shirley, please.

STALLION: You're all assuming it was deliberate. If you can convince Dray I won't kill him, he'll prove it. I accidentally knocked over the heater.

NORMAN: I still do not understand your mentality.

STALLION: And I did so want your approval.

TONY: (*To* SHIRLEY) It's awkward, I've been trying to find the best way to say it.

SHIRLEY: If you want to see me after you leave, the answer is yes. But you'll have to ask me.

STALLION: You're looking at this from the wrong angle. I capitalized on the situation, so that you'd not miss the gym. I merely provided a platform for entertainment. Norman, didn't you enjoy showing us just how aloof and self-righteous you are? It must have been stimulating to express your superiority.

NORMAN: The pot calling the kettle black.

STALLION: Scot, did you get no satisfaction from filling us with your well-versed bullshit? And humour too, granted not everyone appreciated it.

TONY: (*To* SHIRLEY) I'd like to continue to see you after I leave, if that is agreeable.

SHIRLEY: Took your time. It wasn't exactly how I'd phrase it . . . but the answer's still yes.

(*She kisses* TONY.)

STALLION: And look at that, despite ridicule and against better judgment, true love conquers all. With a little help from Uncle Stallion. Whether or not they choose to recognize my part in their love match is irrelevant.

MARCUS: The last kick of a dying dog!

STALLION: Ah, our resident Hercules Poirot. You managed to wave the flag for child liberation and earned good points against the system.

MARCUS: Glad to be of service.

TONY: Let me guess mine. You provided me with a platform for attention. I was the centre of attention for quite a while. More than enough to satisfy my needs.

STALLION: Spot on.

NORMAN: And what did we do for you, Stallion?

STALLION: Oh, you know me, I'm not one to blow my own trumpet. I will just say, though, I'll carry the memory until my dying day. You can't comprehend how satisfying it is to have been of service to you all. It's all right, there's no need to thank me.

(STALLION *leaves hall very full of himself. Others are slightly embarrassed as* STALLION *has hit too close to home.*)

SCOT: He certainly pissed on us from a dizzy height.

SHIRLEY: (To SPIKE) Shouldn't you be following the "great one".

SPIKE: Nice to see you're taking it so well. I'd better leave after all. The air in here is very thick.

(*He exits.*)

BLUE: What makes me sick is he'll probably wriggle out of any trouble over the fire.

NORMAN: People like friend Stallion never get their come-uppance.

TONY: After a patch of slight adventure, it's back to near

normality in the Lodge.

SCOT: (*Whistling tune of song*) Back to the mouldy dump.

BLUE: Where's that from?

SCOT: It's the Lodge song. Remember it, Shirley? I can't
remember who made it up. (*Sings:*)

Down in the mouldy dump,
Down old Lodge way.
Where we get pushed about,
Fifty times a day.
Egg and bacon we don't see,
We get sawdust in our tea.
That's why we're gradually
Fading away.

The aunties smash the windows.
We get the blame.
Especially Aunty Pat,
She's just the same.
Six o'clock in the morning,
The aunts begin to shout:
"Get out of bed, get out of bed,
Before you get a clout."

(*As* SCOT *sings, the other kids join in, laughing and generally
enjoying themselves.*)

NEW ANATOMIES

Timberlake Wertenbaker

A NOTE ON THE STAGING

New Anatomies is designed for a cast of five women and a musician. The roles are distributed as follows:

1   ISABELLE EBERHARDT and, in her Arab persona, SI MAHMOUD
2   SEVERINE   ANTOINE   BOU SAADI
3   NATALIE   EUGENIE   MURDERER   JUDGE
4   JENNY   SALEH   LYDIA   COLONEL LYAUTEY
5   VERDA MILES   ANNA   SI LACHMI   YASMINA CAPTAIN SOUBIEL

The role of PASHA (Act II scene 1) is silent, and should be taken by the musician.

Except for the actress playing ISABELLE, each actress plays a Western woman, an Arab man and a Western man. Changes should take place in such a way as to be visible to the audience and all five actresses should be on stage at all times.

The songs in the play ought to be popular music-hall songs from the turn of the century. Songs 2 and 3 belong to the repertoire of the male impersonator, and song 1 to that of the *ingénue*.

The action of the play takes place at the turn of the century in Europe and Algeria.

T.W.

ACT I

Scene 1

Ain-Sefra, a dusty village in Algeria. ISABELLE EBERHARDT *looks around, none too steady. She is dressed in a tattered Arab cloak, has no teeth and almost no hair. She is 27.*

ISABELLE: Lost the way. (*Steadies herself.*) Detour. Closed. (*Pause. As if an order to herself*) Go inside. (*Sings, softly, Arabic modulations, but flat:*) "If a man be old and a fool, his folly . . ." (*Burps.*) That's what it is. (*Takes out a cigarette and looks for a match through the folds of her cloak.*) Match. (*Forgets about it. Sings:*) "If a man be old and a fool, his folly is past all cure. But a young man . . ." What it is is this: (*looks around*) I need a fuck. (*Pause.*) Definitely. Yes. (SEVERINE *enters. She is a slightly older woman, dressed uncomfortably for the heat in a long skirt and jacket.*) Trailed . . . (*To* SEVERINE) Trailing behind me.

SEVERINE: Come inside.

ISABELLE: Inside? Trailed: the story, I know. Stealing it.

SEVERINE: You have a fever.

(ISABELLE *remembers her cigarette.*)

ISABELLE: Matches. Stolen. (*Louder*) You stole my matches. (SEVERINE *finds the matches, tries to light* ISABELLE'*s cigarette.*)

(*Apologetic*) Desert wind: makes the hand shake. (SEVERINE *lights two cigarettes and sticks one in* ISABELLE'*s mouth.*)

Pay for my story with a match. European coinage!

SEVERINE: You need rest.

ISABELLE: No, later. (*Burps.*) Found out what it was. What was it? Ah, yes. It was: I need a fuck. I need a fuck. Where am I going to find a fuck? Bunch of degenerates in this town. Sleeping WHEN I NEED A FUCK. It's the

299

European influence. Keeps them down.

SEVERINE: Come inside, Isabelle.

ISABELLE: "Please go inside, mademoiselle, and stay there."
Out of the wind. Saw a couple of guards earlier. That'll do.
One for you, one for me. I'll give you the younger one, rules
of hospitality. No? Sevvy the scribe prefers a belly dancer,
eh, dark smooth limbs and curved hips. Or the voluptuous
tale. Your face looks like a big hungry European cock. No
offence: not your fault you look European. Must find those
guards. (*Stares.*) Coolness of the night as it filters through the
sand. The smell of sand, Séverine, do you know it? It's like
the inside of water. Smell . . .

(*She leans down and falls flat.*)

SEVERINE: Isabelle, please . . .

(*They struggle to get her up.*)

ISABELLE: You going to write I couldn't walk straight enough
to find a fuck? They'll want to know everything. I'm
famous now, not just anybody, no, I'll be in History.
(*Near retch.*) They hate me, but I forgive them. You tell
them . . . that when the body drags through the gutter, it
is cleaved from the soul. Tell them the soul paced the
desert. They take baths, but lice crawl through the cracks
of their hypocritical brains. Bunch of farmers. Wallowing
in the mud of their plowed fields. Turnips, cabbages,
carrots, all in a line, all fenced in. (*Cries.*) Why do they
hate me so? I didn't want anything from them.
(*Pause.*)
Si Mahmoud forgives all. Si Mahmoud paced the desert.
Heart unmixed with guile, free. Why aren't you writing
all this down, chronicler? Duty to get it right, no editing.
(*Burps.*) Edit that.

SEVERINE: Please, Si Mahmoud. Let's go in.

ISABELLE: Listen. The dawn's coming. You can tell by the
sound, a curve in the silence and then the sand in the
desert moves . . . Write down: a third of a centimetre,
they'll want to know that in Europe.

(*Pause.* SEVERINE, *resigned, sits with* ISABELLE.)

When I was growing up in the Tsar's villa in St
Petersburg . . .

SEVERINE: Geneva.

ISABELLE: What?

SEVERINE: You said Geneva earlier.

ISABELLE: Did I? Yes, ducks . . . must have been Geneva.

SEVERINE: (*Delicately*) Your brothers . . .

ISABELLE: Didn't have any.

SEVERINE: You said . . .

ISABELLE: I was the only boy in the family.

SEVERINE: Your brother Antoine . . .

ISABELLE: Beloved. (*Makes a gesture for fucking.*) Didn't.
Would have.
Nasty little piece got her claws in him first. No, did.

SEVERINE: Si Mahmoud, the truth.

ISABELLE: There is no god but Allah, Allah is the only God
and Muhammed is his prophet.

SEVERINE: What brought you to the desert?
(ISABELLE *makes a trace on the ground.*)
It's in Arabic.

ISABELLE: (*Reads:*) The Mektoub: it was written. Here. That
means, no choice. Mektoub.

SEVERINE: Your mother?

ISABELLE: No choice for her either. The Mektoub.

SEVERINE: You told me she was a delicate woman. What gave
her the courage to run off?

ISABELLE: Even the violet resists domestication.

SEVERINE: But in the 1870s . . .

ISABELLE: Séverine, it is a courtesy in this country not to
interrupt or ask questions of the storyteller. You must sit
quietly and listen, moving only to light my cigarettes.
When I pause, you may praise Allah for having given my
tongue such vivid modulations. I shall begin, as is our
custom, with a mention of women.

SONG I

VERDA MILES *as a Victorian girl in frills.*

301

Scene 2

Geneva. A house in disorder.

VERDA MILES *takes off her ribbons, puts up her hair and covers herself with a shawl, becoming* ANNA, *a woman in her late thirties, with remnants of style and charm.*

ANNA: And then the children . . . They won't stay.

> (ISABELLE *and* ANTOINE *appear.* ISABELLE *is 13, dressed in a man's shirt and a skirt much too big for her.* ANTOINE *is 16, frail and feminine.*)

ISABELLE: Antoine, Antoine. Don't let him frighten you.

ANTOINE: (*Near tears*) Drunken tyrant.

ISABELLE: Let's dream.

ANTOINE: He threatened to hit me. Brute. I have to go away, now.

ANNA: (*Paying no attention to any of this*) First Nicholas, not a word . . . He must have come to a bad . . . Too many anarchists in the house. It's a bad influence on children.

ISABELLE: Oh yes, let's go away. We're in Siberia. The snow is up to our knees, so hard to move. Suddenly, look, shining in the dark, a pair of yellow eyes.

ANTOINE: I have no choice. I'll have to run away and join the army.

ISABELLE: I'll come with you, we can take Mama.

ANTOINE: The army's only for boys.

ISABELLE: We can't leave Mama.

ANTOINE: I wish I was a girl. He doesn't treat you that way.

ISABELLE: I'm strong.

ANTOINE: He'll kill me.

ANNA: If only Trofimovitch had allowed some fairy tales, even Pushkin . . . not all these Bakunin pamphlets at bedtime.

ISABELLE: It's snowing again. Darkness. Another pair of yellow eyes, glistening. Another. We're surrounded. Are they wolves?

ANTOINE: (*Joining in reluctantly*) No, those are the eyes of our enemies.

ISABELLE: You're shivering.

ANNA: And now Natalie . . .

ANTOINE: I'm cold. It's too cold up there. I want to go further
south.

ISABELLE: The Crimea, lemon groves.

ANTOINE: "Knowst thou the land, beloved, where the lemons
bloom . . ." No, I want to go further south. Far away.
The Sahara.

ANNA: And Natalie's so good with . . .

ISABELLE: Our camels are tired.

ANTOINE: That's the sort of thing Natalie would say.

ISABELLE: (*Offended*) The transition from Siberia was too
sudden. I haven't acclamitated.

ANTOINE: Acclimatized.

ANNA: It's all so difficult.
(*Flute music.*)

ISABELLE: This stillness.

ANTOINE: Dune after dune, shape mirroring shape, so
life . . . weariness.

ISABELLE: How rapidly the sun seems to plunge behind the
dunes. This stillness.

ANTOINE: Let us rest, my beloved.

ISABELLE: I'll build our tent. There's a storm coming, I can
see the clouds.

ANTOINE: There aren't any clouds over the desert.

ISABELLE: That's what Natalie would say.

ANTOINE: You don't understand, the corners of a dream must
be nailed to the ground as firmly as our tent: no rain in the
desert.

ISABELLE: A wind then. Listen, the wind's galloping over the
dunes.

ANTOINE: It's a sandstorm.

ISABELLE: Quick. Where are you? I can't see you.

ANTOINE: Here, come here, my beloved.
(*They throw themselves into each other's arms, roll on the
floor.*)
Beloved.
(*Their embrace lingers.*)

ANNA: Natalie mustn't . . . she's too good with (*Notices the two children.*) Antoine, I'm not sure you should . . . with your sister . . . like that.

ISABELLE: We're playing, Mama, we're dreaming.

ANNA: Are you too old? I don't know. The poets . . . But Natalie . . .

ANTOINE: Wants us to behave –

ISABELLE: Like Swiss clocks. Tick tock.

ANTOINE: Tick tock.

ANNA: You mustn't . . . She is sometimes a little . . . but she's the only one, she's so good with dust. I don't seem to manage very well. There's so much of it and it's complicated finding it. I wasn't brought up to . . . But this new world of Trofimovitch, where it's wrong to have servants, well yes, but what about the dust? I suppose when the revolution comes, they'll find a way, deal with it.

ISABELLE: We don't mind.

ANNA: Natalie . . . wants to leave us.

ANTOINE: Even Natalie can't take the beast any more.

ANNA: Isabelle, she's always been very fond . . . Tell her she absolutely mustn't . . .

ISABELLE: She's free.

ANNA: But Trofimovitch . . .

(NATALIE *enters. She is a tightly pulled together young woman. An awkward silence and a sense that this is not unusual when she comes into a room.*)

Natalie, I was saying . . . to abandon your home . . .

NATALIE: How can you call this pigsty a home?

ANNA: Darling, a young lady's vocabulary shouldn't include . . . Your family . . .

NATALIE: Family. (*Looks around at them.*) In a family you have first a mother who looks after her children, protects them, teaches them . . .

ANNA: Didn't I? You knew several poems of Byron as a child.

NATALIE: A mother who teaches her children how to behave and looks after the house, cooks meals, doesn't let her

304

children eat out of a slop bucket –

ANNA: Trofimovitch says meals are a bourgeois form of . . .
But don't we have . . .

NATALIE: When I cook them. And secondly in a family a
brother is a brother, a boy then a man, not this snivelling,
delicate half girl. You've allowed him to be terrorized by
that drunken beast.

ANNA: Natalie, his mind, philosophy . . .

NATALIE: Philosophy, don't make me laugh. Yes, and finally
in a family you have a proper father, not that raving
peasant, who's driven us to this misery and filth, who's
now trying to get into my bed at night.

ANNA: He's not always very steady at night, he must have
thought . . . He didn't notice it wasn't his . . .

NATALIE: (*Exploding*) And you defend him. My mother
defends the man who's ruining all of us, you defend the
man who's trying to seduce your own daughter. You
won't leave that filthy lecherous drunk, you prefer to ruin
us.

ANNA: Leave him . . . go . . . where?

ISABELLE: Natalie, love forgives.

NATALIE: Love, that spittle of stinking brandy. Love?

ISABELLE: (*Gently*) "Love has its reasons . . .

ANTOINE: . . . which reason cannot fathom."

NATALIE: The two of you with your books!

ANNA: (*Feebly*) Isabelle is right . . . She doesn't mind . . .

NATALIE: At her age you love anybody, even beggars, even a
snivelling brother. (*To* ISABELLE) I'll come back and get
you later, then you can come live with me in a real home,
with a real family, with my husband.

ISABELLE: A husband, Natalie. That's different. Is he dark?
Is he foreign? Does he visit you only at night and wrap
you in a blinding veil of torrid passion? A secret husband,
how wonderful, like Eros and Psyche. Does he let you
look at him?

NATALIE: What are you talking about? I'm marrying
Stéphane.

ANTOINE: Stéphane, the shopkeeping weed. He's driven you to that?

NATALIE: You're one to talk, you fine figure of manhood.

ISABELLE: He does look like a dandelion, you said so yourself.

NATALIE: He'll soon be my husband and I'll have him talked about with respect. We'll be very happy.

ISABELLE: How? If he knows you don't love him.

NATALIE: Love, look where that got us. Oh, I tell him I love him, men like to hear that, sometimes I tell him I adore him.

ANNA: To lie . . . I'm not sure . . .

NATALIE: I can't have you at the wedding. I explained he was too ill. Stéphane's family's a little upset I'm foreign. But they'll see, I'll make a wonderful home for him. (*Pause.*) I must get my things. Don't tell him, it won't do any good. (*She leaves.*)

ANNA: I don't understand, what have I done? But you, my babies, you'll never leave, no, you couldn't now. What did you say, Isabelle? Torrid passion, yes, I think, with Trofimovitch, it was . . . He was so strong, so convinced, impossible to think clearly . . . And then, how wrong it was to have servants, husband, hypocrisy of the sacrament, he said, and how my life made millions suffer. Would you have preferred a big house? You see, there are so many rules when you . . . The doctor says a frail heart . . . There's no choice when your heart is . . . (*She drifts off.*)

ISABELLE: At last the silence descends on the darkening dunes. How still is our solitude, my beloved, how still the desert.

ANTOINE: Let's stop here.

ISABELLE: Yes, let's grow old together and watch the hours stretch on the ground.

ANTOINE: (*Moving away*) Beloved, forgive me, but I must.

ISABELLE: I can't see you. You sound so far away.

ANTOINE: I don't have the strength any more, forgive me . . .

ISABELLE: Where have you gone? Oh, please. Abandoned,

alas, nothing to do.

ANTOINE: (*From off*) But wait.

ISABELLE: Wait . . . and all around me, death. (*Screams.*)
Dead.

Scene 3

Geneva, a few years later.

NATALIE *and* ISABELLE.

NATALIE: Dead?

ISABELLE: Dead. Both of them. Mama first, almost
immediately after she received Antoine's letter. It broke
her heart, those years of silence, not knowing, her frail
heart. And then the letter from the Legion! Antoine a
Legionnaire, he'll never survive.

NATALIE: It might be just the thing for him. Turn him into a
man.

ISABELLE: He didn't even tell me, the coward, the traitor. He
must have planned it for months in secret. And then a
cool letter describing life in the barracks and, now,
marriage. I'll have to find him before it's too late.

NATALIE: And him? Drank himself to death?

ISABELLE: Poor Trofimovitch. He'd begun to put his ear to
the ground listening for the sound of the revolution. He
said he'd hear it when it came, he still had the ear of a
Russian peasant. And he despaired of the silence. When
Mama died, he . . . turned and twisted crumpled himself
into a knot and kept his ear to the floor, but this time I
think he was listening for her. "Three be the ways of love:
a knitting of heart to heart – that's Antoine and me – a
pleasing of lips and eyes, and a third love whose name is
death." That's Trofimovitch and Mama. It's from an
Arabic poem. Trofimovitch taught it to me. There's a
similar one in Greek . . .

NATALIE: Mama should have taught you to sweep instead. If
I'd learnt properly when I was young my mother-in-law

wouldn't have found so much to complain about. But Stéphane has been very patient. I'm lucky. (*Takes in the disorder.*) We can start on this house. Stéphane thinks we'll get a lot of money for it, sell it to some English aristocrats. They like these gloomy old places.

ISABELLE: The house belongs to Antoine. He'll want to come back here and live with me.

NATALIE: He'll want his own little home now.

ISABELLE: "And the screen of separation was placed between us."

NATALIE: The house belongs to all of us. Your share of the money can help towards the expense of having you live with us, and you'll have some left over for your marriage. I wish I'd been able to bring some to my husband, although he never reproached me.

ISABELLE: What's marriage like?

NATALIE: We're doing very well with the shop now and soon we'll build our own house, a big one.

ISABELLE: I mean at night.

NATALIE: You get used to it.

ISABELLE: Brutal pain and brutal pleasure, and after, languor. "And the breeze languished in the evening hours as if it had pity for me."

NATALIE: You've been reading too much. You mustn't talk like that to men. When they come into the shop you must be seen working very hard, dusting things very carefully. That always inspires young men. We've thought a lot about Stéphane's cousin. He has a flower shop and he won't mind the fact that you look so strong. You could help him in the garden. You'd like that.

ISABELLE: Does he grow cactus plants?

NATALIE: They're the wrong plants for this climate.

ISABELLE: It's the wrong climate for the plants. I'm going to Algeria.

NATALIE: The thought of marriage frightened me too, but I'll help you make a good choice. You'll need a roof over your head.

308

ISABELLE: No rain in the desert, no need for a roof.

NATALIE: We're in Geneva and I'm here to protect you until you're safely married.

ISABELLE: Geneva of the barred horizons. I'm getting out, I need a gallop on the dunes.

NATALIE: You'll forget all that when you're married. You'll forget all those dreams.

ISABELLE: (*Looking at* NATALIE *for the first time*) Poor Natalie, left the dreams to look for order, but order was not happiness.

NATALIE: You always made fun of me, you and Antoine, but I always cared for you and I'm determined to help you. When you understand what life is like without the books, you'll understand me, you'll see.

ISABELLE: Geneva to Marseilles by train, Marseilles to Algiers by boat and then a camel for the desert.

NATALIE: That's enough now. It's your duty.

ISABELLE: Words of a Swiss preacher, song of the rain on the cultivated fields.

NATALIE: You have to obey me. You have no choice.

ISABELLE: Trofimovitch told me obedience comes not from direct fear, but fear of the rules. I have no fear, he always said I was the bravest.

NATALIE: He had no right to treat you as if you were an exception. (*Pause.*) You're still so young, we won't force you. We'll give you a year, even more.
(*Silence.*)
If we sell this house, we can take a little trip to Algeria. I want to see what they have over there. They say Arabs are very stupid and give you valuable jewels and clothes for trinkets. Will you agree to that?

ISABELLE: The desert.

NATALIE: Stéphane's arranging the papers for the house and then he'll get us all passports. You couldn't get one by yourself.

ISABELLE: Antoine, we'll gallop over the desert.

NATALIE: I'll be so pleased to sell this house. All buried at last.

ISABELLE: Antoine!

Scene 4

Algiers. ANTOINE *in a crumpled civil service suit sits smoking, tired, grey.* JENNY, *young and very pregnant, is bustling.* ISABELLE *is staring out and* YASMINA, *a servant, is polishing something, extremely slowly.*

JENNY: (*To* ANTOINE) Why doesn't your sister ever help? She hasn't lifted a finger since she's been here. She talks too much to the servant. I have enough trouble making that woman work. They're so lazy, these people. She's said more to that girl than to me. Call her over, Antoine. She never listens when I talk to her.

ANTOINE: (*Weakly*) Isabelle.

(ISABELLE *turns.*)

JENNY: Please remember that Fatma is a native and a servant. They don't respect you if you treat them . . .

ISABELLE: Her name isn't Fatma.

JENNY: Their names are unpronounceable. We call them all Fatma.

ISABELLE: Her name is beautiful: Yasmina. Poor girl, they tried to marry her to a cousin she hated. It was death or the degradation of becoming a servant. I'll write about her.

JENNY: I wouldn't believe anything she says. Help me polish some glasses. I can't trust Fatma with them.

ISABELLE: Throw over a cigarette, will you, Antoine.

JENNY: Women shouldn't smoke. It makes them look vulgar, doesn't it, Antoine?

ISABELLE: Matches.

JENNY: And you work very hard for your cigarettes. They don't grow on trees. Some people have to pay for everything and soon we'll have another mouth to feed.

ANTOINE: Isabelle'll help us when she sells some articles.

JENNY: She won't sell any by just sitting around smoking.

ISABELLE: Inspiration doesn't come frying potatoes.
(ANTOINE *laughs*.)

JENNY: You always take her side. You don't care what
happens to me. She hasn't even offered to knit something
for the baby.

ISABELLE: (*Bored*) Yasmina will help me find something.

JENNY: I'm not going to put some horrible native cloth
around my beautiful new baby.

ISABELLE: I'll get Natalie to send you my collection of poems
when she goes back. Do you remember that beautiful one
of Lermontov Mama used to recite, about the young soul
crying out its entrapment in the womb? The dumb joy of
the mother but for "a long time it languished in the world,
filled with a wonderful longing and earth's tedious
songs . . ." how does it go?

ANTOINE: (*Awkward*) I don't remember.

ISABELLE: "Could not drown out the last sounds of
Paradise . . ."

JENNY: You're jealous, that's all, because you can't find a
husband. Natalie told me how you frightened Stéphane's
cousin away.

ISABELLE: He looked like an orchid.

ANTOINE: You're worse than Arabs, you two, fighting about
nothing.

ISABELLE: Is that what they teach you in the barracks?

JENNY: He's not in the barracks any more. He has a very good
job.

ISABELLE: Sitting on your bum, staring at numbers.

JENNY: And he'll be promoted soon.

ISABELLE: To longer numbers.

JENNY: If you don't ruin his chances. You've been heard
talking to the natives in their own language. There's no
reason not to talk to them in French.

ISABELLE: (*To* ANTOINE) You hate it, don't you, this life?

JENNY: People are becoming suspicious. This is a small
community.

ISABELLE: Tick tock, a Swiss clock, the needle that crushes

the dreams to sleep.

JENNY: You think food just appears on the table. It has to be paid for.

ISABELLE: And only ten miles from the desert. You might as well have stayed in Switzerland for all you've seen of it.

ANTOINE: I did see it. It's not how we dreamt of it. It's dangerous, uncomfortable, and most of it isn't even sand.

ISABELLE: Freedom.

JENNY: Life is much cheaper here than in Switzerland. We'll go back when we have enough money to buy a decent house.

ISABELLE: "Oh the bitter grief of never again exchanging one single thought." Remember how we knew all of Loti by heart and we dreamt of moving, always moving.

ANTOINE: Life isn't what we dreamed.

ISABELLE: It could be . . . the rolling movement of camels, movement, Antoine.

JENNY: Rolling stone gathers no moss. I don't want my baby to be poor.

ISABELLE: Remember when we followed the Berber caravan and we had the sandstorm, oh, my beloved . . .

ANTOINE: I saw the Berbers. One wrong move and they slit your throat. They don't like Europeans.

ISABELLE: Not Europeans with guns, but we could talk to them. Freedom.

JENNY: You keep talking as if Antoine was a slave. He has a good job. We'll be able to take holidays, have a house. That's freedom: money.

ANTOINE: I see how things are now.

ISABELLE: What dictionary are you using? The Swiss clockmaker's or the poet's?

(*An Arabic flute, offstage.*)

Or his? Listen. I hear him every evening, but I've never seen him come or go. He's just there, suddenly, calling.

JENNY: It's probably a beggar and he'll come asking for money. Chase him away, Antoine. They carry diseases these people. It's bad for the baby.

(*They ignore her. She shouts.*)

Go away, you savage, go away, go away!

(*Silence.*)

(*Embarrassed*) I'm so tired and nervous. This isn't a
friendly country. It's not easy to have a baby. It doesn't
happen all by itself.

(NATALIE *enters, arms full of materials and clothes.*)

NATALIE: It's wonderful how stupid these people are. They
give you things for nothing.

ISABELLE: The word is generosity, gifts of hospitality.

NATALIE: Look at this one, it's worth a fortune, that
embroidery, that detail. They're terribly clever for
savages. Look at this woman's cloak.

ISABELLE: It's not for a woman.

NATALIE: We'll be the first shop in Switzerland to sell these
oriental things. They're all the rage in Paris. You could
even model some of them, Isabelle. Here's a woman's
dancing costume.

JENNY: Give it to me.

NATALIE: I can't wait to get back. We'll make a fortune.

ISABELLE: I'm not coming back with you.

NATALIE: Nonsense.

(NATALIE *continues to lay out the clothes.* JENNY *wraps her
face in a veil.*)

JENNY: I'm in your harem. You're the sheikh. Oh, come to
me.

ANTOINE: You look grotesque.

JENNY: You're so cruel. I'll hide behind my veil.

ISABELLE: That's not a woman's veil. Women in the desert
don't wear veils, only the Tuareg men do.

(*She starts dressing* JENNY.)

It should be wrapped around the head and worn with this.
This is called a jellaba. It can be worn in any kind of
weather. The hood will protect you against the elements,
or against the enemy. It's very useful for warriors.

JENNY: I don't want to be dressed as a man.

ISABELLE: Why not? The baby might end up looking like an
Arab? He'll run away from you into the desert.

313

NATALIE: You look lovely. Don't tease her, Isabelle. When you're pregnant you have these caprices. I couldn't wear red or walk into the house without making three turns in the garden.

ANTOINE: It's like the Arabs. They'll never do anything without going through fifty useless gestures.

ISABELLE: The word is courtesy.

(ISABELLE *takes a jellaba and puts it on, slowly, formally. Freeze while she is doing this. Once in it, she feels as at home in it as* JENNY *obviously feels awkward.*)

NATALIE: And they gave me this in secret.

(*She takes out a captain's uniform.*)

ANTOINE: Someone they killed probably. They have no respect for human life. You see how dangerous they are.

ISABELLE: "Always behave as if you were going to die immediately." Remember when we were Stoics and we tried to live in that barrel for a month?

NATALIE: (*Going over to* JENNY *and putting a "feminine" scarf over her head*) I'm afraid reading is a hereditary disease in our family. I would keep books well away from your children when they're young, otherwise it's very hard to wean them from all that nonsense when they're older. If only we could get her married, she's forget all those books, but it's the quotes that drive men away. I'm glad Antoine, at least, is saved.

(*As* NATALIE *is saying this* ISABELLE *is putting the captain's jacket on* YASMINA. *The two girls giggle,* YASMINA *doing a military stance.* JENNY *suddenly notices them.*)

JENNY: Don't do that, it's . . . blasphemy.

ISABELLE: Why, do you think clothes make the monk?

ANTOINE: Isabelle looks like all our recruits. No one would know you were a girl. Is this male or female?

(*He puts on a jellaba, joining in the game.*)

JENNY: If anyone sees us, we'll be ruined.

ISABELLE: (*To* ANTOINE) Let's go to those dark dens in the Arab quarter and have a smoke.

ANTOINE: If they recognize us (*throat-slitting gesture*).

ISABELLE: We'll say we're from Tunis. That'll explain my
accent.

JENNY: You can't go out. What about me?

ISABELLE: Come, Antoine, for at least one evening, let's go
back to our dreams.

NATALIE: I want you to come with me to the market.

ISABELLE: I told you I won't help you cheat those people any
more.

NATALIE: I'm only trying to save some money.

ISABELLE: One evening, Antoine.

(*They begin to go.*)

JENNY: Ooooh – ooooh my stomach. I think I'm going to
faint. Don't leave me, Antoine.

ISABELLE: You have Natalie and the "captain".

JENNY: Oooh. (*Doubles over.*) Put your hands on my forehead,
Antione. It's the only thing that'll help.

ISABELLE: Why don't you just tell him you want him to stay
instead of acting ill, hypocrite?

NATALIE: Don't upset a pregnant woman, Isabelle.

ISABELLE: Antoine . . .

(ANTOINE *goes over to* JENNY *and puts his hands on her
forehead.* ISABELLE *turns to leave.*)

NATALIE: What are you doing?

ISABELLE: I'm going outside.

NATALIE: A woman can't go out by herself at this time of night.

ISABELLE: But in these . . . I'm not a woman.

Scene 5

The Kasbah. ISABELLE, *alone.*

ISABELLE: If, down an obscure alleyway, a voice shouts at me:
hey you, shopkeeper – I'll not turn around. If the voice
pursues me: foreigner, European – I'll not turn around. If
the voice says: you, woman, yes, woman – I'll not turn
around, no, I'll not even turn my head. Even when it
whispers, Isabelle, Isabelle Eberhardt – even then I won't

315

turn around. But if it hails me: you, you there, who need vast
spaces and ask for nothing but to move, you, alone, free,
seeking peace and a home in the desert, who wish only to
obey the strange ciphers of your fate – yes, then I will turn
around, then I'll answer: I am here: Si Mahmoud.

Scene 6

The desert, ISABELLE, SALEH *and* BOU SAADI *are sitting passing
around a pipe full of kif. They are very stoned, from lack of food
and the hashish. Long silences, then rapid bursts of speech. The
poetry must not be "recited". For the Arabs, it is their natural form
of speech.*

SALEH: "The warrior was brave. Alas the beautiful young man
    fell. He shone like silver. Now he is in Paradise, far from
    all troubles."

ISABELLE: Was he fighting the Tidjanis, Saleh?

SALEH: No, Si Mahmoud, that is a song against the French.
    (*Silence.*)

ISABELLE: Tell me more about the wise men.

SALEH: Usually they're sheikhs who have been handed their
    knowledge by their fathers and then give it to a son. They
    live in the monasteries. We'll stay in one tomorrow.

BOU SAADI: But sometimes they wander and look just like
    beggars.

SALEH: There used to be very many, but the French are
    getting rid of them.

BOU SAADI: You must be careful what you say against the
    French, Saleh, it was God's will they become our rulers, it
    was written.

SALEH: Have we not read it badly?
    (*Silence.*)

BOU SAADI: One of the most famous marabouts used to live
    not far from here. Lalla Zineb. Many people visit her
    tomb.

ISABELLE: A woman?

BOU SAADI: Not an ordinary woman.

ISABELLE: But a woman?

SALEH: What difference does it make, Si Mahmoud, if she was
wise? They say she predicted the victory of the French
and then died of grief.

(*Silence.*)

If it is wisdom you seek, Si Mahmoud, you should spend
some time in the monasteries. We could take you to the
one where the leader of our sect lives.

ISABELLE: And you my friends, what have you found in the
desert?

SALEH: I had a cousin who had a beautiful white mare. She
was fast, exquisite. He'd had her since he was a boy. She
was his treasure and his love. One night, she disappeared.
He searched for months and found her at last in the camp
of a few Tidjanis. He waited until the night to get her
back, but someone must have seen him because he
stumbled on her body on his way to the camp. Her throat
had been slit, his beautiful white mare. Some time later he
managed to kill the man who had stolen her. It's only fair,
a mare is more valuable than a wife to us. But the Tidjanis
told the French about it. They're very friendly with the
French. He was judged in the city and then sent away to
forced labour in a place called Corsica. Very few men
come back from Corsica and then only to die. That's the
law of the French.

BOU SAADI: We were born crossing the desert, but now we
have to ask permission to go to certain places.

ISABELLE: Was it better to always fight the Tidjanis?

SALEH: It was our custom.

(*Silence.*)

"She said to me:
Why are your tears so white?
I answered:
Beloved, I have cried so long my tears are as white as
my hair."

ISABELLE: One day we'll understand, Saleh.

SALEH: Ah, Si Mahmoud, perhaps you will, you're learned.

BOU SAADI: We'll leave a few hours before dawn. I hope you're not feeling too weak, Si Mahmoud.

ISABELLE: No, my friends, but why didn't you tell me to bring food? I've eaten all of yours.

BOU SAADI: We're used to this life.

SALEH: "She said to me:
    Why are your tears black?
    I answered:
    I have no more tears, those are my pupils . . ."
(CAPTAIN SOUBIEL *enters*.)

CAPTAIN SOUBIEL: You there, who are you and where are you going?
(BOU SAADI *and* SALEH *jump up, acting increasingly stupid as the* CAPTAIN *stares at them.* BOU SAADI *in particular almost caricatures "oriental servility".*)

BOU SAADI: We're traders on our way to El-Oued, Allah willing.

CAPTAIN: Don't give me any of this Allah business. The three of you are traders?

BOU SAADI: This is a young Tunisian student on his way to the monasteries down south.

CAPTAIN: Monasteries, we've just had a report on those monasteries. Fortresses, that's what they are, hotbeds of resistance. All those sheikhs with their wives and slaves pretending to teach religion when they're shouting propaganda against the French. Don't talk to me about monasteries. (*Stares at* ISABELLE.) A Tunisian student, we've had a report about that too. You're not very dark.

BOU SAADI: Men from the city are lighter than us. Much sun in the Sahara.

CAPTAIN: Can't he speak for himself? What's your name?

ISABELLE: Si Mahmoud.

CAPTAIN: Si Mahmoud. You two, go make some tea.

BOU SAADI: We have no tea.

CAPTAIN: Well, then, go have a piss and don't come back

318

until I call you. Stay where I can see you and you stay
here. (*Has a good stare and then becomes extremely
courteous.*) Remarkable, I must say, remarkable. I
wouldn't have known. I'm honoured. You've become a
legend in the Legion: it's one thing to go out looking for
some Arab scum criminal, but a mysterious young
lady . . .

ISABELLE: My name is Si Mahmoud.

CAPTAIN: You can of course rely on the honour of the French
Army to keep your secret. Ha, ha, you Russian girls are
extraordinary. One of them blew up the Tsar or his cousin
the other day and now we have this young thing living it
out with the Arabs. They say Dostoevsky does this to you,
gives you a taste for cockroaches. But, Mademoiselle, if
you wished to see the country, you should have come to
us. We would be only too pleased to escort you and you
would find our company much more entertaining than
that of those sandfleas.

ISABELLE: You shouldn't speak of the Arabs in that manner,
Captain. They resent it.

CAPTAIN: You must tell me how to run the country,
Mademoiselle. It'll pass the time as we travel. Dunes get
monotonous.

ISABELLE: I am travelling with my friends, Captain.

CAPTAIN: What? Are there more of you? Do we have a whole
boarding school of romantic young girls?

ISABELLE: My friends Saleh and Bou Saadi.

CAPTAIN: She calls these dregs of humanity friends. Ah,
youth, the female heart. I admire your spirit,
Mademoiselle, but it is the duty of the French Army to
rescue damsels in distress.

ISABELLE: My friends will look after me.

CAPTAIN: Mademoiselle, I'm here to protect you. These
people smile at you at one day and cut your throat the
next. You see, they have no logic, no French education.
And if they ever found out . . . You're not at all bad
looking you know.

319

ISABELLE: I choose to travel with them.

CAPTAIN: You're quite a brave little character. I like that. I think we'll get on very well. You remind me of a delightfully unbroken young filly.

ISABELLE: Whereas you, Captain, remind me of a heavy cascade of camel piss. Mind you, nothing wrong with camel piss, I just don't choose to have it on top of me. Or, to put it another way, I'd rather kiss the open mouth of a Maccabean corpse dead of the Asiatic cholera than "travel" with you, Captain.

(*Freeze.*)

CAPTAIN: May I see your papers?

ISABELLE: What papers?

CAPTAIN: You must have government permission to travel through French territory.

ISABELLE: This is the desert. It's free.

CAPTAIN: This is French territory, under the rule of law and civilization and we require even sluts to have the correct papers. I'm waiting. I see you have no papers. You there! (BOU SAADI *and* SALEH *come back.*)

Do you know what this friend of yours Si Mahmoud is?

ISABELLE: Captain, the honour of the French Army.

CAPTAIN: We save the honour of our own kind. You'll kick yourselves when you find out. This little Tunisian friend of yours, ha, ha . . .

ISABELLE: Captain, please.

CAPTAIN: This Si Mahmoud is a woman.

(*Silence.* BOU SAADI *laughs stupidly.* SALEH *doesn't react at all.*)

Look under her clothes if you don't believe me.

SALEH: (*Slowly*) Si Mahmoud has a very good knowledge of medicine. He's helped people with their eyes and cured children.

CAPTAIN: Probably told them to wash. It's a woman I tell you. You must be stupider than I thought not to have noticed or at least asked a few questions.

SALEH: It is a courtesy in our country not to be curious about

320

the stranger. We accept whatever name Si Mahmoud wishes to give us.

ISABELLE: You knew.

SALEH: We heard. We chose not to believe it. (*To the* CAPTAIN) Si Mahmoud knows the Koran better than we do. He's in search of wisdom. We wish to help him.

CAPTAIN: Wisdom? That's the story she's spreading. I think it's more like information to pass on to people who don't belong here, like the English. They're always using women for this sort of thing. They can't forgive us for having produced Joan of Arc. You have ten days to bring this agitator back to the city. You know what happens if you don't.

ISABELLE: I'll appeal.

CAPTAIN: Yes, in Paris. It's never wise to refuse the protection of the French Army. A good journey.

(*He leaves.*)

ISABELLE: I'm doing no harm . . .

BOU SAADI: It's not a good idea to irritate Europeans. It's best to pretend you're stupid and keep laughing. I'm very good at it. Saleh is learning very slowly.

ISABELLE: I want nothing to do with these people. Why won't they let me alone? Ah, my friends, it's written I must leave you, but I'll come back, I'll come back.

SONG 2
(*Optional*)

VERDA MILES as a colonial soldier.

ACT II

Scene 1

A salon in Paris, VERDA MILES, SEVERINE, LYDIA, EUGENIE, ISABELLE, *and* PASHA, *a servant.*

SONG 3
VERDA MILES *as a young man in Paris.*

LYDIA: Isn't she extraordinary? Do you know I am almost in love with that man about town. And it was so kind of her to come and sing for my little salon.

EUGENIE: Ah, but your salon, such a setting for an artist.

SEVERINE: Don't be a hypocrite, Lydia. She knows everyone is at your little salon. And I've been invited tonight because you want me to write a story on her.

LYDIA: What she is doing is so important – for us.

SEVERINE: Lots of women have gone on stage dressed as men. It shows off their figures.

LYDIA: When Verda Miles is on stage, she *is* a man.

EUGENIE: And "man is the measure of all things".

LYDIA: Do interview her, Séverine.

SEVERINE: You can't interview English people, they don't know how to talk about themselves.

(PASHA *comes in with a tray of champagne.*)
I say, is that real?

LYDIA: No, it's just Jean. But the clothes are real. I had them copied from the *Arabian Nights*.

SEVERINE: The Countess Holst has one, a genuine one, but he's not as convincing.

LYDIA: And she had to sleep with the Turkish Ambassador to get him.

EUGENIE: When I was in Cairo I thought of bringing one back

322

with me, but it's cruel to take them out of their
natural environment.

LYDIA: Why don't I engage Verda Miles in conversation? You
can simply listen.

SEVERINE: You'll make it too philosophical and I'll miss the
story – if there is one.

LYDIA: My dear, you can't talk philosophy with English
women, they think it's something naughty their husbands
did as boys. No, I'll start with dogs.

EUGENIE: (*Seeing* ISABELLE) Lydia, what do I see? Ah, there,
there is a true one, I can tell. A young oriental prince,
look at the simplicity, the dignity. Oh, do present him to
us.

SEVERINE: It's even an Arab who looks a little like Rimbaud,
the Countess will be green when I tell her. How very
clever of you.

LYDIA: Yes, that's quite a find, but that's not a real Arab
either. Much more interesting, you have there a young
woman who travels with the savage tribes in the Sahara.
Her name's Isabelle Eberhardt. Russian, I think, she
won't talk much about herself.

SEVERINE: Eberhardt's a Jewish name.

LYDIA: Yes, well, they're all nomads, aren't they? She had
some troubles with officials in North Africa and she's
come to Paris to ask the French Government to help her.
She's very naïve.

SEVERINE: She must be to think the Government will help
anyone. Does she have enough money to bribe them?

LYDIA: She seems to have left everything behind – somewhere.

EUGENIE: The nomadic spirit, it's so noble, so carefree.

LYDIA: She knows almost no one here, but look at her, she
could become quite the rage. You might help her. I
believe she writes.

SEVERINE: Oh dear, descriptions of the sunset in
sub-Wordsworthian rhymes. So many interesting people
would still be remembered if they hadn't left behind their
memoirs.

(LYDIA *has been waving* ISABELLE *over.*)

LYDIA: Pasha, more champagne please.

SEVERINE: (*Courteous, intrigued*) Would you like some champagne, mademoiselle?

ISABELLE: Is that what it is? It's good, I've had six glasses already.

EUGENIE: (*With an exaggerated Arab salutation, or an attempt at one.*) I am so delighted. I too have been There.

ISABELLE: ?

EUGENIE: Why didn't we discover it before? All those trips to Athens and Rome staring at ruins when we had the real thing all the time in the Orient.

(ISABELLE *chokes on her drink, coughs and spits.*)

ISABELLE: Oh, forgot, used to the sand. Sorry, Lydia.

EUGENIE: The Homeric gesture, is that not so? (*To the others*) You can't imagine what it's like to see lying in the sun, or mending shoes, men of such consular types, all clad in white like the senators of Rome. Each one with the mien of a Cato or a Brutus.

LYDIA: There's Verda, excellent.

(*Champagne.* ISABELLE *drinks another glass.*)

VERDA: No, I never drink. (*To* ISABELLE) What a charming costume you have.

EUGENIE: The flowing simplicity of the African garb, so free, so . . . Athenian.

VERDA: I'd like to copy it. You see. I have an idea for a new song, it would be an oriental melody, exotic, and with that costume . . .

ISABELLE: It's not a costume, it's my clothes.

VERDA: Of course, that's what I meant. Do you know any oriental songs?

EUGENIE: Those oriental melodies – so biblical.

ISABELLE: (*Very flat*) Darling, I love you, darling, I adore you, exactly like to–maaa–to sauce. When I saw you there there there on the balcony, I thought . . . (*hiccups.*) That's all I know.

LYDIA: They have the most beautiful breed of hounds in

Egypt. They're called Ibizan hounds . . .

ISABELLE: I ate some cat in Tunisia. They said it was rabbit,
but I could tell it was cat, I found a claw. It tasted all
right.

EUGENIE: I found them so admirable in the simplicity of their
needs. A population of Socrates.

LYDIA: What made you decide to sing men's songs, Miss
Miles?

VERDA: I started singing on the stage when I was 3 and at the
age of 6 I had run through most of the female repertoire.
By the time I was 7 I thought I would have to retire. But
then, one night, I noticed by chance – if there is such a
thing as chance – my father's hat and cape hanging over
the back of a chair. You see my father was also in the
music-hall, as was my mother, who was Scottish. That is,
her father was Scottish. As I was saying, I saw the hat and
cape and put them on. I went to the mirror and when I
saw myself I suddenly had hundreds of exciting roles
before me. I've been a male impersonator ever since. It is,
how shall I say, much more interesting, much more
challenging to play men. There is more variety . . .
more . . .

LYDIA: More scope. How well I understand you. I myself
occasionally scribble. Oh, not professionally, like
Séverine, not writings I would necessarily show.
Although, of course, if Séverine did ask to see them, I
might, just as a friend . . . Do you know that in order to
write seriously I must dress as a man? I finally understood
why: when I am dressed as a woman, like this, I find I am
most concerned with the silky sound of my skirt rustling
on the floor, or I spend hours watching the lace fall over
my wrist, white against white. But when I dress as a man,
I simply begin to think, I get ideas. I'm sure that's why
Séverine is such a brilliant journalist, she always dresses as
a man.

SEVERINE: My dear Lydia, you know perfectly well I wear
male clothes so I can take my girlfriends to coffee bars

325

without having men pester us.

VERDA: (*Nervous*) Of course I never have that sort of problem because I am always with my husband. And I love to wear women's clothes. My husband says I am the most womanly woman he has ever known.

SEVERINE: Lydia was quite falling in love with your man about town.

VERDA: It's puzzling how many letters I get from women, young girls even. Sometimes they are so passionate they make me blush. One girl quite pursued me. She sent flowers to my dressing room and every time I performed I would see her, up close, staring at me. It was most disturbing. And her letters! At last, I had to invite her to my dressing room. I let my hair all the way down and wore the most feminine gown I could find. And then I gave her a good talking to. She never came back.

SEVERINE: Have men never written you love letters?

VERDA: Yes, but that's different. That's normal.

SEVERINE: Normality, the golden cage. And we poor banished species trail around, looking through the bars, wishing we were in there. But we're destined for the curiosity shops, labelled as the weird mistakes of nature, the moment of god's hesitation between Adam and Eve, anatomical convolutions, our souls inside out and alone, always alone, outside those bars. Do you love normality, Miss Miles?

EUGENIE: I was never considered normal. At school, my dancing master said my feet were perfect examples of the evils of anarchy. My deportment had revolutionary tendencies and the sound of my voice, I was told, was more raucous than the Communist Manifesto. No amount of hours spent practising in front of empty chairs taught me how to engage a young man in conversation and at last my poor parents said in despair, let her travel. I have not been unhappy, but I would have liked to be useful, or at least a philologist.

LYDIA: I think normality is a fashion. Here we are, five

women and four of us are dressed as men. And I'm only
wearing skirts because there are some German diplomats
here and they're very sticky about these things. I believe
the century we're entering will see a revolution greater
even than the French revolution. They defrocked the
priests, we'll defrock the women.

VERDA: We'll lose all our strength.

SEVERINE: Tell us about the desert, Miss Eberhardt.

ISABELLE: Sand.

LYDIA: Can't you help her, Séverine?

SEVERINE: Do you remember the Marquis de Mores?

LYDIA: Spanish? Stood around looking passionate? With an
American wife? He hasn't been seen in ages.

SEVERINE: He was killed down there. His wife – you know
what Americans are like – has taken it very personally. She
wants the French Government to find out what happened.
It seems they're showing a most unusual lack of curiosity.
(*To* ISABELLE) We might persuade her to send you down
there to collect some information. I'd like to go myself. I
smell a story which might be quite embarrassing to some
people. We could travel together. I'd enjoy that.

ISABELLE: Do you really like women?

SEVERINE: (*Seductive*) Have you lived in the Orient and
remained a prude?

ISABELLE: Me? Ha!

SEVERINE: There are thousands of women in this city who
would do anything to be made love to by me. But I like
women with character.

ISABELLE: I'm not a woman. I'm Si Mahmoud. I like men.
They like me. As a boy, I mean. And I have a firm rule:
no Europeans up my arse.
(*Freeze.*)

VERDA: I really must go. My husband . . .

ISABELLE: Did I say something wrong?

EUGENIE: The nomadic turn of phrase: so childlike.

SEVERINE: I don't like vulgarity. I'm afraid I can't help you.

ISABELLE: You look just like Captain Soubiel now. He wanted

327

to "protect me". And there was something to protect
then. (*Drinks, hopeless.*) I spent nine months working on
the docks of Marseilles to pay for this trip. Loading ships.

SEVERINE: Too bad it was a waste.

ISABELLE: Yeah, it was written. Too free with my tongue.
Too free.

(*She drinks another glass and passes out.*)

LYDIA: I'll have to teach her some manners. I'm sorry.

SEVERINE: That spirit isn't for corsets. Look at her. She's
younger than I am and she probably has malaria, who
knows what else. Nine months loading ships – that's the
work of ex-convicts. What a story.

LYDIA: She's ruined everything tonight.

SEVERINE: I'm not sure . . . No, I'll help her.

(*The melancholic sound of an Arab love song . . .*)

Scene 2

A zouaia (monastery) in the desert.

SI LACHMI, SALEH, BOU SAADI *and* ISABELLE.

ISABELLE: (*Slightly out of it*) Oh, these happy, these drunken
hours of return.

BOU SAADI: (*To* SI LACHMI) It was written Si Mahmoud
would come back to us.

SALEH: He can now become one of us, a Qadria.

ISABELLE: I wanted to possess this country. It has possessed
me.

SI LACHMI: There are at least a hundred different Sufi orders,
but the Qadria is one of the oldest.

ISABELLE: I've been in such a hurry to live.

SI LACHMI: We are also the most numerous.

SALEH: There are more of us than Tidjanis.

SI LACHMI: You will have twenty thousand brothers.

ISABELLE: The senses have tormented me.

BOU SAADI: The Qadrias are bound by links of affection.

SALEH: And solidarity, limitless devotion.

ISABELLE: A certain languor in these sands.

SI LACHMI: You'll be safe in our territories.

ISABELLE: Take off at last the grimacing, degraded mask.

SI LACHMI: All our monasteries are open to you.

ISABELLE: This is my property: the extended horizon.

SI LACHMI: Keep this chaplet, it'll protect you.

ISABELLE: The luxurious décor of the dunes: mine.

SI LACHMI: There is no dogma. We believe only in the equality of all men and gentleness of heart. You must also show absolute obedience to your sheikh. Our founder, Abd-el-Qader was most loved for his friendship with the oppressed. He loathed hypocrisy, all lies. You must be generous and show pity to all.

ISABELLE: And wisdom?

SI LACHMI: That comes later, Si Mahmoud. You're still young. Free yourself first from the vulgarity of the world.

ISABELLE: Doesn't the word Sufi come from the Greek *sofos*, wise?

SI LACHMI: It comes from a Berber word that means to excel. But that isn't important. Try to be a brave and good man, that's all we ask. (*Pause.*) So you have been visiting France?

SALEH: Si Mahmoud has been asked to find the murderers of a European called the Marquis de Mores.

ISABELLE: Oh yes, I'd forgotten. He was an explorer.

SI LACHMI: The *French* have asked you to look for his murderers?

ISABELLE: Not exactly the French. His wife.

SI LACHMI: Indeed.

ISABELLE: She gave me a lot of money. I should make an effort. Why would anyone want to murder an explorer?

SI LACHMI: He himself was not French?

ISABELLE: I don't think so. Why?

SI LACHMI: I am fascinated by the European tribal wars. They are more bitter than ours, but are conducted with much more subtlety. I am learning much from them.

SALEH: We kill people we don't like openly, in battle.

ISABELLE: You think it was the French themselves who
    wanted to get rid of him?

SI LACHMI: God alone knows the hearts of men. Do the
    French know with what purpose you've come back?

ISABELLE: I don't hide anything. I'm not a hypocrite.

SI LACHMI: We don't forbid prudence, Si Mahmoud.

SALEH: You're our brother now. We'll help you.

ISABELLE: If Allah's willing I'll find the murderers, if
    not – then I suppose it's not written they should be found.
    Does poverty allow the possession of a horse?

SI LACHMI: We don't deny pleasure. Each follows his own
    capacities.

    (*During this last exchange, the* MURDERER *comes in, unseen.
    He strikes with a sabre.* ISABELLE *turns just in time to avert
    it and only her arm is struck. The* MURDERER *is caught by*
    SALEH *and* BOU SAADI.)

    What's your name, you dog?

BOU SAADI: That's a Muslim brother. Do you know what
    you've done?

SI LACHMI: What's your name?

SALEH: Who ordered you to do this?

MURDERER: Allah.

SI LACHMI: God told you to kill a brother?

MURDERER: That's a woman.

SI LACHMI: It's no business of yours who this person is if we
    accept him as our brother. You question a sheikh?

MURDERER: Allah ordered me to kill that person who offends
    our law.

SI LACHMI: What law, fool? My sisters dressed as young men
    when they travelled. Who are you to judge? Who told you
    to do this?

MURDERER: Allah.

SALEH: Or the Tidjanis, or the French?

    (SI LACHMI *hands the sabre to* ISABELLE.)

SI LACHMI: You may kill him.

    (ISABELLE *seizes the sabre, then stops herself.*)

ISABELLE: Why? (*Gentle*) Have I offended you without

330

knowing?

MURDERER: You have done nothing to me, but if I have another chance, I'll kill you.

ISABELLE: Strange . . . I don't hate you. No, I forgive you. But I did you no harm.

MURDERER: You're offending our customs.

ISABELLE: But that's why I left *them*. (*Throws the sabre down.*) No, you're an instrument, but why? A riddle . . . Brothers, if it was written that I must die . . . But so young, without understanding . . . no. I can't die in this silence. Don't let me die here. Don't let me disappear, without a trace. Who wants to do this to me?

Scene 3

The courtroom in Constantine.

ISABELLE *and the* MURDERER. *As the* MURDERER *speaks, he changes into the* JUDGE.

MURDERER/JUDGE: "An angel appeared to tell me the Marabout of the Qadrias, Si Lachmi, would be proceeding to El-Oued accompanied by Miss Eberhardt who called herself Si Mahmoud and wore masculine dress, thus making trouble in our religion". This, Miss Eberhardt, is what the accused has to say in his defence. Have you anything to add?

ISABELLE: There is no law in the Muslim religion that says a woman may not dress as a man.

JUDGE: There should be. It's unchristian. Why do you wear it?

ISABELLE: It's practical for riding.

JUDGE: Women have traditionally ridden in dresses.

ISABELLE: Side-saddle! Imagine me joining a Qadria charge riding side-saddle. I'm greatly admired for my riding.

JUDGE: Did you say you joined a battle, Miss Eberhardt?

ISABELLE: (*Modestly*) Just a small raid. The sun was rising, it seemed covered in blood. There were about a hundred of us and . . .

JUDGE: Who were you fighting?

ISABELLE: Must have been the Tidjanis.

JUDGE: I hope it was not the French, Miss Eberhardt.

ISABELLE: No, no . . .

JUDGE: You've been heard to complain against the French.

ISABELLE: France could help this country so much, with
medicine, technical knowledge. But for some reason it's
making the people here worse off than they already are.
The Arabs will soon hate the French even more . . .
(*Stops herself.*)

JUDGE: You seem very friendly with the Arabs.

ISABELLE: I'm a Qadria, that's why I'm sure the murderer
is a Tidjani and was paid to kill me. I don't want him
punished too severely, but if he gets away with it, I'll no
longer be safe.

JUDGE: Why don't you return to Europe?

ISABELLE: I belong here.

JUDGE: Are you not a European?

ISABELLE: No, that is, not now . . .

JUDGE: You were born in Europe, Miss Eberhardt, you are
also a young woman.

ISABELLE: I'm not . . . (*Stops herself.*) I belong in the desert.

JUDGE: These are troubled times . . .

ISABELLE: I'm not doing any harm.

JUDGE: You've already driven a simple, ordinary Muslim to
madness by your behaviour, Miss Eberhardt. If only these
people were civilized, we could allow your wanderings.

ISABELLE: You don't want me to travel?

JUDGE: We must ask you to refrain from visiting places where
your presence might cause an unpleasant incident.

ISABELLE: I'll stay in Si Lachmi's monastery.

JUDGE: We particularly do not want you in the monasteries.

ISABELLE: I'll travel further south.

JUDGE: Miss Eberhardt, we feel your presence would be a
provocation anywhere in the desert.

ISABELLE: Oh, no, oh, please.

JUDGE: I'm sorry to put an end to your gallivantings.

ISABELLE: You – it's you. You've been trying to get rid of me all along.

JUDGE: We're trying to establish order.

ISABELLE: You're terrified of me! Your order is so fragile.

JUDGE: May I point out, Miss Eberhardt, that a man was recently sent to prison in England for a much lesser offence than yours.

ISABELLE: What? He took a walk on the beach?

JUDGE: This Mr Wilde had a perversion of inclination. You, Miss Eberhardt, have perverted nature.

ISABELLE: You mean nature as farmed by you to make you fat.

JUDGE: We will of course imprison your assailant.

ISABELLE: My friends, my brothers, where are my friends?

JUDGE: But you're to stay out of the desert. For good.

ISABELLE: Fenced out. Always!

SEVERINE: Fenced in, Isabelle, all of us.

Scene 4

ISABELLE *and* SEVERINE.

ISABELLE: Blocked. Detour. Blocked again. Need some absinthe. Buy me an absinthe, girl scribe.

SEVERINE: I thought Muslims didn't drink.

ISABELLE: Shouldn't. Do. Have you seen how supple Arabic writing is? Not like that French print. Need some absinthe. Si Mahmoud is dying of thirst. Hang on my every word, steal my story and won't give me to drink. European!

SEVERINE: I'm trying to keep you sober for Colonel Lyautey. It would help if you made sense.

ISABELLE: Make better sense with absinthe. Understand the world then: nice blurr. "Alas my soul for youth that's gone."

SEVERINE: You're 27!

ISABELLE: Lived fast. Too many detours and had to run.

SEVERINE: Here comes the Colonel. Try to behave yourself.

ISABELLE: The French: camel piss. I forgive them.

SEVERINE: He's an exception. The Arabs like him.

ISABELLE: Europe has taught them ignorance.

SEVERINE: Isabelle – it's your last chance.

(COLONEL LYAUTEY *enters*.)

Colonel. I've heard so much about you.

LYAUTEY: And I about you, Séverine: your pen strikes more terror in the heart of the French Government than the rattle of the Arab sabre.

ISABELLE: His speech jingles like his medals.

SEVERINE: Colonel, you wished to meet Isabelle Eberhardt.

LYAUTEY: (*Bows*.) Si Mahmoud.

ISABELLE: My sister married a dandelion. I was courted by his brother, a radish, no, his cousin, an orchid, and here's a multicoloured bouquet of medals bowing before me. The grace of Allah follow your footsteps, master. (*Bows down to the ground*.) A drop of absinthe for the poet's soul, Colonel, to remember Paradise.

SEVERINE: Colonel, you must excuse her – she's been so badly treated.

LYAUTEY: I've wanted to·meet you for some time, Si Mahmoud.

ISABELLE: Yeah, I'm famous. All bad. They hate me. Why?

LYAUTEY: Bloodthirsty mercenaries defend the boundaries of convention, Si Mahmoud, and your escape was too flamboyant. You remind me of the young Arab warrior who wears bright colours so he'll be seen first by the enemy.

ISABELLE: Ah, you're the firing squad. Here. (*Points to her heart, spreads her arms*.) Scribe, take down the martyr's last words: Si Mahmoud, heart without guile, dies, crossed by European civilization . . .

SEVERINE: Colonel, I'm sorry . . .

LYAUTEY: It's all right. I like refractory spirits.

ISABELLE: Why do compliments in French always sound

translated? I hate flowers, that's why I like the desert.
Barred by the hedges now. Are you very brave, Colonel,
to have picked so many medals?

LYAUTEY: Yes, Si Mahmoud, and so, I'm told, are you.

ISABELLE: With me bravery is a languor of the instincts. Are
you languid, Colonel?

SEVERINE: Isabelle, stop playing.

ISABELLE: Why? Travelling show: examine here the
monstrous folds of uncorseted nature, the pervert seed
that would not flourish on European manure. Complete
with witty and scientific commentary by our own Sevvy
the Scribe, straight from Paris . . .

SEVERINE: It's hopeless, we had better go.

LYAUTEY: Wait. Si Mahmoud, I don't like hedges either. I
come from Provence: it's dry there and barren. And you
can still hear in the walls the echoes of chivalry and
nobility, what you have here, what we're destroying.

ISABELLE: I believed in French civilization once. Is it the
climate that makes it rot?

LYAUTEY: The wrong ones came. You used to travel with the
Qadrias.

SEVERINE: Isabelle can go places where no other European
would be safe.

LYAUTEY: Do you want to travel again?

ISABELLE: When I came out of hospital after my wound, the
dunes had shrivelled. I wondered if they'd been empty all
the time.

SEVERINE: You were ill. You know you want to travel.

ISABELLE: "Anywhere, anywhere as long as it's out of this
world." Let the little cloud of oriental perfume that was
my soul vanish. No trace.

LYAUTEY: They say, Si Mahmoud, you're a young man in
search of knowledge.

ISABELLE: Was.

SEVERINE: She's accepted by all the marabouts. It's only the
French who prevent her from returning.

LYAUTEY: My predecessors have a lot to answer for. (*To*

ISABELLE) The Zianya sect is known for its pious and disinterested leaders. The Qadria have great respect for the Zianya.

ISABELLE: How do you know all this?

LYAUTEY: You forget, I love this country.

ISABELLE: "The tongue is a man's one half."

LYAUTEY: "The other the heart within." And who can judge the heart? Have you heard of the Zianya leader, Sidi Brahim?

ISABELLE: Even our marabouts look up to him.

LYAUTEY: Would you like to visit his school?

ISABELLE: Can't. It's in Morocco.

LYAUTEY: I can get you in.

ISABELLE: Is it written that Si Mahmoud shall speak to Sidi Brahim, that wisdom might be gained at last?

LYAUTEY: What will you need?

ISABELLE: A good horse.

LYAUTEY: When can you leave?

ISABELLE: Tomorrow.

SEVERINE: Morocco. She'll never come back, Colonel.

LYAUTEY: You can only stay five months this first time, Si Mahmoud. Please tell Sidi Brahim the French will help him if he wishes to extricate himself from his enemies.

SEVERINE: I see. The conquest of Morocco.

LYAUTEY: Not this time, I hope. But Si Mahmoud will tell you that country is devastated by marauding tribes.

ISABELLE: Too much bloodshed, yes.

LYAUTEY: We would help, no more.

SEVERINE: Shall we call it then the digestion of Morocco?

LYAUTEY: I'll expect you in Ain-Sefra in five months, Si Mahmoud, and then we'll have long chats about this country. How did my predecessors not appreciate you?

ISABELLE: From the point of view of bread and Swiss cheese, the love of the desert is an unhealthy appetite.

LYAUTEY: What idiots not to have understood you. Poor Si Mahmoud.

ISABELLE: Poor Si Mahmoud.

SEVERINE: She loves pity, Colonel.

ISABELLE: We Slavs are like that. We love the knout and then we love being pitied for having suffered the knout. And you, chronicler, must make no judgments. We souls of the desert (*hiccups*) love the knout.

LYAUTEY: Five months then. Your word of honour. I'll find a way of thanking you, Séverine.

SEVERINE: It may be too late, Colonel, you should have found her before.

LYAUTEY: They should have found me before. It may be too late for me too. Territories exploding, violence sowed and reaped, so unnecessary. Only you, Séverine, it's not too late for you.

ISABELLE: It's never too late for the chroniclers.

SEVERINE: But that's not what you meant, Colonel, is it?

LYAUTEY: No.

Scene 5

Ain-Sefra. Same as the first scene, a few hours later.

ISABELLE *and* SEVERINE.

ISABELLE: Very strict at the monastery. Walk towards the gate and a shadow bars your path. But Sidi Brahim let me pace. He understood Si Mahmoud had been too often locked in. His son lived in another quarter. There were many young men of great beauty in those rooms, and we don't hate love. But I couldn't join. They would know I was not completely a man, and also, much of that was gone. Slowly, slowly, the torment of the senses opens to the modulation of the dunes. Only a ripple here and there betrays the passage of the storm. Sidi Brahim wanted me to go further south and describe the country to the Colonel.

SEVERINE: Why didn't you?

ISABELLE: Promised I'd come here.

SEVERINE: You had more than a month left.

ISABELLE: If a man be old and a fool . . . suddenly, suddenly Si Mahmoud felt a shiver of fear. Suddenly my destiny: forgot the script. So I thought I'll come back, word of honour, and Si Mahmoud is important now, not broken.

SEVERINE: Shouldn't you get some rest? You must be coherent if you're seeing the Colonel later.

ISABELLE: Always coherent. It's the letters that get scrambled.

SEVERINE: I must go in. I feel faint.

ISABELLE: Hard work chronicling. Kept you up all night unravelling the Mektoub. Rest. Will you write my story? Practical guide for girls with unhealthy desires. With diagrams for the Europeans, the Cartesians. They couldn't fence in my tongue. Poor Sevvy, sweet scribe of uncartesian appetites, rebuild your dream.

SEVERINE: Will you find your way?

ISABELLE: Stay outside, head against stone and the soul more pure. If a man be old . . . but a young man may yet cast off his foolishness. I'm not wise, I'm not wise. (*Feels something, sticks out her hand.*) Rain? It doesn't rain in the desert. Mirage. No, rain, that's nice. Sleep in the rain. What's that noise?

SEVERINE: Thunder probably. There have been storms in the mountains. Don't wander off.

ISABELLE: Make my report to the Colonel, then wander off. Tell them Si Mahmoud . . .

(*But* SEVERINE *has left.*)

The rain. Get clean that way, wash the traces and the letters. Fresh sand, new letters.

(*She lies down.*)

Scene 6

Ain-Sefra.
SEVERINE, COLONEL LYAUTEY *and the* JUDGE.
SEVERINE: Drowned!
LYAUTEY: We came too late.

SEVERINE: Drowned in Ain-Sefra.

JUDGE: In the middle of the desert? That's no place to drown.

SEVERINE: A flash flood. The whole native quarter washed
away.

LYAUTEY: My men rushed down. We couldn't find her.

JUDGE: It's said she didn't even try to save herself.

SEVERINE: Our rebel warrior, Colonel.

JUDGE: Close the file. This person must be officially forgotten.

LYAUTEY: We found some journals. Would you like to see
them, Séverine?

SEVERINE: With pleasure.

    (*They walk off, arm in arm.*
    Lights fade to blackout.)

NOTES ON THE CONTRIBUTORS

DAVID CLOUGH   Born in Zambia in 1952 and brought up in Africa, England and Ireland, he is now married and lives in South London. *In Kanada* was originally inspired by reading the short stories of the Polish writer Tadeusz Borowski, based on his experiences in Auschwitz. The first intention was to write about life in the camp, but as David Clough learned more about the author and his tragic suicide, the work grew into a play which raises much wider issues, drawing attention to the underlying parallels between the ideologies of right and left and to the perversion of human values in the name of social change. Rather than trying to be biographical, *In Kanada* sets out to be a parable based on fact – essentially anti- or a-political. It was first performed at the Old Red Lion Theatre in Islington on 16 March 1982 by the Public Property Theatre company, directed by Phil Young.

NICK DARKE   Born in 1948 in Cornwall, he trained as an actor and worked with Peter Cheeseman at the Victoria Theatre, Stoke, as an actor and director for six years. His first play, *Never Say Rabbit in a Boat*, was premiered at Stoke in 1978. There followed *Landmarks* (Lyric Studio, 1979), *A Tickle on the River's Back* (Theatre Royal, Stratford East, 1979), *Summer Trade and the Lowestoft Man* (Orchard Theatre Company, 1980 and 1981), *The Catch* (Royal Court Theatre Upstairs, 1981), *Say Your Prayers* (Joint Stock Theatre Company at the Riverside Studios, 1981) and *The Body* (Royal Shakespeare Company at the Pit, 1983). *High Water* was first performed by the RSC in Newcastle and at the Warehouse, London, in 1980. Nick Darke's television film *Farmers Arms* was shown at the 1983 London Film Festival and subsequently on BBC2. He is a recipient of the 1979 George Devine Award.

JOHN FLETCHER   Born in Kent and went to grammar school and Cambridge University. He has lived for fifteen years in Somerset, where he has worked as farm labourer, shepherd, scaffolder and cider maker. He has written many plays for radio and television. In 1982 his first stage play, *The Marvellous Boy*, about the Bristol boy poet and suicide Thomas Chatterton, was performed at the Bristol Old Vic. *Babylon* is his second. He has written many articles for magazines on such diverse subjects as ecology, social history and nuclear disarmament.

He is a Catholic, Member of the Brotherhood of Ruralists, and is on the Polish Co-ordinating Committee of European Nuclear Disarmament.

Babylon has Fallen was co-produced by the Orchard Theatre Company and the BBC Radio Drama Department. The first stage production was by the Orchard Theatre Company in 1983, and the first radio broadcast was on BBC Radio 4 in February 1984.

ELLEN FOX   Born in 1954 in Toronto, Canada, she came to the United Kingdom in 1974, where she is now a resident, living in London. Her first play, *Ladies in Waiting*, was performed by the Penguin Theatre Company, Ottawa, in 1981 (and subsequently by the Liverpool Playhouse Upstairs in 1982, and the University of Bridgeport, Connecticut, in 1984). For this play she won the Thames Television Playwright's Award and was given the post of Resident Writer with the Hampstead Theatre in 1981. *Saving Grace* was first performed at the Soho Poly Theatre in 1981 and led the way into radio drama when she adapted it for BBC Radio 4 in 1982. She has since written *Foreign Exchange* for the BBC World Service and has been commissioned to write a new play, *Passing Away*, for Radio 4's Afternoon Theatre in 1984.

In 1983 BBC Television commissioned her play *Medicine Man*. They have also commissioned her to write the film adaptation of Jean Rhys's novel *Voyage in the Dark* (producer Kenith Trodd). Other plays include *Conversations with George*

Sandburgh after a Solo Flight across the Atlantic (1982) and *Clinging to the Wreckage* which has been commissioned by the Traverse Theatre Club, Edinburgh, for 1984.

LENNIE JAMES Brought up in care from the age of 10, he was fostered when he was 16. *Trial and Error* is his first play and was written for a weekend drama school but was never performed. At the last minute he submitted it for the National Youth Theatre/Texaco Playwriting Competition and won the prize for the most promising playwright under 21. He wanted to give a fair view of life in care but did not base the character of Tony on himself, although he has met people like Tony. He divides his time between studying for his A-levels and acting at Shiftwork, the Youth drama company at the Lyric Theatre. After A-levels he hopes to enter drama school.

TIMBERLAKE WERTENBAKER Grew up in the Basque country near Saint-Jean-de-Luz, France. Now lives in Brixton. After taking a degree in philosophy, she worked as a journalist in London and New York. She spent a year teaching French in Greece and wrote two plays, which were performed on the island of Spetsai. Her first play, *The Third*, won an all-London playwright's award and was produced at the King's Head Theatre Club in 1980. *Second Sentence* and *Case to Answer* were also produced that year, the first by the Brighton Actors Workshop and the second by the Soho Poly and Central Casting, Ithaca, New York. She spent the next year with the Women's Theatre Group and wrote two plays for them, the second of which was *New Anatomies*, first performed at the Edinburgh Theatre Workshop at the 1981 Edinburgh Festival. In 1982, she wrote *Inside Out* for R. A. T. Theatre and *Home Leave* for the Wolsey Theatre, Ipswich. She became the Arts Council writer-in-residence for *Shared Experience* in 1983 and translated *False Admissions* and *Successful Strategies* by Marivaux for the Company. She also wrote *Abel's Sister* for the Royal Court Theatre Upstairs and adapted *New Anatomies* for BBC Radio.